© 2018 McSweeney's Quarterly Concern and the contributors, San Francisco, California. ASSISTED BY: Rita Bullwinkel, Caitlin Van Dusen, Angela Hui, Jeff P. Jones, Matthew Keast, Emily Mathe, Molly McGhee, Laura Van Slyke, Zoe Young. WEB DEVELOPMENT: Brian Christian. ART DIRECTION: Sunra Thompson. COPY EDITOR: Daniel Levin Becker. FOUNDING EDITOR: Dave Eggers. EXECUTIVE AND EDITORIAL DIRECTOR: Kristina Kearns. MANAGING EDITOR: Claire Boyle.

GUEST EDITOR: Nyuol Lueth Tong

ENDPAPER ILLUSTRATION: Anuj Shrestha
INTERIOR ILLUSTRATIONS: Sunra Thompson

MCSWEENEY'S PUBLISHING BOARD: Natasha Boas, Kyle Bruck, Carol Davis, Brian Dice (PRESIDENT), Isabel Duffy-Pinner, Dave Eggers, Caterina Fake, Hilary Kivitz, Nion McEvoy, Gina Pell, Jeremy Radcliffe, Jed Repko, Julia Slavin, Vendela Vida.

Printed in the United States.

PART I - BIOGRAPHIC DATA

opy of this form for yourself and each member of your family, regardless of age, who will immigrate with you. Please
l questions. Mark questions that are **Not Applicable** with "**N/A**". If there is insufficient room on the form, answer on
numbers that appear on the form. **Attach any additional sheets to this form.**

nt or concealment of a material fact may result in your permanent exclusion from the United States.
e first of two parts. This part, together with **Form DS-230 Part II**, constitutes the complete Application for
gistration.

First   Middle Name

s *(If married woman, give maiden name)*

t *(If Roman letters not used)*

| 5. Age | 6. Place of Birth *(City or* | | *(Country)* |

8. Gender
◯ Female
◯ Male

9. Marital Status
◯ Single *(Never Marr* ◯ Widowed ◯ Divorced ◯ Separate
Including my present ma rried _____ times.

nited States where you intend to live, if   11 d States where you want your Permanent
ZIP code). Include the name of a person   Re *ard)* mailed, if different from address in item #1
(in erson who currently lives there).

Telepho
13. Present Address *(S ess) (City or Town) (Province) (Country)*

Telephone Numbe one Number *(Office)* E-mail Address

Name   First Name   Middle Name

ce of Birth of Spouse

ent from your own)   17. Spouse's Occupation

18. Date of Marriage *(mm-dd-yyyy)*

First Name   Middle Name

| 21. Place of Birth | 22. Current Address | 23. If Deceased, Giv Year of Death |

EDITOR'S NOTE

by NYUOL LUETH TONG

T HERE IS A GENRE called migrant literature. It covers works by immigrant writers, often about the immigrant experience. Among its chief concerns or themes are displacement, movement, belonging, homecoming, departure, arrival, assimilation, bilingualism, and so on. I suppose we can fairly assume this collection of stories by immigrant writers belongs to that tradition. As immigrant writers, creative spirits caught between worlds whose boundaries are ever shifting, often resulting in more displacement and migration, it is comforting to know there exists a coterie to which belonging is conceivable.

That said, we should embrace this veritable genre with caution, for despite its liberating possibilities, it also preserves the very logic of our exclusion, namely our "foreignness," our "otherness," often deployed as a mark of inferiority, marginality, and disposability. In other words, it relegates our works to the periphery of provincialism, outside the so-called canon of world literature. Migrant literature is not only a constitutive part of global literature but also arguably its most vital, exciting, innovative element, concerned as it is with exploring themes and questions that are universal and timeless, yet urgent and humane. All the pieces in this issue exhibit this irreducible quality.

I PLEDGE ALLEGIANCE TO THE BUTTERFLY

by MARIA KUZNETSOVA

WE HAD BEEN LIVING in Gainesville for a year when Officer Friendly told my third-grade class you could call 911 from home and the cops would show up within minutes. Nobody else seemed as stunned by this revelation as I was, but that was no surprise. I had been released from ESL at the start of my second fall in America, and there were a lot of things I was slow to learn.

Like, for example, why people called me Rod. I thought it was because I was Russian or just scrawny, but one day, Billy Spencer sang "Have I told you lately that I love you…" at me and I figured out it was Rod for Rod Stewart because I had a bit of a mullet. Mama chopped it off, but the name stuck. The only people who used my real name were my teacher Mrs. Thomas and my ESL friend Raluca—or I should say ex-friend, because she moved back to Romania over the summer without telling me. I tried not to take it personally.

Autumn called me Okey Dokey, which was definitely closer to Oksana than Rod. We only talked after class, when we walked to the lobby so she could meet her mom and I could cross the street to meet my grandmother behind the clump of palm trees where I made her wait.

But the day after the officer's visit, Baba was flirting with Mr. Trevors the crossing guard by the front entrance, dangerously on display. Kids swarmed around like the ants in our kitchen, looking for their buses or parents or just their friends to walk home with, and nobody seemed to notice her. Baba squeezed the crossing guard's arm, her fiery hair flying in all directions, her pink dress flailing about her high-heeled veiny legs.

Autumn spotted her. "Yuck," she said. "Your mom is even older than my mom."

"That's my grandma."

"Oh," she said, disappointed. "Well how old is she anyway?"

"No clue. Eighty, ninety, something like that." No one at school had seen her before and it made me twitch. I said, "You really think if I call the cops they'll come?"

Autumn's eyes grew wide. "Yes, yes!" she said. "Call the cops!"

"What do I say?"

She rubbed her hands together. "Say 'Help! My grandma is trying to kill me!'"

"Alright," I said. As Baba caressed Mr. Trevors's arms and then his stop sign, it sounded like the truth.

"Okey dokey, Okey Dokey. I'm flying away," Autumn said, flapping her hands up and down like wings, which had to do with her saying the Pledge of Allegiance to the butterfly instead of the flag every morning. She flew off to her mom, a silver-haired lady who waited for her in a Jeep, merciful enough to never step out and embarrass her.

But Baba had no mercy for me. I approached her with my head down, incognito. Thankfully she had taken a step away from her prospect.

Mr. Trevors was a nice bald war veteran. He lifted a hand at me and said, "Have a nice day, Rod—I mean, Oksana!"

Baba winked and strutted away. She leaned toward me and said, "Such biceps!"

"A cop came to class," I told her. "He was nice."

"Some are," she said. Then she told a boring story about one summer in Odessa in 1957 when a police officer named Bobik wrote a song about her legs.

The sun baked us as we walked along Main Street, also known as Prostitute Street. It was covered in broken glass and only had a couple of palm trees on it. It ran along the Pic 'N' Save where Baba took me to get a doll once a month, Dick's Adult Video, and a gas station with an inflatable alligator at the front. Lizards scattered at our feet. There were always a few kingdoms on the ground, looking like deflated balloons. Men put them over their things to have sex with the prostitutes.

I never saw actual prostitutes there, but sometimes men would honk or slow down and shout at Baba and she didn't know why. Mama and Papa said not to tell her because she needed the attention since her husband had just died, her daughter had kicked it a while back, her morning work at the lab was unpaid, the Soviet Union had collapsed, she had to share a room with me, her family had been gutted by fascism and anti-Semitism, the world was cruel and unwelcoming, et cetera.

She got one honk and tittered. "Your grandma still has it all, doesn't she?"

"Are you eighty or ninety?"

She laughed. "Eighty or ninety what, dear child?" She realized what I meant and pretended to choke me. "Fifty-one years young. Hardly old at all, infinite imbecile!" Then she walked ahead of me, like she didn't want to be associated with me, either.

At home, I knew Mama was napping because it was quiet. If the TV was on, she was applying to jobs and drinking white wine or calling her friends or her mother, who lived in a place called New Jersey, or just silently weeping. Everyone my parents knew back in Ukraine was in New Jersey now, but we were stuck in Florida because that was where Papa had found a job as a physicist for the university. It didn't seem like such a great job to me because he also had to deliver pizza for Dino's.

While Baba smoked on the balcony I went to the room I shared with her. The carpet was brown and swallowed up cicadas. The walls displayed photos of Kiev and Baryshnikov framed in a heart. Our beds were separated by a nightstand with a sad photo on it and that was all the furniture there was room for. The only thing of mine was the pile of dolls by my bed.

Baba's cigarette smoke wafted through the window. I had to act fast before I lost my nerve. I took a breath and put my hand on the receiver and pictured Officer Friendly in his black uniform. He was tall and handsome and had a mustache. He winked at me when I said, "You'll really be there if I need help?" Then I imagined Autumn clapping her hands and dialed.

"911, what's your emergency?" said a lady's voice.

"Um," I said. "I just wanted to see if this worked?"

"Honey, is there an adult I can talk to?"

"Nobody here speaks English," I said, hanging up. My heart pounded. I had done it! Then the phone rang and I picked it up.

"May I please speak to your mother or father?"

I hung up again. It rang a third time, and I heard Mama grab it. She used her careful English voice, which was nothing like her Russian voice. She sounded nicer in English.

"Oksana Victorovna Konnikova," she called. I approached her with my best angel face. Her skin was paler than usual, making her dark eyes and hair even more striking. She was tragically beautiful and her eyes were filled with desperate rage. I was tan, light-haired, and hideous. "Tell this lady nothing is wrong here," Mama said. She shoved the phone in my direction and it looked like a weapon, like a rocket launcher from *Doom*. Baba crushed her cigarette with her high heel on the balcony and she looked menacing, too. I screamed wildly.

"Help!" I cried. "My grandmother is trying to kill me! Help!"

I wept and choked and ran off the balcony and past the SUN BAY APART-MENTS sign and the pool all the way to the lake with the mossy trees and smelly ducks, and I stared at the water, remembering the Dnieper, which flowed outside our Kiev apartment, where I slept in the living room with Mama and Papa while my grandparents lived on the other side of the city and nobody ever called me Rod. I wasn't there long when Mama dragged me away by the ear.

"Dearest God I don't believe in," she said. "Tell me, what have I done to deserve this child? Did I commit murder in a past life I don't believe in? Genocide? Was I Stalin himself? Did I smother a litter of puppies?" She glared at me near home. "The police are on their way, poor idiot. You must tell them everything is normal."

Baba was drinking cognac on the balcony, thrilled by this turn of events.

Papa was in his Dino's uniform eating pizza standing up. There was sauce on his nose.

Baba wagged a finger at me and said, "*I* was young and sharp once, but *you* are young and dim-witted, and one day you will be old *and* dim-witted, don't you see?" She lifted her glass and smiled slyly. "I hope your officer has a nice juicy rump!" she added, squeezing the air with her hand for emphasis.

Papa dropped his slice and shrugged and picked it up and ate it anyway.

"You see?" Mama said. "Normal family."

They were knocking as soon as we walked in. The woman had short hair and the man was definitely not Officer Friendly, or even friendly.

Officer Friendly was young and energetic and this was a tired bearded man. He greeted my parents curtly and walked over to me.

"Do you realize what you've done, young lady? We could be spending our time helping people who actually need it," he said.

"I'm not that young," I said.

"We are profoundly sorry," Papa said.

"Very profoundly," Baba said, circling the man like a vulture.

"Tea?" Mama asked, but they did not look like they wanted tea.

The officer turned her down and circled the apartment, the coffee table we ate dinner on, the lawn furniture we used inside, the tiny TV with its foil antennae, the sign Papa had hung up that said IT'S NOT ALWAYS THIS MESSY HERE... SOMETIMES IT'S WORSE, and the stained green couch that sunk to the floor. Then he studied Mama and Papa and Baba, who, with their thick accents and garage-sale clothes, were probably even weirder to him than our apartment. I tried to make eye contact to show I was not happy being tied to this place or these people, but he didn't look at me. When he finished his inspection, he squatted next to me until we were eye to eye.

"Do we understand each other?" he said.

"No calling unless I need help," I said. I didn't know what else to do so I saluted him.

"Enjoy your day," said the female officer, and they were gone. It was already getting dark out. The cicadas chirped. I had messed up big time, but I was thrilled.

"What were you thinking, you fool?" Baba said. "They could throw you in jail!"

"This feels like jail," I noted, and Mama sent me to my room without dinner.

*   *   *

At lunch, I sat by Autumn instead of alone. She was weird, but I couldn't afford to be picky. She had greasy blonde hair and freckles and wore dresses big enough to fit a mother. Billy Spencer grinned a wild dog's grin at me, like he was amused I had a friend, but I didn't care. Autumn didn't tell me to go away, so I told her about the cops.

"What did you say?"

"I said my grandma was killing me."

"I didn't think you'd go through with it. You get in trouble?"

"Had to skip dinner but food at home sucks anyway."

"Not bad, Okey Dokey," she said, impressed.

I opened my lunch box. It held a slew of items Mama had put in just to torture me: crackers with cream cheese, a hard-boiled egg, and a tomato, which were nearly redeemed by a container of herring. Cream cheese always smeared all over the box.

Autumn peeked inside and shrugged. "Find out how old your grandma is?"

"Fifty-one," I said.

She nodded slowly and took a bite of her PB&J.

"My mom is forty-eight. She adopted me."

"How old is your dad?"

"No dad, no dad," she said gleefully, almost singing the words.

"You just live with your mom?"

"Basically," she said. "We barely talk because she's always working. She sucks."

"You're lucky. My mom's always home. My grandma too."

"How annoying," she said, biting my tomato.

I dipped my finger in a smear of cream cheese and licked it up. Autumn did the same and looked like she wanted me to keep talking.

"Mama and Baba are always home but we never *do* anything. When my dad said we were moving to Florida, he was all like, the beach, the beach, we'll spend so much time at the beach, but we barely go, anytime I ask they're like, we're too tired. And I'm like, What's the point of living here if we never even go to the beach?"

Autumn nodded with great understanding. "Family," she said, and she shook her head like an ancient person.

Papa brought home a pizza nobody had claimed from Dino's a few days later and set it on the coffee table. The table had come with the apartment. Somebody had scratched FUK SUN BAY in its center. We ate on plates that said FAT IS BEAUTIFUL. Baba bought them at a garage sale before she knew what it meant.

We ate sitting on the floor. Mama poured vodka for the grown-ups, Sunkist for me, and sliced a tomato and a cucumber and pinched salt over them. A jar of sauerkraut appeared out of nowhere, and a few boiled hot dogs. The pizza looked like cheese though it was a little roughed up. I bit into my slice and spit it out into a napkin.

"Yuck," I said. "There's sausage in here."

"What you are given, you will eat," Mama said.

"I'm sorry, darling. I should have warned you," Papa said.

"I'll just pick it off," I said, avoiding Mama's glare. "It was a surprise, that's all."

"A surprise?" Baba said. "Ha! You know what was a surprise? One day, when we were starving in the Urals during the war, Mama baked us a delicious meat pie. We said, 'Mamachka, what's in this pie? It's so savory.' And she said, 'Oh it's Old Syomka.' The family dog. She said, 'Syomka is with us forever now.'" Baba laughed and slapped the table. I spit up my cucumber.

"Oksana, behave!" Mama said. "Do not waste food."

"That's disgusting," I said.

"Disgusting?" said Baba, not without glee. "It was life, dear child. We got through it. Even my poor father," she said. "It was kind of beautiful, in fact. Mama was right. I never forgot that poor creature."

"A touching story of sacrifice," Papa said, forking a tomato.

Papa and I played *Doom* and later Baba and I got into our beds. Her bed was an arm's length away from mine. I could reach out and touch her if I wanted to. She picked up the photo on our nightstand, which showed her, my grandpa, Papa, and his sister holding baskets of mushrooms in the woods. Two-fourths of the people in the photo were dead, which I recently learned could be simplified to one-half. Papa's sister died of a weak heart before I was born, and my grandpa, according to Baba, died "of being a Soviet male."

I only knew my grandfather as a man in bed who smelled like dying, dusty and sour. Whenever Baba made me bring him medicine, I held my breath. When I heard I'd have to share a room with Baba in America, I worried she'd smell that way, too, but she just smelled like too much flowers.

I couldn't sleep. I hugged my doll Lacy and thought of the dead and what it would be like to eat your dog. The chirping cicadas and sirens outside didn't help, either.

"The police came to my house once," Baba said after a while, sensing that I was up. "The NKVD, in fact. This was just after the war. I was about your age, darling. They came in the middle of the night and took my father away."

I waited for her to tell me what happened next. It took me a moment to understand there was no more story.

I went on a late drive with Papa the next weekend. Our car was a brown Mercury with a tan roof with holes Mama had taped up, and he was proud of it. He had never had a car or driven before. He played the B-side of *The White Album* and we zipped along the highway with the windows down, hot air blowing in our faces. We picked up two hitchhikers, a couple who said they had just gotten married. Mama hated when he did this, but Papa said he had a car, he had gas, and goddamn it if he wasn't going to help people go places.

"We won't forget this," the man said when we dropped them off near St. Augustine. We drove a little further and got out and walked to the water. It was oily and ominous, a monster that could swallow me whole, but a dark beach was better than no beach. Papa held my hand. When he wasn't working, he spent his evenings playing *Doom* with me or pasting photographs of his father and long-dead relatives in albums on the balcony.

"It's not all bad here, is it, Oksana?" he said, putting an arm around me. A bonfire blazed in the distance, the flames eating up the darkness.

"I like the beach. I wish we'd go during the day."

"Soon, child. Soon." He looked up at the sky. "My father used to take me and my sister out to the country to look at the stars, the constellations. I have forgotten most of their names. Though there's Orion," he said, pointing out the archer and his belt. He lit a cigarette.

"Papa?" I said, after a while. "What's it like to have someone close to you die?"

He looked at the stars again as if they could give him an answer. The waves licked the shore and the tops of my feet.

"Sad," he said, and then he put out his cigarette and said it was time to go back.

He drove for a while without saying anything. *The White Album* finished but he didn't turn the tape over. He spoke again when we were almost home.

"When you lose someone you love, they stay with you. My father and sister—they're always nearby. I can picture how they would react to almost anything, and sometimes, I even talk to them. So in that way, it's not so sad, kitten, because I am never alone."

This made me spring up, like there was a psycho in the backseat ready to slit our throats. The hair on my arms stood up. I peeked behind me, but no one was coming for us yet.

Autumn came home with me and Baba after school one day. As we walked down Prostitute Street, Baba got three honks and tossed her hair. Though she had started dating Mr. Trevors, it didn't stop her from having fun. Autumn thought it was hilarious Baba didn't know about Prostitute Street.

"I get younger by the minute, don't you see?" Baba said.

"Definitely," Autumn said. Baba pinched her cheeks and declared her a good influence.

Every morning, as sad Principal Bates said the Pledge over the loud-speaker, Autumn and I held hands and said the Pledge to the butterfly. October had rolled around, so we sometimes said the Pledge to the pumpkin instead. Mrs. Thomas would roll her eyes and say, "Silly hippies. Flower children," but she didn't punish us.

When Autumn entered my room, she sneered and I thought it was because I shared it with Baba, but it was because of my dolls.

"Dolls are stupid, Okey Dokey. They're just there to make you think all you're good for is having babies. That's what my mom says."

"I thought you don't care about your mom," I said. I saw this was the wrong answer and said, "I hate babies."

"Do you even know how babies are made?" she said.

"Sure." I told her a man and woman get naked and roll around under sheets and moan sometimes because it hurts. I didn't mention the kingdom because I didn't know what the man put it on for.

"The man puts his thing in the woman's hole and squirts into it," she said.

I gasped and put my hands to my private parts. I would never do something so disgusting. I slowly released my hands and the world came into terrible focus.

"The man puts a kingdom on his thing if he doesn't want to make a baby," I said.

She snorted and patted my arm. "That's called a condom."

"A condom?" This sounded less magical. I liked *kingdom* better—a word Raluca had taught me—a mystical gateway between man and woman and family. After that, I pretty much waited for Autumn to leave. I was tired from knowing how everything worked.

By the time Autumn and I were saying the Pledge to the turkey, the lab where Baba worked mornings offered her a real job. This was apparently a cause for celebration, though it meant she would no longer pick me up from school. Mama would replace her. This was slightly better but still annoying.

"A nice surprise," Baba said, putting on lipstick in the hallway mirror.

"We're very happy for you," Mama said, not without bitterness.

"We must go out," Papa said, clapping his hands. They decided on the Outback, because it was supposed to be nice and was close by. Baba put on a sparkly black dress and curled her hair. As they got ready, I noticed that nobody told me to change.

Mama said, "Do you really want to come, kitten? We may be there a while."

"We're getting blasted!" Baba announced. "Surely you are not interested."

"Of course she should come," Papa said.

"I want to stay here," I said. If they didn't want me, then I didn't want them. Besides, I had never been alone in the apartment before. In Kiev, Mama and Papa had left me home to go to the movies sometimes. I would stage plays with my dolls and do all their voices.

"We won't be long," Papa said, squeezing my shoulder.

"We'll bring something back for you," said Baba, but she hardly cared. She was looking in the mirror.

"Goodbye, little idiot," Mama said. The door slammed shut behind her. I was glad to be rid of them and do all the things I couldn't normally do.

I danced around in my bikini. I blasted Ace of Base. I ate cold nacho cheese with my fingers, which was much better than cream cheese. I tried to read a few pages of Baba's romance novels, but I didn't understand what was going on. I touched all of the walls with my hands. I did a few cartwheels. I jumped on Mama and Papa's bed. I pulled three cicadas out of the carpet with Mama's tweezers and flushed them down the toilet. I drowned the ants by the sink.

The darkness crept in. It was windy out and a tree branch scraped against the balcony. It sounded like a person. I played *Doom* but it only made me scared. I grabbed my Amy doll from my doll pile and hugged her hard. The noises grew louder and I was certain someone was coming for me. I decided it was one of Papa's dead. I would be smothered. I called Autumn and hoped she could calm me down.

"I'm home alone," I said. "I'm freaked out."

"Your family left you?"

"Not for good, just for dinner. They'll be back."

"Too bad," she said. Then she added, "That's not normal."

"It's not?"

"Not really. But it doesn't matter. Who cares if they don't love you? Fly away now," she said, and then she said she had to go. I heard laughter before she hung up. I still had never been to her house but I assumed the only laughter there came from TV.

I didn't know how to fly away. I flipped through the album Papa was working on, thinking it would put me to sleep. It started off boring, but then I found a photo that filled me with revulsion and horror. Papa was my age and my grandpa was pretty young. They stood in a field of tall grass in their underwear, holding sickles. I could see the outline of their bulging things, things I now knew had brought Papa and then me into being. I slammed the album shut and screamed. I screamed again and clutched my doll but nothing happened, nobody came, not the cops, not the neighbors, not my grandfather, not Autumn, not Raluca. I cried until I tired myself out and curled up on the couch and a million years later the key was scraping in the lock.

"What's wrong, little idiot?" Mama said, putting a hand in my hair.

Papa and Baba emerged behind her looking worried. They were all happy and red-faced.

"I got scared," I said, sitting up. "I heard noises. I thought a robber was going to kill me."

"You are safe now, poor creature," Papa said.

"If you don't want us to treat you like a child, do not act like one," Mama said.

"Besides," Baba said, "if a robber broke in, what would you expect us to do, infinite fool, fight him off?" She didn't care about my suffering. She didn't care that I didn't ask to get born or to be all alone one day.

Before I could answer, she put a hand on my wrist. "You should have seen the waiter. As handsome as a young Baryshnikov! And on the way home, a man rolled down his window and told me I was beautiful." She pranced around like she was queen of the world. I couldn't be near her anymore.

"Those men think you're a prostitute," I said.

"What?" Baba said.

Papa froze and Mama dropped her purse.

"Main Street is Prostitute Street," I said. "Everybody knows."

"Well!" Baba said, clutching her necklace. She looked from me to my parents, who looked at the floor. "Of course it is, you little idiot," she said. "Of course it is. Of course I know that. You are a devil," she said, and then she walked slowly toward the balcony, like a doll running out of batteries. Papa didn't look at me as he followed her. I didn't know she already knew.

Mama smacked me. "Are you happy now?"

"Delighted."

Mama was so upset she didn't even lecture me. Baba returned eventually with a splotchy face. She said, "Until you apologize, I am not speaking to you, do you understand?"

"Works for me," I said.

I stayed up in bed until Baba came in, carrying her heavy perfume scent. She got under her covers and turned away from me, coughing a phlegmy cough. Her back heaved and I remembered how my grandfather had smelled and wondered if she had smelled like him all along, if she just used perfume to cover it up.

When Mama picked me up from school, I decided I had outgrown my dolls. We took all the dolls from my doll pile and tossed them in a black plastic bag.

"It's nice to get rid of some things we don't need, isn't it, darling?" Mama said.

"Dolls are for idiots who want to have babies," I said. "I don't want a baby and I don't want to be anybody's mother."

Mama laughed. "You have some time to change your mind, silly child," she said. But when we dragged the bag to the dumpster, she looked weepy. Her hand dug into the back of my neck, making me wish I still had my mullet for protection against her touch.

"Why the rush?" she said. "I don't want you to regret this later."

"I won't," I assured her.

I grabbed the heavy doll bag and dumped it in the trash. Dust and flies flew up in its wake. Mama sunk her claws into my shoulders and her face was like the ocean at night. "I have no job. I have no father. My mother is old. I don't even have a country anymore," she said. "But I have you. You are my greatest achievement. Do you understand?"

"Ow! That hurts."

"It better, little devil, it better," she said.

She was fuming as we ditched the dumpster, but a smile crossed her face when we turned the corner. I followed her gaze across the parking lot, where Mr. Trevors was escorting Baba home. She still hadn't said a word to me though a week had gone by since our fight. They stopped near a palm tree and he backed Baba up against it and kissed her madly. Her hands were raised above her head like the talons of a pterodactyl.

"Your grandmother has a zest for life," Mama said, turning me away from this disturbing scene. "She is an inspiration to us all."

The next time Papa took me for a drive, Autumn and I were saying the Pledge to Santa Claus. We zipped past a cracked-open armadillo drowning in a puddle of its own blood and guts. When he turned down *Breakfast in*

America, I got nervous, thinking he would tell me something awful, that he was dying or that Baba was going to marry Mr. Trevors.

"Oksanka Banka," he said. "It seems you do not hate it here after all, am I right?"

"It's not bad."

"You know how when you are in a maze in *Doom*, you have to walk along the same wall to ensure you are moving forward? But sometimes, you may find you are in center of the maze, going in circles instead of finding a way out."

"So what? Then you just follow a new wall," I said.

"Exactly," he said, but I didn't get it. He cleared his throat. "A Jew once said, 'The foxes have their dens, the birds have their nests, but the Son of Man has nowhere to lay his head.'"

"Which Jew?"

"We are leaving Gainesville at the end of the month."

I gripped my door handle like it might disappear. I tasted tin. I thought of Raluca, how she must have felt when she heard this terrible news. "Are we going back to Kiev?"

He gave me a sad smile. "We are moving to Worthington, Ohio. I found a better job at the university there."

I kicked the dashboard and wailed. "Nobody asked me," I said. Papa pulled to the side of the road. He gave me a Dino's napkin and I wiped my face with it though it was greasy.

"This will be good for all of us. Your mother will be happier. We'll have more money. I won't have to deliver pizza. You will be happy too, in time."

"But why leave if I'm already happy here?"

"You have to think of the good of the family, dear Oksana."

I looked down at my hands. They were covered in dried-up flecks of pizza sauce.

"I would like to be an orphan," I said.

Papa pulled back onto the road. "One day, you will get your wish," he told me.

Back home, Mama was slapping herring on a Dino's pizza as consolation. Baba orbited her as she wiped away my tears. Her heels crunched into a cicada. Mama said, "We already have a new home in Ohio, kitten. It's much bigger—a two-story condo."

"Does this mean I won't have to share a room with Baba anymore?"

Baba looked like she was going to say something, but then she turned away and put a hand to her face.

"You won't, dear girl. Your grandmother is staying here," Papa said.

Baba folded her arms over her chest as Papa explained that she loved her job at the lab and her new friend Mr. Trevors and that her independence was important to her. I looked from my parents to Baba and wondered if I factored into a single thing they did.

"That's fine," I told Baba. "Because I hate you anyway!"

She didn't seem angry—she seemed amused if anything—but Mama dragged me to my room. "Oh, who was I in a past life I do not believe in?" she said. "Was I Genghis Khan? Yezhov? Nero, perhaps?" She regarded me with scorn. "Were you born without a heart? What did your grandmother do to deserve such treatment?"

I knew there was no good answer so I thought of a bad one. "Maybe she was Stalin in a past life," I said, and Mama slapped me.

"You, Oksana," she said, "cannot joke about Stalin."

"But you can?"

"I know what Stalin means. I have suffered the pain of anti-Semitism."

"Stalin died a long time ago. What pain?"

She thought for a moment and said, "Collective pain."

I turned over what Mama told me in my head as I tried to sleep. I figured a *condo* was different from a condom, but I pictured me and Mama and Papa living inside a giant two-story condom in Ohio. It sealed us in until we ran out of air and suffocated. I would have preferred a kingdom, but, as usual, nobody asked me.

I searched for Autumn in the school parking lot the next morning to tell her I was leaving. Her Jeep pulled up by the side entrance. A dark-haired man was driving, her mom was in the passenger seat, and Autumn was in the back with a big white dog. She was babbling and they were laughing, and it looked like even the dog thought she was hysterical and they were thrilled to be together, all of them. She had betrayed me.

There was more bad news inside the classroom. Officer Friendly was back and this time he was there to talk about drugs. He stood next to a big glass display of pills and syringes and other exciting things I hadn't thought about putting in my body until that moment. He tipped his hat at me and winked. He was still tall and handsome and his mustache was even bushier.

I could hardly look at Autumn. She made me sick.

"I didn't know you had a dog," I hissed.

"You mean Muffins?" she said. "I love Muffins."

"Maybe if I had a dog and a nice family I would have given up my dolls earlier," I said, but she just frowned and shrugged.

She smiled at Officer Friendly with her dumb greasy hair and over-sized dress and I realized I didn't know her or anyone in Florida at all. I understood Raluca completely. I too would disappear without telling anybody. I wouldn't leave a trace behind.

As soon as Principal Bates got on the loudspeaker, I jumped on my chair. The students below me whispered and stared, but I didn't care. They could have belonged to my doll pile. They were garbage now. When Principal Bates began the Pledge, I shouted:

I pledge allegiance to the butterfly
Of the United States of butterfly
One butterfly, indivisible, under butterfly
With butterfly and butterfly for all!

This didn't create the dramatic effect I wanted, so I knocked over the drug case. It didn't even break. Billy Spencer whooped madly. Autumn covered her face with her hands, but the officer and his case didn't matter to me, none of it mattered, it didn't matter that Autumn had flapped her hands and said "Fly away, Okey Dokey" as Mrs. Thomas grabbed me by the ear and pulled me to the front office, where I had to sit and wait for my family.

"Shame on you," Mrs. Thomas told me. "And today of all days, what will poor Officer Friendly think? This is a good school, not without its problems, but we love our country, and so should you," she said. "Baby Bolshevik," she muttered. "And to think, I never once called her Rod…"

I sat across from the principal's office, which had glass walls. Principal Bates was perched over a pile of papers, munching on a cafeteria pretzel. The only time I had been there was my first day of school when Papa told me my name would be hard for people to say. "Now you say *O* as in *octopus*, *K* as in *kite*, *S* as in *Sam*, *A* as in *apple*, *N* as in *Nancy*, *A* as in *apple*," he said before he told me to have a good day. He took a few steps away and turned around to add, "The rest will be hard, too." That seemed like a long time ago.

Baba was walking down the hall a while later. She wore a gold suit and her hair danced around her shoulders. She had never been inside and looked a little lost. She stopped and turned, talking to somebody I couldn't see. It was Officer Friendly. I worried he'd think she was weird, but he was nice—they usually were—and she laughed and ran a hand over his badge. He gestured toward her brooch and tipped his hat and walked off. She tilted her head and admired his butt. I loved her so much I wanted her to die.

She nodded at me and marched into Principal Bates's office without knocking. She never sat down, she just wagged her finger at him and walked out before he could get a word in. He was a short sad man and he watched her with his mouth open.

"What a ridiculous thing to be punished for!" she said as she grabbed my hand and marched me out. She spoke to me for the first time in a month when we hit Prostitute Street.

"You have another week here, child," she said, kicking a lizard aside.

"What would you like to do one last time?"

I got sunburned almost as soon as we hit the beach but nobody cared. Papa blasted Dire Straits from his radio. Mama and Baba didn't chase me with sunblock, they let me build sandcastles as the gulls squawked above me. I decorated my castle with tiny pastel clams and we ate soggy Subway sandwiches and Papa and I kicked a soccer ball around. He'd just bought a camera and took pictures of us for a new album.

I walked to the water and looked at the horizon. The sand was warm and welcoming and I wanted to melt in it.

Baba came up behind me. "Soak it in. You won't have water like this in Ohio."

"There is nothing in Ohio."

"I believe there are lakes. But you'll have other things, child, like snow and farms and your own bedroom." She sighed. "Of course I could go with you. But I'm not ready to give up on myself yet. I like it here. The storms, my paramour, my job, the pool..."

"The cicadas. I'll miss how annoying they are," I said. A plane flew over our heads with a banner for a seafood restaurant. "I'm sorry for what I said, Baba. I didn't mean to hurt you."

She laughed. "It took you long enough! But I forgive you, dear. I know all this has not been easy for you, either."

"You do?"

"Of course. But you have no idea how you have lifted my spirits. All of you," she said, sweeping her hand past me to my parents, who sat on the hood of the Mercury drinking beers.

She had lost everything: her country, her youth, her father, her daughter, her husband, and soon us, and yet she hummed and toed the water and wiped her face and said she was going for one last swim and I watched her head rocking above the waves and knew she was happier than I had ever felt.

Mama lifted her bottle at us when we returned to the car. She was drunk and happy. "Dearest God I don't believe in, what have I done in a past life to deserve such bliss? Was I Florence Nightingale? Maybe Akhmatova..." She gave Papa a kiss that made me squirm.

We picked up a hitchhiker on the way back and Mama didn't complain. He was young and limp-haired and he bobbed his head like he was listening to a secret song. I sat between him and Baba in the back and she kept reaching over to squeeze his bicep. He told us to drop him near Flagler Beach, and Papa made us all get out on the side of the road and asked him would he take a picture of us, it was our last trip together, and my face burned as we posed. Then I asked the man if Flagler Beach was where he lived and he laughed and said it wasn't, but maybe it could be, and he thanked us and walked through the brush to the ocean.

Back in the car, Papa put on "Ticket to the Moon" and as Mama and Papa and Baba sang wildly with the water brimming around us, I knew I would never have a family of my own. I couldn't carry the weight of their pain or get to the bottom of it. One day they would all be dead and I would make sure I felt nothing. When the song was over, I closed my eyes and imagined I was drifting up into the sky and by the time I opened them we were almost home.

MRS. KATEGAYA'S CURSE

by CASALLINA KISAKYE

MARCH 3, 1996
    Mrs. Kategaya lost her job today because she's been poisoning us. Students are getting sick after meals and at first no one was concerned, until some parents complained and Headmaster was forced to act. Mrs. Kategaya swore her food was not the culprit and pleaded to stay, to no avail. Then, she whispered some strange words no one understood and followed up with an announcement that she'd put a Curse on the school. I do not like Curses.

March 16, 1996
Before the sun rises each morning, the headboy, Juma, rings a deafening bell to rouse us from sleep. Harriet says Juma is a prince in the Busoga kingdom and he wants to marry her. (Harriet also claims her father is an ambassador in America, even though we all know she's the daughter of Dembe, the musician who died of AIDS. No one says this to her, of

course. We are not cruel.) As soon as Juma awakens us, our first task is to immediately (and also neatly) make our beds. We have to move fast because the last two girls to finish must mop the dormitory floor. Because we sleep on double- and triple-deckers, the girls on the top beds inevitably end up on cleaning duty. (It's quite difficult to make your bed while maintaining your balance on the railings.) That used to be me, until I gave Harriet half my pocket money and shined her shoes so she'd switch beds with me. Now I can't afford to buy *sumbusa* from the market, but at least I'm no longer mopping the floor.

The electricity has been going off in the mornings. There are whispers that this is the Curse at work but power outages are not unusual. The problem is it's dark when we wake and we cannot see a thing. Girls have been falling off the top bunks as they attempt to climb down. We trip over each other when we kneel for morning prayers. And in the darkness it is impossible to make our beds properly and neatly. One Saturday every month, Headmistress inspects the girls' dormitories and chooses a winner based on the most perfectly made beds. Our dorm wins the competition every time. Until today. Miss Nabukenya, our housemother, was not pleased. But what could we do? We can't see.

April 7, 1996
It has rained every day since Mrs. Kategaya left. We no longer have the market on Saturdays. Sports Day was cancelled. The flooding has become so serious that one of the cows drowned.

April 21, 1996
Brian is the new student. He's a *mzungu* from England. His parents are missionaries. All the girls are fascinated with him. Even Patience, who usually has no interest in boys, lets him borrow her mathematics textbook. We follow Brian everywhere and we touch his skin, which we have only

ever seen on TV. His skin is whiter than Amita's, the Indian girl in our class last year. (She did not return this year and I'm glad. Headmaster allowed her to keep her hair long while the rest of us have to shave ours off, and I thought that was unfair.)

Brian is now the most interesting boy, even more than Edgar. I like Edgar. He's the best student in our class and lets me copy his answers on tests. One time we snuck away from the assembly, and Edgar asked if he could stick his finger inside me. I let him and afterwards he ran off. Later I told his cousin Ruth and, as happens with her, soon the whole dormitory knew. Of course Harriet had to top my story, so she shared that a "real man" had done the same to her: Mr. Kizito, the P7 teacher.

On Sunday when we were fetching water from the well, Brian fell and seriously injured himself. We wondered if this was the result of the Curse, but Patience pointed out that Mrs. Kategaya left before Brian arrived, so why would she punish him? Brian tried to stand and screamed, "Oh, my leg!" This has become his new name, *Ohmyleg*. Even our teacher, Miss Miriam, is calling him that. "Ohmyleg, please pass out the pencils." "Ohmyleg, who is the president of Rwanda?" And he answers to it.

May 9, 1996

The nation held its first presidential election today, but the biggest issue here concerns what to do about the grasshoppers that have invaded our school. They are everywhere—outside, in the dining hall, in the classrooms, in our dormitories and showers. (Miss Miriam remarked that the manner in which these insects have encroached on our lives is symbolic of our current political climate. Then she laughed and laughed.) At first we were excited to catch the grasshoppers because Miss Nabukenya was frying them for us to eat. But now they are starting to frighten us, especially at night when all we hear is that very loud chirping, as if they are preparing to attack.

May 13, 1996

A story has spread that the Curse brings creatures into our dormitories at night as we sleep. Some of the girls are so afraid that Miss Nabukenya allows them to sleep on the floor of her residence. The twins Babirye and Nakato swear they've seen these creatures but can't agree on whether they look like ghosts or animals. Then last week at supper, Harriet said she too had seen them in our dorm. There were three or four and they looked like human skeletons with no flesh on their bodies. No eyes either, but somehow they could see where they were going. Patience, who questions everything, asked what exactly the skeletons were doing. Harriet pointed to me and said they were standing over my body as I slept. And that wasn't the end of it. She added that one of the skeletons picked up my towel, wiped its body with it and placed it back at the foot of my bed. Patience wanted to know why the creature chose my towel, and Harriet theorized that they are plotting to take me away. All the girls were terrified, but I simply laughed because I knew Harriet was lying.

Harriet and I were best friends since kindergarten, until the day came to choose our school colors. Each student belongs in yellow, green, blue, or purple. Your color is important. When we're not in our red uniforms we wear our colors, and we also put them on for Sports Day, when your color is the team on which you belong. Harriet decided we were both to be in blue but I had already chosen yellow. (It reminds me of my mother: she had a bright, yellow gomesi she only wore for weddings and she looked so beautiful in it.) Harriet never forgave me for going against her decision, and ever since then she finds ways to punish me. I do not believe anything she says because she invents stories. Like when we came back from holiday and she told everyone she had spent New Year's in America, even though Ruth saw her watching the fireworks at the Sheraton in Kampala. I'm not sure there are any skeletons. But for now, I have thrown away my towel and I'm using my clothes to dry off after I bathe.

May 26, 1996

Mr. Mukisa, the P4 teacher, was run over by a *boda-boda*. Ruth said his body was nearly ripped in half but he's alive. (How does Ruth know everything? She's like a rat that lives in the walls, eavesdropping on people's conversations.) Of course *boda-bodas* destroy lives every day. My own Uncle Sessanga lost a leg to one. But it is becoming harder not to blame all these happenings on the Curse.

June 7, 1996

Six girls have disappeared. The Pearl of Africa Revolutionary Army abducted them, and the government is negotiating with the group to release the girls. Headmaster reassured us that the Pearl is not as serious a threat as other rebel groups in the north. (Edgar noted that these groups will become more dangerous because the presidential election was rigged. Headmaster ordered him to stop talking.) In the meantime, the school has hired additional guards and our night classes are ending earlier.

June 10, 1996

The school clinic caught fire last night. No one knows what caused it. We stood in our nightgowns watching the flames, as the older boys ran down to the well and returned with water buckets. The building still stands, but most of the supplies were destroyed. I told the girls the school needs to give Mrs. Kategaya her job back to put an end to this Curse. For once Harriet agreed with me. In fact, she has written her mother asking her to consult a witch doctor. Patience, as usual, insisted that Curses are not real, and neither are witch doctors, or *abasezi*, or Father Christmas.

June 28, 1996

It finally happened: the Curse touched me. Today, for the first time, I was punished with the bamboo stick.

During school hours we must only speak English. Headmaster says this will prepare us for a "global future." Except for Ohmyleg, English is not anyone's first language, although most of us are fluent at this point. But every once in a while you forget a certain word and say it in Luganda, and then you're in trouble. Or you finish lunch (we are allowed to speak Luganda during meals), and then return to class and speak without switching back to English. The rules are confusing.

Miss Miriam was late, most likely from spending the night at Headmaster's residence, since Headmistress is away this week. (One night Ruth forgot her handkerchief in the classroom and when she went back for it she saw Miss Miriam and Headmaster standing close, with his hand resting on her backside. Another time Ruth heard Miss Miriam whisper to Miss Nabukenya that Headmaster is "filling.") As we waited, I told the girls about my mother visiting me in my dream last night. Patience said the dead cannot visit you and that those are stories "bush people" like to tell. (Patience thinks she's so clever because she lived in America as a baby.) I was so angry and before I could stop myself I yelled, "*Komanyoko*." Everyone gasped and went silent. Patience promised she would tell Miss Miriam I used foul language, in Luganda no less. Then Harriet started a chant, "*Omuwala afudde!*" The other students joined in. Edgar pointed out that they were all in fact speaking Luganda but this went ignored.

When Miss Miriam arrived, Patience told her what I'd said, of course leaving out the part where she called me a bush person. I tried to defend myself but Miss Miriam was very upset with me. I swore I wouldn't cry during the punishment, but as soon as I laid down on the floor and felt that first strike from the bamboo, I burst into tears. The class was quiet so my cries seemed very loud. When it was over I went outside until I could stop crying. Today I hate everybody.

July 2, 1996
Snakes. Snakes, everywhere. Thankfully they are the *namagoye,* the blind, non-venomous kind, which you're not supposed to kill. Nonetheless they manage to scare us each time we stumble onto one slithering across the schoolyard or curled up in a corner of the classroom.

There is still no sign of the Pearl Girls, as the newspapers are calling them.

July 15, 1996
Headmaster was arrested. According to Ruth, he was stealing money from the school and using it to build his new house in Jinja. (I hope this means Mrs. Kategaya has completed her cycle of revenge and the Curse will end.) Headmistress was rolling her body in the grass and screaming at the policemen as they led her husband away. Everybody looked sad for her. Except Miss Miriam, who just sucked her teeth.

July 30, 1996
First the chickens died. Mr. Kizito, who is acting as headmaster, said they were poisoned and threatened to dismiss the school guards for allowing it to happen on their watch. Then all of the goats were found dead. Miss Nabukenya has begun wearing her Rosary daily and when we asked her why, she replied that the animals are an omen of what will come.

August 19, 1996
Miss Miriam lost her baby. A few weeks ago we started to notice her body was rounder, and Harriet finally asked her if she was pregnant and she said yes. (Patience asked who the baby's father was, since Miss Miriam is not married, and she answered, "God.") This morning Miss Nabukenya informed us that Miss Miriam is in the hospital because the baby came out too early. She explained that sometimes this happens to women's

bodies and there is nothing we can do about it. Later, though, Ruth told a different story.

There is a group of older girls and boys who sneak out after bedtime and gather in the backfield where we hold Sports Day. Usually they will have gotten their hands on some *waragi* from the school guards, and they will drink and play and do whatever girls and boys do in the dark. Last night the group noticed smoke coming from the teachers' compound. They thought it was another fire, but when they went to investigate they saw that the smoke was in fact a dark mist surrounding Miss Miriam's house. A few moments later they heard Miss Miriam scream. Everyone was frightened and there was talk about whether or not to go into the house to help her. But somebody pointed out that the mist indicates spirits are present, and it is best not to get involved or else they come after you.

The spirits took Miss Miriam's baby. The Curse has claimed a human life.

September 1, 1996
Many of us are sick with malaria, which has turned our dorm into a makeshift hospital. This whole ordeal has been worsened by the shortage of medicine due to the clinic fire. We can't sleep at night because our bodies ache terribly. It is truly unbearable and I'm beginning to wonder if we all might die.

October 13, 1996
Visiting Sunday was today. We put on our uniforms, shined our shoes, and made the beds until they were perfect. The dining hall was decorated, and the cooks served *matoke* and beef, not the *posho* we usually eat. Term scores were released and rankings were posted on a wall in the classroom. I normally land between twenty-one and thirty-five, but this time I came in at nineteen. Edgar was number one, of course. Patience was second,

and I smiled because I know how much it bothers her that she's not the best. Harriet was sixth, and this also made me happy because it means her parents won't bring her presents for making the top five. Ohmyleg came in last, and Ruth (twelfth) heard his parents complain to Mr. Kizito about "privacy" and how the rankings are "not appropriate."

But the biggest reveal of the day was that the Curse has been undone by Mrs. Kategaya's death. She had a heart condition, and Patience, who still maintains she does not believe in these things, explained that Mrs. Kategaya's passing means the Curse died with her. And she's right. The Pearl Girls were freed last week after the group came to an agreement with the government, (although Ruth says two of the girls are pregnant). Miss Miriam has returned to us, and even though she no longer smiles, we are thrilled to have her back. Mr. Mukisa is also out of the hospital after recovering from the *boda-boda* accident. We are no longer suffering from malaria. The electricity has consistently stayed on for the past several weeks, and there have been no sightings of grasshoppers, snakes, or skeletons.

The Curse has been broken.

October 29, 1996
Edgar was found hanged in his dormitory. He used a bed sheet, while we were at lunch. Ordinarily we would get all the details from Ruth, but for the first time ever she did not speak. Her eyes were wide and she was shaking uncontrollably and breathing loudly, but she didn't cry. Miss Miriam had to hold her because it looked like she might collapse. Mr. Kizito was shouting, "This is not right." I thought he was going to cry. Miss Nabukenya and the other housemothers were weeping. We were sent back to the dorms for the rest of the day, and everyone was completely still and silent. We were all thinking the same thing, that perhaps we'd been wrong about the Curse. And if so, which one of us would be its next victim?

At night no one could sleep so Miss Nabukenya allowed us to keep the lights on. Later, Patience pulled out her trunk and produced the much-coveted packets of biscuits her parents bring back from America. She passed them around to the entire dormitory. I gave out the *kabala-gala* Aunt Marjorie sends me, and more girls shared their snacks. Harriet allowed those without shoe polish to use hers. The twins Babirye and Nakato, who sew very well, offered to mend anyone's torn uniforms. Another girl gave up her spare soap, and another her extra Vaseline. It went on like that all night.

In class the next morning, Miss Miriam instructed us to each write a letter to Ruth.

Dear Ruth,

When someone dies, at first you don't cry. I didn't even cry at my mother's funeral. Until, without warning, the tears come. And you cry all the time, every single day. You can't control it. You wonder if you're going to die from crying. Then one day you stop. Not because you want to, but you just do. So you return to your life. It's never the same, of course, because you are forever changed and the tears will emerge occasionally. But by some miracle your heart keeps beating.

January 6, 2004

I did not return to school after the end of that year. My father could no longer afford the fees, and to be honest I was grateful. Today I work as a housegirl for a family in Kampala. I'm able to send money home and best of all, my mother still visits me in my dreams.

I think we all managed to beat the Curse. After Edgar's death, Ruth transferred to Gayaza. She is now at Mbarara University with plans to be a nurse. Patience received a scholarship to attend university in America, and apparently she's in a relationship with a woman. (I can't confirm that last part, but it came from Ruth and she knows everything.) Harriet is at Makerere studying to be a teacher. She's engaged to marry the son of a Member of Parliament, the closest thing to a prince. I think of her often, especially when a song by Dembe comes on the radio.

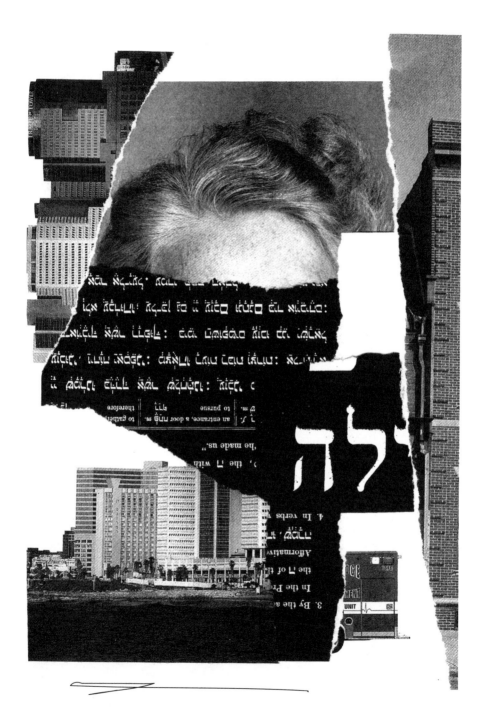

THE ANATOMY
OF EXILE

by ZEEVA BUKAI

T HAT YEAR THE UNEXPECTED heat had the neighbors gathering on the stoops of the Calliope Garden apartments. From her second-story window, Tamar heard the murmur of their conversations and her children shouting as they played catch. The late September sun was a blood orange in the Brooklyn sky and Avenue C sidewalks that had baked all day at ninety-eight degrees shimmered.

Salim brought his dinner plate to the kitchen. "See you downstairs?"

"You don't need me there." She scrubbed the dishes hard, wondering if he heard her displeasure over the gushing faucet. She could feel him behind her weighing his next move, knowing what he would do before he did, and held still. He wrapped his arms around her, hands splayed on her collarbone, thumbs curving into the hollow at the base of her throat, softly and then with a bit of pressure, just enough to let her know there was strength in them.

"None of this makes sense without you." He nuzzled her neck. "Besides, Shira will beat me with a rolling pin if you aren't there."

He waited for her to laugh. She leaned her head on his chest instead, thinking not of their next-door neighbor but of the steady heartbeat beneath her ear, as familiar as her own. The belt buckle on his chinos, the blades of his hips jutting into her back, his breath a warm cloud. This is me truly alive, she thought with despair.

"Does Shira think I mistreat you?" Salim gently rocked her.

"No, only that you work too much. She and Aaron are here more than you are."

He gave her butt a proprietary squeeze. "I want us to have everything."

"I know." She thought of the house for sale he'd taken her to yesterday. Far from here, on the other side of the borough. "You don't mind if they join us for the Sabbath, do you?"

"No." He began to pull away.

"Because," she rushed on, "they're like family to us, like a mother and father." She tried to control the quaver in her voice. "Even Estelle. On a good day, she's almost an auntie to our children. You've seen her talk to Ari. How she encourages him to build things."

"Tamar," he kissed her cheek. "It's not a good idea to get so close."

She tried to grab hold of his hand, but he was too quick for her and stepped out of range. She went back to the dishes, soaping the forks and spoons. "I had everything once. Even when we had nothing."

The door clicked shut behind him. To the empty kitchen she said, "We had time then for dancing and afternoon naps."

The apartment was oppressive without him and the children to distract her. She quickly rinsed the silverware and then changed into her favorite yellow dress, enjoying the feel of the seersucker grazing her knees. She unpinned her hair, an impulse she would normally have ignored, except that today it reminded her of those summers on Kibbutz Magen, picking peaches with the other scouts and dancing like goats around a campfire.

All day the heat had made her homesick. The heat and the scent of honey cake that still lingered though Rosh Hashanah had ended days before. This morning she thought she smelled the jasmine tree that had been in her front garden in Tel Aviv, but it was only the fabric softener. The fragrance burst out of the washing machine and when she hung the clothes on the line she had the disquieting thought that home wasn't grounded in one particular place, but existed in the scent of a thousand objects.

She kicked off her slippers and before she could talk herself into a pair of shoes descended the stairs barefoot. Outside the warm dusk engulfed her. A few neighbors had set out folding chairs near the entrance, a short distance from where children played Red Rover near the corner of East 4th Street. The youngest were led by her daughter Rachel in a game of Red Light Green Light. Her son, Ari, tall for his age, was a giant next to them. The children fell in giggles when he froze mid-stride, his hands clawing the air, a goofy grin on his face. She smiled and he beamed at her. As a toddler he'd always had a hank of hair falling into his eyes. That hadn't changed, nor had the stare that dug into her as if he could see into her heart.

Salim waved to her. The men around him were dark and foreign. Their gruff laughter, their accented talk enveloped in the aroma of cheap cigarillos.

The women greeted her. Shira Geller gave her a quick hug.

"Isn't it a marvelous night?" She tucked a strand of hair behind Tamar's ear. "I don't think I've ever seen you with your hair down. You look like a girl. I had no idea it was so long and so wild, too."

A flush stained Tamar's cheeks. Shira's hair was perfectly coiffed, dyed a deep chestnut, coiled into a chignon. No one looking at her plump figure would guess that during the Second World War she had starved, or see in the mild planes of her face the death of a beloved son. No one knew that more often now she had to put her husband, Aaron, to bed, and when he woke tuck his feet into a pair of leather slippers, strip him of his cotton pajamas, bathe him, and shave his face. Only her daughter was difficult to hide. Estelle wore sunglasses and earmuffs all year long. She was sensitive to light and sound, a result of having spent fifteen months in a sewer below their Berlin apartment before the family was caught and freighted east. She was the same age as Tamar and, though Shira encouraged Estelle to mix with the neighbors, she stayed nearby, ensuring that Estelle remained calm.

Tamar thought of the effort it had taken to cultivate this friendship. Five years and one month they had lived here and each week she'd visited and listened to the Gellers' troubles. She tried to please them with cakes and stories, to be a daughter, a mother, a sister, a confidante, to be a woman who secured her hair in a bun, who wore shoes, who didn't dress in homemade clothes. She ran errands for them, shopped for them all so that she could form an attachment to people who would care about her, people with whom she could belong, and who understood what it meant to abandon one country for another. Sometimes Tamar imagined Shira calling her daughter. Now all she'd worked for would be severed if Salim got his way.

Shira pointed to an empty beach chair beside her and Estelle.

"I was saving this one for you," she said, and then, "Are you alright?"

"Of course," Tamar patted Shira's hand and greeted another neighbor before Shira could probe further.

She wasn't ready to tell her about Salim and the house for sale in the new development east of Canarsie. They'd left the kids home with their eldest daughter, Ruby. The day was overcast and the faint stench of sewage had drifted out of the sanitation plant on Flatlands Avenue near the Paerdegat Basin. She had held her breath until Salim asked her what the hell she was doing and exhaled so quickly she'd felt lightheaded. His exasperation had made her shrink into the corner of the car's passenger seat. She had wanted him to take notice and draw her back with a word or an arm across her shoulders, the way he did to woo her after an argument, whispering in her ear how much he needed her, kissing the back of her neck until her head grew too heavy to lift. And each time she would turn to him, a sunflower bowing to the sun, forgiving him. But he'd been too intent on showing her the neighborhood to pay attention to anything else.

"They have everything here." He had pointed to the strip malls that lined Ralph Avenue. There was a supermarket, an International House of Pancakes, a bank, a Woolworth's, a dry cleaner, a bridal shop, and a Chinese restaurant.

The stores were big and overbright, something she had come to expect of American shops where merchandise was always on display. In Israel her favorite stores were small and half-lit, sundries shops selling paper and ink, calendars, and leather-bound travel journals whose blank sheets were like dares. She loved the tiny groceries that popped up every few blocks, tucked into a corner of a building, smelling of freshly ground coffee and spilled milk that soured in the afternoon heat. There was barely room for the proprietor to maneuver around stacks of goods, and yet they knew exactly where everything was and if they didn't have it they'd order it for her special, telephone the next day or the following week, address her by name so that she felt valued, even cared for. Here she was just another consumer, one of the masses, anonymous and unseen, her money the only thing speaking for her.

Shira placed a hand on her shoulder and looked at Tamar's bare feet, worry deepening the creases around her eyes. Tamar was grateful Shira didn't voice her concern.

"Did you hear?"

"Sorry." Tamar said. "What did I miss?"

"Aaron has a doctor's appointment next week. Can you come?"

"Of course."

"He gets so nervous. Maybe if you join us we can make a pleasant day of it."

"I'm happy to go." Tamar knew it was Shira who grew anxious whenever Aaron had to see a doctor.

Shira squeezed her hand. "We're good friends."

"Yes," Tamar said, thinking they were her only friends. The other neighbors weren't much more than acquaintances, people with whom she visited, brought a cookie tin to, but in whom she couldn't confide, couldn't say "I don't belong here." Shira seemed to understand this about her, and on days when it was hard to shake off the homesickness she would roll up her sleeves and say, "Come, let's make strudel." They would make the pastry from scratch. Aaron would roll butter into each thin layer of dough. He'd call her *maideleh* and tell her stories about Berlin. His life, like her own, was sheared in two, before and after. In the before he was head engineer of the Berlin central railroad, a good position with a fine salary. The after was something else entirely, hiding under the street where they had once lived in style with servants and tutors, a weekly gardener, a grocer boy who delivered produce to the kitchen door, until the morning the Gellers were caught. Though he rarely spoke of the after, it was always there, a sinkhole ready to pull him down. As he spoke, Tamar would peel and core tart green apples, slice them, and add golden raisins, cinnamon, and sugar, the same recipe she and her mother had baked Friday mornings for the Sabbath before her father died.

A car gunning its engine broke into her thoughts. She followed its path to McDonald Avenue, catching sight of the oak trees and the Dutch colonial houses across the street, the Church of the Annunciation on the corner with its green lawn spanning half a block, tempting her the way the kibbutz had tempted her to run barefoot through fruit orchards and fields of tall grass. Further along Avenue C was the school where Ari and Rachel were in the fifth and sixth grades, and, a few streets beyond, the high school Ruby attended. All of it familiar now; she knew this neighborhood almost as well as she knew Tel Aviv. She didn't want to begin again, to be a stranger in another strange place. If she had to stay in America, then she wanted to stay here, though when she'd first seen the apartment at the Calliope Gardens she'd hated its long, dark foyer and two mean bedrooms spearing off the hall. Seeing her reaction, Salim had cradled her face and said, "Remember what I promised you."

"A fortune in five years and then we go home."

Until yesterday the words had been her mantra, but then he'd taken her to that new development with its model homes and identical townhouses with screen doors and pitched roofs. Acres of derelict lots heaped with slabs of concrete and steel girders twisted and bent. Where the ground was left undisturbed, weeds grew taller than men. Hardly any of the streets were completed.

"This was once a landfill site. Amazing, isn't it? What they can do with garbage here?"

She had swallowed back the old despair, knowing he'd already made up his mind about the place and if she said no, not this time, he'd accuse her of ruining their lives, of not loving him enough, not sacrificing enough, of forgetting what they'd learned long ago in the Scouts—the good of the collective was more important than the good of the individual. "Aww, Tami," he'd say. "You know I'm doing this for us."

They drove down roads where bulldozers had exhumed broken toasters and mattresses, busted television sets, and legless coffee tables. He stopped the car on a block where there was a row of attached homes on one side and a weed-ridden lot on the other. At the corner was a hill of sand she knew Ari would love to climb, but imagined it full of sharp objects and thought about how and where he would be cut, the length and depth of the wounds, the blood difficult to staunch.

Salim came up behind her, his hands on her shoulders. "Can you see it?" he said, his chin a pendulum moving back and forth along her scalp. "Our future here."

At the thought of that future, her toes curled into the concrete. A breeze blew across Avenue C, drawing a faint rustle of leaves and the aroma of something wet in the air. Her neighbors chattered on about whose child was sick with mumps, whose husband had lost his job, who was pregnant, who had died, and had anyone seen the latest *Vogue* pattern? Salim was deep in a circle of men. His stance almost indolent, one hand in his trouser pocket, the other holding a cigarette; ribbons of smoke threaded round his fingers. She was seventeen the first time he'd kissed her. It was their last summer before he was drafted into the army. They'd traveled to Kibbutz Magen to harvest peaches, the fuzz a terror on bare flesh. After a night of folk dancing he took her to the orchard and tossed his shirt on the ground for her to lie on. They faced each other, shivering, their foreheads touching; he smelled of smoke and caramelized peaches; their toes burrowed into the soil like worms.

Now she recalled how he'd pulled her into that house for sale—her feet bricks dragging behind her, through the kitchen with its fancy dishwasher, up the short flight of stairs to the master bedroom, private bath, and walk-in closet.

"Tell me you can resist this," he said.

She could, she absolutely could. When had she ever wanted such things? When had he?

He crossed the hall. "This can be Ari's." He pointed to a small blue room. "He'll be a bar mitzvah in two years. I can't see him sharing a room with his sisters forever. Can you?"

His logic was a serpent. She trailed behind him downstairs to "Rachel's" bedroom, where a sliding glass door opened onto a tiny patio and a con-crete yard with a narrow strip of dirt.

"Remember the small garden we planted on our balcony in Tel Aviv? We could do that here."

Sturdy weeds straddled the perimeter of a three-foot fence. This was nothing like the dahlias and lilies on their *mirpehset,* or the bougainvillea that had greeted them at the entrance to their old building.

"Is it safe?" she asked, apprehensive at how easy it would be for someone to climb the fence and molest her daughters. "People could break in."

"You always look for the hair in the soup." He gave her a gentle shake.

"You know what the best part of this place is? There's another apart-ment. We can rent it. We can be landlords." He took hold of her hands.

"Think of it, Tamar," and then, "I put a binder on it. We're in contract."

Tamar felt Salim's attention on her.

"Anything wrong?" He mouthed the words.

She shook her head and he resumed his conversation with Ibrahim Mahmoudi, their upstairs neighbor, an Arab from Jaffa. The men spoke in Arabic. Sometimes she forgot that Hebrew wasn't Salim's first language. Before they married she'd asked him what it was like to be an Arab Jew in an Arab land.

"Not much different from being an Arab Jew in a Jewish land," he'd said, and then changed the subject, as though she couldn't know what it meant to be an outsider. She hadn't then. It struck her now that he might be more comfortable in Arabic, even though he was fluent in Hebrew. She had never considered him a foreigner in Israel. There were so many immigrants there and he rarely spoke about his childhood in Syria. His life, the one she knew, began in Tel Aviv at the age of ten.

He and Ibrahim were the same height, though Ibrahim was bulkier

around the middle. It disturbed her to see similarities in them, her preju-
dice, she admitted, the way they spoke with authority on all subjects, the
way they behaved with their children, though she wanted to believe that
Ibrahim took the strap to his boys with more regularity than Salim did;
they were rarely indulgent with women and rarely affectionate in public,
patronizing, cautious with a touch of tyranny. They spoke of money, of jobs,
their talk a bit clumsy, their accents thick, eyes intent, sometimes flicking
toward the women if they were too loud. Neither looked easy in his skin, not
even Salim who was ready to put good money down on a house where the
carpeting smelled of naphthalene and the living room had wall-to-ceiling
mirrors. Their reflections had caught half a dozen times. Salim had struck a
pose and grinned in that triumphant way she'd seen only twice before—on
the day Ari was born and when he'd finally obtained their visas to America.
She closed her eyes, fighting a bubble of nausea, fearing that if they bought
the house they'd never go home to Israel again.

"Why do you insist on standing?" Shira patted the chair next to her.
"Sit down."

Besides her husband and children, the Gellers were the nearest thing
to family she had here. They took an interest in her and her children,
brought them small gifts, remembered their birthdays, invited them for
tea on Saturday afternoons.

Tamar sat in the chair. Even on this warm night Estelle wore her pro-
tective gear: earmuffs and sunglasses. Sometimes Tamar wondered if she
didn't have the right idea, setting the world on mute. Tamar touched her
shoulder and Estelle swung around, scoring her fingers through the muff.

"It's you," Estelle said. Her relieved smile changed to consternation.
"Your hair."

"Different, I know." Tamar wrapped the bulk of it around her wrist
like a rope, then let it fall over one shoulder. "I see you've got a new muff."

Estelle rubbed a hand over a circle of white rabbit fur. The old one, though beloved, had become ratty and bald. Poor Shira, Tamar thought without irony, appearance was everything to her.

Tamar closed her eyes and felt the day drain from her, the homesickness like a low-grade fever she couldn't shake. All afternoon memories of their last night in Tel-Aviv had haunted her: the suitcases stacked in the empty living room, the children sleeping fitfully in their beds, her and Salim standing on the balcony like sentries over the city. The scent of jasmine was almost cloying. Between the white Bauhaus buildings, they glimpsed the sea, moonlit and wavering. Sounds from Dizengoff Square burbled through the neighborhood and the Cameri Theatre on the corner of Frishman had just let out. Theatergoers flooded the quiet streets as they made their way to their cars and apartments. Chekhov spinning in their heads: Nina, Masha, Treplev, Tregorin, the gun, the samovar ready to fill teacups made of porcelain so thin they were almost transparent. "Where did they find those costumes?" she heard one say, and then as a group passed directly below them a woman cried, *"I'm in mourning for my life."* Laughter shot into the trees. She and Salim, two stories above, buffeted by the sounds of home.

Darkness fell in increments over Avenue C: cerulean blue turned to indigo, indigo to black and then blacker still. Insects swarmed the street-lights, some no bigger than a speck of dust while moths so large they could hardly flap their furred wings for the weight hovered like spacecraft in the glow.

She watched with envy their ability to fly anywhere they wished. Yet all their energy was spent on a lamp on this street. She was turning to ask Shira what time the doctor's appointment was when she saw Aaron Geller exit the building. If Shira was like a mother to her, Aaron was like the father she had lost at fourteen. He had died at the breakfast table on a Saturday morning in June while reading the editorial in *Haaretz*. Her mother said she had screamed his name, but Tamar didn't remember making a sound.

Aaron moved his chair against the wall. He didn't like anyone coming up behind him. His hands rested on his knees. They were large and dangled like a child's mittens from the sleeves of a coat. He was eight years older than Shira, tall, white-haired, a bit stooped in the shoulders. He lit a pipe and a scented cloud of cherry tobacco floated above him. They exchanged a greeting and he dug into his pocket and offered her a candy. He always had sweets for the neighborhood children. When she shook her head he said, "Take it, my dear, you look like you could use one today."

She smiled, "You know me too well," she said, and unwrapped a butterscotch.

He puffed on his pipe and patted her hand. Their talk meandered to the days before the Second World War. She loved listening to his stories, though sometimes he lost his way in a conversation or forgot where he was and he would search for his wife and daughter and find in their faces a landmark he recognized.

Now he watched the children bound from stoop to curb, playing tag. Some were dressed in pajamas ready for bed, moist from their baths, waiting for their mothers to take them in, not wanting to miss a second of the evening with its symphony of crickets and insects singeing their wings on the lamps above the lintel. Someone turned on a portable radio and the song "Sealed with a Kiss" played. Conversations stopped and started like threads picked and dropped; Tamar didn't follow any of them. Her daughter Ruby ran up to her.

"I'm taking the kids to the pizza shop for ices. Dad gave us money," she flashed the dollar bill in her palm. Rachel and Ari hung back as if they expected her to say no.

"Fine." Tamar watched them dash away so bright and tall, so American in their Converse sneakers and printed T-shirts. One day she feared she wouldn't know them.

Intent on this thought, she almost jumped out of her chair when Aaron lurched to his feet. He stretched his arms and rumbled like an airplane engine, moving toward the children on the far corner of the block, leaving his pipe smoldering on his seat. Shira said she was going upstairs to get a shawl. Tamar nodded, but didn't offer to go with her. Aaron boomed, "I'm going to get you," and stalked after the children. They were delighted. Their feet pounded the pavement as they ran to the end of the street, close to where Tamar and the neighbors sat. When they reached the corner they spun around, dodging Aaron, surprising him with their agility and sure-footedness. His hands remained outstretched, no longer as an airplane but straight out, ready to haul a child up by the collar, allowing them to escape at the last minute. Shrieks of joyful terror filled the night each time Aaron drew close enough to grab a swatch of cotton. She and a few of the other neighbors whistled and clapped, urging them to run faster. On the third turn, when the children reached Building D, Aaron finally captured a small boy by the scruff and the others gathered and took hold of Aaron's arms and legs. The littlest ones climbing him like a tree, burrowed their hands into his pockets to find the candy they knew was there.

At first he seemed to enjoy their exuberance, chuckling at their antics, pretending to smack their inquisitive hands away, but the children dug in, refusing to let him go. Aaron staggered under their weight. He searched for a way to break their hold, hooting with laughter as they tickled him without mercy, their small fingers drilling into his flesh, until the tallest and boldest, a boy with a military crew cut, pushed the little ones aside. He held a toy revolver to Aaron's chest. Aaron's gaze fixed on the boy's hand, and he stumbled backward when the boy gave him a shove with the gun. The children loosened their grip and Aaron set off in earnest. Now the pack of them gave chase, led by the boy with the revolver. They ran Aaron up and down the block. The perimeter grew shorter with each lap, so that soon he was running in circles. Children swarmed around him. They looped their arms together so he couldn't break free of the human chain and in one voice began to shout: "run, run, run, run." Aaron lunged to the right, then to the left. He hesitated then teetered in the center, trapped.

Tamar walked to the periphery of the circle, calling to Aaron to come and sit down. She expected him to stop playing and chuckle his way out, ruffle a head or two, but instead he raised his arms in the air and began to jog in place, knees high, breath coming in quick spurts. The children's voices grew louder and in response he ran faster and called out a series of numbers. His face, gray and contorted, glistened with sweat; his shirt was soaked through and still the numbers rang from his lips, each like the strike of a bell. The kids fell silent.

"Aaron," Tamar called again, but it was obvious he couldn't hear her. Salim and some of the other men cocked their heads to listen. Shira appeared at the entrance, a shawl draped across her shoulders. She took in the scene and rushed to the circle. The children grew frightened and stepped aside. Nothing, it seemed, could stop Aaron. He looked like a terrified clown. His pant legs hiked up, revealing pale, delicate ankles. Moving slower now, his body shook with each footfall. Shira grabbed hold of his shoulders and still he continued until she pressed her nose to his.

"Do you know me?" she said.

He stopped, his ribcage expanding and contracting with effort. Shira attempted to steer him back to the chair, but he was pinned to the spot. His hands, like loose plates at the end of his arms, were at an awkward angle, the wrists having been broken and never properly set. His eyes tunneled into Shira's. Minutes passed before his face lit with recognition. He raised a fingertip to her cheek then dropped to his knees. His body hit the ground, sending the last bits of candy in his pockets rolling across the concrete. The children, thinking he was still in the game, converged.

Shira screamed and everything quieted. Only the faint crackle of the fluorescent lights could be heard, and the far-off hiss of cars as they sped down Ocean Parkway. Someone had turned off the radio. Estelle bolted out of her seat and ran to her parents' side. Earmuffs and sunglasses clattered to the ground. Mothers shooed their children upstairs and the men who had been too deep in their conversations before crowded around the Gellers. Salim extended his hands toward Aaron, intending to lift him, but at the last moment jumped out of the way when a stream of piss gushed from Aaron's pant leg and a foul smell rose from his body.

It was Ibrahim Mahmoudi who pulled the lever down on the fire-alarm box and it wasn't long before they heard a siren. "What can I do?" Tamar asked. She tried to shut her mind to Estelle's howling, wondering if that was how she had sounded when her own father had died. Shira cradled Aaron's head in her lap and told all who'd gathered, "Please go home, he's going to be fine." Her stockings were torn at the knee; her skirt was hitched too high, exposing the metal tabs on her garter belt, the shawl a bundle on the ground.

Tamar had the urge to cover her up, knowing Shira would be mortified at the sight of her own dishevelment. "What can I do?" she asked again.

"Take Estelle home," Shira said, "and call Aaron's sister in Florida. The number is in the blue book on the counter."

Tamar slipped an arm around Estelle's shoulders just as the fire engine and ambulance reached their block. "You've dropped your muff," she told her, trying to draw Estelle away from Aaron's side, but she refused to budge and held onto her father's shirttail that had come free of his waistband.

When the ambulance pulled up to the curb, Estelle finally relinquished her hold; the revolving lights and noise overwhelmed her. Tamar gave her the earmuffs and sunglasses and Estelle put them on, turning away as a paramedic placed a stethoscope on Aaron's chest and then, when he couldn't find a heartbeat, performed CPR, counting out the breaths, pumping cupped hands over Aaron's heart, the frail ribs fracturing under the strain. Twenty minutes later, Aaron was strapped to a gurney and put into the ambulance. Shira was beside him and they drove off. This time there were no flashing lights and no siren.

Estelle pressed her face into Tamar's neck. She had never realized how heavy Estelle was; had always thought of her as far too slender. Now she had to use all of her strength to remain upright.

"Estelle, please."

"Ma?" Ruby said.

Tamar looked up to see her children, their faces like moons, wide and vacant. She had no idea how long they'd been there or what they'd seen. *I should go to them*, she thought, knowing they must be frightened, but couldn't manage a step with Estelle clutching at her. Salim told Ruby to take Ari and Rachel upstairs. He placed a kind hand on Estelle's shoulder and told her not to worry, but she only buried her face deeper into Tamar's neck. Her hands snagged in Tamar's hair.

"Well, Shira's not going to stick around this place. Not after today. You okay?" His cheek rubbed against hers, abrasive and welcome. "You can thank me later."

"For what?"

"I put a down payment on the house. It's ours."

"The house?" She felt off-balance, as if the ground had shifted, but it was Estelle tightening her grip.

"Don't you see," his breath filled her ear, "it's fate. The house came to us just in time."

He drew himself up. "Poor Aaron," he said, and strode into the building.

Her gaze fell to where Aaron had collapsed. Gently, she pried Estelle from her side and told her to fold the beach chairs and when she was done to go home and wait for Shira, who would return soon. When Estelle finally let her go, Tamar felt weightless. Her feet, pale as wood stripped of its bark, were inches from the pool of urine and the shawl Shira had left behind. There were cracks in the concrete where blades of grass emerged. She bent down and tore them out by the root, recalling the anemic backyard in the house for sale where the pavement had buckled and levered due to shifting landfill. To test its depth, she had taken a branch and slid it into a gap in the concrete; she had to reach far down before it sank into solid earth. The effluvia of the underground washing over her wrist. She was about to tell Salim what she thought of the house, how it all seemed so precarious, another move, uprooting the family again, investing their life savings in something that rested on little more than sand, when he turned to her full of longing and said, "Please let me have this."

An autumn wind blew. She wrapped the shawl around her shoulders and picked up Aaron's pipe beside the stack of beach chairs. Still warm, it smelled of burnt cherries. In the churchyard on the corner the lawn glowed blue under the parish lights, beckoning her. The gate was unlatched. She let herself in and ran past the lilac bushes. The grass fragrant and wet with dew as she wormed her toes into the soil. The air brimming with a thousand scents, and Salim calling her name, urgent, searching in the darkness.

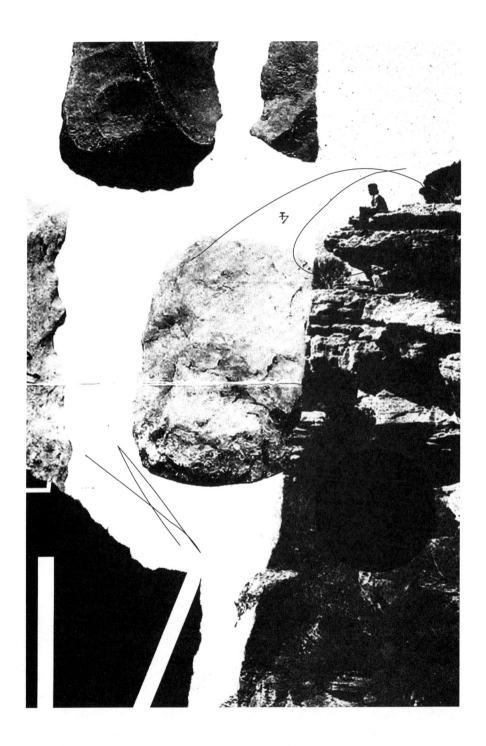

MY MOUNTAIN IS TALLER THAN ALL THE LIVING TREES

by ESKOR DAVID JOHNSON

M Y MOUNTAIN THAT I live on is not much to speak of and if you go by what some of the foreigners who come around this way say then it is really more of a hill, or even a mound. But I've never been anywhere foreign myself, nor do I want to at this point, and Barbados is about as flat as the bottom of a pan. Even on the ground you can see for miles around just by standing on the tips of your toes. So you can just imagine the view from my mountain, which is very near the town of Karata, whose people keep goats to race on weekends or kill and cook if they are too slow. I know this because when I squint I can see all their business over that way, though it is not to say I recognize any faces from so high up. There was once a day when one of the goats escaped from its rope-fence enclosure and wandered off into the confused roads, across the devilgreen land, up and down through ditch and hole until climbing my mountain and there licking my face where my cheek became my jaw. I did not have any sapodillas or oranges or cherries to give so it stayed with me only a few minutes before going back from where it came.

The people of Karata are aware that I live here and are on good terms with me. This began with them taking the detour during their walks to pass by my mountain and wave hello. Now they tend to shout from farther away. Sometimes they invite me down for a wedding or First Communion but I do not much like the taste of goat anymore and so I haven't been to Karata either. When I do need food, it is from the rainwater in my gourd or the trees around my mountain, which are sapodilla and orange and cherry—though some now have termites for veins and do not bear. I only take fruit from one of them a day, which I can look down and choose before making the walk. So you see? There are the birds and the sun and moon and the charcoaled corpse of a pine that was on its way to reach the clouds before it died, and that is it. My mountain is taller than all the living trees.

In general I do not face Karata because there is not much to look at apart from their lives and the beginnings of the sea on the horizon and also because most of the people who come to see me do so from the opposite way. I do not much like being snuck up upon and even though by the time someone is making their way up my mountain it is quite impossible for me not to have noticed, I would still rather I see them coming from all the way. The land in that direction is bush and farming plots cut from the bush. For me to not spot a visitor approaching they would have to not only avoid all the flattened clearings but also hope it is a windy day so I confuse their rustling of the bushes as nothing special. I no longer sleep much and, in the hours I do, it is simply ridiculous that anyone would think to visit then, though life has not been without its surprises. A woman was from Peru and a sleepwalker, moving like a drunk shadow in the field. I cannot say what it is that woke her but she right away took to screaming so loud the fireflies around her outed their lights. It was some time for her to notice my mountain. She headed over and climbed up and screamed again when she saw I was at the top. Who would have thought I was there without first knowing it, a mole-faced man whose hands have started to shake? She said she was camping and was from Peru and was a sleepwalker and did I know where she was. Over there is the town of Karata, I answered, but she'd come from that way where the stars are bunched tightest. It had already rained for the night, the cold dampness of a fever hung low.

She pondered the blackness. The grass here hides a tricky beetle whose song is a long hiss, so at night it can sound as if my mountain is in a nest of snakes. There are also snakes, real ones, but not nearly as many as the hissing would have you think and they do not have poison in them. But the woman from Peru did not know any of this and I could see in the anxious way her eyes darted to the insects' calls that she could not decide which terror to brave between serpents and a man. She asked if I knew the time and I told her I did not. "I never walk longer more than an hour," she said aloud, "so it is not more after than two. I would always know the time when I am little." This talking as if she were alone calmed her and she went from a stand to a crouch, speaking at me about other childhood oddities: always knowing north even when spun around many times, walking in her sleep if she lay on her back. "But I am more comfortable if I sleep this way so this is the matter," she said. Then I told her that most people walk through their lives in a sleep, too, except they never get the chance to wake up. What bad manners of the mind to pass through life in a dream. She liked that.

When she slept it was with a rock as her pillow.

In the morning the sun faces my mountain from across the long yawn of land the woman from Peru had crossed. She grew sweaty with it and woke up itching and was making her way down before turning back to say thank you while once touching my foot. When I was sure she was gone I went down to pick my fruit. I do not know if her body still rises itself up to walk an hour north at night, but I do not see why it would.

Anyway, that meeting was a coincidence and you should not think I spend my time waiting for sleepwalkers to come my way. Most of my visitors believe I am where they find me. A few have believed it for so long they no longer expect to be proven right, as is true of those who go high enough in the air to see the whole earth is round. On finding my mountain they do silly things like wet their pants or sing—not all lunacy comes from delusions. I can tell apart the foreigners from their walk, which not only lacks the waisty roll and tumble of the country people around here, but also wanders, searching for whichever direction is left. Even when they are still specks no bigger than a cherry seed I notice the vague maybeness of their steps, a tender shuffle that comes from trusting the current of a journey more than its sense. When they reach my mountain there is always a pause while their senses catch up to where they stand.

Unless the opposite is true and it is instead a peppered heat that has driven them all this way. There were once two men approaching equally distant from each other and my mountain and running like maniacs. This was in the dry season when footsteps crack like knuckles. I did not like their animal rush, even more so after the barrel-built one running through the canefields to my right galloped on all fours when he tripped rather than right himself. I decided it was him I would hit with the rock I had picked up from my foot since he looked more solid of figure, better able to handle a misplaced throw to the head should I miss—my aim is not very good—and the other was already belabored by his own high-knee running.

Soon they were close enough. But when the space between them had narrowed as at the bottom of a valley, they set upon each other with the futility of wave and shore, one too persistent and the other too stubborn, and I could not throw my stone in the tangle of limbs. Neither wanted to hurt the other man but instead keep him back from my mountain. I would not say the burly one won, though it was he who first touched the bottom of my mountain, for as he climbed closer I saw how deeply his face had been shred open by the ground and how pebbles poked from his cheek. Through spittle and blood he spoke of their race across three continents and an ocean, then of the fellowship between them that had turned sour. They were both without names—he on my mountain had never had one and he below had had so many as to not remember which was first—and had come in search of new ones. "True ones," said my bald, bloody fellow. "How can a man speak with certainty when there is not a word to know that man by?"

My name is Itawadilela, which means he who greets with fire. I know it is mine as a child comes to know its own reflection: it moves as I do. And as there is no place for another to tell you which figure you are in a mirror, so is there no allowance for them to pin your fate to a word.

I said this loud enough that they could both hear. The lower one, lanky as a vine, crept up my mountain to be nearer. I asked why they did such terrible battle against the other when their hopes were the same and they said, "The news is that you speak to but one visitor a year," which was a little true, because after the man with two limbs I saw no one else for thirteen full moons. "I have nothing to call you," I said, but in their pleading and crying and reaching for my hands my heart was moved. "Your names are Wax and Wane," I said, and when each asked which was for whom I took a sapodilla from my lap and bit into it. A quick cloud made the sun blink.

I believe I am the center of a game played by the children of Karata, though the rules are still not clear to me. In it, they send an emissary to ask me questions, but only to get a particular answer, or maybe as a distraction. Even now, schoolchildren from Karata are coming with giggles in their uniforms. I can see them: khaki shorts and skirts just above the knees, button-down shirts the yellow of fallen bananas. They sing for most of the way, a birdsong babbling that is still music. The smaller ones are in danger of becoming stragglers, and must often catch up to the rest with quick little steps that leave them panting. The taller bunch wear their bags with just one strap on the shoulder. All of their collective courage stalls closer to my mountain until, a few feet from the bottom, they are silent.

A girl shouts up, "Afternoon, Sir."

I nod.

"Sir, you know it have a big storm coming this way? The storm big so." She stretches her arms wide and spins around. Some of the others laugh and steal glances up at me. Their bravery spreads like a rumor.

Now that she has found her voice (and her voice is the voice of them all) she dares some steps uphill. She has a shallow chin that causes her mouth to hang open when not speaking. Black blemishes spot the skin on her arms.

"Well if is look you need to look for a place to stay from the rain it always have by my Granddad house. You must be know him, he pass this way before. He does wear a hat like in them cowboy films and have a dog big so. You know who I talking about, right? A curly hair man, but he have a baldhead in the front."

By now she is well close to my feet and talking all the louder. Her head mirrors mine to occupy my vision. I have not said anything.

"You don't want to listen to what I saying, Sir? You come to stay forever, eh? How you going to stay forever? Just like that?"

I do not much believe in the wisdom of children, as others seem to, nor do I believe in their innocence. Down there, some of them have made their way to the other side of my mountain and are picking up pebbles to fit in their pockets. As I turn to see, I hear the loud girl taking more steps up.

"What you go do with all the time if you stay forever, Sir? You don't want to go?"

More of them scurry around. A girl climbs the sapodilla tree. Boys throw pebbles. Everywhere I hear them bleating.

"You want to watch everybody go and you don't have to?"

I stand very quickly to push her down, and as she flails for a grip all she grasps are loose rocks that dislodge with her. She tumbles all the way, hitting the grass with a bounce on her shoulder. The rest of them scream and run away trying to throw things up at me but it is difficult to fight and flee. The talking girl is the last to leave, hanging the battered arm loose at her side, wincing when she tries to move it.

Sometimes the children come with good cheer and smaller numbers; these days are good. Sometimes it is with the malice of a wild herd and then I wish that they, too, could be kept behind rope, or done away with on weekends.

A big storm is coming this way. Two afternoons later the air smells of a cent pressed beneath the tongue. By the evening the beetles do not hiss the dark welcome. I spend the last hours of sunlight lashing together my shelter. Though it cannot grow anymore, the dead pine still has branches that are as strong as they are supple. Its body stands just beyond a rock's throw. The twine to knot the branches together I find in the farming plots, untying them from the waists of sapling plants and the sticks meant to keep them straight.

Going so far away from my mountain is a difficult thing to manage. Being on the ground means that I cannot tell as well who may be coming, and being on the side facing the field means that I cannot see Karata. In such moments the hours go faster if I stay facing my mountain and keep in mind how difficult it is for someone to climb it without practice.

What I make is a flap of branches tethered down by more twine, the gaps in its lattice padded by mud mixed from orange juice. It is fastened to the side of one of the giant stones that had been too heavy to move, so that once tucked under, my back to the stone, one arm holding my ceiling down tight, I am a bird beneath a wing. Along the branches are rows of termites, reminding me at once of a traveler from Africa who said how delicious a meal termites can be just before the rainy season, sautéed with no other oil than that from their flesh and promising a light, nutty flavor. Unlike ants, termites have been known to build nests taller than a man, piled together from chewed wood, dirt, and feces. The clouds pry low. When it starts to rain the hairs of the soil stand on edge.

Because the rains always come from the direction of the sea, I know that my mountain will protect me. For safety, I am not even at its foot, but still close enough to huddle in its wind-safe shadow. Pressing my ear to the dirt I listen for the sound of the thunder-before-thunder, as I know is done in some parts of Bangladesh. Nothing ever happens when you want it to.

What comfort could I have given the man with two limbs? One arm and one leg on opposite ends as if leaning diagonally. His skin was warped and dangled loose around the face and neck yet cinched tight everywhere else. He could have been a Blackman or an Indian but there was no hair on his head to tell. I mean to say that he was a fearful sight bobbing through the fields on his way to Karata. "No one," he would say to me afterwards, "even help me get here." Unless you count the young boy along the way that had lent him a plank of wood to press on. "Man like me, you have to learn your way through the scruff." This story that I am telling you happened long before, in the year of the wildfires.

He had first been walking to the old pine, which still lived at the time, green as a frog's back. Then on getting close he paused, took in the tree, and changed course to come to my mountain. The sun at that hour was in his eyes: even squinting tightly he could not tell if I was there.

"Hello?" he said. "Hello!" he shouted.

"Hello, I am up here," I said. "You cannot see me because the sun is in your eyes."

He picked up his plank and shielded his brow with it. He balanced well without it.

"Well kill me dead!" he said. "Who gone and put you up there? They wasn't lying, no. Who gone and put you there?"

"Would you ask the same of that old pine you were just watching? My answer is the same as its own."

He laughed. "Oh yes it's some pretty lyrics you have. Pretty, pretty lyrics."

This man could not climb my mountain nor did he try. In fact even then he still seemed in a hurry. Between his laughs he glanced at the horizon from whence he'd come.

Seeing me seeing him, he began, "They send me to the jail for beating a man to blindness. They did. But you put a man in a room as long as he can reach lying flat on the ground, lock the door and tell him he can't leave until you say so…"

His missing arm pointed to his missing leg. "They had do plenty to me before then. But you put a man in a room with no windows and tell him he can't leave? You don't need much more than that."

So he had escaped, and I could tell by his pause that he wanted me to ask him how, so I did not. Instead I asked of the arm and leg. He clenched up like a secret, the two rows of his teeth sliding together into one grimacing line.

"Gangrene," was all he said.

What a life to live, where even to see from a regular height is a day's worth of effort.

We could hear the cracking of bushfires coming to life now that the sun had found its angle. Most of the fires started with kudzu, which is like ivy, and fast-growing. Koreans had flown it in some months before to save the land from erosion. The kudzu spread and then died, drying up into waiting tinder as the days got hotter. At night the sky was kept awake by long legs of fire kicking its underbelly. I would remember the scent of those orange evenings. Nothing is malicious in the smell of a natural fire. Still, had the man with two limbs made his journey to me an hour later, he may well have found himself wrapped up by those burning vines.

He did not stay long that first day, hobbling on to Karata where a cousin waited with ironed clothes. The next afternoon he was back in a one-armed blue shirt that crackled with starch when he moved.

"So it's how many questions I get to ask you?"

"People pick their own habits."

"Well my habits is I is a talker. You good with that? You like you could—aye—aye—aye—" A wind had come to push him down, and would have, had he not hop-hop-hopped and righted himself. "Ha!" he coughed a laugh. "I tell you it's plenty they do to me!"

He wanted to know if there was anything a man could do to forget everything but *now*, as an animal does. I told him even an agouti remembers where the traps from last year were set, so every new season hunters have to trick them in new ways. Still, he went on telling me about what he would forget if he could:

"It had a day I walked around with a gun in my pocket. You ever do that? Man, you can't watch people the same after." And the footrace he'd lost on the first day of school and seeing his brother get married and gangrene. He only checked my face whenever he said a joke, to see if I found it funny, and, though I did not, it was his constant checking that eventually made me smile.

"Ha!" he laughed.

Before leaving that day he whistled. The tune was blue as his shirt, cutting through sheets of night dark like a scythe. I did not know what song it was. When he shut his lips, I heard the whistle still ringing in my skull as if the bones in me were quivering.

"Boss," he took to calling me some days after, "I had come to ask you 'bout this dream I had last night. But you know what I figure on the way here?" He sometimes propped his plank behind him so that leaning back against it he could better look up when talking to me. After asking a question he would raise both his eyebrows until the wrinkles rippled past his forehead up to his exposed scalp.

I began: "A man came to me once who believed—"

"On the way here I figure your dreams don't mean nothin'. It just come like a reflex. Like if you smell pepper then you sneeze, that's all a dream is, your head sneezing at night. Somebody ever ask you to explain a sneeze? Right, right. I thought so." After that, if ever one of us sneezed, he shouted, "Wake up! Ha! Wake up!"

He could be serious, too. On a cool afternoon he came late and held a plastic flute in hand. The mad chorus of birds were running their mouths.

"My cousin have a little daughter she raising over there. A bright girl, if you see she read... you does really wish they could stay just so. Watch what she give me today." He held up the flute and then played from it, a light tune that should have been happy—a song the sound of sweetbread left outside until the gnats found it. He did not laugh *Ha!* or look my way.

That night a jeep drove through the bush toward Karata, its lights howling terrible against the black. It parked and men got out. I watched them walk to one house and then another, knocking on doors and sometimes stepping in. Some hours later they left. The man with two limbs did not come the next day.

I asked him once if it would not have been easier for him to have stayed his time in the jail.

"Nah it could never really be easy so," he said soft, as if others were listening. "How that go look for them to do that?"

"But you do not think—"

"Chuh! I mean watch you and all. If I was to say you couldn't go past this little space so, how you go take that?"

"Yes, I would not like that," I lied.

"Yes man. You ever see what it does be like over so anyway?" He pointed beyond the horizon.

"Once," I said. I thought a little. "They tried to do plenty to me, too."

"Ha!"

Always he made music. Sometimes from instruments he'd put together—pebbles in a bottle, rubber bands stretched over a can—but mostly from whistling. My bones would hear him when he walked from Karata and then shiver again later as he left, his high tones wavering away like a woman in a dress running. He did not always realize when it was he whistled. Now and again, looking silently at the dusk's flames, each of us deep in the solitude of his own longing, sound would come leaking from his mouth without tune or direction. If I pointed that out to him, he would not remember having done it.

I offered him this: suppose this power to forget, he had already learned it, and on so learning chose to turn it on itself, remembering it no more. He liked that. "That come like a bulb getting so bright it blows," he said. Yes, I said, but thought to myself, more like a snake swallowing itself from the tail up.

Then he brought me food. It was a grilled snapper on a plate he balanced on his head through his slow, slow progress. The fish was cherry-skin red and from where I sat looked tiny enough to fit whole into my mouth. He had two forks in his pocket, dropping his plank to offer me one. "She not too bad, you know, my cousin," he shouted. "You would have to be plenty terrible not to cook up a snapper right." Because of the plate on his head he could not look up as he normally did, staring straight into my mountain instead. How would he get it to me? The fish would fall flat into the dirt if he tried climbing. I wondered if his cousin had left it to soak in garlic and salt the night before or had tossed it fresh onto the fire as it was. When you eat fish, the smell stays on your lips for hours after and flies smell it on you. Right there on my lap I had a pile of peeled oranges, enough to last me until the new morning, when I would take from the cherry trees.

"Boss," said the man with two limbs. "It not gonna swim again if I throw it back in the water, you know."

So I went down from my mountain, and we ate.

By dark, I am soaked. The land is smothered by a wet night. The sky is bigger than it has ever been, big as a face leaning in so close its skin is all you see. Its thunder sounds personal—I want to shout back at it. My arms ache from keeping the roof above my head, one moment pulling it down from where the wind would snatch it away, then pushing it off my chest to keep from suffocating. So you see? Even the air can drown you. So much of the mud between the branches comes loose once dampened again that it is not at all difficult to keep an eye on my mountain. It shakes and leans along with the trees. When there is lightning I make the mistake of seeing somebody on top and start toward it, but the storm sits me down again. Who would be out on my mountain at a time like this? Still, when I sleep, I have the dream of going up my mountain and the top getting higher the more I climb.

This is better than the other dream I sometimes have, which is the dream of walking on the ground. In it, my mountain can be far away or it can be close. If it is far, I spend my time walking to it and do not make it. If it is close, when I make it, it is not my mountain. It is a different one.

It came to bother me, the lie I had given the man with two limbs. What was wrong with my space of land that I would want to find others?

We were eating from a bag of peewa and spitting the black seeds as far as we could. "Them men them still using stone to sharpen they blade," he said, spitting. "The best thing to do is use a piece of hard leather."

The farmers from Karata had spent a lot of the mornings cutting and clearing as much dried-up foliage as they could, leaving fewer targets for the heat to incite into fire. When he was with me, the man with two limbs commented on all the farmers' doings.

"It have plenty, plenty uses for them ashes, too," he told me. "Mix that up in your soil so and your produce growing plenty, plenty."

As he talked more about his other life as a farmer, I began to choke on a peewa seed. Seeing my troubles, he used his plank to strike me on the back while I pressed at my stomach until, just as spots began to dot my sight, the seed popped out, dropping barely past my toes. His final tap with the plank threw him off balance and he fell to the ground. When I turned to thank him, as sprightly as he'd seemed, something in me could not stand the sight of his apparent decrepitude. I grew sad for seeing him on the ground. The hand I used to help him up I did not use for anything else the rest of the day.

That month he had come with food and music and I had grown fat on the ground. I learned the kind of woman his cousin was through her food. Her macaroni pie was light as a conversation and the bread soft as washed skin. But in the week that her daughter came down with a fever, the okra tasted of nights up late.

The habit I had picked was to eat with him, but what was down there that I had to go see? My appetite changed after the peewa seed. I noticed flavors in the food that had not been there before. Her worries became my own—I would finish only half the portions the man with two limbs brought me. Once I took the meal into my hands (breadfruit oil down, broth leaking to my elbows) and climbed back uphill to eat it there alone. He looked at me only a little and coughed a lot when he spoke. We talked about more things to forget while the wildfires bloomed.

For five days he did not come. All the noises startled me, a loud bird screeching overheard, the high whine of a goat. My bones were waiting for his music and I chastised them for it. Once, the moon was low and close, filled to the brim with so much light it might have split at the sides. Carefully, after checking that no one was coming my way, I lifted my head to it and tried to whistle.

On the sixth day he came in silence and my hands started to shake on seeing him. "Boss," he said, "it's some real craziness in that house I in." I did not say anything. He lowered the plastic container from his head and put it on the ground to open its lid. In some seconds its scent had reached me, meat still warm and calling. My hands were shaking. Then I was on the ground with my back to him, eating.

"That same shortman I mentioned that does be coming to check my cousin"—the flesh was burnt-sugar brown and slipped right off the bones as my teeth touched it—"well he come the other night talking about how he could build her a house, he does do some building work"—the peppers made me warm up to the ears, I tasted cardamom and excitement—"and just so she have all this marriage talk up in she head. You would swear no man ever talk to her before"—my face low down into the bowl, slurping gravy from the edges between bites—"and you already know it's plenty quarrel between me and her over there... like that goat hitting your belly right. Ha! Yes, she start to outdo sheself cooking now that this shortman coming around talking about two-story house with gas oven"—to get to the marrow I had to close my lips tight around the end of a bone and suck it out, as a mongoose does to an egg—"but if I end up not able to talk some sense into her the wedding could be in two weeks and all. I come to check if you could make it? You hearing me? You go come?" I stopped.

What was wrong with my space of land that I would want to find others? What was down here that I had to go see? Suddenly I felt ashamed of my hunger, its weakness. Staring into the bowl made me dizzy. "Come, it's not like it's a far walk," said the man with two limbs. "And if you get lost on the way back just watch for that pine tree over so. Ha! I swear you could see it from the next side of the island and all, never see something so tall."

I turned to face him. "Why did you come here?" It was strange to hear my voice this loud. I had forgotten it could echo.

He wobbled as he rattled away. "Easy easy it still have the two weeks to think it over one of them young boys say he looking to make the altar but the varnish they find old and dry up so they looking to get more plus it does take its time settling, too—"

"Why did you come here?" I said again. He understood.

"Well, you know how they are so… man ask for a trial… thought we was free men here… spend my life in a room with no windows? Ha!… tell a man he can't leave?… Ha!… Ha." But he also saw that I would be of no help, the trickle of his words drying up as I stared. Then he turned around and began to hop away and, as if waking up, I realized that he was about to climb my mountain and I realized that if he had had another leg and arm he would have used them to climb my mountain while I was eating.

I picked up a rock near my foot and threw it against the back of his head. He fell and bled into the earth. All his sound spilled out of him. That night, for the first time, I had the dream of walking on the ground. In fact, this is why I do not sleep much anymore.

*   *   *

The main difficulty in building my mountain the first time was just finding the privacy to do so. No one will say much to a man they see carrying a stone in his hands, except if he carries it to a pile already higher than their waists. So whereas I had moved the first stone in peace, by the end of that day not a passerby could avoid involving themselves.

At the time, my strength could be seen through the skin. Most observers knew better than to offer their help. Those who brought me rocks anyway had them refused: to this day some of those rocks have remained just where they dropped them. To move the boulders, I had to flip them face over face from farther out in the bush where they'd been nestled together in a wide cup of dirt. I could only manage such an effort twice, abandoning the third one but a few steps from the greater pile. "But look at this," someone had said, holding her son's hand to point it for him. "But look at thiiis."

I worked at night, sweating hot in the sky's shadow. The sun made too many people brave. Without it I could ignore whether or not it was blood running down my legs. In the light, I wiped away the red-crusted residue.

Each day they resurged:

"Don't stand so close before something fall on you."

"Excuse Sir, what you doing this for? All this work and you could have built a house with a backyard already."

"Ask to see if he need water."

"The base he making not wide enough. That thing go fall."

"Look at this. Look. At. This."

"Go find the schoolmaster and tell her come."

Word was spreading that I was here.

They stopped when my mountain grew taller than them and they grew silent in its shadow. One day I spoke for the first time in months: "Alright,

I am tired now. And over there are your homes." That is all it ever takes. They retreated like ripples from a stone. By the time the moon had shed five new faces all the trees but one received my words as they would rain.

But the morning after the storm my mountain is shorter than it should be, and on climbing it as soon as the winds tire, I see how much work I have to do, how much of its body has been scattered. There is no choice of food but cherries: most of the oranges and sapodillas have been stripped off their stems. I slip on the wet backs of rock on the way down and hit my head. I see the flash of stars behind the sky's veil.

All that day the people of Karata trek the mud road beyond my mountain to check their lands for damage. The cane stalks are strewn. Where there were farming plots are now big, brown puddles. What they can salvage, or what they need for rebuilding, they ferry back in long trains of men and goats.

Without the strength I had the first time, rebuilding is difficult. My joints are broken levers bending the wrong way. On each trip I leave soggy plops of footsteps in my wake. Twice more I fall, my face so low down to the earth I cannot see farther than a child can jump.

Seeing my mountain smaller than they have remembered it in a long time, some of the townspeople find their old courage and offer help from a shout away, perhaps thinking that I am not up to so solo an effort again. Always I turn away their friendliness with a wave, then, when they get closer, with soft words of independence.

I have heard it said that nothing that lives lives alone, but how can that be when I have seen snakes slide away from their broken shells at birth without a look back? Unlike ants, termites do a poor job of making their way home if separated, but, unlike ants, any termite can become king or queen and start building anew. If I did not finish, how would my visitors know where I am?

* * *

Usually from the top of my mountain I would have been able to tell much earlier that something was amiss with the people of Karata, but now that my vantage is on the ground it is easier for them to sneak on the edge of my vision. This begins in the evening, when still a man offers help, despite a day of my saying no. He does not move along. "That's too much to handle on your own," he shouts. "It's whole day you looking like you going to break your back."

To show him my back is fine I pick up the biggest stone near me and hold it with one hand straight above my head. He cannot hear my shoulder creak under the weight. He does not move along.

Another man with a big dog stops to whisper with the first. They have their hands on their hips and gesture with small movements. I realize I need to get on top of my mountain.

Once there I see two more men and a woman are on their way. I see, too, that there is no one left clearing out the farming plots though the land is still ragged.

"Mr. Man." The second one tunnels his voice through his hands for it to reach me. "It's not no crime to need help. We going and start to walk over to you." I shout no. Those others have spread themselves out. Together, the five of them step toward my mountain.

A rock slips out beneath me and *clackclackclacks* down. The half-moon stares like a lazy eye. The hissing of snakes wells up in my ears; wings the weight of an eyelash flutter in the breeze. I feel the thunder-before-thunder in my soles.

"Look, you need help. Is just talk we looking to talk." It is the second man again, with the dog. His hands are up and open to show he holds nothing, grazing the edge of the dark curls past his hat. On his arms, I recognize blemished spots. I feel the thunder-before-thunder beneath me. They are all close. "You need help. Come down so we could talk. Let us help."

Why should I go anywhere when the world comes to me? Why should I be on the ground to talk? For people who do not have a mountain the world is without knowing, like a book held too close to the eyes. How could their words make sense if I were down there pressed next to them? The thunder-before-thunder is beneath me.

What do they know of what I have done? "Were you there when I touched a cripple on the head with lavender oil?" I say, turning in tight circles to see them all. "She moved her toes for the first time. Did you know that?" Their steps are slower, but they do not stop.

"My mountain was in a magazine!" I say. This man and his dog do not know that. A Ghanaian with a heavy mustache had brought me a copy as a gift and showed me the double pages where from a distance someone had taken its picture (and though I have never been as far away from my mountain as the picture-taker must have been, still I could recognize it, because no other mountain looks like mine).

"How will anyone even find me, if I come down to talk?"

"You can always come back," says the spotted man. "No one taking nothing from you. It's just talk." The dog has run ahead. It has a black, sad face. They have sent it to bite me and dig up my mountain. I remember the stone from before is still in my hand and I take aim.

The man is stern now: "No more of that. Nothing else have to dead."

"Everything that lives long enough learns that life is elastic, like chewed-up sap," I say. "Its weakness is in trying too much to stretch longer."

To burn him: I had to cover the body with a bed of kudzu thick enough for anyone passing by not to notice. But no one did pass by on that day, a silent one with a sun ripe for arson. He was heavier than you might expect. It was not until I had let more of the blood seep of out his skull that I could even move him about to fold into those roots.

"What that have to do with it? You are idle and advantageous," says the

MY MOUNTAIN IS TALLER THAN ALL THE LIVING TREES

spotted man. He points and he is clear: "That pine never bother nobody and look what you do."

There are many uses for dead trees, as any man of labor will tell you. Ash can give new life to fields when mixed into the mud with goatshit. It was with a terrible mercy that I had found embers from a just-dead blaze and breathed them back to life amongst the roots, his limbs. "That pine had reached for too much," I tell him.

They have spaced around my mountain on all sides. Their hands are behind their backs and that dog is pawing the ground before it. From beneath me there is the rumble of a laugh digging its way to the surface. I will throw the stone.

Some mountains are hot and tempestuous on the inside. Some volcanoes are best left sleeping. Where were these men to see how many before were willing to lose their way in finding my mountain? Had they faced the Turk with his loud questions and his pistol? The woman so light she gripped the soil during strong winds? Did they know what becomes of a life eaten from the inside until it is unable to climb, or the sound it makes in its final panic? Young elopers had arrived on a clogged night with the heat of lust all in their eyes. On the verge of my giving them my blessing, they screamed at the idea of joining lives, as if waking up, and parted in separate directions. Ha. So you see? Not everything you are looking for is what you want to find.

FIVE PETALS
PROUD

by AYA OSUGA A.

S EIJI WAS AT HIS mistress's house at the approximate time his son
died. Len, his American-born son, had been stationed in Afghan-
istan against Seiji's wishes.

Seiji was in bed in Tokyo, away from home. The lingering chill of
early March left aches in his seventy-year-old joints when he left his
mistress's warm body to take the call. It was his wife Hana, the call,
long-distance from Los Angeles, the first in a week. There was silence,
then—"It's Len"—that was all she said before she could no longer speak.
Seiji understood then; their son was dead.

He returned, his head a rock in the down pillow. Len had been on his
second overseas tour. It was a desire sparked at sixteen while watching the
World Trade Center reduced to dust and office paper, a desire that turned
into a career three years ago when he enlisted with college diploma in
hand. Since that day Seiji had prepared himself to receive this call, but
he'd buried this thought deep in the back of his mind, the same place he
buried fears of his own mortality so that he could sleep at night.

His wife said servicemen turned up at their California home, told her it'd happened two days prior. He died courageously, they were grateful for his sacrifice. *Your* sacrifice, they added. The men were in full dress, lapel pins colorful like Jolly Ranchers.

"Has something happened?" Maki, his mistress, said.

"That was Hana."

She frowned. She hated when he said her name.

"My son is dead."

"Oh." She clutched her forehead. Her skin was taut for a woman past forty. She was very thin, her hair thick like silk spools. "Are you sure? I just saw on the news last night. The fighting's been subdued, they said."

He scratched his scalp in annoyance. "I'm pretty sure I heard correctly."

"Did your wife provide any details?"

Maki ran her hand up his knee. She broke the seal on the Cohibas. A twinkle of red embers. "I hope this takes some edge off," she said. "I'll prepare breakfast right away." The smoke parted like a silky curtain as she walked off.

His wife would have complained. "Disgusting, that smoke in our clothes. Ashes in the carpets."

Maki murmured in the kitchen. "...the ashes?"

"What?"

She popped her head into the room. "I said, what will you do with your son's ashes?"

"He'll go in *our*—" he corrected himself. "In the Katsuragi tomb."

She straightened herself apologetically. "It's just—well, it's just, you know, when you remove yourself from the government registry, you give up your right to enter the family tomb. He's an American, isn't he?"

Their stay in America was meant to be temporary. Len was born during their fifteen-year foreign residence with Takei Corp. When the mandated time was up, Hana decided that their son would be educated at an American university, and nothing, not even Seiji's retirement and relocation back to Japan to start his private consulting business, could stop her. Even after Len's acceptance at a Tier 2 school she'd insisted on staying, and so for the past ten years he'd commuted to see them.

But during their final encounter six months ago, Len had toppled Seiji to the ground, knocking the air out of his lungs. He'd come to dinner at their California home before leaving on his second deployment. At sixty-nine, Seiji was still athletic, though leaner, shorter. He dyed his grays. No one had yet offered their seat to him on public transportation, a fact he took great pride in.

Seiji had been drinking, as usual, and yelled at his wife that the rice was dry.

"We still have an entire pot left," Hana said. "Can you please *gaman* and eat it?"

This made his buzz fade a little. "Are you talking back to me?" he said, banging his chopsticks on the table.

His wife looked down at her plate.

"Dad, leave her alone," Len said. "The food is good."

"I'm the man of the house. I work all day long," Seiji said. "If the rice is dry don't I deserve a new bowl?"

"You're drunk, old man," Len said.

Seiji stood from his seat. He stumbled around the table and grabbed Len by the collar. He leaned his face into his son's. "Is this how you speak to your father?"

As Seiji lifted the collar, Len suddenly stood and shoved his forearm into Seiji's chest. Seiji landed on his back, breathless.

His wife screamed.

Len sat back in his seat. "I only nudged him, I swear," he said calmly.

Seiji retreated to the bedroom, coughing. He wondered when it was, exactly, that his respectful, obedient son had been replaced by this complete stranger.

Seiji spent the morning on the phone with Japan Airlines, growing all the more impatient with the stolid operator: "Thank you for your business! Before we can help, please verify your phone PIN. Sir, that's incorrect, do you need to reset? Okay, a new PIN will arrive by postcard in three to five business days. Sir, you can't attempt another guess, please wait for the postcard."

Finally he managed to bark, "You listen to me. There's been a family emergency." She brushed off this salvo: "I'm so sorry. Flying today will be difficult. I'm sorry. I'm very sorry."

Even though he'd dealt in them his entire life, suddenly Seiji despised the verbal wrappers for the word *no*.

"So, tomorrow," he said.

"I'm very sorry," the high-pitched voice said.

Seji counted on his fingers: one, two, three days since he had died. Len's ghost was still likely in the mortal world. He would need prayer in order to reach the golden bridge of the underworld, he would need prayer during the judgment. He would need all the help he could get.

"Maki," he called. "You pray too, Maki."

Seiji bowed his head and put his hands together at his forehead. In any other circumstance, the *tsuya* would have been held yesterday. Friends and family would have gathered to guard the body from the darkness, shared stories, kept the candles and incense illuminated through the night. Today, the body would have been cremated.

Seiji blinked. He couldn't remember what came next. Were they supposed to meet again four days after the funeral, or fourteen? What color were the chrysanthemums? As he racked his brain, the one custom he could remember was the *shijukunichi.*

The rites should have been familiar. Only a decade ago, in 2000, he'd entombed his mother. The cemetery workers heaved open the large slab rock of their ancestral tomb, sweat forming on their foreheads like teardrops. In north Tokyo, the cemetery and its cherry trees became a quiet respite against the skyline of high-rises, billboards of half-dressed preteens.

With the tomb exposed, Seiji counted the spaces. The first belonged to Seiji's great grandfather, who'd descended the snowcapped mountains at the turn of the century to take a copywriting job in the city. He died in the 1923 earthquake and fire that engulfed the business district.

The second plot was his great-grandmother, who had died of heartache shortly after.

The third was his father, whose remains were left in Manila during World War II. His plot was occupied not by an urn but by a smooth stone. He had been a large man, standing just shy of two meters, with a booming voice that resonated through the walls. Seiji was only five when the notice arrived home, his father's body made small by the vast land, interred forever overseas with canteens, money, and an Imperial banner riddled with red knots and bullets.

The fourth and fifth plots were his grandparents, who turned to ash in the air raids.

His brother claimed the sixth space. When the war ended, polio claimed the grit-stained alleys and the children who shined shoes. The adults wouldn't allow Seiji to see his brother; it was bad luck for children, they said, to see other dead children, so he sobbed outside in the hall.

The slab removed, the tomb was a mere hole in the ground, dusty in the light of day. Into the seventh spot, Seiji carefully placed the urn of his mother, a woman who had outlived her husband by more than fifty years and never remarried. He then watched the priests pray, the slab eclipsing a shadow over the empty spaces that still remained.

"Well, what did they say?" Hana asked on the phone.

"Tomorrow," Seiji answered.

"I might be late picking you up," she said. "Lennon's friends are gathering."

He couldn't recall how long had it been since she was eager to hear from him. Lately she'd been more excited by her Ashtanga yoga class than by his homecomings. He somehow knew she was calling from the bedroom landline, beneath which they'd stored two sets of divorce papers, both unsigned.

"I received an email from Lennon's friend today," she said. "Listen."

Mr. and Mrs. Katsuragi, my name is Sgt. Glen Nolan. My parents run a small pharmacy in Allentown, Pennsylvania. We're all reeling from the news. Lennon and I trained together. A great man, the absolute best. Once, I wanted a tattoo and asked him to write my name in characters, and he let me use his character. I argued, "Hey, my name is Glen, not Len," but he said Len means virtuous, so now he is tattooed on my arm.

"Tattooed on my arm," Seiji repeated. "Idiots."

"Why?"

"Is *Glen* the same as *Len* these days?"

"I think it's sweet," she said curtly. "The military also sent me a list of Lennon's personal items. This is a lot for me to do on my own, you know. You're never here for the important things."

"Complain to the airline, then."

Through the receiver he heard the indifferent rustling of paper. "Books.

iPad. Space blanket. Weapons lube. Running shoes. Tactical gloves. Camera. Steel coffee mug. A Hilton towel."

"Your amulet is in there?" he asked.

She was quiet.

"Maybe it was on him," he said, an attempt at consoling.

"Yes." He could almost hear her tears.

When the deployment orders came through, she'd driven an hour to the shrine in downtown. The charm was pentagonal in shape, wrapped in orange felt, blessed to ward off evil. She bought two and kept one for herself, inside her purse. It was the one piece of culture that remained with her outside the house.

He was about to ask if she was alright when there was a knock on the other end of the line.

"I should get that," she said.

He heard the pattering of slippers, the tiles too cold for her feet. There was a relief in her voice when she opened the door. A woman's voice. Some talking, sniffling, he made out the word *hero*, then a pause. They must be hugging, he thought. He despised that, the hugging, as if they'd been friends for decades, entering your personal space. Whoever this woman was likely stepped into the house without taking off her shoes.

"Mrs. Fischer," she said, having picked up the receiver. "She brought over some pie. She mentioned Arlington."

"Arlington?"

"She said American heroes are given proper burials there."

"In a coffin?"

"With full honors. Guns fired in salute and everything."

"We have a family tomb, Hana."

"Mrs. Fischer said it's the greatest honor."

He pictured his feather-haired, button-nosed neighbor, always grinning and hugging for no occasion.

"Is that the lady who makes pies? Adding sugar when fruit is already sweet. That's why she's fat," he said.

She clucked her tongue, then hung up.

Prior to that pre-deployment dinner, Seiji had witnessed his son's truculence only once: at fifteen, he'd shoved a *chikan* on a crowded train in Japan. The jab was swift, confident, decisive. This unfamiliar gallantness had mortified Seiji. He pulled his son aside and dragged him off the train.

But the roots of this daring originated long before, Seiji considered. It was the year his wife stopped packing bento boxes. While Len was in elementary school she'd packed him a lunch box every day, setting the alarm for when the sky was still dark.

By the time the darkness faded, the plastic container was replete with recipes she'd learned from cookbooks, family, and old neighbors who'd all sent their children to school this way. Glazed mini-meatballs, carrot flowers with grated yuzu, baked shiitake stuffed with prawns. Breakfast sausage preened to look like a baby octopus. Hana even cut shapes out of the seaweed and assembled them into a face over the rice, so that each afternoon Len would be greeted by a smile.

But one day Len arrived home and slid the uneaten lunch onto the kitchen counter.

"Too busy to eat today?" Hana asked.

"I hate the bento, Mom," he said. "Why can't you just give me money to buy pizza from the cafeteria? Pack me a Lunchables or PB&J, like everyone else."

"They clog their bellies with garbage."

"But they make fun of me," Len said. "They say the seaweed looks nasty. They say the fish smell is gross."

It was clear on his face—Len had succumbed to America.

Later, in the privacy of their bedroom, she cried.

"What does he know, he's just a boy," Seiji consoled her.

But this made her cry even more. "You don't know anything."

Unable to bear the sight of her crying, Seiji slept downstairs. He was awakened the next morning by the rustling of aluminum foil as his wife wrapped a ham sandwich.

"I'm going to pay my respects," Seiji said to Maki. "You come, too."

Their little Pomeranian yipped at her heels as she grabbed a sweater.

Once, cherry trees had only been planted in cemeteries, and it made sense to him now as he drove along a highway embossed with white tips. Soon each dark branch would be heavy with pale pink blossoms—like dots on an impressionist painting, like popcorn glued on a tree—but up close each flower would be perfect, each of its five petals proud. For two short weeks the city would teem with flowers, then the petals would scatter, masking the concrete streets. It will be a late bloom this year, he thought. It's been a very cold year.

It was on a day similar to this when he flew to the United States as a newlywed some twenty-five years ago, leading the offshore expansion for Takei Corp. It was an ambition he'd prepared for, working so hard that he did not meet his wife until the word *bachelor* stopped sounding like a status symbol and just sounded like loneliness. She was a bright-eyed girl, not so much a pretty girl, short hair carefully blown into curls that rested on her shoulders. At twenty-seven, she was one of the unsold Christmas cakes in the office: an unmarried woman past her expiration date despite being seventeen years his junior. She giggled nervously when he asked her to dinner, and she rested her head on her wrist until the end of dessert, nodding to his every story like a bobblehead doll. For the first time in many years he discovered he genuinely enjoyed a person's company.

She helped him put on his suit jacket the morning the floor chief announced his promotion. He'd start in their U.S. office, build their international franchise. "Work hard in America," floor chief said. And even though he and Hana barely glanced at each other, she pinched the cuff of his arm, and on their walk home she stood so close waiting for the traffic light that their pinkies gently touched.

His mother cried, "Who, my dear, will protect our family tomb if you move overseas?" But he assured her this was just temporary. They would return soon. They'd be home at the end of the year to pass the new year together.

Part of Seiji had been excited to cross the waters and see for himself a country potent enough to bring his father's *sokoku* to physical destruction. He worked to integrate his wife into the neighborhood, correcting her English as she fumbled with pronunciation ("I want a bowl of lice"), bringing her to each house delivering department-store-bought cookies shaped like doves. His wife hummed songs in their sparse house as she unpacked items they'd just received as newlyweds.

In the far land where their son was born, they named him Lennon after the songs she'd hummed. *Imagine there's no country...And the world will live as one.* At forty-five, Seiji embraced his first son, cocooned in a blue blanket and beanie. For short they called him Len, which in Japanese meant virtuous, honorable, selfless.

Seiji and Maki arrived at Yasukuni. They walked under large iron arches shaped like the symbol π. They walked up to the main pagoda: tree-trunk pillars wore deep lines like an old man's hand. He arrived there first and already had his hands together as Maki caught up. Their claps resounded hollow across the sterile grounds. "My father's name is enshrined here." Seiji felt compelled to speak in a low murmur, the area silent save the fluttering of pigeons. Seiji was not a religious man but here he felt calm. In nature he felt

God: during autumn, in the ginkgo leaves that framed the shrine a glorious gold; during summer, in the way the cold stone darkened from the rain.

In the stillness of the grounds he felt the young soldiers whose remains were never recovered, who took off on suicide missions on aircraft or submarine shells—*gyokusai*, people called it, their death likened to scintillating, shattering glass.

As Seiji and his mistress walked the path to the museum, the word *Arlington* lingered in his mind. Was Hana really considering putting their son into the ground with maggots and frozen, foreign earth?

"Do you think it was a mistake that I ever moved to America?" he asked.

The spring breeze blew warm between them. "I don't know," Maki said.

He knew what she wanted to say. If Len were her son, she'd said previously, she wouldn't have allowed him to join the military. And if he had divorced his wife sooner, maybe they could have had a son of their own.

They walked through the shrine's museum beneath submarines and Zero-sens, suspended on lines, suspended in time. He thought about the type of ammunition his son must have carried. A big rifle slung across his back, a tactical vest heavy with metal.

Seiji had not seen his son in war gear. At the send-off ceremony, he wore fatigues with an American flag patched on his bicep. Seiji had not recognized his son as the band played military songs and people waved flags, and Len hugged them both and said, in perfect English, "I love you guys."

The scene had been all too familiar. Seiji sent his own father to war this way, two lines of uniforms castanetting past a sea of red-striped Imperial flags. The entire village had turned out for the event. They sang:

> *You and I, we're cherry blossoms.*
> *When we bloom, it's unavoidable, our petals'll soon fall.*
> *If so then let us, let us scatter splendidly.*

In the eerie stillness of the museum Seiji read the letters of a fifteen-year-old boy. He read the letters, loaded with hope for his siblings, and guilt for surviving his mother and brothers-in-arms, and love—of the Emperor, of family, of country.

Seiji thought of his own father's letter, arriving home in a long brown envelope. How his mother, knelt in the wooden hall, gripped wrinkles into it like those forming in her green kimono and in between her brows.

"A patriotic death is the happiest death," he'd written. "If my countrymen can live, if we can form pillars of our nation." Seiji did not understand these words but tugged at his mother's kimono as she sat him down and told him, with tears in her eyes, that they would go see him at Yasukuni.

Seiji recalled the night of Len's enlistment. Len had gathered college friends—teammates, fraternity brothers—to set off sparklers in their backyard, filling Dixie cups with lukewarm beer. They toasted under the star-spangled flag, wrestled on the grass. How ungrateful his own son seemed in comparison, how ignorant. How cavalier he was with his own life that he'd volunteer for *another* war, one that was not his own. In the back of Seiji's throat lodged a sensation he just couldn't swallow.

As Seiji and Maki exited the museum building, she nudged him on the arm. "Will you be alright for a moment? I need to check on Taro."

Taro, the Pomeranian Seiji had bought her five years ago, gnawed the furniture because Maki never trained him otherwise. He'd once been the size of two knuckles, exposing his flocculent belly to pedestrians passing his glass case, sloppily tagged with fat marker: 225,000 YEN.

"Do you think that's pricey?" she'd asked.

"It's a new grad's entire month's salary."

She'd paused, then asked, "What would be the cost of maternity?"

Maki was pushing thirty-six at that point. They had met after his mother died and they had already been together five years, a period too long to walk away but too short to commit to starting another family. He'd tried to fill this pregnant void by buying her Louis Vuitton bags and shoes, but she'd become more vocal about the issue, eyeing strollers and diaper bags with a wistful yearning.

As they'd exited the store cradling the little puppy, he stuck out his small red tongue and licked Seiji's arm. Seiji dropped his shoulders and smiled. After all, he considered, it wasn't as if he could speak any less to this "son" than to his real son.

Len almost never spoke Japanese. The weekend he had come home from his sophomore year in college, he had strapped a surfboard to his car at dawn and not returned until lunchtime.

"*Doko ittetanda*," Seiji looked up from his newspaper.

Len stalled in the patio and, as if addressing one of his friends, shouted, "Out with Travis, Dad. The swells. Epic, epic, epic. I almost died!"

Seiji frowned. "*Omae*, heavens, I addressed you in Japanese."

Len started explaining in his broken Japanese, and then he got stuck. But, excited, he continued to explain. The waiting. Sitting in the dark water. The fear. The quiet. Waves humming into shore. The sun-cast orange and gray clouds climbing the horizon like mountains.

"I saw God, Dad. It was, like, *whoa*," he said.

"Mercy, your language," Seiji said. "Has your inattentive mother neglected your studies?"

Once again, his wife had proven incompetent. She was the one who'd allowed Len's mother tongue to lapse, just like she was the one who'd refused to leave America.

Walking back from the museum on the shrine's stone pathway, Seiji was filled with dread: in the days ahead they'd need to select an urn and assist the priest in preparing Len's soul and name for the afterlife. He wondered if perhaps Maki could take over the duties instead.

He glanced at his mistress. She smiled back.

Hana had always been odd, he mulled. She was what the neighbors called *hijoushiki*—lacking common sense. The salient nail sticking out in a line of nails. When she attended his mother's funeral she bowed at all the wrong times, to all the wrong people.

As he passed the wooden pagoda of the shrine he turned and took another bow. The trees rustled above like silver coins. Prior to this week, Seiji hadn't thought much about lineage, but when he did, he remembered his mother's nighttime tales of duty and bloodshed, and he was happy to be a Katsuragi. Marriages into the Imperial family. Warlords who carried on in the wake of betrayals, falls of the clan. Men of few words who maneuvered their aces and deuces.

He remembered the tombs he'd once encountered: nature had reclaimed the mossy monuments belonging to families that had long since died out. As Len had no children, Seiji too would eventually need to make arrangements to break down the tombstone, remove the ashes and move them to the communal space marked only MUENBOTOKE. The departed souls with no kin.

Suddenly, exhaustion overcame him. He told Maki he wanted to be left alone. They returned home, where he collapsed into the down pillow, his body once more a rock, and did not wake until the distant horizon started turning from black to blue.

At the airport, he called his wife.

He didn't quite know what to say, so he said out of habit, "Do we have food in the house? Should I bring home seaweed or caviar?"

"The moms have been coming over," she said. "We have three tins of whole-grain lasagna. Burritos, Krispy Kreme. They've been so amazing."

"You know I can't eat that type of food," Seiji said. "Can we give them away?"

Hana made an exasperated noise. "You know, sometimes you can be so—"

"Who's going to eat them, then?"

"It doesn't matter," she said. "Friends brought them. For us."

Ever since the ham sandwich replaced the bento, various new foods had invaded Seiji's home. Hana's eyes seemed open to the myriad of cultures that surrounded her. After a twelve-inning Little League game, a teammate's mother suggested she bring home something called calzones, a neatly tucked-up pizza. Then came the ribs dripping in fat, the fiery lamb vindaloo, the Chinese fortune cookies that occasionally topped the dinner table. Len's classmate, Mark, invited their family to Seder dinner where his mother served matzo, kugel, gefilte fish.

Suddenly Len was having birthday parties at roller rinks and laser-tag centers, with long tables of kids eating hot dogs and cookie sheet cakes with frosting called simply "electric blue."

And every time Seiji returned from a business trip or a long day at work, Hana and Len were laughing about some new television series they had started watching or some other inside joke.

Seiji learned not to change the topic when the duo's conversations became animated, but instead retreated into his study, where he would call his mother.

Hana sounded hasty on the phone. "We'll talk about it when you arrive. You can eat out if nothing in the refrigerator suits."

A voice echoed through the high ceilings of the terminal. "Flight to Los Angeles..."

"But you'd be eating on your own. I'm not leaving the house."

"Alright, well. You can join or not," he said. "See you at the airport."

"Like I said: I might be late."

"I'll be at arrivals, then. Until you pick me up."

Seiji waded through the aisles of business class. Lodged in the back of his throat was something hard he couldn't quite swallow. A little girl ran past him in dinosaur steps, giggling down the aisle.

Seiji picked up the carry-on case that she'd knocked from his hand and found his seat next to an elderly man. Folds of skin bunched under a garment stinking of moisture. He clutched a guidebook in a meaty hand weathered like a vintage mitt.

The flight attendant addressed them simultaneously. "And this is your first visit to the U.S.?"

The Mitt looked up from his guidebook. "Miss, would you have any recommendations for a good beach?"

The attendant smirked. "I'll bring you a list of tourist beaches."

She turned to Seiji with an immigration form in hand. "And you, sir? How long will you stay?"

The way she looked at him reminded him of when he'd first arrived in America. He remembered how people had heard him speak and looked at him with a hastiness, a haughtiness. It was not dissimilar to the way Seiji himself gaped at the illegals sitting in U-Haul parking lots. Selling star maps on Hollywood Boulevard.

Seiji had told himself that this was not *his* land of opportunity, merely one for the firm. He, a man of business—no, *he* had not crossed the desert on foot; rather, he'd flown first class on an airline—ironically called American—across the sea.

Still, neighborhood kids pulled at the sides of their eyes, calling, "China!" And at the supermarket with his wife he'd heard someone murmur, "Speak our language or leave." And, speaking his slow, accented English, he had encountered the same look as the one worn by the flight attendant this very moment.

He smiled courteously at her. "I can't seem to remember."

Behind him the girl shrieked, accompanied by noises of struggling and seatbelts.

Seiji glanced to his side. The Mitt was breathing loudly, each breath gurgling in his double chin.

He rang the attendant bell and asked for a drink.

His whiskey arrived. As the first chill sip hit his tongue, he felt instantly better.

Halfway through the flight he was jerked out of his buzz. The girl behind him giggled and kicked his seat again. The thuds echoed in uneven intervals like sandbags hitting the ground.

Her small hand reached around and grabbed his reading light.

Seiji turned back and saw that the girl's mother had dozed off, her head tucked awkwardly into her shoulder like a crane. He said loudly, in Japanese, "Whose undisciplined child is this? I'd like to see the faces of the shameful parents who raised her like an animal."

The mother scrambled awake. She frantically pulled the girl's hand away and apologized.

Seiji heard his neighbor whisper, "I'd never put a child in business class." He looked up to see their trays like mirror images, two glasses containing amber liquid that lustered like honey.

He felt a sudden affinity for his neighbor. "Did you select the Nikka?" he asked.

"Single malt."

Seiji raised his glass. "My name is Katsuragi."

The man smiled. "Daidoji. But people call me D-Cup."

Seiji glanced at the man's chest to assess whether he was, in fact, wearing a bra. He hoped he was inconspicuous in his gesture.

The man noticed his gaze. "It's a joke," he said. "Nobody calls me that. Although if you want, you can call me Akebono."

Seiji smiled. "Akebono's 1993 season was absolutely legendary."

"This must be your first time going to America also," Akebono said. "You look nervous."

Seiji lied. "My son moved there ages ago," he said. "On a company transfer. He... he has this much younger wife. Now they barely show up at my house."

Seiji was unsure why he lied; he attributed it to his delightful whiskey buzz. After all, what a sobering task to explain why he was seventy and his son twenty-five.

"He's an ungrateful one," Akebono said.

"Things come up, you know. When he first moved, he was supposed to stay six months. Then it got extended five years, then another ten..."

As he uttered these words, Seiji thought about his mother, how each time he flew home to see her she'd aged a little more, remembered a little less.

And some years later he flew to see her through her last days, thin with age, her spine crooked from osteoporosis. He'd taken fifteen-year-old Len to the entombment, Len's wallet chain flashing from his black pants, and together they watched the cemetery workers remove the slab rock to reveal their lineage, the lapis-colored urn of his mother weighing heavily in his hands.

Akebono leaned into him, his soft folds trapping Seiji's elbow. "I'd tell your son to be careful with a younger wife."

"What do you mean?"

"Just speaking from experience," he hissed, alcohol and sourness rank on his breath. "The Americans, they're different. Cheesy pick-up lines don't embarrass them."

"I see."

"Even if they're directed at your wife." Akebono raised his eyebrows knowingly.

"Oh, I'm sorry," Seiji said.

"Cowboys," Akebono sneered. "Anyway, just make sure that she doesn't have some young buck on the side. For your son's sake."

Seiji tried to forget what Akebono had said. But these words weighed on him even after Akebono passed out in the seat next to him, snoring lightly. Outside the window, thick clouds piled upward like a big tree. Seiji thought about the cabin air circulating the plane, collecting sneezes, coughs, sighs, baby vomit. He shortened his breath.

He asked for an *oshibori* and wiped his hands and face. Behind him the girl settled in watching cartoons. Ahead, the television monitor displayed blue humanoids from a recent Hollywood blockbuster.

He grabbed the remote control to change the channel and noticed the numeric keypads on the back.

He found his credit card and awkwardly started dialing.

"Hello?"

Seiji heard a familiar voice. He hung up, put the phone down. Then he dialed again.

"Hello?" the voice said again.

"Hana," he said.

She switched to Japanese, having realized who was calling. "Did you miss your flight?"

"I'm calling from the plane."

"What? God. Isn't that like twenty dollars a minute?"

"Are you at home?"

"Yes," she said.

"Who's with you?"

"Nobody." She sounded surprised.

"No one in our house?"

"*No.*"

"Where are you?"

She was quiet, the seething in her voice. "I'm in *Lennon's* room."

He pictured her among surfboards, bookshelves of English texts. In his buzz he could see a blurry buff figure sitting on his son's bed.

"Are you having sex in our son's room?" he asked.

"Have you lost your mind? *I'm—*"

"Tell me why you did it, Hana," he asked. A tingling sensation was building in his throat. His breath was short, his face hot from the whiskey. It no longer mattered to him whether there was a figure there or not. "Hana," he repeated his wife's name.

His wife's voice was a buzz through the line. "Mrs. Fischer had to help me receive the servicemen at our home this week. Because I'm alone. I'm always alone."

"No, tell me why," Seiji said again. Black flickers crowded his peripherals. "Tell me why you let Len enlist."

There was heat behind his eyes. He shook the phone. "I come home and he's already enlisted and there's nothing else I can do."

The tense tone of his voice caught the girl's attention. She stood to peer around the seat.

"And you let him. *You* let him. Even an idiot can tell you. War's not a tea party, people aren't selling brownies. People go to war to die."

Hana's voice was calm. "Lennon knew all of this."

Akebono was awake and looking at him intently. Seiji turned away. He felt as if the entire plane were staring at him. He lowered his voice. "*You* let him. Dammit, Hana," he said.

Behind him, the girl yanked off her headphones. "You can't say that," she said.

"Excuse me?" Seiji said.

"That's a bad word. You can't say that word."

He ignored her, turning his attention to the phone. "I worked hard so he wouldn't go hungry. So he wouldn't ever have to shine shoes."

He wanted to say how he'd failed their only son, except he couldn't get the words out. Through the phone he heard Hana sobbing.

The girl was indignant. "You can't say that word. Mom, he can't say that word."

Seiji grew irritated. He waved his hand at her.

He heard Hana's voice. Vindictive, quiet as a mosquito. "You know what the unit nicknamed him? They called him Captain America."

Seiji's face was hot. He could feel Akebono's eyes boring a hole through the back of his skull.

The girl hummed, *"Dammit dammit dammit dammit."*

He turned around to look straight at her. *"Urusai!"* he yelled.

She froze. Then her face wrinkled, mouth opening wide to reveal her baby teeth. As her daughter's crying filled the cabin, the mother apologized without so much as making eye contact. She took off down the aisle with the girl in her arms to avoid any further interaction.

As the sound of crying grew faint, Hana's voice came through the static-colored line: "Len's body is coming home on Friday. None of this will bring him back, Seiji."

Seiji found himself in a sea of silence, the sadness of a man discovering his son's lifeless body, his father and unborn grandson and his entire heritage held inside it and expired as a single breath in this very instant. He hung up. He felt nauseous.

Then he remembered.

He remembered the discolored Japanese children's books baking in the sun, on sale for five cents on their driveway. The scattered sunscreen bottles, the cancelled family vacation when Len decided he'd rather drive to San Clemente to camp on the beach with his girlfriend.

He remembered his wife turning seven hundred dollars of that vacation money into a Rusty surfboard. The way Len carelessly ripped off the red bow.

He remembered, as they arrived in Japan for his mother's funeral, Len being a stranger there. He remembered Len picking at his cuticles when store clerks made him repeat his heavily accented phrases. The pusillanimous stares watching Len apprehend the *chikan*.

And he remembered Len in a mess of Little League uniforms, clambering over boys double his size to see the starting lineup pinned to the corkboard. Seiji remembered staying with Len long after those boys had left, fingering the black of his printed name over and over and over.

He remembered Len running down the empty roads of the Great Plains on their first family trip, toward a horizon where the fields met the sky. Seiji sat mesmerized by the roads, twice as wide as anything he'd seen in Japan, when he heard Len faintly, a dot in the distance: "I love it here!"

And Seiji remembered the hospital room, bare and frigid and bright. The nurses rolled Len in, swaddled like a pupa in a thick blanket. Seiji had rocked the baby, the heir to the Katsuragi name, pressing his cheek against the soft fuzz of the small head. And a few months later lying side by side, he felt the baby roll over to bury his fragile, sinless body into the groove of his arm. And he remembered the diminutive breaths coming from the little nose and a creak of a yawn as Seiji turned on his side to wrap an arm around him ever so carefully.

And then, finally, Seiji remembered the Sunday he taught Len the forkball. As he adjusted the ball between his son's small fingers he was reminded of his own childhood huddles, joining shoulders with other children who'd lost their fathers in the war. He'd chuckled at this sudden recollection. Len learned the wrist-snap on his first try, and afterwards he lay on the cold grass, a darkened cap glittered by spiraling ash seeds. He looked so free. Dirty, they returned under the salmon-colored sky, hushed along by the soprano Santa Ana winds. Then, out of nowhere, Len asked about his grandfather. Seiji carefully removed a sepia photo from his wallet: a young man, unsmiling, in a uniform and cap. Dark, luminous eyes pointed straight to camera. "It's a copy," Seiji said. "Grandma has the original." Len took the photo and stared back at the man, his first-ever connection to the military; he stared at the photo in silence until they reached the top of the block, where they could see the light from their living room window. As they reached the yard they could smell Hana's cooking, and, walking into the house, Seiji took in the smell, deep, like the first time he had smelled the nape of her neck.

Seiji heard a noise and turned around. The mother had returned; she averted her eyes as she sat down. The little girl had fallen asleep in her arms, the fine hair of her hairline fluttering, round stomach rising and falling quickly. Seiji found it difficult to imagine Len had been this age once.

The in-flight announcement sounded thirty minutes prior to landing. Akebono wiggled trying to bring his seat upright. The flight attendants hovered, reminding passengers to fasten their seatbelts as the plane descended to earth.

Outside the plane's window, clouds streamed past the bluest sky. Seiji tried to pray for his son, still wandering this lonely Earth. From the tiny window he wondered how the sky could remain so serene. Is this a vindictive God, one that purposefully took his son away, one that instilled hatred in their hearts? Where are you, God, he thought, staring into the clearest blue. I need your grace to get through this.

The large body of the plane landed with a thud, bounced once, and rolled to a stop. Has Len's body landed already on this soil, he wondered, delivered in a large cargo plane with other boys' bodies, wrapped in a flag and repatriated home to heartbroken parents—wounds, bullets, all?

Seiji wondered if Hana was waiting at the airport or would even show up. He looked up to see the metallic handles of the overhead bins, shiny from use.

Akebono heaved as he stood up. "Well, I wish you a pleasant journey."

"You were asking about beaches." Seiji turned. "My son really loved Hermosa. It gets cold at night, but the sun dips behind the waves and fills the peaks golden. It's breathtaking."

Akebono shook his hand.

As Seiji looked back to the monitor, a flight map appeared, their route highlighted in yellow. They'd crossed the Pacific. Behind him, there was listlessness in the mother's voice. Silently Seiji stood and retrieved her suitcase. The girl clung to her mother's pant leg.

The woman looked surprised, then bowed her head thank you.

Seiji waited in line at immigration behind a dread-locked backpacker, an Arab businessman in *kandura*, a mother asking her kids to translate the immigration form. When it was his turn, the officer asked, "What's the purpose of this visit?"

The man swiped Seiji's weathered green card and said, "Welcome home."

Seiji stood for a moment, looking at the pleasant-faced man. Then he took a step back and bowed deeply.

Seiji passed under a large American flag, a photo of President Obama, and a sign that enthused, WELCOME TO THE UNITED STATES OF AMERICA. The land that killed his ancestors. And the land that Lennon loved.

He called his wife as he walked the terminal halls. She answered, her voice nasal. "I'm already here."

His heart grew full listening to Hana's soft breathing through the receiver. He understood then how Lennon had felt, watching the event that inspired his enlistment: office papers from the Twin Towers, scattering like cherry blossoms across the sky. With a tenderness he hadn't felt in years, he said, "Maybe we can spread Len's ashes over the Pacific."

She said nothing. Then, "He'll need his wetsuit."

He smiled.

He saw his wife waiting on the other side of the railing as he rolled his luggage cart up the slope. There were tears, the estranged pair united only by their sorrow. He hugged her frail frame and wondered when it was exactly that she'd aged past her rosy complexion, when her worries had started to show on her face. And they drove back on the Pacific Coast Highway, sitting in a silence that only a familiar couple knew, the only solace in the land, the sunset fading purple and orange against the twilight of the city, against the salt spray of the Pacific, the dusty brush smell of the hills.

THE WALL

by MERON HADERO

W HEN I MET HERR Weill, I was a lanky ten-year-old, a fish
out of water in ———, Iowa, a small college town surrounded
by fields from every direction. My family had moved to the
United States a few weeks earlier from Ethiopia via Berlin, so I knew no
English, but was fluent in Amharic and German. I'd speak those sometimes to strangers or just mumble under my breath to say what was on
my mind, never getting an answer until the day I met Herr Weill.

I was wearing jeans with a button-down, a too-big blazer, and a
clip-on tie, waiting in line during what I'd later come to know as a
typical mid-'80s Midwest community potluck, with potato salad, pasta
salad, green bean casserole, bean salad casserole, tuna pasta salad casserole, a good three-quarters of the dishes on offer incorporating bacon and
crushed potato chips and dollops of mayonnaise. The Norman Borlaug
Community Center had welcomed us because one of the local bigwigs
had been in the Peace Corps in his student days, and he'd cultivated an

interest in global humanitarianism. He'd heard of the new stream of refugees leaving communist dictatorships in the Third World, found us through the charity that had given us housing in Berlin, and arranged for the NBCC to orient us, get us some new used clothes and a place to live. They also invited us to Sunday meals, which were the best ones of my week.

On this particular Sunday, I'd walked into the recreational room transformed by paper cutouts of pumpkins and bundled ears of multicolored corn. Cotton had been pulled thin across the windows, and dried leaves pressed in wax paper taped to the wall. Beneath a banner (which I couldn't read) was a plastic poster of a woman with a pointed black hat on her head, her legs straddling a broom, haunting grimace bearing missing teeth, as if I didn't already feel afraid and alienated in that space. Next to this monstrosity stood a very benign-looking real-life man with a wool scarf and wool coat, who wiped away a bead of sweat as he eyed, then looked away from, then eyed again a pretty woman across the room who was picking through a basket of miniature candy bars.

In German I said to no one in particular, "Why doesn't he just talk to her?" Nodding at the man with the wool coat, I continued, "What's he waiting for, permission from his mother?"

Then, from a deep voice behind me, I heard in German, "There was a woman in my life once. I looked at her the same way."

When this stranger spoke these words, I recalled the moment a few months back in West Berlin when I was playing soccer with Herman and Ismail, two Turkish brothers who lived on Friedrichstrasse next door to me. Our improvised playground was this plot close to the Berlin Wall where someone had tied a piece of yarn between two old halogen lamps, a makeshift goalpost. Sometimes I'd aim not for those feet between the metal posts but far beyond the Wall. This was in defiance of my mother's strict command to stay away from "that horror of a serpent."

Wasteful and risky, she called it when I'd told her twice before that I'd sacrificed a soccer ball to the GDR. She was wrong to worry that I'd get in trouble for my antics—I never did. But she was right that I'd been wasteful. We had nothing as it was, and the embarrassment of buying a toy must have been infuriating to her because strangers slandered her with cries of "welfare woman" and "refugee scum" when she walked down the street anyway, just to get groceries or some exercise, and when they saw her carrying something as frivolous as a soccer ball, they'd shout louder, with more spit in their breaths and more rage in their eyes. I knew this, I'd even witnessed this, but for some reason I couldn't help that sometimes, after running circles in the tiny paved playground that pressed against the barricade, I'd visualize this little grounded balloon between my feet soaring to the other side of that imposing wall that seemed to challenge my very sense of freedom, and so I'd close my eyes and kick hard. Herman and Ismail could never—or would never—clear the hurdle, but I'd done it twice already, and the third time I launched the ball just over the barbed wire, I heard a loud grunt from somewhere beyond, and saw the ball come soaring back toward us. I caught it and was stunned. Herman and Ismail yelled at me to send it over again, but I knew it would have broken my heart some if we'd kicked it back and never had it returned. I'd have held tight to hope, I'd have gone back to the spot and waited, I'd have lingered in the playground anticipating a reply, whether or not another ever came. So I convinced Herman and Ismail that we should retire our game, and to make sure of it I put a pin through the ball and let out the air.

This is how I felt standing in the potluck line that October day, looking at the man looking at a woman, hearing this response in German said back to me, the first words I'd understood in this new country spoken by anyone other than my parents: "There was a woman in my life, once. I looked at her the same way," the man had said in German, and I replayed this in my mind as I stood there frozen, not daring to say a thing, holding onto my words like I held that returned ball on the playground.

Johannes Weill went ahead and introduced himself and said everyone just called him Herr Professor Weill or simply Herr Weill because he once was a dean at the college who'd won some big international award, and so it stuck. He told me I was famous in town, too. I pointed at myself, wondering what he'd heard. "You're one of the Ethiopian refugees, right?" Herr Weill asked, then said, "I've been waiting to meet you. The whole town has been talking." I nodded, just beginning to trust in this conversation, in the sincere interest of his tone, in his perfect German, in which he continued, "To answer your question, the man in the wool coat is trying to think of a way to impress the girl, of course."

"Stringing together a sentence might be a good start," I suggested. "His opener is obvious. As she's picking through the basket of candy, ask her what kind of chocolate she likes."

Herr Weill took off his round glasses and squinted in a way that severely exaggerated the already deep lines that crossed his face. He held his glasses up to the light, like he had to make sure that I was real and not a speck on his lens or something, and after this pause he replied, "It's not always easy to find the right words, you know."

"Maybe you just have to know the right language," I said.

"Well, if you don't learn English soon, you'll end up like that man in the wool coat, with no way to say what's on your mind or in your heart, except to some old German guy you meet waiting for spaghetti and ham-balls," he said. "And that doesn't sound like a good way to spend a childhood."

"Yeah, I'm working on it," I said.

"I could teach you English."

"Then you must not know," I said. The part I didn't say was "just how poor we are."

By now I was taking modest spoonfuls from the big Tupperware containers so as not to show just how poor we were. Not to overstate how eager I was for spaghetti and ham-balls, I pursed my lips to hide my watering mouth, and turned away hoping he wouldn't hear the faint rumbling of my stomach.

I finally decided to take bacon that was in strips *and* in rounded patties.

"It's true," Herr Weill said. "I didn't teach languages. I was a professor in the arts, but I do know how to teach."

"But a tutor costs money, and the problem is—"

"A money issue?" he asked and waited, but I didn't respond.

"You'd be doing me a favor," he said. "It has been ages since I've spoken German to someone face to face—spoken German to anyone at all. It would be quite nice to have a new friend to talk to."

I turned to face him. A friend, he'd said, and I nearly repeated him. "I would like a friend to talk to as well," I confessed, unable to stop myself from smiling openly now. We shook on the deal, and I bowed slightly in the Ethiopian way as I said, "Nice to meet you, Herr Weill."

I'd go to Herr Weill's on Mondays, Wednesdays, and Fridays after school. During our early conversations, it was a relief to land on his doorstep after the six hours in a school where no one understood anything about me. My silence, my inability to grasp the very words being said in class, including my own name—mispronounced by the teacher taking the roll. The pungent food I brought for lunch that I ate with my hands. My solitary play at recess that usually involved creative projects with flowers, rocks, wood, whatever I collected from the patch of wilderness on the edge of the playground. My need for expression took on non-verbal forms in those thirty minutes of freedom outdoors. I contributed nothing to the class discussions, and understood almost nothing as well, except during our math hour (what a short hour), my favorite subject, that universal language. Math and art, the only things I cared about. After these exhausting days,

I'd walk the mile of country road to Herr Weill's tidy brick house, and it mattered that he always seemed pleased to see me.

Before I went up the walkway that perfectly bisected his perfectly manicured lawn, I'd always straighten my coat, tuck in my shirt, and inspect my shoes. He'd greet me in a suit and wing-tipped shoes, hold out his right hand for a handshake while his left arm was held behind his back, like he was greeting a dignitary. His wispy white hair was always parted in the middle in an unwavering line from which thin strands were combed toward his ears. When those strands would flop as he was talking excitedly, shaking his head and index finger while making a point, he'd simply smooth his hair back down once he'd said his piece, that meridian reemerging just so. He had an unfussy home: no phone, sturdy furniture, lots of these framed silhouette paintings hanging on the walls. He'd set out tea and bread, cheese, and meats, and he always made me a to-go box to bring home to my mother. He was well regarded in town, and so my parents quickly warmed to the idea of these meetings, and especially the free English lessons. Whenever I asked my parents a question about English, they'd say, "That's one to remember for Herr Professor." Herr Weill and I would usually meet for about two hours. My mother didn't have to worry about finding a sitter or some inexpensive after-school activity for me three days a week. Herr Weill was a blessing, she always said. Father wasn't particularly religious, but he agreed. Herr Weil was a blessing.

We worked through a basic English textbook that had a cartoon of a red schoolhouse with a big sun shining down actual rays of wavy lines, something any preschooler could have drawn, if he had no imagination. We sat with this workbook for an hour and spent the rest of the time speaking German. At first, I was surprised by how much I had to say. With both my parents spending long hours at work cleaning the chemistry lab by day and applying to training programs at night, and with no one to talk to in my neighborhood or at school, I had filled my days with so much silence that my time with Herr Weill was an unexpected outpouring.

Herr Weill didn't reveal very much that first day, but opened up just to tell me he had been a refugee once, too, and had left home when he was a teenager because a war scattered his whole family. He spoke slowly and said little, but it was also an outpouring, I could tell. From then on, we talked often about these things, like conflict, violence, war, fleeing from it and the way it makes you tired and confused whether you're running or still. We talked about scars, invisible and visible, instant and latent ones, all real. How hard it is not to keep losing things because of conflict, even once it's far away, miles or years away, and yet how life fills up with other things all the while. At the end of that visit, he said, "It's a relief to be able to chat with someone around here about something other than Chuck Long," whom I'd never even heard of anyway.

The second time I visited Herr Weill, he gave me a leather journal so I would always have someone to talk to, if only the blank page. I wrote in German so that I could show it to Herr Weill if he ever asked to see it. I was always jotting down notes about my life, about the things I'd encounter and wanted to think about, conversations that were mostly reflections of what I longed to say and hear.

Li is from China. I've been sitting next to her in the back of the room ever since last week when we were the only people in the class without costumes for Halloween. She told me a secret, her family fled from the first country, and she asked me if I knew what she meant and I did. I told her I even knew what it meant to flee from the second country, and also to leave the third country, and that made her smile. She has a pretty smile. And she's really good at drawing. And geography. Maybe because she saw me writing in this journal, she gave me a box of pens today. She always has these nice pens she draws with that have little pandas on them. She gave me a whole box. How did she know I love pandas? Her English is worse than mine. When she handed me the pens, she said something like, "Your book." I tried to say, "Thanks, pandas are my favorite animals," but she didn't respond. Maybe underneath, it really went like this, or could have:

    Me: How's everything?

     Li: I'm fine, how are you?

    Me: I'm fine. I've just been writing in this journal that my best friend gave me.

     Li: What are you writing about?

    Me: Oh, just about life and love and things like that.

     Li: Wow! I brought you pens so you can keep writing in your book.

    Me: Thanks, pandas are my favorite animals!

     Li: Mine, too!

    Me: I'll dedicate this journal to you.

     Li: I'd like that very much.

Later, I will try to tell Li that Herr Weill is taking me to the college library. It will be closed for Veteran's Day, but he has a "ritual" to go every year the day before on November 10th. He thinks I might like it there, too.

Every November 10, Herr Weill would go to the college library to see what he called his German collection. Before we met, this was the only German he heard all year. He'd read German books out loud, and it was the only German he spoke all year, too. Herr Weill and I took a bus to the library. The roof of the bus had these little gold stars painted onto it, and I thought that was a fine touch. Unlike in Berlin, you could look up at night from any point in this town and see the stars anyway, but still, it was nice to be reminded of a clear night sky on a cold morning.

Herr Weill knew everyone at the library, and they all came over to say hi and see how he was doing. He introduced me to the research librarians and other staff. They took us to a very small room made of glass that reminded me of an elevator I'd once seen in Berlin. The room had two chairs in it and shelves for books. He gave the research librarian a stack of bits of paper with numbers and letters, and about a half hour later, the librarian rolled a cart over to our little room. The cart was full of books, maps, newspapers, photographs, most of them dusty as if they hadn't been touched all year.

We spent the whole day there with these items. So we could keep up our energy, Herr Weill snuck in breakfast, lunch sandwiches, a snack, and a light supper. I wrote down everything I could about what I saw in our glass room because it was such a standout day. I saw:

— *Café Elektric*, a silent film with Marlene Dietrich and with no ending because it is said to be lost. Herr Weill thinks the end was later lost in the war because that's the nature of war, to leave stories incomplete and rob us of our resolutions (we also listened to Marlene Dietrich sing in *Blue Angels*).

— *The Threepenny Opera* by his "namesake by coincidence," Kurt Weill, also a refugee. The song I remember was about mercy being more important than justice and Herr Weill said he listened to it every year to see if he'd come any closer to deciding whether or not this was true, and, if it was true, what it required of him or what it eased in him, so he said.

— Poems by the poet Rilke.

— A few pages of *Zen and the Art of Archery*, which Herr Weill had been reading a few pages at a time for years, each year. We took turns reading aloud. He said Zen doesn't believe in language, so it's best to give the pages space, months, years to breathe. He folded over the top, a tiny bend marking where we would pick up next November.

— News clips from November 10, 1938, because of the treacherous anniversary of Kristallnacht. Herr Weill says it's important to acknowledge an anniversary, even the ones that mark tragedy. This was around the time he left Germany and became a refugee, which I can tell he doesn't like to speak about. He said very little about 1938 except that some things we can't help but to remember, and some we must struggle to forget. I forgot to ask him which things are which.

— Old maps and new ones because Herr Weill said that the borders can change on you, so you have to keep watch, keep checking in. Through the maps, I learned some more about Herr Weill and my old home:

- Herr Weill was born in 1920 not in Berlin, but in a suburb. By the time he was two months old, the city had grown at least three times because someone moved some lines on a map. So he was born just outside of Berlin and grew up in Berlin, having lived in the same house all his childhood. I saw the old map of Germany in 1919 and in 1920. He called it something else, Weimar.

- He pointed out the borders of the Jewish ghetto that he said had walls of its own when Germany was called something else, the Third Reich, but he didn't call it that himself, he said.

- We looked at a map of Germany after WWII with Berlin in the eastern part of the country. This was before the USSR built the Wall, but still there was West Berlin with borders around it, a floating dot in the Communist bloc. Herr Weill said, "It's a very uneasy thing to live life surrounded by enemies." I knew this to be true.

- A satellite map outlining the wall built in 1961. From this point of view, it had none of the order I always associated with the Wall.

- On a modern map of West Berlin, I pointed out where our studio was situated in the shadow of the Wall on the Western side, which looked the same as the shadow that fell on the East. I pointed out where Herman and Ismail had lived. I also found the general location of our playground, and also where I liked to sit by the Spree and watch the boats when I lived in the East and where I liked to sit by the Spree and watch the boats in the West just like I liked to watch the boats when we went on vacation to the banks of Lake Tana.

I will always remember the way Herr Weill quoted me back to myself after that day, saying, "You say you lived with your family 'in the shadow of the Wall on the Western side, which looked the same as the shadow that fell on the East.' In this, you have pointed out the main aspect of a wall that these damn architects never seem to grasp: no matter which side you're on, its shadow is cast on you." He'd say it at random times, and reflect on those words in a way that made me feel understood.

At the end of our visit to the college library, Herr Weill wished me a happy eve of Armistice Day, his favorite holiday, marking the end of World War I, a "war to end all wars, a day that for a moment must have seemed to promise eternal peace, for a while." I asked, "Why celebrate a day that was a lie, there was no armistice to end all wars," but Herr Weill replied, "Even if a promise isn't kept, it doesn't mean there has been a lie." He said we'd do this again next year, and being let in to this annual ritual gave me the feeling we'd be friends for a long time. Before I left, Herr Weill invited me and my parents to lunch at his home on November 11, but I told him my father didn't have the day off and my mother wanted me to help mend the winter clothes we'd been given while we were still wearing our fall clothes.

November 14, sunny, freezing, so cold that recess is getting shorter so we've been playing inside. I started to pass notes to Li in the back of the room:

— Monday: Do you like me? Yes, No, Maybe
  Li answered by drawing a doodle of a cat sleeping on a chair.

— Tuesday: Want to play after study time? Yes, No, Maybe (circle one)
Li answered by drawing a tic-tac-toe board and putting an x in
the middle.
— Wednesday: No note (playing it cool)
— Thursday: Would you like to share my juice box today?
Li drew a sun with sunglasses on it!
— Friday: Can we play tomorrow in the park?
Li wrote the words to the Pledge of Allegiance.

I couldn't tell if Li and I were growing closer or missing each other.
There were few friends in my life. Ismail and Herman had left Germany
just before I did, and the only letter I wrote was never forwarded, just
returned unopened, wrong address. I couldn't write my friends back home
because my parents said it was unsafe to tell them where we'd escaped
to. Though I barely talked to Li, she was my closest friend at school. I
longed to know her better.

I brought my heartache to Herr Weill, tentatively. I eased into the
subject, asking Herr Weill, "When I first met you, didn't you say there
was a woman you looked at once with longing?" He lifted his brow, and
revealed that, sure, he'd loved a woman once. They were neighbors in
Berlin. He was shy, she was shy. He'd carry her groceries, walk her to
school sometimes, tried to show her he was a dependable rock in her life,
and he had it all planned out in his mind: when he graduated from high
school, started a job, and had enough money to take her out in style, then
he'd ask her to dinner. But the war happened, and it didn't end in time.
They both walked into the war, never reconnecting. She was always good
to him. Her name was Margareta.

I asked him, "If you never married her, did you ever marry anyone else?"

"Almost once, but it fell apart. Then another time almost, but it
slipped through my fingers. That seemed like as many chances as I was

going to get. But I every so often wonder about Margareta, just like I wonder about many things from back home that eluded me," he admitted.

"Do you regret not pursuing her?" I asked him.

"You see," he said, "one always regrets a lack of courage. In one form or another, that's probably the only kind of regret anyone ever has."

"So you tried to find her again later?" I pressed, testing my own feelings about Li against his answers and experience.

"No, I haven't tried to find her yet," he said. I didn't feel the need to tell him the obvious, that forty-five years seemed long enough to wait. But I was shy, too, so I could understand where he was coming from, which made me even more upset. I decided that I'd need to learn from this, to be bolder than he was in matters of the heart, and I came up with a name for my plan to win Li ASAP: Operation Panda Margareta, which was both my favorite animal, the animal I imagined Li also loved, and the name of the woman Herr Weill had once loved.

I talked to Herr Weill about it and he seemed charmed, understood that something as monumental as Operation Panda Margareta would need to be dramatic, carefully planned, and very strategically implemented. The next time I saw him I showed him my idea, which he thought seemed adequately heroic:

OPERATION PANDA MARGARETA

9:15:   Sneak into the principal's office while Principal is out for his daily smoke/walk
9:16:   Play the Jackson 5's "ABC" over the PA
9:17:   Read a poem for Li
9:19:   Run!

I worked on the plan on my own, especially writing the poem, which took time since my English was still halting. A couple of weeks later, I was leaving school to visit Herr Weill and go over last-minute details for Operation Panda Margareta, recite the poetry, test out the cassette player my dad had loaned me, and go over the book I'd checked out from the library on operating a PA system, when I noticed Thomas Henry—sweet quiet farm kid—come down the front steps of the school, walk up to Li, and, without saying a thing, put his arm around her in a familiar way, like he'd certainly done it before. Behind his ear he had a panda pen, and my heart was sinking. I fumbled for the poem in my pocket, and I almost did what I had meant to do, read these words to Li, declare my feelings. When Thomas and Li walked by, I tried to catch Li's gaze, but I couldn't quite keep it.

I stopped writing in my notebook after this, and just before winter break Li began sitting with Thomas and his friends up by the front of the room. I joined a soccer club and cut back on my visits to Herr Weill's. I made all kinds of excuses, but the truth is as my English improved, other barriers came down, too, just like Herr Weill predicted. I was discovering more about my classmates, that it turned out they also found it fun to watch the magic tricks that Benny the crossing guard practiced on his breaks and also liked playing in the cleared fields surrounding town. They pranked me by teaching me dirty words but telling me the wrong definition (for about a week, I thought *cabbage* was an insult, *artichoke* a sin to say). I pranked them by showing them sophisticated, "worldly" ways to dance and shop and roller-skate that were ridiculous and hilarious and got us all kicked out of a few establishments.

So in this way, Herr Weill and I drifted apart, allowed ourselves to become somewhat untied from each other, and let the ebb and flow of life move us along our own paths. I'd still go by from time to time, after chatting at the community center and making plans to meet some weeks, until eventually, with weekend matches to play, I stopped going to those Sunday potlucks, too. When I did come over, Herr Weill would put out meats, cheeses, and breads as always, and I allowed myself to imagine he did this whether I came or not, set out this spread every afternoon, that he wasn't going out of his way for me on these haphazard visits. By the spring, my parents decided it was time for us to move again, this time to move toward something: a new job for my father pulling us away. A better job, no longer washing lab instruments but now getting training in a hospital in a town that American doctors avoided. And so we packed our bags again, I hoped for the last time.

Herr Weill and I wrote letters for the first few months after this, but then I guess I just couldn't keep up, or just didn't. The letters piled up, four unanswered ones from Herr Weill that I'd only read quickly, meant to answer but hadn't, life becoming something else by now.

We nearly met again, almost, just after November 9, 1989, when suddenly and unexpectedly the Berlin Wall fell. My first thought upon hearing the news was where were Ismail and Herman, and maybe they could reclaim our lost soccer balls. My second thought was did Herr Weill see the news and what did he think/do/say? I tried to look up Herr Weill in the phonebook, but he still didn't have a number listed, so I told my parents what I wanted to do and they reluctantly let me take the car to visit him the next day, November 10. I managed to get to the library before it closed. I went to Herr Weill's usual desk, but he had left. When I asked, the librarian said Herr Weill had come by for just a short visit, and I'd missed him by hours. I requested that old copy of *Zen and the Art of Archery* and saw he'd gone through a few more pages, advanced six unobtrusive folds since the time we'd read this book.

I retraced a path I'd walked so many times, driving that road through the fields and wooded brush. I drove right by his house at first, looking for a large home, circling back, puzzling over how modest it actually was. The paint was faded, but the mailbox was new. The lawn was strewn with leaves, some soggy and patted down and some fresh atop that cover, like he hadn't cleared the yard in weeks, maybe all season. It was too late to ring the bell, I told myself. It would have been awkward to visit unannounced then, and I realized I hadn't worked out what I'd have said, anyway. I could sleep in the car and knock in the morning. But it was hard to sleep that night for some reason, and I found myself clearing his lawn with my bare hands of all those messy leaves and filling up his mulch bin. I finished just after dawn, then stayed to pull the tiny weeds that had just sprouted up in the cracks on his pathway leading to his porch, which already had an American flag flying for Armistice Day ("Armistice Day, flags display," Herr Weill once said). I drove into the quiet town, the shops on Main mostly closed, yet all with bright red, white, and blue banners hanging in the still morning. I passed my old school and the community center, circled back down by the college, saw the movie theater and the roller rink, each taking on an aura of reverence that a quiet holiday brings.

I thought I might look up Li and see if her family had managed to stay still in her second country. She'd have been sixteen, a junior in high school, but I never got the courage for that, either. I imagined she was getting ready to go to homecoming with Thomas, maybe thinking about buying him a boutonniere and he asking her what color her dress was so he could find the right corsage. As I was filling up the gas tank to make the trip back, I wondered already if I'd regret not looking for Li and I knew I'd regret not having stopped by to visit Herr Weill, our friendship that I'd once thought would last for years already somehow in the past. At least after clearing his lawn, I'd left him a note, simply the first page in the journal he'd once given me and that I still carried around from time to time. On top of the torn-out page, I wrote: *11/11/89, To my first friend in my fourth country on the event of the end of the Wall. A heartfelt and happy Armistice Day.*

Then, in faded ink and smudged lettering:

October 15, 1983:
To Herr Weill: Thanks for this journal. It's terrific.
To Journal: Welcome to my life! Herr Weill is my first friend here so far. We have some things in common and some not:

My favorite food: wurst with kraut and mustard. Also dorro wat or kitfo with injera.
Herr Weill's favorite: schnitzel because his mother used to make it and it is "comfort food."
My favorite movie: *Casablanca*, ever since they played it at the American Consulate because it was about refugees.
Herr Weill's favorite: *Casablanca*! He says it's a story about true friendship.
My favorite season: I hate the cold because of the way it makes you cry, but I love reading next to a fire.
Herr Weill's favorite season: he loves the vigor of the cold, but he hates the snow, too mushy when it melts.

So what else can this mean but that we both love the fall?

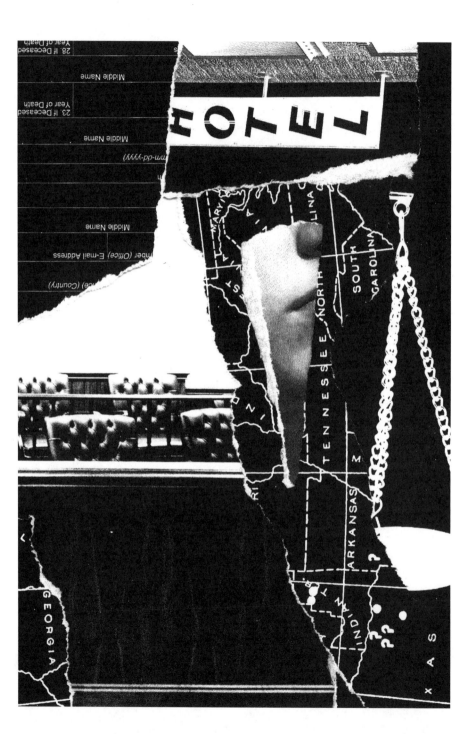

AT THE EDGE OF OMAHA

by JOSÉ ANTONIO RODRIGUEZ

I'm nervous, I say
Over dinner
In a Holiday Inn.
Nothing to be
Nervous about, says
My colleague who's already testified.
Tomorrow you say,
Yes I'm the one
Who translated
Those phone calls.
And she rolls
Her eyes, relishes

Another morsel
Of Salisbury steak and potatoes.
Here I wish
More than anything
That I could be
Her, convinced that this
Entire enterprise
Crowned by a judge
And his gavel
Is a mere formality,
That the men in orange
Are crash test dummies,
That the defense attorneys
Are performers
Playing at picking apart
The terms I chose
For the entertainment
Of the courtroom audience.

But what if
I mess it up, I say.
What if I say
The wrong thing,
Lose the case.
Some expert
I'd be
Then.
    Won't matter,
    she says,

they're Mexican
and on trial
in the Bible Belt.
They don't stand a chance.

CAPPUCCINO PLEASE

by EDVIN SUBAŠIĆ

T HE FIRST TIME I ran into Lucia I was on a quest for a refuge from the refuge. I needed a little time to myself in order to stay sane, away from the crowd in the camp. She worked at Café Ekatarina the Great on the main strip across from the only movie theater in town. Although the town had changed its citizenship to Croatian, many of its places were still remnants of Yugoslavia. The ghosts of the old country were still everywhere, after the dream of the united South Slavic tribes had burst and evaporated. It dissolved into lonely bubbles floating through the air. The movie theater had been conquered by Yugoslav actors—grandiose Rade Serbedžija, farcical Miki Manojlović, or the eternal partisans such as Ljubiša Samardžić. Even Tom Cruise and Demi Moore, their immaculate Western image, their brilliant new Hollywood poster on the theater's wall, couldn't eradicate the ghosts from the old, musty screen and the squeaky, shabby seats.

Lucia asked me what I wished to drink as soon as I entered the café, before I sat down. It was late afternoon and there were only a few regulars. A group of high-school students was sitting in the dark corner opposite the entrance, drinking coffee and smoking. Their backpacks scattered all over the seats. I asked for a cappuccino and a glass of water. She sized me up and asked me if I had money to pay. I threw a twenty-kuna bill on the table. She turned away and left in a jiff without saying a word. She joined the high-schoolers. They exchanged a few words and glanced at me. They knew I was a Bosnian refugee, fresh out of the camp, looming like a ghost. Besides, my Bosnian accent was obvious.

The last few days had been good to me. I had money in my pocket. I'd found some work. Although we officially weren't allowed to leave the camp premises without permission, never mind to work under the table, some of us decided to take our chances. The week before, I had dug gas lines. Everywhere the machinery couldn't get to, our group of young refugees burrowed by hand. We were paid by the square meter. In spite of picking and shoveling from sunrise to sunset, I'd made only a few kuna. Digging in the woods entailed cutting stubborn tree roots. I had done only ten meters the first day. I was hungry and somewhat disappointed. The palms of my hands were covered in blisters. That whole day my meal consisted of a single bread slice spread with butter, which I had saved from the previous night's dinner. I was fighting the firm soil and hardy tree roots while being starved of food and confidence.

The next day I dug twenty meters and was proud of myself. I was hopeful. I thought that if we stayed here longer, I might be able to become a new person, not a charity case. I might even call it a home until our return. That way this new reality would be bearable. Before we left home Grandma had told me that we'd find our way back again. She'd seen it in her dreams, as she had once dreamed that Grandpa would return alive after being taken away by the Germans in World War II. Three months after the war ended he appeared on her doorstep.

It was worth it—to spend a quarter of my wage on a cappuccino. I felt human again. Lucia finished her conversation with her friends, occasionally glancing at me. I heard them calling her name and I adored it right away. I loved the way they raised their intonation on the first syllable. Then she disappeared behind the bar. Five minutes later she returned with plain espresso.

"Here," she said, "it's free." She threw it in the air. The tiny brown espresso cup bounced and slid toward me.

"I hate making cappuccinos," she continued, her hands resting on her hips. "Just drink the damn coffee. It takes forever to make those milky drinks. It's on the house."

"Huh?" I nodded, my eyes wide.

"That's all you have to say?"

"Why, what?"

"Is that all?"

"Huh, yes?"

She turned around and marched away, her steps short and fueled by fury. She stood by her friends' table and lit up a cigarette. She murmured something and they laughed. She looked at me, her eyes spitting fire.

I sipped the coffee without hurry, listened to the music. The dark room felt good, safe, even though I'd managed to upset my host already. I decided to ignore what had just happened. I had come here to stay away from people and their tempers. This coffee would give me enough of a break to be able to return to the camp again for another night of noise, stink, and luminous dreams. I'd wake up in the middle of the night and listen to the people's breathing, unable to grasp where I was or why I was there. Through the infinite, dulling darkness of our vast warehouse room echoed recurrent coughing, moaning, and squeaking of beds as people tossed and turned. Our air reeked of filthy socks and stale sweat. I'd panic and run outside in the night, gasp for the fresh morning air that smelled of grass and water.

I immersed myself in the placid dawn, listened to its silence and thought about now. Everyone at the camp contemplated either the past or the future. I couldn't. I didn't want to think about what happened south of the border. I didn't want to reflect on anything. I just wanted to be: be able to enter a café and sit without worrying that someone might enter it drunk and armed to the teeth, looking for me or someone like me. Tonight I wanted to be able to breathe fresh air in peace.

A week before leaving home, I'd had an extraordinary lucid dream. In that dream I found myself in a brick house, a stranger's home, enormous and foreign. The strangers' faces around me spoke English, and I understood them for some reason although I'd never learned English before. I understood I was in America, but the setting seemed to be in northern Europe, maybe England—wet, drizzling, and lush green. The America I knew from the movies was enveloped in sunlight, dry and dreamy. It must've been all the talk I'd heard about the looming exodus into a scary, unknown world. I woke up steamed in my own sweat.

That morning my mother found a rocket-propelled grenade in front of our house. We called the police. They said we were lucky. It didn't detonate because it hit the roof at a low angle and rolled on the ground. Shingles broken in pieces lay over the edge right above my bedroom in the attic. Everyone knew who did it. Our new neighbors had been drinking the night before and thanks to the brandy they had missed. The police knew it, too. Dad's old friend, a policeman, stayed behind and whispered in confidence. His advice for us was to leave as soon as possible. The word was we were next on the list, whatever that list might be.

My dad didn't want to leave. He said that we couldn't just abandon our home and live on charity somewhere in the world. My parents cursed. My grandma cried. She had survived World War II only to witness another war five decades later. That morning, I knew we'd pack soon.

*　*　*

I kept working while I lived in Grad, the camp for war refugees from Bosnia supported by a German charity. Every time I found a job, I felt more at home. I was myself and away from the past. I had no time to go back for another coffee. I helped on a construction site, mixed concrete and delivered it to the bricklayers. We worked from sunrise to sunset. The last rounds we made in the dark with the help from the nearby streetlight. The concrete mixer rumbled while me and another kid from the camp—the blond twin brother with crazy eyes who wouldn't shut up the whole time—kept feeding and emptying it. We were rewarded with a bit of cash and a feast. The owner of the estate, a wealthy *Gastarbeiter* from Austria, treated us with roasted lamb, pork, and lots of beer. We didn't stop until we were so drunk that we couldn't find our way back to the camp. We got lost in the middle of some field, freezing our drunken asses off in the cold night. We found our way somehow, stumbling through the fields of corn, dogs barking in the distance, smelling our skin permeated with beer and meat roast. By then we were almost sober. The crazy-eyed twin had been talking the whole time, blabbering about anything that had happened in his and his brother's childhood.

I shared the money I earned with my family and asked my parents to buy some real food. I had a few kunas left and the next few days I returned to Lucia. I persevered and asked for cappuccino, but she kept bringing me plain espresso, banging the cup and saucer in front of me. She muttered "It's on the house" or "I'm not making that cappuccino." She stared me down and then walked away, leaving me wordless and furious. Then she continued to ignore me and talked to her friends who regularly stopped by after school. She smoked a cigarette and stood in front of their table. I caught her sometimes gazing in the mirrors on the opposite wall, spying on me. Our eyes met in one of the fragmented pieces of irregular shapes slapped on the walls randomly, artistically. I suppose it was a design pattern which I didn't get. I was too young to understand designs and looks, or too ignorant to think about it.

All I wanted was to see Lucia make me that cappuccino, and I would pay for it. I was worth it. Although I was just a young man, an ordinary but uprooted soul without relevant history or future, I wanted her to admit that I was worth that effort. I demanded respect. And I would ask her every time until she did it. The truth was I liked her, and I didn't know why. The mirrored walls in the café must have played with my mind or my heart.

A few weeks later I ran out of luck. I couldn't land a job. It got cold in mid-October and the work season tapered off. People didn't need help. One day, out of the blue, an older woman living down the street from the camp asked me to help her clear out the garden—to harvest and cut the corn stalks. Then she asked me to clean up around the house, scrub the chicken coop clean, run some gravel around, and fill the ditches carved by last spring's rains.

At the end of the day, she said she didn't have any money but she'd made me a supper with dessert. I could eat as much as I wanted. The scrawny old woman who moved like a pendulum had already set the table on the patio. She also brought a jug full of homemade white wine and two bottles of sparkling water. She left me alone with the food and wine and disappeared behind the backdoor. I shrugged and dug into it. I ate the hot beef goulash the color of her brick house, the salad of lettuce and onions, fresh homemade bread, and *kiflice*—walnut and butter cookies. While I ate I kept making spritzers and drinking them as if they were water. When I got full, I left the patio table and wandered into the garden. I sat on the bench under the yellowing grapevines, holding the jug, which was now half-empty. I continued sucking on it until the last drop.

An hour later, she came out of the house. Her eyes fell on the empty jug. "*Gospode bože*, oh my lord, I can't believe you drank all that wine. You're too young to drink that much."

"*Znam gospodjo*, I know, ma'am, but I did it and that's all I can say. Now I gotta go home," I replied.

"Home?"

"Ha ha ha," I laughed hysterically. "Home? Huh, what home? What am I saying? I meant back to my bed, the bed on top of the beds on top of the beds. Hope I can climb in."

I stood up. Suddenly the world turned upside down. Or the right way, since my world had already been upside down. I decided I needed a walk to sober up before returning to the camp. I paced as straight and as dignified as I could. I followed the imaginary line that the road construction workers had etched in when they laid the asphalt in the street a few decades before. It led me to Lucia.

She was behind the bar, washing dishes. I saw her reflection in the mirrors. Her loose curly brown hair, high arched eyebrows, dark round eyes, mouth shaped like an angry bird, and full lips bursting with confidence. She must've been about my age, maybe a senior in high school. She was a beautiful ghost stuck behind impenetrable mirrored walls.

As soon as I sat in my usual empty corner behind the entrance door—a partially confined booth shielded from intruders, the oncoming guests—I realized I had only two kunas left in my pocket. Not enough for a drink, not even a plain espresso or a glass of water. I dug into the pockets of my pants, then my black leather jacket with zippers, ran my fingers through various compartments—both the real and the fake ones. I had gotten the jacket earlier that week when Caritas brought a load of used clothing. It was a great rock-and-roll leather jacket. I liked to think it had been worn by a member of the Clash or Milan Mladenović from EKV. Ragged and cracked in several places, it still looked impressive. I wanted to show it off in front of Lucia.

Not even the secret sections of my jacket would help me. I realized

Lucia was watching me from the corner of her eye. I couldn't back out now. I couldn't just disappear. I knew if I left now I'd never be able to come back. My pride wouldn't let me. Yes, even a refugee kid can have his pride and hold onto it as if it were everything left of life. In the end, it was all I could carry with me. My despair made me mad and turned me into a fool.

Suddenly, I had an idea. I could order cappuccino. As always, she'd bring espresso and say it was on the house. A few minutes later, she approached my table, her beautiful face gracious and welcoming—no trace of the usual attitude.

"Cappuccino, please," I beamed nonchalantly. My eyes fixed on hers, not a flinch to offer. I was good, I thought. Perhaps all that wine was good for something.

"No problem," she said, smiling back and keeping her eyes on mine.

She vanished behind the bar again and I heard the sound of the espresso machine. A pair of middle-aged men sitting at the bar kept ordering white wine spritzers. White wine was the drink of choice here. People downed it as if it were their last. Now I'd barf all over the floor at the mere thought of drinking another spritzer.

The two men tried to strike up a conversation with Lucia. She gave them short replies, looking away the whole time. Then the usually closed door behind her opened up. An older man with thick square eyeglasses, dressed in blue khaki pants and a neatly ironed white shirt, appeared from behind it. He stepped to the register, opened it, and counted the cash. He must be the owner, I concluded. Lucia looked at him, then at me. She was visibly agitated. He talked to her and she nodded silently, still working on my drink. I closed my eyes and focused on the piano melody swelling in the background. I recognized the intro of Djordje Balašević's "Divlji Badem." A wave of nostalgia and the scent of first, secret love in the air overpowered my senses, bounced me back in time, into the permanent refuge of memories.

Several minutes later I heard the cup and saucer clanging. I opened my eyes and there it was, the cup brimming with white froth encircled by a fine brown line. I couldn't believe my eyes. She had made cappuccino—a perfect-looking one. And I had to pay.

I looked up and saw her stunning phantom face. It shone in the limelight.

"One cappuccino for you." Her smile lingering.

"I can't pay." I heard myself blurting it out in a hurry.

"What's that?"

"I have no money." I grinned sheepishly.

"Okay, now what?" Her smile disappearing.

"I don't know."

"You Bosnians—"

"Huh?"

"You think you can simply walk in here, just like that, and say—" She frowned and blushed, unable to finish the sentence, trying to contain and hide her distress.

"You didn't mind it before, when you brought me espresso instead of cappuccino." I switched to my defensive mode. Suddenly, I wasn't as confident as the wine had made me.

"Why are you here? You're not allowed to leave the refugee camp. That's what they say."

"Who?"

"Everyone, the TV and the radio."

"Well, yes… I suppose you're right. But who's going to arrest me? You?"

She glanced at her boss, who had been watching us. She frowned and shrugged. "Maybe I am." Her voice mellowed. She looked away, somewhere above my head, and sighed. "Never mind, just drink your cappuccino. It's on me."

She strutted back to the register, fed it with cash and nodded at her boss. Then she retreated to her friends' permanent camp in the opposite corner. They looked in my direction at once for a moment and then returned to their conversation.

I emptied the glass of water she'd brought with the coffee. My mouth was parched. The alcohol had squeezed every drop of water out of my flesh. She kept her eyes on me. She observed me carefully, as if the mirrors were her microscope lenses. Her eyes glistened. I'd never seen that look before. I had been deceived. It was all a part of an act—a charity performance. Today our show was interrupted by her boss's presence. She was helpless. I was naked.

I couldn't let her do this to me. Yes, I lived in the refugee camp right outside the town. Yes, I wore charity, ate charity, slept on charity. And I came here just to run away from people, to buy some time before something came my way. Something better, perhaps a ticket to Germany or back home. No, I couldn't. I regretted that I had tried to play her instead of just getting up and leaving. At least I'd still have my pride and think of her as someone from another world, perhaps a dream. I lifted the cup full of cappuccino, held it high for a moment, and then poured it into the empty glass on the table. She gaped at me, her lips apart.

I stood up and ran out. I found myself on the other side of the street, staring at the movie posters in front of the theater. It was deserted, still too early for movies. The clock on the wall ticked sluggishly—five o'clock. Showtime was at eight. I scrutinized Tom Cruise and Demi Moore in their perfectly clean, flawlessly white military uniforms. I sought an answer. I wished to sober up or to wake up, perhaps in the movie, somewhere in America, where I'd finally finish this transitioning business that had begun the morning I left my home. Anything would've been acceptable except returning to the place where everyone was in limbo and everyone was fed up with everything. Where people didn't shave for weeks and stood in lines for the shower, toilet, or food, fighting over their turn. Where babies cried and children ran around aimlessly as if it were all a game—a pretend game.

A week later, the Germans drew our names. We left the same day. Six months was enough, more than enough. The clotheslines, burdened with worn-out clothers, swayed sluggishly in the wind that carried the smell of Ariel detergent across town to the northern borders, toward a new life. The children's screams, the lost, wary faces of adults standing in line for polenta and a cup of yogurt. The beds infested with people of all ages and backgrounds. Every new day in the camp took a toll on its residents. With time, we'd get lost in its reality and become adrift and desolate—runaways from our asylum. This was the Grad I knew. And that part was easy to forget.

Five years later in Boston, at Café Sarajevo, I run into the crazy-eyed twin, as talkative and annoying as he's ever been. Some things never change. He and his brother left the camp a month after my departure.

"The day after you left a girl came to the camp looking for you," my former coworker and co-refugee says. "She wanted to talk to you. She looked very sad."

"Lucia?"

"Yes, that was her name. She worked at that pub, downtown by the theater."

I put my beer down, nod to the bartender.

"Another round?" he asks, his short haircut revealing his insolent Slavic head, his forehead wide and imposing.

"How about a cappuccino?"

He scowls, hesitates for a moment, and then edges toward the espresso machine. Five minutes later I have my cappuccino—steaming, frothing, welcoming, and comforting, but utterly flawed. I gaze at the rapidly deflating foam in the hopes of answers. I chug my beer and pour the cappuccino into the empty glass, all the while the bartender's eyes are fixed on mine, clearly indifferent. He shrugs and brings me another beer. I stay in my seat, my face propped against the bar, resting on my forearms. A few minutes later I leave a twenty-dollar bill on the bar and walk toward the door, the crazy-eyed twin laughing in the background, the walls around me melting like glass.

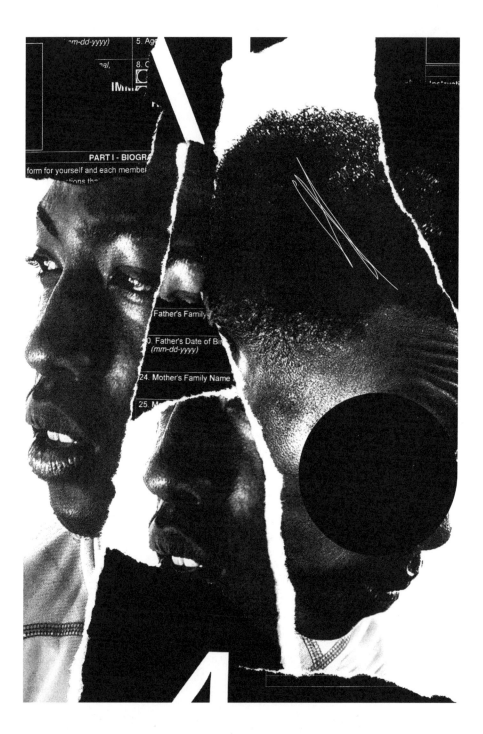

HENNESSY
AND
RED LIGHTS

by MARCUS BURKE

I HAD A CRUSH, A very hard one, on Trina the second I saw her. She was new on campus. It was the first semester of our sophomore year. Like a vulture I watched her from afar, circling her, waiting for an opening to get closer to her. But it wasn't until the second semester, when we took a Rock and Jazz Experience seminar together, that the whole nonsense with us started. Dr. Rash was leading the class in a discussion on Louis Armstrong. We'd just listened to "What a Wonderful World," and I don't know what the hell Dr. Rash's point was exactly but he started in on some misguided idea about how Louis Armstrong's success transcended racism because of how he was able to travel all around the world to play his music. "Being that he was a black man and all."

After he finished his point, the room hung in an awkward silence.

Prompted by nothing, this quiet little white boy sitting at the top of my row wearing too-tight jeans, scuff-covered cowboy boots, and a flannel shirt raised his hand.

"Louis Armstrong was a rich black man and he did it all from working hard," he said. "Don't you think he'd be disappointed to see how minorities are exploiting the government, demanding affirmative action, using up all that public assistance?" He paused his little rant to spit a brown wad of chewing tobacco into a water bottle.

"Not today, devil," someone said from the back of the room. This was the first time I'd heard Trina's voice. The whole room put eyes on her. She continued. "No! What the hell does the fact that Louis Armstrong was successful have to do with affirmative action and minorities using government assistance? See, that's why I can't with you white boys. Y'all be doing too much."

She sucked her teeth in full you-go-girl glory and something about her gangsta growling at Quiet Boy turned me on.

Quiet Boy looked back at Trina from across the room. "Everything! It has everything to do with it," he said. "Louis worked hard, why can't they?"

Now, I have no idea what the hell Quiet Boy intended to do, but he stood up. Initially I was slightly amused, but when he stood I felt fire in my bones.

"Sit ya ass down, white boy." Trina's voice boomed across the room and Quiet Boy turned and took a step in her direction. He'd taken no more than a step before I found myself standing inches away from his pimple-ridden face.

"Really, you ain't 'bout to do shit." I clapped my hands in his face. "What you wanna do?" I took a step back, giving him a chance if he wanted to swing, but he just stood there and said nothing, his eyes trained on the floor, fear wilting his shoulders inward, so instead my attention turned to Dr. Rash, who'd stepped between us.

"And all this is okay with you?" I asked.

"Gentlemen, please return to your seats."

Realizing that this little exchange would probably get back to my basketball coach, I bit down on my jaws and started back toward my seat. As I walked up the aisle I looked over across the room at Trina, and she winked at me. "White boy, ain't 'bout that life," she said. And even at the height of being pissed off, feeling like I needed to put my hand through something, as I looked at her, we both smiled and laughed. I got to my seat and Dr. Rash went back up to his podium at the front of the room and promptly ended class.

Dr. Rash kept me and Quiet Boy after class. He tried to get Trina to stay but she just kept walking as he called her name up the hallway. He lectured me and Quiet Boy, rambling on about how it was unacceptable for us to be having such outbursts in his class, and just to shut him up I agreed to shake Quiet Boy's hand. He made us walk in opposite directions when we left the room.

I got down to the lobby of the music hall and Trina was sitting on one of the couches around the big black grand piano. I smiled at her and she started walking toward me.

"These country boys out here in Pennsyltucky be tripping, huh?"

I agreed and we both laughed and started walking up Academic Row toward the gym. Trina's from Brooklyn, and like every person from Brooklyn she's very proud to be from Brooklyn. She had all types of shit to say about people from Boston, and I let her have at it. New Yorkers always hate on Boston, happens all the time. Really I didn't care what she was saying or what trash she was talking about my city as long as she kept walking close enough for me to smell her perfume. Her sister locks were jet-black with red tips. It was no surprise when she told me she was Trinidadian. Me being a Jamaican, she had plenty to say about that, too.

Usually I have no patience for Trinis talking bad about Jamaicans, but I was too lost in her eyes to care. Like a key in a lock we just clicked. As we walked it felt like we'd known each other for ages. I don't know who held who first, but before I knew how it happened we were holding hands. It just felt right, like we were supposed to be holding hands, and I just went with it. Until we ran into Mitch, Lil' Sticky, Hurk, and Tunka walking out of the gym.

They started yelling *Oooo* at us, blowing us kisses and carrying on. I dropped her hand immediately and tried to ignore them and kept walking toward the gym.

I really wasn't embarrassed. My teammates, they're like family—you can't choose them, you're just stuck with them, and I don't know who started it but there's a locker-room game our team plays all over campus called Paparazzi. The game is if you're spotted with a lady and someone snaps a picture of you and whatever you're caught doing, the picture is printed and hung up all over the locker room.

I noticed Trina wasn't next to me anymore and I turned around and her brown eyes narrowed on me and she stuffed her hands into her hoodie pocket and turned away from me so fast her locks swung up in the air as she walked in the opposite direction toward the girls' dorms. I stood there as the crew drove by in Hurk's red Chevy Blazer, still making a scene, catcalling us out the window. I walked after her. "Trina, wait," I hollered. She tossed her hand in the air. "Naw, it's okay," she said. "Talk to your friends." I stopped and glanced back and Hurk and company were gone. I turned back and so was she.

She skipped the next couple of classes and funny enough I ran into her in the training room at the end of the week. We were lying on tables opposite each other. I was hooked up to the electric stim machine for my jumper's knee, and she was getting ultrasound done on a deep bone bruise on her upper thigh. I hadn't even realized she was on the track team but I did notice her sprinter's thighs. She finished her treatment before I did but she lingered around the training room sitting near the ice baths reading a book. When my treatment finished I walked over to her.

She looked up at me. "What you want, scary boy?"

"I wasn't scared or embarrassed," I said. "I was just caught a bit off guard."

"What caught you off guard?"

It felt like a trick question.

"Can I borrow four dollars?"

She laughed. "For what?"

"A burrito, I haven't ate lunch yet. Have you?"

"So you're asking me to buy you lunch but when your teammates see us together you act like you don't know me. You gonna run if they see us?"

"But I really don't know you though," I said.

"Well, you tried dumb hard." She sucked her teeth and stood up. "Well, come on. Let's get you a burrito."

And just like that we'd started something.

We exchanged numbers and hung out in her dorm room that night watching reruns of *Intervention* on YouTube. We ordered pizza and blazed outside in between episodes.

We connected quietly. Intimacy was our key, and we tended our secret garden religiously. We could run our mouths all night talking about whatever, really, and some nights we'd just get high and hold each other and be silent. As the months passed it was clear we were becoming something and nothing at the same time.

We both had very different lives in the athlete world on campus. We both had appearances to keep up and we never really tried to break into each other's worlds and I liked that about her. I never showed up anywhere with anyone on my arm and that was okay. Even though I spent three or four nights a week at her place there was never the illusion of monogamy between us. On the days we weren't together, we simply weren't. Out of sight, out of mind. Though sometimes I did wonder what she was up to, I never asked. There were days I thought maybe I wanted something more with her, but I wasn't sure she'd ever got past that day outside the gym.

One time she mentioned it. We were in bed and she sort of rhymed and then laughed at me. "We cool, but I see you, playa. Too cool for Trina when you're with your boys, huh? Basic as hell. I see you, playa."

We existed mostly in her room. We had no proper claim to each other and as the months went on a kind of tension built between us but we wouldn't fight. We'd just go offline. We'd go our separate ways and do things to make each other jealous, but like a boomerang eventually we'd return to our old rhythm of seeing each other. And this is how it was with us, hot and cold. In our offline months, sometimes I'd see her out with other guys, she'd see me with other girls, and maybe that was a part of our game, seeing who could pretend they didn't care the most. We rode out the rest of the school year like that, being something and nothing.

The next school year started no different. Trina was the first girl I saw when I got to campus. And after one too many consecutive nights together we went offline again and for the first time, for whatever reason, when we weren't talking it bothered me. I'd been looking forward to seeing her the entire summer. That was a scary development. By the time preseason rolled around in October, we'd fallen in and out of each other several times and our periods of silence were becoming longer and longer. At first we'd messed around on each other respectfully—we never spoke on it but teammates were off-limits—but things got messy at the end of last school year and now I didn't know what the rules were.

By the time the basketball season started, me and Trina were in one of those spells of not talking, and this is when I met Chellissa. We hooked up the night of our first home game. We'd danced all night. I wasn't sure who she was and I didn't know she knew me until she reached up and pulled me down by my neck and whispered, "I saw you score points tonight at your game, Andre Battel from Boston." She led me to the door. I'd only had seven points. Before I'd passed out in Chellissa's bed that first night, I looked at my phone and realized Trina had texted me earlier in the day asking if I'd go to a formal with her. I felt bad about not even responding. I had no good excuse, so I set the phone down and nestled my face in Chellissa's curls and passed out.

Me, Lil' Sticky, Mitch, Hurk, and Tunka packed into Hurk's red Chevy Blazer for a blunt ride. All of us nursing serious hangovers. On the second rotation of the blunt we pulled up to a red light. Tunka cut the music down and spun around, body dangling over the passenger seat, and began telling us about how he and Trina had had their ways with each other last night in his dorm room. Now, I know I'm violating some part of the bro-and-ho code, but something like aggravation began churning in my belly as Tunka delivered the play-by-play. As Tunka ran his mouth, Hurk bit down on the blunt, turned, and rag-dolled Tunka's storytelling ass back down into his seat with his free hand.

"We smoking or trading lies, my nigga?"

Hurk lisped at Tunka and smirked as he passed him the blunt, then turned the music back up. Them two are always a finger-snap away from scrapping, always manhandling each other. Tunka's 6'7", and the only person bigger than him on the team is Hurk's 6'9" bull-strong ass. Hurk's a sophomore, Tunka's a freshman. Hurk be getting off on that seniority shit. Me, Lil' Sticky, and Mitch, we stay out of it. Them two are too big and too light-skinned for us to be playing Gandhi.

"Niggas talk more than bitches these days, I swear," Hurk said.

The light turned green and we pulled off.

Tunka reached over his shoulder and passed me the blunt, then crossed his arms over his chest. "Ain't nobody lying," he said. Pouting like a baby, his shoulders dropped and he slouched down into the seat as we cruised through the Amish Market.

Regardless of the fact that I had woken up in Chellissa's bed this morning, I was bothered. Nothing I could do about it, so I inhaled, swallowed smoke, and held the feelings there, in my chest. I'm out of order. All of us athletes run on the same party circuit; it's the land of the pretty people, everyone sharp-angled, tight-muscled, searching for a new flavor of the moment to try.

So with this in mind, when Trina starts talking about love and swearing she wants to be with me—lies, I say. She's got other guys, and some of them are my teammates, and it's all good. As far as the squad goes there are only two rules.

Rule one: no smashing your homie's girl.

Rule two: don't nobody have a girl.

Girls come with the territory when we're in season. We're ballplayers. They're more of a weekend party thing. With class, practice, film session, weightlifting, and the post-practice ice bath, ain't nobody got time to yo-yo back and forth with a girl on a weeknight. Girls require attention, entirely too much attention.

As we rounded the entrance to campus, we all put on our hoods. Hurk let down all the windows to air out the car. High enough to sleep off our hangovers, we parked and everyone headed back to the dorms to nap.

As I walked to my room all I could do was shake my head. I promised myself no more fucking with Trina. Knowing nothing about nothing is one of my finer qualities in life.

On the weekends, when we're free, there's no pre-gaming—we halftime. By the time we hit the streets to party, it's 'bout half game-over for all of us. That night before I headed out to halftime with the fellas I stopped in front of the mirror and said aloud to myself: "Chellissa, Chellissa, Chellissa, whose room will you end up in tonight?"

I winked at myself, hit the lights, and rolled out.

Still bothered, thoughts of Trina and Tunka pop-rocked around my brain the entire walk over to Hurk's place, but I'd convinced myself I was over it, over Trina, by the time I knocked on the door.

I was the last to arrive. As soon as I got into the living room, we crowded around Hurk. He gripped the Crown Royal bottle by the neck and held it out and we all tapped the cap. The ceremonial splash hit the floor. Tunka took the bottle to the head and gulped, passed the bottle to me, and I did the same. The Crown Royal had been in the freezer all day, and it was sliding down with an icy-warm after-tingle. The bottle circled the room from Hurk to me to Mitch, Tunka, Lil Sticky, and back.

I could feel the promise I'd made to myself waning to mere suggestion. Trusting myself after I've been drinking is one of the bigger jokes I've been playing on myself lately.

We were having a mixer with the girls' track team that night. Trina's a sprinter and Chellissa's a high jumper. Pretty good chance they'd both be there. They're teammates. Messy, I know.

With the bottle polished off, we'd reached our level. As we walked down to the cars we split up in twos: me and Hurk, Tunka and Lil' Sticky. Mitch ducked off in his car, claiming he had a booty call for the night, but don't nobody know what he be up to. We rode around campus in a procession, picking up our various bird flocks, gearing up to party.

We stopped to pick up Chellissa and her friends from the freshman dorm. She had on a pair of stiletto Timberlands, a white fur–hooded puffy coat and a white spandex catsuit smothered in little silver lightning bolts. She might as well have been naked. All her teammates wore variations of the same outfit in different colors. She hardly looked at me as they walked to the car. Even though we'd had sex that morning, I could tell that over the course of the day something had changed. Who knows who she'd been talking to or what she'd heard. We were texting after my nap and all I got was one-, two-, or three-word responses.

The cold air stung my eyes as the girls piled into the backseat of Hurk's Blazer. They hardly said hello and I looked up in the rearview mirror. A few of them were sucking in their cheeks and squinting their eyes as they fixed their makeup, looking into little pocket mirrors. Midway through the ride, one of them tapped on the overhead light and they broke out into a selfie photo shoot. My head felt like a shaking snow globe, and I closed my eyes, their voices echoing in my ears.

The mixer was in full swing as we pulled up. I could hear the bass from the party vibrating the siding on the house. A couple of circles of people were drinking from red Solo cups and smoking cigarettes near the back door. We let Chellissa and her girls out first and me and Hurk hung back to smoke our last blunt before we headed in. A few minutes passed and Lil' Sticky and Tunka rolled up on the car, smacking the hood. We ignored them. They scampered off and we finished smoking.

We ashed the blunt. It was well past halftime, more like fourth quarter, for both of us as we stepped out of the car. The music pulsed through me as we walked into the party's warm smog of body funk, sour beer, and cheap perfume. By this point in the night, the beer pong was done and the whole spot was for pushing up and grinding on each other in the two big rooms or finding a private spot to freak. I looked around and Hurk was gone and for a second I felt lost. So I walked over and disrupted a couple making out up against the fridge and got a can of Pabst Blue Ribbon because we're classy.

One of the rooms had red lights; black lights were in the other. I stepped out of the hallway into the room with black lights. The smoke coming from the smoke machines made everything hazy, gray and blue.

It was hard to make out anything more than flailing limbs and jolting torsos as my eyes adjusted to the darkness. When my eyes fully adjusted, across the room Chellissa's white spandex catsuit was glowing at me in the black light, her head bobbing up and down a few inches away from knocking into the ceiling fan. She was tethered around Tunka's waist, her stiletto Timbs crossed behind his back, Tunka hoisting up her ass as she hula-hooped herself into his crotch. I leaned against the wall beside the doorframe and sipped my beer, watching them melt into each other.

'Cause regardless of how big the cut, out here there are no scars.

I chugged the rest of my beer. A delicate hand stroked my neck and Trina stepped next to me, linking her arm in mine, watching the party with me.

"When you gon' stop chasing these lil' young hoes?" She elbowed me in the ribs. I don't know if she knew what I was looking at or if she just said it, but with her hand on my neck I looked down into her coffee-brown eyes and felt something in my chest loosen, bud or bloom. She ran her hand down my face with a "hmmm" and somehow, from somewhere, she produced a bottle of Hennessy and raised it to my lips and I grabbed it and took a swig. I looked down at her looking like a little brown angel, wondering how the hell she'd found me in here. She smiled, her big white teeth gleaming up at me in the shadow of the white smoke playing in the hallways separating the red and the black lights.

Trina snatched me to her. "Fuck that lil' bitch, come on."

She took my hand and led me into the room of red lights. We danced for about five or six songs and passed the bottle back and forth. Trina's hips are everything. She's a hot-blooded Trini; she's been winding up her hips to soca her whole life it's like her bones are cartilage. We'd been grinding on each other until we both sweated through our shirts and it slowed us down none, so sweaty and wet it was like we were wearing each other.

The music slowed down. She leaned her head on my chest. We were slow winding on each other. I took the last swig of Hennessy and held the bottle upside down and it slowly dripped on the floor. She pulled my arm to her and began licking the last drops. I did the same until my hand dropped the bottle and we started kissing.

I lost confidence in my Jell-O-legged ability to stand and I stepped us to the side in front of the couch and fell back onto a mound of coats. Trina stood there twirling her locks and looking down at me. A smile greased into her lips and she hopped down onto my lap, straddling me. She leaned down and curtained off our faces inside of her draping locks.

At some point during the lap dance I either blacked out or fell asleep. I can't remember how we made it from the mixer back to my dorm room. I awoke to the sound of metal creaking, the sound of Trina grinding her teeth as we snuggled. I could've let her stay the whole night but I just felt like she needed to go.

Here's the trouble.

Me and Trina existed mostly in her room. The first time she was officially in my bed it was a me, her, and Hurk Eiffel Tower–type situation. Hurk was on his recruiting visit, and me and Trina were offline when he and I happened upon her in the cafeteria. We told her we had Hennessy and she came over and it went down with the three of us. It was all in good fun and the secret stayed amongst us and I liked that about her. At that point I didn't even know if Hurk was joining the team the next year, so I flirted with the idea of still properly dating her, but it only took a few months for the idea to die. We were already sort of talking to each other before our little group situation jumped off, so about a month later, when the dust settled, we began flirting and texting again. It took a little longer for me to finally get her to come through and kick it. Trying to be proper, I even got her a Valentine's Day present and everything. I took her out to BJ's for chicken wings and bought us a few vodka lemonades, and we blazed on the side of my dorm. Once we got to my room we were in the sheets before I could even put a movie on.

After we finished I asked her if she wanted to still watch something or maybe smoke again. I was even down to just sit and talk to her, but she looked away from me, side-glancing the floor, and said she should probably leave. I didn't tell her to go, didn't want her to go, but I wasn't going to stop her either. We went offline for the rest of the year after that.

See, the situation with Hurk I could handle but this shit with Tunka I cannot.

So I laid in bed with her, I tried to remember how it was that we made it back to my dorm room, remember what I had said. Lord knows what I'd told her in the past, in post-nut bliss. A lot of my memories from our old nights were foggy, but I knew I'd told her about shit back home—caught slipping—how I blame basketball for my not being in the country when my grandma died, how sometimes I wonder if she was mad at me for not being there. We'd almost post-sex drunk-cried together a few times after these talks. I'd told her entirely more than I should've. Girls are good at capitalizing, catching you slipping. So maybe shit with us was a bit deeper than surface, but that does not mean she knew me. If I were to show her the real me, whoever that is, she'd no longer know me—and again, would we not be back at square one?

Under the warmth of the blanket, she started stroking my chest, and her touch blasted an electric-cold shiver all over my body and I sprang to my feet and turned on the light. She sat up squinting at me, half-awake, and before I could even think I just said it.

"Put your clothes on. I'll walk you out."

"Really, Andre? It's four in the morning. I can't just sleep here a few more hours?"

She sucked her teeth and got dressed.

I watched her and my teeth were grinding. It felt like midgets were hitting tennis balls around in my head. I closed my eyes and rubbed my temples and remembered that I had a lifting session with Coach T in the morning, and all I really wanted was a blunt and some sleep.

As I walked her out the whole energy was different. I don't know what to call it but I could feel it, something sliding between us. Maybe even then she understood better than I did. I gave her a hug as she leaned her back against the door, about to leave. She looked me in the face all genuine, and sadness wiggle-twitched under the corners of her eyes and under her lips.

"Andre, why do we keep doing this?"

Entirely too drunk for the discussion, I countered, "What is it we're doing, Trina?"

"Don't play with me. All this back-and-forth between us."

I leaned my elbow on the door and kissed her on the forehead.

"Get home safe, aight."

I looked down at her and her face turned lemon-sour.

"You're an asshole. Dogging bitches out at 4 a.m. like a basic-ass fuckboy."

She shook her head at me slowly. "I bet your grandmother would be real proud of you. If she could only see you now."

I bit down on my jaws and my cheeks burned. The midgets were now dribbling figure eights on my brain, and I clenched my fists as I watched the gold clutch that I'd given her for Valentine's Day dangling from her wrist as she spun and walked away and all I could do was shake my head.

I walked back to my room as the dial on my headache cranked up. I got a towel and stuffed up the bottom lining of my door, turned on the fan, and opened all the windows.

I grabbed a piece of paper from the floor to roll my blunt on. I sat down at my desk in the dark, smoothed the paper, and began to break up the buds. It wasn't until I was done breaking up and had the blunt gutted that I realized I couldn't see enough to roll up and clicked on my desk lamp.

In the light I looked down and it was like life was just fucking with me. Because after Trina had brought up my grandmother, I looked down into the eyes of Nana Tanks's smiling face and realized I'd been breaking up on her funeral program the whole time. It must've fallen from my dresser. I sort of laughed, 'cause sometimes that's all you can do. I saw red. I felt a volcanic fire in my chest, my entire temperature rose, and I just couldn't handle it. I brushed the weed onto my desk, kissed the portrait of Nana Tanks, and tucked the program into my desk drawer.

Now all I wanted was sleep. I turned out the lights and got in bed and my eyes began to sweat as I thought about what Nana Tanks would think if she really could see me now. I couldn't imagine what she'd say, but I knew she wouldn't be proud. In the tar blackness, I listened to the birds sing as the water fell from my eyes, stinging my cheeks, and again I promised myself: no more party nights, fuckin' with Trina, Hennessy, and them red lights.

THE COBBLER AND THE ACOLYTE

by ILAN MOCHARI

H E WALKED ON HIS hands on the trimmed green stadium grass, his legs stretching toward the sky and his ankles squeezing a soccer ball. Using the strength of his lower legs, he lofted the ball in the air as he flipped forward. His head swung up to whack the descending ball. The ball rocketed toward the goal as if it had been kicked.

It was the first time my mother saw my father.

Her teach-English-in-Israel program had distributed tickets to a semi-pro soccer game in Tel Aviv. She took her first snapshot of my father after observing his forward-flipping header. During the game she photographed the entire team. My father's build bespoke push-ups and pull-ups. His thick shoulders and chest distinguished him from his lithe teammates, though all of them had those soccer thighs, sinewy at rest and pulsing at play.

After the game, she approached my father, who was speaking to his older sister. They went to a bar on Allenby Street, near the southern part of Tel Aviv where the Eretz family—my father, Eli; his sister, Miriam; and their parents—all lived. Soon my mom and dad were holding hands and strolling Tel Aviv's prominent promenade. It was a balmy night in early spring, eleven months before I was born.

My paternal grandparents moved to Israel from Libya in the early 1950s, when my father was two and Miriam four. They changed their last name from Aard—which means "land" in Arabic—to Eretz, which means "land" in Hebrew. All this my father explained to my mother on the night they met. He also confessed to the biggest crime of his life: he'd lied about his birth year and fought in the Six-Day War at age fifteen. After helping subdue the Egyptians, he joined a group of infantry reinforcements storming the Golan Heights. His best friend from the neighborhood, Dov, was killed in the effort.

Following his three years of service, Eli returned to Tel Aviv. By day he worked at construction sites and by night he played soccer. Sometimes he helped his father, Baruch, who'd established a shoe-repair business on a busy connecting road near the Tel Aviv Stock Exchange. But I paint a false picture of the post-military Eli if you imagine him then as a tranquil civilian, eager to slouch toward quotidian commonplaces following an upright military stint. Something about my father remained coiled throughout his adult life—even after he followed my mother to the United States and married her.

They both liked to wake up early on Saturday mornings. My mother, who wrote for *Forbes*, typed her stories on our basement computer: one of those trendy Commodore 64 machines from the mid-1980s. I loved watching as she typed, mainly because she hadn't learned how. She clacked out her copy with her index fingers, looking down at the keyboard and then over to her pile of notepads on the right.

While she worked in the basement, Eli took me on errands in his black Ford pickup. The inside of the truck smelled of extinguished cigarettes, newly sliced leather, and freshly sawed lumber. My father—I called him Aba, Hebrew for Dad—trafficked pounds of leather because, like his own father, he owned and operated a shoe-repair business. Eli's store was on a corner of Queens Boulevard, across the street from a Citibank and down the block from a popular bowling alley. He kept the lumber in the truck for spontaneous projects—shelves for store supplies, a coffee table for the area where customers sat and waited. He loved woodworking in early morning, before customers arrived. And sometimes he woodworked at home. He'd spend hours sawing and sanding in our garage after dinner, smoking cigarette after cigarette and loading his honed wood into the truck.

Most Saturdays, we drove to an outdoor shopping mall with a colossal parking lot. Our destination was a hardware store called Pergament, which opened at seven. A doughy scent filled the lot, emanating from the adjacent bagel shop. I slept en route, using the passenger-side window and door as a pillow. One Saturday, I awoke to find a small pinkish imprint dimpling my right cheek, its source the tiny chrome nub serving as the door's push-down lock. Inspecting my dimple in the sun-blocker's mirror, I awaited my father's commentary. The dense muscles of his forearms twitched. His work-callused fingers drummed on the steering wheel. His hands were like ospreys in their coloration, a dark caramel top with a chalky underside. His right hand stopped drumming and reached for the Marlboros in his front pocket. He held the cigarette's tip to the truck's lighter. After his first drag, he addressed my dimple in his accented, present-tense-only English. "Barry," he said. "Deese watt happen when you stay up too late."

* * *

My maternal grandparents lived in a suburb called Douglaston, ten minutes from our house in Bayside. Most Friday nights, we dined with them. When it was time for dessert, my grandmother, Roslyn Jakob, distributed coffee mugs and sugar spoons. Then she brought two small bowls to the center of the cherrywood kitchen table: one with orange packets of Sanka, the other with pink packets of Sweet'n Low. Beside the bowls was a plate stacked high with chocolate-filled rugalach.

During dessert and the card games that followed, I fled to the basement, where Bernie Jakob kept an office. I spun in Bernie's swivel chair and toyed with percentages on his adding machine. I played with his ink stamp, stamping DUPLICATE on blank 1040 tax forms with loudly dramatic thuds. I switched the typewriter ribbon from red to black and back again. I clanged out my name in both colors in all capitals, appending fanciful titles: BARRY ERETZ, ANCHOR, CBS EVENING NEWS; BARRY ERETZ, QUARTERBACK, #14, NEW YORK JETS; BARRY ERETZ, AUTHOR, *A BRIEF HISTORY OF THE DIPLODOCUS*.

One Friday night, Bernie asked me to fetch a blank index card from his office. When I returned to the dinner table, he handed me a sharpened pencil from his shirt pocket. "Now Barry," he said. "Above the pink line on that card, I want you to write—in regular letters, not cursive, so your father can read it—I want you to write: 'Expressions and pronunciations my father should learn.'"

I did as I was told. Through it all my father grinned, his thin purple lips peeling back to reveal a mouth of yellow, misaligned teeth. A yarmulke, from the evening's drunken Sabbath proceedings, still covered his head of robust black curls, attached by a bobby pin. He and Bernie smoked their respective Marlboros. The bright orange tips faded to grimy grays as they banged their ashes at intervals into a weathered tray of dull silver. My mother and Roslyn cleared the dessert dishes. My grandfather dictated and I copied.

Bernie slid the index card across the table to my father, who said, "Tank you." They adjourned to the den while I swept the floor. When I finished sweeping, my grandmother told me to go to bed. I went to the bedroom I shared with my father whenever we slept over. Though it wasn't my earliest remembrance of my parents staying in separate rooms, it was the first time I sought an explanation. Roslyn, tucking me in, said, "Your mother likes to go to sleep. Your Aba likes to keep drinking with your grandfather."

"Are they getting divorced?" I asked.

"They just like to do different things in the morning," Roslyn replied.

I hugged her good night, absorbing traces of her late-night fragrance, a bath of Sanka and cigarettes and Topol toothpaste. While the fragrance was distinctly hers, her bony ribs and hips, piercing my arms each time we embraced, belonged also to my mother. Nor did the resemblance stop there. In her newlywed pictures, the young Roslyn mirrored my mom: shoulder-length hair of the darkest brown, the hue of watermelon seeds, falling straight down around taut, slightly sanguine cheeks. Both women were 5'8", ample in the upper body and long in the torso. And both Roslyn and Rachel had sharp, pointed chins. In art class, whenever I tried drawing their faces, what I began with was not an oval but an ice-cream cone, V-shaped at the bottom and topped with a semicircle.

The next morning, while my mother slept in the room she had grown up in and her parents smoked and ate Grape-Nuts and read *Newsday* at the kitchen table, my father and I went to Pergament.

We bought a sixty-pound bag of cement mix, plus gravel, sand, and four wheelbarrows of pink brick. Eli urged me to try lugging the sixty-pound bag from the store to the truck on my scrawny right shoulder. "Aba, help," I cried, unable to take more than two steps. My father was halfway to the truck with the first wheelbarrow. He sprinted back to me, leaving the bricks in the middle of the parking lot. He hoisted the bag onto his shoulder. His armpits were soaked, his white tank top clinging to his rugged frame. He finished loading the truck with the help of two Pergament employees.

On the drive back, with our windows down and the black leather seats baking in the morning sun, my father asked me to open the glove compartment. I found the index card I'd written out the night before. "Udder side," he said. Before I could turn the card over my father seized it from me, flipped it, and handed it back. To my surprise, the "udder" side was blank. I looked to him for an explanation. His eyes were on the road. "You know Morris?" he asked.

The question seemed like a non sequitur. Sure, I knew Morris. He was one of my father's regular customers. He had a thick black mustache and he bowled several nights a week at Hollywood Lanes, the alley near Eli's shop. He'd made his money somehow; Eli told me it was through the stock market. He spent his nights trying to get his photo on the Hollywood Lanes Wall of Immortality, where there hung twelve gilded plaques commemorating the men who'd rolled perfect games.

"Morris," continued my father, "he tell me, Eli, you want to be reach, you need to write down you goals. I say, Morris, okay, but only one ting wrong. I can no write."

"You can write in Arabic or Hebrew," I said, shifting in my seat.

"But Ara-beak and Hebrew, Morris can no read," he said.

"You can translate. Or ask Mom to translate."

"Watt she know about becalming reach?" he asked.

"She's a business writer. She knows a lot about it."

"Deef-rent tings, Barry."

By the time we returned to my grandparents' house I'd penned three of Eli's goals on the back of the index card:

To own my own store—no landlords—within the next five years.
To use my leftover leather to make sandals of all sizes—babies, kids, adults— and to sell these sandals in my own store, other shoe stores, and catalogs.

To start investing in safe, big corporation stocks like IBM and GE.

I returned the card to the glove compartment and followed my father around as he unloaded the truck and placed the supplies beside my grandparents' driveway. The surface of this driveway resembled a tic-tac-toe board. It was a three-by-three grid of concrete squares, each as wide as a highway lane, so that the entire area easily accommodated two vehicles side by side. Bernie drove a maroon Oldsmobile 98; Roslyn had a brown Nissan Sentra. Both cars still sat in the driveway when Eli finished unloading. He wiped his forehead with the neckline of his tank top. "You got to be sheeting me," he said. He sent me inside to ask my grandparents to park on the street.

I felt the cool kiss of circulating central air as I entered the house. I eased the screen door shut so it would not slam, keeping a promise I'd made Bernie a few years earlier, when I was ten. Then I shut the main door so no air could escape, consistent with another boyhood promise.

I found my grandparents at the kitchen table, smoking and collaborating on a crossword puzzle. From their brown, AM-only radio perched atop the fridge, with its manual tuning dial and knobs labeled BASS and TREBLE, came a replay of Governor Cuomo's State of the State address. Empty plates and coffee mugs sat unwashed in the sink, and I knew it would be my duty to scrub them if I weren't helping my father. I waited for Bernie and Roslyn to notice me.

"Welcome back, Barry," said my grandfather after a minute or two, putting down his pencil. "You've already done more work than your mother will do all day."

I looked to Roslyn. "Your mother's still sleeping," she said scornfully, though it was not yet eight o'clock.

"Maybe she's tired," I said.

They exchanged glances. Then they returned to me. "Do you want something to eat?" asked my grandmother.

"No, thank you," I said. "But Aba wants you to move your cars." I could practically hear my father's restless fingers drumming loudly against his thigh.

"Aba," muttered my grandfather. His slow enunciation of the three-letter word was an adagio of disdain. He was a bald, skinny man, his Adam's apple prominent, his jaw rigid beneath a trimmed gray-white beard. He leaned back and reached into the pocket of his brown corduroys for his keys, which he slid clanking across the table to me. "So, your Aba sends his kid to ask the tough questions," he said.

"Bernie, you did say you'd move the cars," said Roslyn. "Barry, are you sure you don't want some juice? It's awfully hot outside."

"No, thank you."

"Make sure your father rolls up the windows," said Bernie.

As soon as I reached the driveway my father ripped the keys from my hand and left me on the front lawn. He maneuvered each vehicle into snug street spots. He left the windows open and I said nothing.

I lingered beside him as he appraised the vacant, damaged driveway. Black cracks snaked across the gray surface like lines on a palm. Through the wider cracks burst yellow-rimmed dandelions and unkempt grass in pallid tufts of beige. My father wiped his brow with the strip of his tank top covering his left shoulder. He sensed what I was thinking. "Eef you grandpa want heeze car keys, he calm out here," he said.

He dropped to his knees and fingered the concrete, prodding between the cracks. Next he put his ear to the ground and knocked hard with his knuckles, like an old-school doctor performing an auscultation on your chest cavity in advance of applying the stethoscope. His diagnosis: "Tree hours, I tink," he said. "Tree hours, eat luke like new."

He set to hammering the driveway, bashing the widest cracks until tributaries appeared. The force of his percussive slams seemed to shake the neighborhood. The blows were crepitant and destructive, like the whacks of a lumberjack. Bit by bit, the surface became smithereens. Every few minutes he ceased pounding and used the claw of his hammer to extract grass and dandelions and concrete chunks, yanking them up and out. I gathered them all into a mixed pile on the lawn. He hammered and clawed; he clawed and hammered. Sweat flowed down the crevices of his cocoa-colored face, dripping from his nose and chin onto the driveway's upturned clods. He removed his sopping shirt, which was almost transparent in its wetness, hugging and revealing his upper body. He wrung it out and placed it on the ground. It looked more like a rag than an oft-laundered shirt of stitched white cotton.

When eight of the nine boxes on the grid were complete, my father handed me his hammer. "Try," he said. Down on my knees, I took several fruitless thwacks at the top center square, replicating my father's rapid right-handed motion. The concrete looked the same as it had when I'd begun. The bones in my hand stung from gripping the hammer too tightly. My father sighed. "You keeding me, Barry," he said.

"I'm only trying to help," I said.

"Maybe your mom need help waking up," he said.

After this motivational remark I wound up for my mightiest strike. I swung so hard that the hammer flew from my hands upon contact with the ground and caromed toward my face. The claw side gashed my lower left eye and upper cheekbone. With my fingertips I felt myself bleeding. I rose to retrieve a bandage from the house. I'd taken three steps when my father shouted: "No."

"I need a Band-Aid," I said, and kept walking.

"Barry, *bo*!" he yelled. And I froze.

Bo was shorthand for a Hebrew phrase meaning "come here." I'd been trained from my younger days to respect *bo* as the ultimate command, the utterance my father resorted to when he meant business, when to disobey would brook the risk of feeling the real power in his forearms. He'd only smacked me once, when I'd not heeded a *bo* at age eight, but his open palm still singed my cheek whenever he said this punchy word.

I staunched my bloody lower eye with the sweaty neck of my T-shirt. My father raised his hands toward my face and I flinched. He grinned. "I not gonna heat you," he said. He licked his fingers and used them to swab my cuts. His callused fingertips felt abrasive yet warm on my open skin. After he cleaned up the blood, he let me go inside to seek a Band-Aid. "I hope you mom ease awake," he said.

I found Rachel in the bathroom, brushing her teeth. She washed my cuts and applied two tiny bandages to my face; then she urged me to wait in her room. I sat on her unmade bed. Amidst the quiet of a suburban Saturday, in a residence where windows and doors were shut to keep in the central air, I still heard my father's hammering outside. Then the hammering stopped. I crept toward the front of the house.

The door had been opened. I peered through the screen and listened as my mother berated my father in English. Her sandal-clad feet were inches from his discarded tank top and the pile of refuse I'd shoved together. He remained on his knees in the driveway, nodding at everything she said, as if her speech were another distraction in his quest to get it all done in "tree hours." Ordinarily they argued in Hebrew, to prevent me from understanding. Now their quarrel was in English; I wondered if it was for my or my grandparents' benefit. "You kept Barry out here in the heat for two hours?" she shouted.

Eli grinned. He tossed the hammer in the air and caught it by the handle. "You such a woman," he said. "Deece no watt we really fighting about, ease eat?"

"You're not thinking about what's good for Barry," she said.

"But you no care on udder Saturdays when you typing you articles. Only today."

"Has he eaten breakfast? There's a bagel store right next to Pergament."

"Ease no big deal. Ease not even nine o'clock."

"No big deal a twelve-year-old is working in the sun on an empty stomach."

He chuckled. "Believe me, Rachel, he no working. And eef eats beag deal to you, maybe you wake up earlier."

At this point my grandmother put her hand on my shoulder. "Barry, maybe you should go to your room," she said. From the kitchen my grandfather shouted. "Let him listen, Roz. It's no good keeping him in the dark." She rolled her eyes and led me back to my room. She sat me on my bed and offered to make me pancakes. "They're getting a divorce, aren't they?" I asked. She opened a dresser drawer. She smelled my pajamas, refolded them, and shut the drawer. "I don't know, Barry," she said. "I honestly hope not. At this point your guess is as good as mine. You want those pancakes?"

I nodded. After she left I went back to my mother's room. I found Rachel sitting and reading the *New Yorker* on her unmade bed. Her forehead was sweaty. "So you've been out there playing contractor with your father again, have you?" she said, suppressing a yawn. "Are you his brick-and-mortar acolyte?"

"What's an acolyte?"

"Barry," she moaned. She wanted me to look it up.

"Just tell me what it means for once."

"Look it up next time you're downstairs," she said. Bernie had the Random House *Unabridged* on a shelf in his office. In my arms it felt as heavy as the bag of cement mix. She removed her glasses and placed them on the night table, beside a stack of *Forbes* back issues. "Are you guys getting divorced?" I asked.

"We're trying to work things out," she said. "You can't agree on everything when you've been married almost thirteen years."

"Okay."

"Your father is going to be out there for another hour or so," she continued. "So how about I take a quick shower and we eat together?" I nodded. She left the room. I opened a *Forbes* to its table of contents, hoping I'd find her name among the bylines.

*   *   *

A few days later my father woke me at five so I could accompany him to work. When we arrived at the store, he handed me a thick silver key. I twisted it within the palm-sized padlock and helped him push up the cage of corrugated metal protecting the glass display window. Minutes later I crouched outside the storefront, vigorously scrubbing the window with Windex and paper towels. The glass lacked any signage save for an orange decal near the lower left corner promoting Cat's Paw shoe glue. When the glass was clean, I went inside and swept the tile floor until I believed its red-black checkerboard pattern would pass my father's inspection. Then I mopped, mindful again of paternal appraisal.

My father sat at his square work table behind the counter. He lined up a dozen or so shoes, all in need of mending for scuffed sides or ground-down heels. With an X-Acto knife he sliced up a slab of black rubber shaped like a stick of butter. Some slices were as thin as cheese, others as thick as bread. With a brush he dabbed each slice with pungent glue before attaching it with his fingertips to the shoe's area of need. Songs from the oldies rock station, CBS-FM, came from a box radio he kept on one of the wooden shelves he'd installed a few months earlier. The morning DJ played a familiar assortment of Elvis Presley, the Kingston Trio, and the Dave Clark Five—songs it seemed like I heard every time I was inside my father's shop.

I continued readying the store for customers. I saved my favorite part for last: the magazines. I had shoved the coffee table against the side wall to do my sweeping and mopping, and now, with the floor nearly dry, I returned it to center stage, in the middle of the customer waiting area. From another shelf I retrieved the dozen or so glossies we kept in the store. All of them were monthlies or weeklies my mother had recently discarded.

Having mended the shoes on his work table, my father inspected my cleanup. He crouched here and there, pinching with his fingers all the dust specks and dirt balls I'd missed, holding them up and shaking his head. He dropped the debris back to the floor and sighed. He glared at me as if I were guilty of looting his shop by dint of sanitary neglect. "Floor steal dirty, Barry," he said. "You know watt *my* Aba do to me eef I leave sheet on da floor in *heeze* store?" He poised his open right hand high up in the air, the one that had slapped me once and only once.

"Yes, I know what he did," I said. In my own hands I gathered the debris my father had dropped. Oh, how badly I wished to wise off, to reply in heated, earnest eloquence, to say: "I know life must have sucked, growing up in Libya and Israel, raised by your Aba, my Saba, the parent you uphold as a lord of discipline but never visit."

"Barry, luke at me when I toking," he said. I looked. He took a step toward me and seized my T-shirt with a closed fist. I dropped the debris. He shoved my face down to the floor until my eyes were an inch from the hairy, sandy pile. He gripped me by the back of the neck. "Aba, please," I cried. "You're hurting me."

He let me go. He sat in one of the plastic chairs by the coffee table and held his face in his hands. I wondered whether his remorseful appearance was a sincere manifestation of instant regret, or a superficial display of the same. Maybe it was both. "Sorry, Barry," he said.

"Don't worry about it," I said. We were silent a few minutes, each of us staring at the floor while a Beach Boys tune played. There was a rapid knocking on the glass door. We smiled and waved at Morris and his sister, Cookie, as if it were just another day at the shop. My father unlocked the door, ushered them in, and locked it again. Cookie, whose real name I never learned, kissed my father's cheek. "Hello, Kook," he said.

Morris turned to me. "Barry, my boy, what's the good news?" he said. "You know, if your father had your brains, he'd own seven shops by now."

"And if you could fix anything like Eli fixes everything, you wouldn't be single," said Cookie. We all laughed. She wore tight blue jeans, sandals, and a black concert T-shirt from the band Duran Duran. She could not have been older than thirty. She had hair of brown curls like her brother, who was clad in a gray Adidas sweat suit.

My father clasped Morris's forearm and said: "Leasen to me, my friend. I tell Barry my goals, and he write eat down." He nodded at me. I fetched the index card from its temporary home inside the cash register.

Morris scanned it. "Eli, you gotta face facts," he said. "You'll never own this place. Your landlord—I know him—wants to own all of Queens Boulevard. He wouldn't sell this space for a million bucks. And as I've told you a thousand times, rent is not your biggest problem. Double your prices. Stop doing free work for my sister and all the young women who smile at you. Believe me, you'll make rent halfway through the month."

My father looked down at the checkerboard floor. I wondered if he felt dressed down in front of his son, or if he gladly suffered didactics from a *reach* guy like Morris.

It was Cookie who looked more offended than anyone else did. She had a hand on my father's shoulder. "Look, Cook, Eli knows this isn't personal," said Morris. "So does Barry. This is just how men talk. Anyway, Eli, goals number two and three are noble. But you should hold off until you've got this store breaking even. Because right now, if I worked at a bank—even the one across the street where they can see how popular you are—I wouldn't give you the time of day, let alone a line of credit. How much do you need to make it through July?"

"I tink eight hundred," said Eli. "Same deal as last time. I pay you one tausand by September."

"Happy to help," said Morris. "I like having a shop like yours around here." He pulled a money clip from his pocket and peeled off eight hundred-dollar bills.

"Want to go bowling at lunchtime?" Cookie asked me.

"I need Barry helping today," said my father. He often gave this answer and I excelled at hiding my disappointment.

"Oh, Kook, I almost forget," added my father. "You heels is ready."
He led Cookie to the back of the shop.

Morris put his hand on my shoulder. "Law school, Barry," he said. "Or
Harvard Biz. You don't need this shit." I turned around to spy on Cookie
and my father. Their hands were on the same shoe. My father's fingers
probed the thin heel, to which he'd glued a centimeter of rubber. Cookie
grasped the straps in front. Morris whispered to me: "How's your mother
doing? What's her name again?"

"Rachel," I muttered back. "She's good. She's doing a story on Wang
Computer."

"Wang Computer," he repeated. Then he whispered: "Why does your
father spin his wheels in the mud?"

I looked up at him, puzzled. He smiled. "Cook," he shouted, "let's go
already. Mom's expecting us for breakfast." She kissed my father on the
cheek and walked back to her brother, the repaired shoes in her hands.

"Take eat easy," said my father to Morris.

"Charge her thirty bucks next time," said Morris.

At two in the afternoon—when our rush of lunch-hour customers was
over—my father hung the BACK BY ___ sign on the door and locked the
store. The blank space on the sign featured a clock with movable cardboard hands, which Eli placed in the 3:30 position. He knelt by my feet
and tightened the laces of my sneakers.

I detested jogging with him but liked his lightened mood afterwards.
We ran straight down Queens Boulevard for what my father claimed was
three miles. Then we turned around and ran on the opposite sidewalk for
another two. I say "we ran," but in reality my father ran as I huffed and puffed
in his wake, falling farther and farther behind until he stopped at a corner
and did push-ups until I caught up. When I finally reached him, I turned

despondent in an instant as he sprang to his feet and began running again.

Walking the last mile back to the shop, we often stopped at a restaurant called Knish Knosh to grab our late lunch. While Eli waited for the food, I hung out and read comic books at a nearby convenience store. Dov Kurti, the convenience store owner, was also an Israeli immigrant. And he was one of my father's best friends. I often pondered—but never asked—whether Eli's affinity for Dov was enhanced by the sentimental coincidence that his childhood friend, who'd perished in the Six-Day War, was also named Dov.

On this particular afternoon I asked my father to buy me a *G.I. Joe* comic: an issue entitled "The Battle of Springfield." Eli looked at Dov and they shared a lengthy laugh. "Someday you understand, Barry," said my father, handing me the paper bag of knishes.

And then one night—or early morning—it was my mother who woke me, instead of my father. "We're leaving," she whispered.

There had been loud fighting—in Hebrew—from the moment I'd gone to bed. What the quarrel was about, I had my hunches: money and me, in that order. With their Semitic sentences flying back and forth I could only pluck the recognizable scraps—like my name—from their verbal volleys. And amidst the Hebraic consonant clusters I discerned certain words I knew: *kesseff* (money) and *by-eet* (house).

But then I fell asleep. And so, apparently, had my father. As Rachel and I prepared for flight, he remained stone-stiff on his back in bed. Peering into their bedroom as my mother packed, I wondered, with an absence of sorrow that alarmed me, if I was seeing him for the final time. In the silent house I heard Rachel zipping shut a gym bag. She kissed my forehead and handed the bag to me and urged me in a whisper to tiptoe down the steps and wait by her car.

In her car, a Honda Civic, we remained hushed as she drove. I clearly heard the clicks of my mom's turn signals. And I noticed that the traffic lights, too, made a clicking noise whenever they changed color. "Do they know we're coming?" I asked.

"No. But it won't surprise them. They warned me about Sephardic men," she said.

"Warned you what?" I asked.

"Barry, your father smacked me in the nose with the back of his hand," she said.

"Why?" I asked.

"There's no why for something like that."

"He hit you for no reason?" I asked.

"That's hardly what I'm saying, but I don't feel like explaining myself right now. What I need to know is, has he done something like that to you?"

"No," I said. I felt I had to protect him. After all, he'd only hit me once, as a punishment. His grabbing of my neck in the shop—it hurt, yet I couldn't truly count it as a punch. I didn't want to. Such an admission would paint an inaccurate picture of my father's severity, color him abusive when he'd merely lost his temper. To confess to being hit, to know that such a confession would lead to my mother claiming that Eli had hit me, too—I didn't want to be a party to that, not while my father lay sleeping like a rock, unable to defend himself from the accusation.

The quiet returned to the car as we rode on. When we were almost there I asked, "What were you fighting about?"

"Money," said Rachel. "He thinks the store is more important than our mortgage, or your college savings."

"He should raise his prices," I said. She briefly took her eyes off the road and stared at me, as if I hadn't the faintest idea about anything.

We rode the rest of the way in silence. When we arrived, we parked the Civic on the lamp-lit street and approached the screen door, illuminated by its bright orange porch light. We walked right past the driveway my father had rebuilt, on which rested the two cars he'd had to move just to begin his work.

PART I - BIOGRAPHIC DATA

10. Permanent address in the United... known (street address including ZIP code)... who currently lives there

give both

12. Present Occupation

Telephone number

13. Pre...

Telephi...

14. Spouse's Maiden or Family Name

15. Date (mm-dd-yyyy) and Place of Birth

...arated

(Country)

Middle Name

...is form for yourself and each member of your family, regardless of age, who will immigrate wi...
Mark questions that are Not Applicable with "N/A". If there is insufficient room on the form, u...
...appear on the form. Attach any additional sheets to this form.
...a material fact may result in your permanent exclusion from the United States.
...his part, together with Form DS-230 Part II, constitutes the complete Application for

3M

AUNTIE SHIRIN

by SANAM MAHLOUDJI

F OR A WEEK IT had been a nonstop party of weed, coke, and
cartoons, until an hour ago when I bailed my Auntie Shirin out
of the Aspen jail for attempted prostitution. In the white Suburban taxicab that bulldozed across the uneven snowy roads, she poked
her head out the backseat window, avoiding my questions. Finally, she
turned around, her cheeks pink and alive, and yelled in Farsi for me to
stop meddling: *"Foozooli nakon!"*

At our hotel, Auntie Shirin marched down the third-floor hallway. She
passed 3E without slowing down. "Not dealing with Houman's drug-in-
duced *kumbaya* shit. Bita my dear, my *joon*, I'm staying with you."

I hovered the plastic card over the wall, and the door opened.

Thirty minutes later she walked out of the bathroom wearing a big,
white hotel robe and a towel around her head. The steam smelled of
sweet chemicals.

Shirin removed the towel and shook out her hair. She lay facedown on the king bed, on top of the cloud-like eiderdown. We'd dubbed my room Club 3M. Me, her son Mo, and all the dipshit kids of our parents' friends. For eleven years straight, since 1994, we'd flown in from New York, Los Angeles, and Houston, as if 1979 and the Islamic Revolution hadn't happened and we were still the most important families in Iran, although this was America and nobody cared. The locals hated us. Not openly, but they had to. I imagined that, like that Pace Picante commercial, they were the cowboys mumbling "Get a rope" when they saw us in all black, buying a thousand dollars in caviar and champagne at the mom-and-pop market.

"Bita *joon*. Bita darling," Auntie Shirin said.

"Yes?" I said, standing at the foot of the bed.

"Fetch me a Fiji and a Marlboro Light." Auntie Shirin turned to her side, her cheek against the white pillow. She raised her arm and pinched at the air. "Be a good girl and do as your auntie says."

"Okay, sure," I said.

In Iran, before 1979, Auntie Shirin had chauffeurs and servants. She was also studying political science. Once she said to me, without an ounce of self-reflection, "Bita, even the chauffeurs talked about overthrowing the king. They drove me to the marches. They hated the Pahlavis nearly as much as me."

Her thick, dark hair splayed out across the white pillow, like ink spilling out on paper. She was a mess and I hated her and I loved her, too.

I walked to the TV, opened the minibar underneath, and pulled out a cool blue bottle. I got a cigarette out of the pack in my poofy ski jacket on the floor, stuck it in my mouth, and lit it on a matchbook from the Caribou Club.

Against my fingers, the printed gold antlers of the muscular animal rose up in silhouette on the black cardboard. This was the club where my aunt was arrested for attempted prostitution. I took a deep inhale of the cigarette, and watched the salt-and-pepper tip turn red. I held out the cigarette.

"Here you go," I said, blowing out the first smoke.

"Good girl," Auntie Shirin said.

She turned over onto her back, fingered the cigarette, and brought it to her face. She looked to the bedside table as if to say, "Put down the water." So I did.

It was 4 a.m. and I was no longer high. Or drunk. Just tired and annoyed, and not just because of the room takeover. I was pissed I'd bailed Shirin out for ten thousand dollars and all she'd said when the cop brought her barefoot to the damp, empty waiting area was "Thank you Bita *joon*" and "How generous" and "I knew you'd answer. What a damn genius I was to call you first, my little lawyer-in-training. That was good practice for you—although you want to be one of those do-gooders. Houman would be going up the wall." Before we left, the cop handed me a large plastic bag and her boots.

Still on her back, Auntie Shirin lay like a puddle soaking into the surface. The smoke rose from her mouth. "Don't you dare knock on their doors," she said now, meaning our friends and family passed out in rooms across the third floor.

I sat down on the tufted floral armchair next to the bed. On the TV, the black-coated newsman stood in a blizzard of white snow, breathing out white air. I pressed mute.

"They treated me like one of their common criminals. I'm disgusted," Auntie Shirin said, and filled her throat again. Her deep-maroon nails sparkled.

"Did they read you your rights? They search you?" I asked.

"Are you kidding? A horrible slob stuck her hand in my ass. I'm going to sue them, you know that."

"I don't know, Auntie. Why don't we just focus on getting the charges dropped?"

She widened her eyes, ashes building on her cigarette. "*Mash'allah* Bita," she said. "For an Ivy League law student, you're pretty fucking wimpy."

I looked away at the silent TV, a new man talking in a blue room, the news always on in our spaces. I thought it was pretty hypocritical that she invoked Allah, given that nobody in our circle actually thought of ourselves as Muslim. Although some ancestor once made the Hajj, circled that big black box, and was known for doing so.

"Don't talk to me like that," I said. "You owe me."

"Attagirl," she said, and smiled.

I rolled my eyes. "You're a jerk, Auntie," I said. I groaned. "This is bad, even for you. At least you didn't go through with it. Right?" I pictured Shirin under a big blob of man, giving herself to him, wanting to.

"That pig. That stupid officer fuckface posing as that Dallas playboy," Auntie Shirin said, and ashed her cigarette onto the floor.

"Do you think they targeted you?"

"For what? Being beautiful?"

I laughed and shook my head.

She stared at me, daring me to speak. I said nothing.

"He said, 'Baby, be my Cleopatra for the night. I want to be your sheik.' I've had it up to here with that shit. So I said, 'Okay honey, I can be your Princess Jasmine, but it's gonna cost you. Gimme fifty Gs.' Bastard."

I laughed. Shirin narrowed her eyes, her oily black lashes folding together. "Where did you come up with that amount?" I said.

"Punish that ignorance," she said. She stretched her arms out in a yawn, pushed against the headboard with her cigarette hand.

"Watch it," I said. Ash scattered behind her head.

Auntie Shirin rolled her eyes, dropped her cigarette into the bottle full of water. "They're so uneducated," she said. "Everyone's a fucking Arab. They don't know anything about the Persians, that we were the greatest civilization on earth. So then he said, 'Okay baby, just walk with me to the ATM.' I'm no idiot. I know an ATM isn't going to give you that kind of money. So I said, 'You're full of shit.' He took out a checkbook and wrote me a check and gave me his entire wallet as collateral. I believed him. I was going to do it, you know."

"It was a trap," I said. "But you're right—why should they care you're Iranian? All they saw was a woman with dark skin."

"What dark skin?" She looked down one arm and then the other. "No, no."

"Please," I said.

"This guy just wanted to humiliate me. He hates beautiful women."

I looked out at the dining table. Ketel Ones, a mirror taken from the wall, rolled-up dollars, Gore-Tex gloves, torn-up ski passes with mangled wires, green soy-sauce packets and used chopsticks from Sushi Olé. On the carpet, kicked-off ski boots, their shiny hard shells. Black-on-black Prada shopping bags. Half-drunk Fijis, red-lipstick-kissed necks, slowly oozing water onto the floor like blood.

I held my stomach.

Shirin groaned. "And those opium-smoking dumbasses," she said. "They won't find out. Let them play their silly games."

She meant the men, like Houman and Dad, who sat playing cards at their round table covered in green felt brought in a roll in someone's luggage. The air would smell of various smoke—sweet, earthy, and floral, crystal tumblers of scotch shining like stars in the soft green sky.

"I told a couple friends from school—no names. One knows a lawyer in Denver. We should meet up," I said.

"I don't need a lawyer, but fine."

"Don't do me any favors, Auntie," I said.

"I won't."

I tipped my head back and stared at the air vent. Gray dust clung to the center slats, like petri-dish fur.

*   *   *

There was a knock at the door. Then, more knocking.

"Go see who it is," Auntie Shirin said.

I walked to the door. Pressed my eyes on the cold ring of the peephole. "It's Mo," I said.

"Don't tell him shit. He can't take it," she said. "But wait." Auntie Shirin twisted to reach the large Ziploc on the floor. Her name—Shirin Javan—scrawled in black marker. She shook it and junk scattered on the white duvet. Matchbooks, makeup cases, phone, black purse. She hurried to refill the purse.

I opened the door. Mo plowed past me, straight to Shirin, whose head was back on the pillow. "The fuck, Mom? Where you been? I've been calling you all morning."

"The fuck what," she said. "Call it female bonding. Show some respect. You don't speak to your mother like that." She propped her purse up on the nightstand.

"Sorry, Mommy," he said. He bent down and kissed her head. He wore all black. His platinum Rolex shone in the bedside light. He was thirty, four years older than me. Mo short for Mohammad.

Mo and Shirin had the same beautiful dark moles on their faces, spaced like constellations, jet-black hair, fluid motions. Shirin smiled. Her eye makeup had stayed on throughout all this—eyeliner drawn slanted like cat eyes, mascara pulling her lashes up and away.

"I'm starved—can we eat?" she said.

Shirin swung her legs onto the floor and untied the robe. It opened up like a curtain and I saw her naked body underneath. She dropped the robe on the bed. I looked at Mo, still crouching over the head of the bed, and saw that he was watching her, too. Eyes full of love. Her boobs were round and stiff and seemed a separate thing from her body. Her tummy flat and tan, her pussy waxed into a razor-sharp V. Not like someone's fifty-year-old mother. I thought of the cop dressed as a Dallas playboy, approaching her, kissing her. The only signs of age were in the veins that stuck out of her hands and her neck.

"Can you believe you came out of this?" she said, looking at her crotch. "Best decision I ever made. One day I went to the toilet to take a shit, and there you were."

Mo rolled his eyes. "Mom, no one else would think this is normal. Be serious."

"I am serious. It's a miracle you're not gay."

Mo laughed.

"Nothing wrong with being gay," I said.

"Talk to me when you have kids, Bita," she said. "No one wants that. My baby boy is a lady-killer. And a superstar, his managing director told me so." She gave Mo a kiss on his stiff, gelled hair. She walked over to the love seat where she'd dumped last night's clothes. A form-fitting black wool dress and above-the-knee Louboutin boots. No underwear. She put them on. Over it, she put on my black coat with the big fur collar. Her dark skin shone. "Let's go," she said. "I could eat a cowboy."

I squinted my eyes at her. She smiled and grabbed her purse. What was she going to get us into today? I got up from the chair, zipped my boots up my calves, and saw the white powder already sliced into lines on the mirror. I leaned over it, took the rolled bill, and inhaled. Mo and Shirin did the same until it was gone. I closed my eyes, breathed in and out. The inside of my nose burned and the bitterness leaked down my throat. I swallowed. And there it was throughout my body: a little flash of joy.

We walked out the hotel room. I checked that the door tag said DO NOT DISTURB, stuffed the plastic key card into my coat pocket, and shuffled through its bills and loose cigarettes. At the elevator bank, a hotel maid was organizing her cart. Shirin acknowledged the maid and then, when she turned, grabbed some tiny liquor bottles and put them in Mo's coat pocket.

The three of us stepped out of the elevator onto the mezzanine carpeted in peach and orange paisley. Gold chandeliers lit up the room. A grand wood staircase rose from the lobby and circled to where we stood. The après-ski crowd sat on velvet and drank wine, tossing back their heads, ordering more than they could drink. They were like us in that way.

We watched down below, our arms on the banister. The guests, fresh off planes, in cowboy hats, fur coats. I counted all the bleached blondes and Ken-doll haircuts.

Bellboys rushed around with luggage. I spent my infancy on planes. Khomeini stepped off a plane from Paris. Planes left Tehran daily with people like us, who could bribe and smuggle their way out. "When did we realize this was for real?" I said to my parents once. "Never," Mom said. "We were more pro-Shah than we knew. When push came to shove."

"These Texans are making me sick. They're a couple cows and oil wells from being complete dirt," Shirin said. "Let's go take over a wing and have a drink."

We sat in the crackle of the mezzanine lounge fireplace. Christmas songs played on invisible speakers. I'd sung them all as a little kid in Los Angeles. I'm sure Mo did, too, in Houston.

American newlyweds sat on the adjacent sofa. They Eskimo-kissed, twirled their wine glasses like they teach you at a wine-tasting class. They looked over at us and left. The fire warmed my body.

"Your mom would have loved this," Auntie Shirin said. "The biggest Christmas freak."

I smiled. Fuck cancer, I thought. And fuck how we distance ourselves from Mom by giving her death a scary, clinical name. I wondered how real Muslims remembered their past. I could barely see her face when I shut my eyes and she'd been dead just ten years.

Mo frowned. "She hated religion."

"No. She hated lemmings," Shirin said. "She loved the parties and Santa."

Sprawled out over the soft burgundy couches, I kicked my black boots onto the wood table with an etched-glass center. We drank mimosas and ate pretzels and those seaweed-wrapped orange things from small golden bowls.

"This is the last time I'm doing this dumb trip, kids," Auntie Shirin said, rubbing the salt off her shiny, dark nails.

"Why?" Mo said.

"They're so boring. You seen the hair growing out of your father's ears? The women act like my old Naneh. The monarchy crawled up their asses and died. Roll me a joint, baby." She passed a bejeweled cigarette case to Mo.

Shirin ordered us straight champagne. I clinked my glass to theirs and then against the edge of the side table as my hand wobbled. I waited for something to break. Shirin smoked her joint and nobody stopped her.

"Your fathers," Shirin said, inhaled and exhaled, "are such losers."

"You're so mean," Mo said. "Dad does good business."

"Hah," Shirin said. "In Iran, they *were* the economy." She looked at me. "Houman and your dad are now selling what? Fake Iranian teabags? With inspirational messages?"

"Yo, the fake part is not their fault. Hello, sanctions," Mo said.

Suddenly, Shahla, Neda, and Leila appeared in front of us. Sisters I could barely tell apart. Houman's brother's kids. Thick hair blow-dried straight, perfectly arched eyebrows, sad sexy mouths. Like me but, if I'm being honest, much prettier. Black pants, tight sweaters, diamonds, fur earmuffs. Somewhere between ski bunny and Playboy bunny and Iranian Ivanka Trump.

"Oh girls. Sit down, girls. Eat. Eat," Auntie Shirin said. "Looks like all you're on is Ritalin and coffee. I don't understand you girls. You eat, you just eat smart. Lunch, okay. Dinner is for pigs. For dinner you eat a nice salad and that's that."

Shahla, Neda, and Leila giggled and two of them flipped their hair from one side to the other.

"We're going shopping. I need a new dress for tomorrow," the girl on the left said, twisting her torso and cocking her head. "Side-boob for real."

"*Da-yumn*," Mo said. "We got the hottest girls. I'll always say that."

"Why do you only date blondes, then?" I said.

"Why you only date Harvard guys?"

"That's different," I said.

"Oh, is it?"

I rolled my eyes. But he was right. Like him, I also sucked at being in a relationship. Who was I to feel superior? Still, I did.

"These Houston boys invited us to a party on Red Mountain," the one in the middle said. "We gotta look on *fi-yah*, yo."

"Mrs. Claus not playing hard to get, huh?" Mo said.

"Oh, shut up. No one's in it for the conversation. *Blaaah, blaaah, blaaah*," Leila said hoarsely. I knew her by her voice: the oldest, the wisest, the one who'd been passing out drunk on tables since she was eleven.

"Let's *vamanos*. It's three," Auntie Shirin said. "Stores close early." She put her hand in the air and waved down a waiter. Not even our waiter. "Check?" she said to some guy in a navy uniform. "Don't have all day."

I was nearly asleep, and stretched out my legs on the coffee table. The man rushed back to the bar. "No more stealing, though," I said. "You're such a criminal."

Shirin smiled.

Mo scrunched his brows. "Huh?" he said.

"Joke," I said, and put my feet on the ground.

When the waiter didn't return, Auntie Shirin stood up and walked out the revolving glass door. She didn't turn back. Mo and I shrugged our shoulders and followed. For a few seconds, I was alone sealed in glass. The world was quiet. Outside, I zipped my coat up to my face, feeling jagged metal against my lip, and drew up my hood. I joined Mo and Shirin under the green awning.

I walked with them over the melting ice and cobblestone. Cowboy hats bobbing up and down with shopping bags. Everyone buying last-minute Christmas presents, and now so were we, I thought. My eyes felt the cold wind. They watered.

Auntie Shirin walked us to a jewelry store that required us to press a button. She pushed it.

"Are we just looking?" I said.

The door buzzed. A security man opened it and we entered. He shut the door and resumed his position just inside. He wore reflective sunglasses and a tight tan uniform, like a caricature of an '80s highway patrolman. He did not smile at us or even look in our direction.

"What shall I get you two?" Auntie Shirin said to Mo.

"For what?" Mo said.

"A new watch? What about you, Bita?"

"I'm okay," I said. "And are you kidding me?"

"You're turning down jewelry?" Auntie Shirin said.

"Shouldn't you take it easy today?" I said.

"*Saah-ket*," Shirin said, meaning shut up.

A sixtysomething woman organized boxes on the other side of the glass counter. She wore a long ivory cardigan. Her dyed caramel hair was pulled back into a loose bun, her posture absolutely perfect. I hated her right away. No matter what we did, we would never be her.

The woman looked up. "Can I help you?" she said.

"I'd like to see your men's watches," Auntie Shirin said as the woman approached.

"Wonderful." She twisted a key into the glass case. Inside the case, the display was a miniature Aspen dripping in jewels. Diamond-stud earrings suspended with invisible string were the snowflakes.

"Nobody needs another watch," I said.

"You know what? I'll take them all." Shirin glared at me.

The woman took a step back. "Oh my. Are you sure?"

Shirin raised an eyebrow. "What do you think?"

"Do you want the prices first?" the woman said. She unfastened watches from the green-and-white felt mountain.

Shirin laughed. "Throw in that necklace, too." Shirin nodded at an emerald choker that doubled as a gondola cable.

"You must really love Christmas," the woman said. "That green is marvelous for the season."

Shirin laughed. She shook her head. "You have no idea."

The woman stared at us. "I'll go wrap these."

"Throw them in here," Auntie Shirin said, pulling out the Ziploc from the Aspen jail.

The woman stared at the pile of watches and then at the empty plastic bag scribbled on in Sharpie. The woman's perfect hair and face powder reflected off the overhead lights, giving her the glow of an angel. She looked back at Shirin and smiled, mouth closed like she'd never felt sorrier for anyone in her goddamn life.

Outside the store, we walked. Auntie Shirin wore her emerald choker—a green gem, an octagon, held onto her neck by a chainmail of gold. It glistened. She'd bought six watches. Spent over thirty thousand dollars.

She swung the plastic bag side to side sharply as she walked.

"What's that bag?" Mo said.

"None of your business," she said.

The sun was out now, the clouds moving fast. The snow on the ground blinded me. I put on my sunglasses.

"Don't embarrass me like that again," Shirin said. Her boots sounded hard on the red brick.

"Embarrass you?" I said. "I was just trying to protect you."

"I don't need your help," she said.

"Come on, guys. Cool it. Let's get a crepe," Mo said.

"Whatever you want, sweetheart," Shirin said. "Give me those vodkas."

Mo reached into his pocket and handed them to Shirin. Shirin stopped, tucked the bag under her arm, untwisted one bottle's top, shot it. Did the same with the remaining two. She tossed the empty bottles into a mound of snow. I considered picking them up, but I didn't.

Soon we approached the line extended from the red-and-white-striped crepe cart. We got into the back, the big Aspen mountain rising up ahead. I felt dizzy and hot. I looked at my feet on the uneven bricks. I remembered something Mom used to say: if someone said, "I like your bracelet," in Iran you were supposed to offer it to them. Just like that. Of course I couldn't ask Shirin to pay me back for the ten thousand dollars. It would be against everything they ever taught me or would expect from me. Besides, the only reason I had the money was our parents gave us money.

"Hey hey hey, if it isn't my favorite people of all time," I heard. I turned around. It was Uncle Houman, with Dad. They had red noses from the cold, their short beards grizzled. They wore big fur hoods and thick parkas. Dad held a cigar in his thick, brown hand. "Where've you been, darling?" Houman said. "I didn't see you last night."

"You know. Defending our honor," she said.

Uncle Houman laughed. "Just relax, honey. Seriously. Relax. Everything's okay." He tilted his head up to the crisp blue-and-white sky, drew his arms wide, and breathed in. "*Ahhhh*," he breathed out a cloud of white vapor. "What could be more beautiful than this? Aspen, Colorado with my beautiful wife and family?" He patted Dad on his back.

Shirin shook her head. "Come on," she said. "You're pathetic. This town is a shithole."

"Order me a chocolate crepe, will you, Bita?" Dad said.

"We've got the poker tournament of the century going on," Uncle Houman said. "It's beautiful." He patted Dad's thick coat again, like he was dusting a pillow. Dad coughed, stretching out his cigar.

Two police officers with mustaches and crepes folded into white paper plates walked past us. Chocolate sauce crawled down the sides of their plates. I watched them. I watched Auntie Shirin watch them. One of them smiled at her and winked.

"Excuse me?" Shirin said, loudly.

The cops turned around. "Excuse who?" the other one said, the chocolate sauce now dripping over his hand.

"Don't you dare look at me," Auntie Shirin said. Again very loudly.

"Now, now, Shirin *joon*. Relax," Houman said. "Sorry, my wife must have had a few too many."

"Look at him. Dirty. Pig," she said.

"Hey," the cop who had winked said. "Watch it."

Shirin looked back at us. Nobody said anything. The cop stood, his feet wide apart. He shook his head and squinted at Shirin in the bright sun.

Auntie Shirin turned again and looked at me, then Mo, and then the fathers. "Wait a minute here. None of you shits are saying anything?" she shouted.

I looked down at my feet. Please let her stop, I thought. I waved people along so they'd pass us in line.

"Now, now," Houman said. "Let's all just have a Merry Christmas. It's fine."

Auntie Shirin looked at him. She clenched her fists. "Shut up," she said, suddenly quieter, her mouth clenched, too.

The cop stepped closer to her.

"Get the fuck away from me," she said. "I saw that face you made. You heard about the Cleopatra bullshit, didn't you? You know who I am, don't you?"

The cop scrunched his eyebrows. "Huh? I can arrest you right now for public intoxication. Want that?"

"I'm not drunk," she yelled. People in line behind us started to walk around us without asking, their heads turning, though, to keep watch.

"Really?" the cop said. "Control that shit mouth on her," he said to Houman. "If it weren't Christmas Eve, I'd put her in jail right now." He walked to the other cop and started to say something. The other cop took out a notepad.

"Shirin," Houman said in a low voice. "What is wrong with you?" He grabbed her hand and shook it.

"I nearly fucked one of their guys," she said.

I watched Houman. He stared right at her and didn't blink. I'd never seen him so still.

"What are you talking about, Auntie?" I said. "Come on. Stop that."

"Mom," Mo said. He looked at her and then at the people watching us.

Shirin looked away, toward the ski mountain.

"She's joking," I said.

Auntie Shirin laughed. A bitter, angry laugh. "What. Do I. Have. To lose?" she asked, glaring at me.

I looked in her shiny, dark eyes. They were wet.

"I don't know," I said.

Mom always said Shirin was the smartest of all their friends. The most

ambitious and daring. Houman and Dad had been serious and respected—
leaders in the community, as undemocratic as it was. I was supposedly
smart, too. The Revolution fucked everyone up. Even Mo and me and
the three Ivanka sisters.

"Please, Auntie," I said.

She shook her head. "I got you idiots presents." She swung the plastic
bag in front of the men. "But I changed my mind."

Auntie Shirin walked away from me, Mo, and the fathers. We stood
watching her. Motionless. She walked away. From the crepe stand. And
the lift-ticket booth. She didn't look back.

She stopped when she reached the base of the mountain, where people
had left skis punched into the snow. I waited for her to turn, but still
she didn't.

She started walking up the mountain. I could feel her leaning forward
and bending her knees. I could feel the hot tears on her face.

Skiers shot down fast, right past her. Surely inadvertently spraying her
with snow. Giving her pause as she climbed. But she kept going. Then
she stopped. She looked up, her neck craning. Her arms reached out. The
plastic bag dangled from one hand, glistened in the sunlight.

Skiers below her now shook snow off their helmets and clicked off
their skis.

Auntie Shirin reached into the bag. I think. She was far away now and
I had to squint. Suddenly, she swept her arm in an arc across the sky. Then
she repeated it. Her hand at the bag. And then her arm across the sky.

In the distance, objects flew across the air. The beautiful, useless watches.

I said nothing. I watched Shirin. I watched the mountain, letting my
eyes travel up past her, up along the slope leading to the top, obscured by
clouds. The mountain looked both soft and sharp. Rock pierced through
powder. I breathed in the cool, crisp air.

Tehran was very dirty, something everyone knew. A city running on smog. The last time I had breathed its air, I was a baby. As a kid, I felt surprised when I learned Iran was mountainous, the Alborz mountains growing just north of the city. Embracing Tehran in its majestic, silent beauty.

I watched Auntie Shirin. I watched myself.

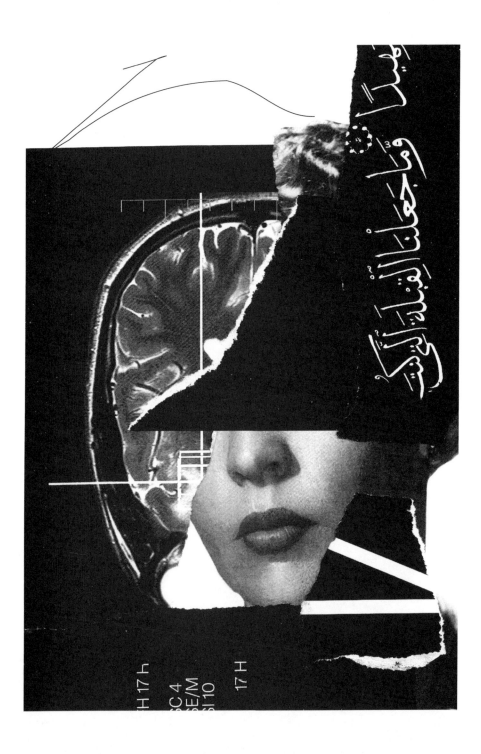

THE FOUR HUMORS

by MINA SEÇKIN

I STAND AT THE LIP of the outdoor market in Istanbul. Behind me is Cooper, my boyfriend, the man I have sex with, who is no man but a boy my age. I'm at an age where I don't yet feel comfortable calling myself a woman. I'm not sure what this makes either of us. Most likely, boy and girl—or girl and guy. The market is crowded and we're having trouble wedging through. I think Cooper wants to be polite. He hates to mow people down. I take his hand to weave through women weighing fruit in their hands, children begging mothers for plastic toys. I run over a black street cat and it snarls up at me, baring a mouthful of tiny white daggers.

We've come back to the outdoor market, open every Saturday, because last week we couldn't decide on the right towel to buy for his family in California. The first time we came to the market we pointed at towels and we touched them. We discussed absorbency. We developed and shared our preferences for which pastel colors we believe to be the best pastel colors. We left the market with nothing.

Cooper wants this purchase to be perfect. He wants to make his family happy. I want him to be happy. We're only here for the summer, college break. Me, to take care of my grandmother, to see my father in his grave. Him, to see that I do these things.

He buys three towels.

He followed me to Istanbul to take part in my summer adventure. Then we coined it *our* adventure. Then he found a job, an internship at the eye hospital near the university. He's a curious person and renowned for being kind. I summon and repeat the words *our adventure* in my head, an incantation, until the letters press against each other with so much speed and force they blur and break and I'm left here, in this market, on no adventure at all, only a mixture of mutated letters in my head.

We make our way out of the market and catch the bus to my grandmother's apartment. The windows are torn open and a breeze moves through. We take turns leaning against the pole because Cooper has given up our seats to a woman with two children. Here, he'd said, gesturing to the seats, his smile as wide as an ocean across his face. They scrambled into the seats, and me, I got up, trying to be as kind as him.

He pulls out his towels from the plastic bag and holds up his purchases. I'll give my mom these two blue towels, and my sister this purple one. What do you think?

I say, I think that's great. They will definitely love them. I am convinced of this because my family loves them, these thin towels. They are much more absorbent than people think.

Should I have bought my sister two towels, too? Do you think it's fair that she gets one but my mom gets two?

Light pours into the bus and we sway on its pole as we swerve through the hilled city. A city with many hills has become that way due to a lifetime of earthquakes. The two children have their small hands on their laps and stare up at Cooper as if in a trance and he beams back. My head has ached for one month. I can't tell if it feels as if I'm in an earthquake or an ocean. Whichever I am more likely to survive.

We take the elevator upstairs to my grandmother's apartment, the one my mother first met my father in before they moved together to America. I tell my mother's story in the elevator ride up. It's a very slow elevator with a heavy door you must heave open and I'm a remarkably fast talker. She was younger than me, I tell him again. I love telling Cooper this because it reminds me that I can do anything, being this age and without children. I'm not allowed to spend the night in Cooper's rented room because it would break my grandmother's heart. Really, we have very little sex here because of these technical, spatial difficulties, and in this way I come to realize he must not be the man I have sex with, but something else, something more terrifying and personal: a man who may know me.

Each time we enter her apartment, Cooper makes a point to wait at the entrance. He's learned that my grandmother wants to greet him. My grandmother opens the door and gestures with her hand toward her apartment. They grasp one another's hands as if to build a lifeline. They cannot speak the same language but they make it a point to communicate. This can make me jealous.

Before we came here together, my mother set up ground rules for us. No kissing in public, because the real Turks won't do that openly. We kiss, instead, when the door is closed. When we are alone in the apartment he sublets near the eye hospital.

My grandmother brews us tea and brings out a plate of cookies. On the television they show the beige wreck of a city after a bomb. My grandmother sits down on her ancient green armchair, her throne. She tells me that America has learned how to fight the new world war silently, killing brown people from the sky with a laser-focused needle. She looks at Cooper to make sure he is eating the cookies. She tells me to tell him what she just said, to translate what she thinks about her president, and about his president.

Cooper is so beautiful. His lips are pink and wide like a flattened heart. They open and close, this beating heart in his mouth, as he listens to my translation, as he listens to what she thinks of those who run her country.

Cooper and I return to the market the next Saturday. We want to purchase another towel, this time for my grandmother. This was Cooper's idea. He wants to return her hospitality.

The market is less crowded today. I follow Cooper's head of yellow hair, as yellow as a dried stalk of corn. We spend one hour touching the towels at three different stands. Finally we pick out two white towels with yellow trim. I tell Cooper that gifts are useful, given that they cannot speak to one another. He nods and points out that it is still remarkable that they seem to understand one another. It is easier to leave the market than to enter it, and when we reach the edge of the thing, we decide to walk to a café. We find one with a French name and strong gunky Turkish coffee. My head pounds.

I think I am dehydrated, I announce. I order two *çays*. Cooper's working on drawing faces.

Where do you start, Sibel? He asks. The temples? The forehead?

Maybe the temples, I say. But I can't draw people.

There is a woman next to us. She has long tan legs, not a natural brown but orange. Her blonde hair is so straight it looks like the ends could cut you. She tells her Turkish friend, in English, that she wanted to come to

Istanbul because of the interesting political things going on. That's what she said, *things were getting so interesting*, and she nodded seriously, holding a ceramic cup of coffee in her hands.

This is terrible, Cooper says. This will just have to be something else, like a building. He cocks his head. He laughs. Look, an ear, out of nowhere.

He begins to draw an eye, maybe my eye, into a crescent moon, and on the television hammered to the wall the president is speaking.

It's not politics I am afraid of, I explain, but people.

Yes, he says. Yes. That's who makes up politics, right? It's definitely my eye he draws, a dark oval that meets the moon at its lowermost crescent point. Cooper has sketched Istanbul, the mosques, and the river. The moon and the stars are above the city, and tiny framed portraits hang from the crescent moon's lower tooth like hair.

I tell him about the news segment my grandmother watched yesterday. The anchor was a woman and the network made sure she looked beautiful. She gave tips on how to identify a person who could set off a bomb. One month ago, before we came to Turkey for the summer, a bomb blew up in a historic site, killing both tourists and Turks. Then they reminded us of another bomb. The segment ended with a woman in a headscarf crying. She held her palms to the sky like bowls. The bomb went off and my children were blown away like scraps of paper.

I translate this for Cooper.

I explain to him what the news anchor said. We must, she urged, look for a drugged eye, a backpack, someone muttering to Allah so he will hear him. I add that I may look like this some days, a muttering person, but because I dress in some sort of western fashion and have a generally polite look on my face, no one will suspect me.

But I'm not sure, I admit to him. I say, I was googling my headache while this happened. I wasn't really watching.

Wow, he says, scanning my clothes, my face. Yeah, your tight jeans and sneakers. He reaches to touch my hair.

Nothing will happen, I repeat. It's you I'm worried about. They can see your head of hair from miles away.

He thinks about this. He pencils faces into the portraits he's framed. He wonders whether this bomb segment was racist, as it would be in America. In the very middle of his sketch of Istanbul, what I thought was the river has become a cemetery. The internet continues to tell me my headache could be dehydration, aneurysm, stroke, brain tumor, worry.

I convince my grandmother to take a taxi to the Bosphorus with me. The taxi hunkers down Nispetiye through traffic before we merge onto the winding two-lane road at what feels like a ninety-degree angle downhill. We drive down the steep hill in a slow, quiet procession. My grandmother wears a blue cardigan and a matching blue knit shirt with black pants. When we finally get to the river and climb out of the taxi I tell her she looks like a movie star. We walk along the water, an alarming, electric blue, for as long as she wants and stop at a café with seats on the river when she gets tired. In the distance, we can make out the Marmara, and the shipping barges multiplying in the horizon. The gulls lift, soar, and fall into the water.

Look at the Boğaz, she says. It's the widest river in the world.

I think it's actually the narrowest, I say, or a very narrow strait.

I'll die before I ever leave Turkey again. Even to visit you and Alara and your mother.

We can come here, I tell her especially because I already am doing so.

Sure, she says. You can stay with me. She gestures again to the river, as if the Boğaz alone is where she lives. She means to say Istanbul.

I already am, I point out.

That's true, she says. *Allah'aşükür.*

The week before, I had confessed to my month-long headache. When I told her about my headache a weight lifted inside my chest as if by crane.

It's a headache located not behind my eyes but at the very back of my head, I'd explained. My grandmother and I went to the hospital but I didn't stay as planned in the machine that first time. I'd pressed the panic button, and the kind man reading my brain released me. Here, I could've sworn he'd said, holding my brain on a petri dish. Take care. And I am trying to, to take care. I google my symptoms each time I have wi-fi. The last time I googled I was led to a page on humorism. The theory of the four humors was first developed in Ancient Greece, but became popular in Islamic medicine, too. This was before science.

Can we go again, to the hospital, I ask my grandmother.

Sure. She orders us tea. Her hand shakes as she hands the menu to the waiter.

It's a weird headache, I say. I can still read while it goes.

That's okay, baby. She gives me a careful look. Do you want me to come with you to the graveyard?

No, I say.

I bought flowers, she says. Did you see them?

No.

I left them by the entrance. You should take them to the grave.

Okay.

When are you going?

Maybe after my headache goes away.

Is he coming with you?

I'm not sure.

The graveyard is a ten-minute walk from my grandmother's apartment. It rests in the middle of the modern city, which makes its presence not an ominous, suburban haunt, but one determined to be at the center of everyday life. Everyday life, after all, built itself around this very cemetery, one of the first modern ones, not made up of the ancient graves that hold the first Ottomans. In the cemetery, you see the steel high-rise buildings in the distance, straight spines working into the sky. I was only there once, last winter, days after Baba died in the kitchen while boiling water for tea. It had snowed the night before so the cemetery was white. At the funeral, my younger sister and I held hands for ten minutes.

The four humors that pump through my body determine my character, temperament, mood. Blood, phlegm, black bile, and choler. The excess or lack of body fluids in you designates how you should be.

I don't know what choler is and when I google it, they bring me to a link asking whether *choler* is a scrabble word.

Who is *they?* asks Cooper when I report my internet finds. We are at my grandmother's, who is tired from shopping for bargains on towels all day. The window is open and a breeze moves through the apartment, carrying cat, gull, and car sounds from the street into the room. We lounge on her sofa and google bodily fluids and Hippocrates the Greek healer, who first worked this theory out. Cooper is so curious about words. He wants to take a magnifying glass to each person he meets to see what they speak. It's not enough to hear them.

My wants: to tell him that I am very unhappy and have been for quite some time. I would say, I think you are so optimistic that you believe nothing could be wrong with me.

When we began dating sophomore year, he told me in his dorm room on his twin-sized dorm bed that he was amazed at how in the time he had known me I had not been sad once. One year later, when Baba died in the kitchen while boiling water for tea, Cooper repeated this statement.

It has not yet been acknowledged that I build walls against others. It is the strongest thing I have built thus far.

Choler, it turns out, is yellow bile. Phlegm makes you sleepy and sluggish, but when mixed with choler you may transform into something suddenly serene and stable. Black bile is melancholy, and blood is the "best" humor, the kind that pumps you into a balanced, patient person. One website deems those who are mostly blood able "to judge people and situations well, and to contain his or her own shifts of moods, as well as those of others."

Wow, says Cooper. He hovers his finger over my computer screen to point out the last sentence, which warns that an excess of blood can nonetheless produce indifference to the fate of others. We agree that many people suffer from this blood condition.

The humors theory prevailed until the nineteenth century, when another man discovered germs. But I believe in fluids more than germs. They say that St. Margaret Mary Alacoque, who was visited by Christ in a yearlong series of revelations, suffered from an excess of blood. She was his chosen instrument, St. Margaret says, but she could not get the others to believe her. Christ asked her to initiate the Feast of the Sacred Heart. Christ permitted her to rest her head on his radiant, torn-up heart. To cure her ailments, the priests decided to bleed her out once a month. They cut her on her white thigh and had her sit in a stone basin. But my understanding of Christianity is limited and mostly googled. I am unsure what they did with her blood.

The second time we go to the hospital, a woman motions for my grandmother to sit down. I smile graciously at her. Her eyes are a rare blue for a Turk. She is a doctor.

My grandmother resists. Oh, but I am not seeing you today. She is.

I am not sick, I say.

What? asks my grandmother.

Who is sick? asks the doctor. She looks at her cell phone.

I have Parkinson's, says my grandmother, but it is not very serious.

Okay, I announce, maybe I am sick. I do not know with what.

I also have high blood sugar, my grandmother confesses.

The doctor is confused. Who is sick? She repeats, suddenly very stern.

Me, I'm sick. My head hurts.

She brings me to a small changing room and hands me a white robe and slippers. My grandmother is behind the door. She asks me if I want her to come in.

That's okay, I say. Thank you.

I am made to remove my necklace before climbing onto the flat bed and entering the white tube. The necklace belonged to my mother and from its gold chain hangs an Arabic prayer, the one Baba taught me. I dip this chain under my shirt's neckline each time I'm at an airport, but in bodegas the men behind the counters read the prayer I carry and nod. When American friends or strangers reach out and touch it, I can always feel their hand on my chest, near my neck, as they ask me what it means.

I have to stay in the machine this time, because both visits have now carved out my savings. It is forever before they pull me out of the MRI machine. The white steel tube reads me. I will myself to feel as calm as a tank full of still water. I think of ways to distract myself. I make up stories of me having sex with strangers, but an image of Cooper and his ex-girlfriend floats in, and I wonder if the ex-girlfriend knows about me. I have imagined us running into one another at bars or at museums or on street corners in New York. I imagine what he would do if it happened. I want to know would he touch her arm, her hand, her back. I want to know would he speak to her with feeling in front of me. I get bored. I begin counting the seconds on my hands with my fingers in groups of ten, because they say that is the only way to get your brain read without having your brain walk out on you.

My grandmother's new medicine arrives at the pharmacy and I go to pick it up. I also buy lavender-scented hand lotion and, on the street, more cigarettes. The man running the newsstand remarks on my preference for menthols and also my strange Turkish accent. I tell him I grew up in America, but to not worry, I am still Turkish. He nods in approval. I am to inject the clear liquid drug into my grandmother's bloodstream three times a day. My aunt, who is afraid of blood, comes over to make sure I do everything correctly. She wants me to put the needle in. I think of myself as one well-meaning, pious man in the mob of villains who bled out St. Margaret. But those who suffer from excess blood are too passionate, which my grandmother is too old for. She suffers from old age, an excess of phlegm, and in paintings on the internet St. Margaret is dressed in black and her moon-shaped white face stares back at me from inside her habit.

We drink tea in the living room as my grandmother prepares a plate of food. She's avoiding me and the syringe in my hand. The news is on, and the new prime minister sits with his colleagues at a table, eating lunch. The new prime minister's wife sits at a table in the same restaurant but across the room. She eats alone, her face to her food. I can see her fork stab eggplant and the red tomato oil the eggplant sits in. She eats slowly. The camera is in her face. The news anchor tells us about her, and about this fact that she does not eat at the same table as her husband and the people with whom he runs the country.

My aunt waves her arm at the screen. We didn't grow up like this, she says. We grew up wearing miniskirts. We didn't even wear long socks.

And now, I say, it's not like you can wear miniskirts any longer.

Nobody needs to see my legs now, it's true. She nods with force and continues. It's the men who need to cover their heads, maybe that will open their brains.

My aunt calls Cooper my fiancé. She inspires the others to do the same. It's unclear whether they know he is no fiancé of mine, that dating does not always work that way in this country or the one I am really from.

What kind of dress will you wear at the wedding, my aunt asks. She pours me more tea and I hold the glass by its thin waist. What shape will the neckline be?

I don't know, I say. But I do like the kind that illuminates the collarbone.

Yes, she says. Did you know mine was like that? My collarbone, we put eyeshadow on it so it sparkled.

I have seen the pictures. They are framed in my family's living room in New York, on the shrine of things they left behind in Turkey. On a coffee table, photographs of each relative, because if they visit us in America they want to make sure they are represented. This aunt did not like the way she appeared in the original photograph of her that we framed, where she was shown graduating from middle school. She brought her wedding photo as a replacement. My aunt is flanked by her own grandmother, and my grandmother, and they stand in a line with their hands on one another's waists, a basket weave of arms in white and black lace. Their collarbones gleam and blur in the photographs, like they'd already become ghosts.

She suddenly looks worried. Is he attached, very strongly, to any family names?

Maybe, I say. His middle name is Bartholomew, after his great-grandfather.

You have to make sure your own names are given priority.

I say nothing. I do want those names, too. To brand my children with a name like my own, one my family can pronounce. But I do not want to give my children an alien name, a mispronounced name, a dead name, a name that other people—strangers, teachers, lovers—bury alive upon speaking. My own name, Sibel, Americans think means a Greek prophet of doom, but the Turks think the name comes from Arabic, meaning a single raindrop between earth and sky. It may also be the Turkic name for an Anatolian goddess of mothers.

At least the child could have blue eyes, my aunt mentions after a while.

I think of my sister, who wears purple eyeliner to summon the green shards in her iris. She shaved off the first syllable of her name and now goes by Lara.

It won't work, I say.

You're right. The Turks have genes too strong for that.

My grandmother walks in with a tray stacked with tiny dessert plates and baklava and fresh cherries. Piles of fruit and fat.

I wouldn't trade all of my grandchildren for one blue-eyed child, she announces.

My aunt is appalled. I never said that's what I suggested she do. I'm only saying maybe something good will come out of it.

She doesn't have much to choose there, you know. She turns to me. We knew long ago that the boys over there would be foreigners. She uses a flat cake knife to lift a baklava from its box and pushes it onto a plate with her thumb. She uses the Turkish word *yabanci*, which formally translates to "stranger" but has come to mean "not Turkish."

My friends have so many sons, complains my aunt, but Sibel doesn't like them.

I do, I say. I do like them. They are very attractive to me.

My grandmother turns to me. She draws the cake knife through the air. Don't say it if you don't mean it. Your Baba, if he hears, his heart will rise from the ground and you will break it again.

Baba is dead, I point out. And he never met him.

My grandmother raises her eyebrows.

How can we know what he'd think.

It isn't that easy to understand, being a father. My aunt exhales.

He's dead, I repeat.

And what about your mother in New York, who works two jobs, only to come home and cook, only to make sure you have a place to settle?

She's there because she would never leave, I say. Because her and Baba said a million times that coming back would be an act of cowardice. And because of Lara.

They decide to ignore me. I tell them my head aches, that I will lie down in bed. I can feel the thing in my head between my ears and it bangs and bangs. I am in bed and think of my aunt, who will be forced now to put the needle through her mother's arm.

Just as I came to Istanbul for the summer with a mission in mind, so did Cooper. His grandmother, after graduating from college in America, worked in Istanbul for two years. This was after the end of World War II. She taught at an American girls' school. The same school is now a coed high school in the green hills of Boğaziçi, its buildings between the river and the flat, wide roads at the top of the hill.

Cooper loves to talk about his grandmother. He does so now in his apartment. Today is the hottest one yet and we put the fan at an angle where it hits my damp neck, his chest. Cooper's apartment has no air conditioner, something he finds meaningful. His place is on a narrow street of crumbling, slanted buildings in the middle of a steep hill. One strong earthquake would bury this neighborhood, although I'm unsure if earthquakes are most effective at high or low elevations.

Cooper tells me that his grandmother never talked about that time in her life. It was before she met the man who would become his grandfather, who, at the same time, was serving in the Philippines.

They say, Cooper continues with excitement, she almost married a Turkish man. I don't know what happened. She came back to California two years later, with a suitcase full of silk scarves, towels, and black charcoal sketches she drew of the women in headscarves. Remember, he says, recalling the one time I visited his family's home in California, we framed those sketches. They're hung up in my kitchen.

They're beautiful, I say. I remember feeling moved and transported before them. I remember having told my Baba that his grandmother worked in Turkey. I'd told him about the sketches and he got upset. Women don't wear all black there, and especially not on their heads, I remember he'd said. He'd paced around the entire island in our kitchen with the intensity of circling the globe. My mother then sat him down by pressing on his shoulders. She'd motioned toward her own heart. Don't tire yourself out, she'd told him, and he'd held her gaze and nodded.

Last winter, Baba died in the kitchen while boiling water for tea.

We sit on Cooper's bed as he digs in his pocket for his phone. It's so hot he's taken off his shirt and he's more excited than he's been all month and each time he sees I've stopped paying attention, he touches my jaw to lead my head from its view of the window and the streets outside to face him, inside this room. His hand is on my jaw, his fingers running over my mouth. His other hand holds his phone to his ear. Finally he manages to get in contact with the administration at his grandmother's school.

I have a strange request, Cooper says on the phone, my grandmother worked at this school when it was a girls' school in the 1940s. He takes his hand off my mouth and his eyes vacantly look into mine. I hear a muffled voice on the other end. Cooper laughs.

Yes, her spirit has sent me back here. Do you happen to have anything of hers, any papers, formal documents?

Outside, a group of small boys throw around a rubber ball and yell freshly acquired insults at one another. They call each other pussies and vaginas and sons of whores. In the distance is the river, and farther back, the tall minarets far enough away to look like needles. I watch them through the thin, skin-colored curtains pulled over the window that looks out to dusty downhill street. A younger sister, or maybe love interest, stands at the edge of their circle. She has her thin arms planted on her hips. She's watching the game. From my spot at the window I see that she wears a green plastic clip in the shape of a bird in her hair. It looks like she wants to join but her brother, this boy, shoves her and her head hits the steps of the building across from us, the building with a window directly across from me. If I threw down a wooden board I could walk across, over the crumbling street and into this home. I look into this window each day.

We are scheduled to visit the school three days later. Cooper wears his loose white shirt and, around his neck, a lanyard holding his hospital ID in a soft plastic case. He wears it everywhere he goes. We wait at the security gate, where we show the guards our identification. We wait for ten minutes before they decide to let us in.

The school is on one of Istanbul's many hills, the security gate planted at the top by the road and residential complexes, the main buildings a few car-minutes down the hill among hard, tall trees. If you walk farther downhill you'll meet the river. The women at administration are very friendly. One asks me in Turkish if I'm an alum, and I tell her a polite no. The same woman gives Cooper a package of his grandmother's papers.

We made photocopies, she explains in English. So it's for you to keep. She smiles at Cooper. She asks if she can help with anything else.

We remark on how kind this gesture is. We stand in the entrance to the school, next to the Turkish flag, and open the package. We remark on how his grandmother looks very similar to a Turk in her photograph ID. Her nose ends in a small hook like mine. We do not know why this is significant.

The package also contains her application essay and her résumé. Her essay is written in a neat, tiny script. She explains that she wants to teach in Turkey because the world is in a very fragile state right now. We have to come together and understand one another's differences in a time like this, she explains. The date on her essay confirms that she applied one week after the end of World War II. In her identification card for the school, they have written out her name and under her name and photograph, her religion. They stamped PROTESTANT in Turkish beneath the rectangular photograph of her face.

That's so funny, he says, she wasn't religious at all.

They had to write something, I say. My identification card says ISLAM.

We continue to sift through her papers, heavy in a packet, light when holding up just one sheet. I want more packages, receipts for clothing and *kebap*, evidence of how she spent time. I want to know how she liked it here. I want to know what liquid humor she considered herself, if she had to choose. I want to see the man she almost married, the Turk. I want to know who broke whose heart in half and who kept which pieces.

I say, this feels like we are traveling through time.

Traveling through time is harder than I thought, Cooper says.

But we're doing it now.

I mean, emotionally hard.

It begins to rain and we want to make sure the papers don't get wet. He slips the papers under his shirt and we run to a wide set of stone stairs sheltered by green trees. In the distance, the river glitters under the sun. He has a peculiar look on his face.

What? I ask.

Don't you want to find your dad's records, too?

I wave my hand through the air. Oh, I already know those. He told me all his high-school stories. He said all the boys spent hours cooking up plots to talk to the American women teachers after class. He said he managed to swing one date with his teacher.

What?

It wasn't a real date, they got tea and *simit* from a café nearby to talk about his most recent exam and also what he wanted to be when he grew up.

They probably have a whole file, though. And with more information because he went here more recently, and the school became bigger and more organized.

Maybe, I say. Maybe I'll go ask.

He stands up. Well?

I make to get up. Why don't we wait until it stops raining?

You don't want to do it, do you?

I do, I really do.

He looks at me. He moves toward me, sitting on the step against the stone wall. He corners me like this.

Look at me, he says, please.

This place reminds me of the place we went hiking in California, I offer.

Last year we hiked for one day in the redwoods and smoked and had sex against a tree. We went off the trail and hiked a hill and there were people underneath us on the path. We could hear their voices climbing toward us. Cooper had his whole hand in me. He reached up into my ribs and held my wet organs in a hard fist. I remember feeling calm. We'd looked at one another, me and Cooper, and he'd continued to use his hand to get something from me.

I know less and less about you sometimes, he says. He's still towering above me, behind him the trees and blue river. I say nothing. His eyes water. I want to take a boat and oar through the blue salt of them. I want to ask him how can you love somebody so lonely. I want to hold his body down like a board for an answer.

He sits down next to me on the stone step. We're sheltered from the rain. I point out the glittering river between the wet trees and bird calls.

The necklace I usually wear each day is now missing. I took it off for both MRIs, and the taking off and putting back on created a schedule I was not used to. I looked for it before our dinner plans. We took the metro to Istiklal, where we padded down the narrow street to Pera, where the buildings look Parisian and have windowsills hosting flowerpots. We show visitors our most beautiful streets, which happen to be the ones the Europeans built in the 1800s, when they came here for business on the Orient Express and needed someplace of their own to stay, someplace less Muslim.

We meet up with my Turkish friends at a restaurant. We dunk bread in eggplant and tomato dips. My friends are in agreement that the nervous energy on Istiklal is enough to make them stay home. They mention that Istanbul is not what it used to be. I mention that Istanbul has always been a place for migrants. By the late 1800s half of Istanbul's population were migrants. They continue to ask me why I came here this summer, when most of my life is in New York, when New York is not dangerous. They text me the dates that they hope to visit so I don't forget. One friend who sits closest to me complains about her boyfriend. How he got her sick. She coughs on our dips and bread.

I think everyone is sick these days, I say. I still can't get rid of my headache.

It's true, another friend says, nodding. Her name is Dilek and she has an opinion on everything. You know, she continues, Americans don't believe in AC sickness?

Not this again, says Cooper. He smiles.

I explain to my friends that each time I get a sore throat from leaving the AC on, or from sleeping with my hair wet, or even the window open, Cooper doesn't think it possible. Every time he says, you were probably already getting sick.

My friends laugh and shake their heads. Dilek bats her eyelashes, these dark webs, around the table, landing on Cooper. Dilek is the daughter of Baba's best friend. They met during high school, years ago, when the country was split up more than it is today, maybe less, but it is impossible to tell. I've known her since childhood. I watch her, thinking of the girl who used to tell me that I played with dolls incorrectly, that I should know more Turkish curse words as well as proper, consistently implemented grammar if I wanted any kind of power. She would take the plastic male doll from my hand and make him kiss the female one.

But it's not possible, Cooper says. He looks around the table at our blank faces. Mine is blank in solidarity, because I know it's stupid to think you can get sick from that but also I do, really, contract a cold from sleeping with my hair wet at my nape. And when everyone tells me it is true, that I will get sick from these things, how am I supposed to believe something different?

I feel good with these friends. I feel *keyif*, an untranslatable word that I have tried to translate for Cooper but for all his love of words he does not seem to understand. It's the first time I have felt *keyif* in months and its closest approximation in English is the feeling of joy. I want to know should I not have brought him here with them. I want to know if, had he not been here, I would have explained to them what I felt. I want to explain to somebody how I've felt.

My friends light cigarettes at the dinner table. I ask one friend for a cigarette, pretending I don't have my own in my purse, hidden in the pouch with a zipper. Cooper shoots me a look from across the table. His face is compassionate, understanding, but he wants to tell me that I will die if I continue this and I expect he does not want me to die. He wants me to stop smoking. But he cannot want everything. He does not know what this cigarette feels like releasing itself in my throat and opening my chest as if with two strong arms. Before we leave the restaurant I find my gold necklace in my purse, coiled up under my hidden cigarettes.

There is something happening in the main square, so our taxi driver, who is upset, tells us he has to take the alternate route. He curses. I tell him it's okay, we have no place to be. Cooper agrees and tells him thank you in Turkish. I repeat it, too, a tranquil thank you, and look out the rolled-down window. I begin to bullet-point the inside of my head with each event that took place in Istanbul, each life zapped off or imprisoned, each public square, nightclub, or metro station now an open-air mausoleum.

Each taxi I take back to my grandmother's passes by the cemetery. We drive by its white gates now and I have still not visited his grave. At night the white stone gates glow and behind their glow the high buildings are lit up for miles. The white stone gates are engraved with a verse from the Koran that tells me every living thing will taste death. Last winter, Baba died in the kitchen while boiling water for tea. We spent the next ten hours on a flight to Turkey. I held my mother's damp hand during the airplane ride. We learned that you can transport a body with you on the same passenger plane you are traveling on or you can have it fly separately on a cargo plane. The funeral house arranges it for you. I must have been on many airplanes on which there was a corpse in the luggage below me. But it is your right to transport this body in any of the given number of transportation means they offer. My sister was our researcher and spokesperson for this information, because, as she mentioned to me and my mother, we had not done anything useful for days. The funeral was here in this same graveyard but the graveyard was different. It was covered in snow and when they lowered his body into his grave some snow fell in, too, with him, which my grandmother said was a good thing, a good sign for him. Not him, his soul. Now it confuses me where I will be buried. Next to my mother and Baba in Turkey, or in America, with the American children I will have?

I put my head on Cooper's shoulder. I scratch and scratch at my neck and my necklace chain breaks. It spills into my hand like gold water.

We spend most nights eating dinner with my grandmother. Cooper and my grandmother are now able to communicate remarkably. Just now, after clearing the dishes, I come back to the living room and there they are, perched on either end of the sofa, speaking using their hands. Their eyes widen and shrink to convey emphasis. Cooper, his hands cupped to form tiny mountain peaks, remarks on how similar Turkey's terrain is to California's and my grandmother looks wistful, absorbed, as if she can see the mountains and trees and blue water of California, a place she's never been. I watch her seeing it and want to know exactly what familiar Turkish mountains she's conjuring as reference, what images her brain builds to fill his statement with shape. Us listeners summon image after image to visualize what we're told but we'll never know what shapes other people use to see.

Cooper picks up an apricot and holds it high in the space between them. He uses a mixture of English and Turkish words to say, look, we are both known to grow apricots. They marvel at the apricot as if it has stepped onto a stage, a spotlight illuminating the small and round performer's orange, edible skin.

The television is on behind them and the news tells of violence at the eastern border. They show men, their faces hidden beneath black fabric, pressing another man's face to the ground until his legs jerk. Each news broadcaster's voice is indistinguishable from the next. They speak only in panicked tones, rising intonations, a tornado of anxiety. It is impossible for me to tell whether the country is divided due to each broadcaster's apocalyptic tone, or whether this apocalyptic tone is due to the country's division.

But they make sure each broadcaster looks beautiful. Today, her mouth is painted red, her hair dyed a plastic yellow. Her smile is faint, visible only on her lips.

I turn to watch Cooper and my grandmother again. Seeing the two of them communicating, as if connected by brain or heart or some other powerful organ I can't make use of in myself, forces me to stand up. I want a cigarette but have no excuse to go outside at this hour, when the two people I love most in this country are right here, communing. I go to my bedroom, Baba's former bedroom. On the wall is a framed photograph of my parents marrying. It's a grainy, almost green photograph. They're dancing, and I can see the muscle in my mother's calf flexed from her high heel. Her hands hold Baba's face. It's hard for me to look at it, his face. Somebody is always looking back.

The next day is hot and clear. A bomb goes off at the airport. It is sometime after lunch and I'm at my grandmother's and we divide up her phone book to call people as we simultaneously take calls, and my mother, she calls, very upset, saying we should have brought my grandmother here, to America, to see the better doctors but of course she didn't listen and of course I call Cooper first although I know he is working at the eye hospital near the university and has no business at the airport because we have planned to leave Turkey together and we are even sitting together on our flight back to New York. I imagine he is finally fed up. I imagine he wants to go home already. That his family, who told him to be careful in Turkey, was correct. They will call me soon, I presume. I imagine they will call me selfish. I imagine what people will tell me when I tell them I have not yet visited Baba's grave. I imagine what Cooper will say to me later that night, at my grandmother's, eating dinner. I don't know what I'm doing here, he will say. He will put his fork down. He will wait for me to explain to him what, if anything, he is doing here. I wait for one hour with no answer on his whereabouts.

Last winter Baba died in the kitchen while boiling water for tea. You have four chambers in your heart. And a diseased heart is unusually large, as large as a metronome.

We see one another later that night. We stand in the kitchen between the pantry and the wall of hanging pans and my mouth is pressed against his. He lets me start kissing him, here in my grandmother's kitchen, despite the rule that says we cannot kiss in public or in the presence of family, and I begin to think I'm this sort of powerful, I'm not that sort of sad. The call to prayer goes and goes and clears up the furniture stacked high in the small room of my head. I want to know what it is that makes kissing feel good. I want to know is it the opening. The balancing out of another bodily fluid: spit, which easily may contain regenerative qualities when shared with another. The humor theories do not mention this. They only mention your own body as containing fluids that you balance by diet, exercise, bloodletting, and other things that are between you and your body. They do not mention what other people can do for you. I want to turn the news off. I want him to open my head. I want to get him alone, without my family around us—especially the English-speaking ones who translate what he says for the others—and demand an answer. I will ask, What are you most afraid of?

Loneliness

Dying

Being lonely

I will put my hand around his white throat to find out which one makes his veins fill.

CHINESE GIRLS DON'T HAVE FAIRY TALES

by RITA CHANG-EPPIG

M Y MOTHER WAITED UNTIL I had moved the last of my boxes into my childhood home before she started in on me. As far as she was concerned, she was granting me a mercy with this reprieve. She turned the knob lock, flipped the two deadbolts, and slid the chain on the door guard into place. One couldn't be too careful in East Oakland. At my previous home in Malibu, my ex-husband and I had used only two of our locks: one on the front door and one on the French doors at the back, which opened onto our terraced patio. On warm evenings, we would lie on our sides on the uppermost tier, watching the waves of the Pacific pirouette dizzyingly toward shore.

"I thought you would have more boxes," my mother said in that tone I knew all too well.

"Life is full of surprises."

"I can't believe you signed a prenup. This is what your American ideas get you."

I dropped the box in my arms, and it landed on the faded mauve carpeting with a tinkle instead of a thud—the box containing my various beauty products, I supposed. In the end, no lipstick, no gilded glass bottle promising a radiant complexion, had been enough to keep him with me or to further my career as an actress. He left for a blonde in her twenties with the laser-cut collarbones of a malnourished fourteen-year-old, and the agency couldn't find me any work that didn't involve me either smoking an opium pipe in a turn-of-the-century whorehouse or doing math in the background while the main characters debated how to stop the comet from reaching Earth.

"I'm going to take a shower," I said, heading deeper into the house. She didn't move to stop me or to trail behind me, listing her grievances. This was about as merciful as I'd ever seen her in my thirty-five years. Even she felt pity for me, and this woman pitied no one, except for maybe those sick kids featured during the television charity drives that she used to make me watch. "Look at how unfortunate those kids are," she would say to me. "And you complained just because we couldn't afford a birthday party for you this year. What they wouldn't give. What they wouldn't give to be you."

She didn't bring up the divorce again until after dinner, when we were clearing the table. She began by humming lightly, which I pretended not to hear. Then she fell silent, as though the absence of sound might unnerve me enough that I would give in and broach the topic. She flounced back and forth in front of me more times than strictly needed while she cleaned, wearing her perfume of cooking oil and dollar-store shampoo about her the way Grace Kelly wore scarves. Funny how I'd never really noticed the scent until Elle Bannon announced during our sixth-grade bake sale, for which my mother had been pressured into volunteering, that she was feeling "nauseous" because something smelled like "deep-fried potpourri."

Finally, she said, "It's because she's white. He's white. I told you this would happen."

"She's younger, and he's an asshole having a midlife crisis. That's all there is to it."

"Then why didn't he leave you for a twenty-year-old Asian girl? You're from different cultures."

"And what culture am I from? Oakland culture? Dental-school dropout culture? I've never even lived outside of California."

"Fine, fine, you're 'American,'" she said, snatching a glass away from me as though rescinding a trophy I had acquired through steroid use. "That's even worse. You Americans with your fairy tales and your love-at-first-sight and your—" She made a gagging sound here. "Generations of little girls raised to think they're princesses. Chinese girls would never be this dumb. We don't even have fairy tales."

"What are you talking about?" I yelled. "Chinese people totally have fairy tales." I had the sudden, irrational belief that if I just argued her down from this claim, then I would be, by extension, right about everything else that she and I had been arguing about my entire life.

"Not the stupid American type, we don't. We have myths. Legends. But not the happily-ever-after Disney garbage you were raised on. We know better."

There was no reasoning with her once the fight had escalated to a certain point. She once maintained, in earnest, that acupuncture was a perfectly effective treatment for cancer (the cousin of a friend of a friend was completely cured). She, a woman with a college degree from Taiwan, espoused something so ridiculous just because to back down would have been to admit that she might occasionally be wrong.

"I think we should take a break from this conversation until we are both calmer," I said, lowering my volume and slowing my pace, doing my best imitation of my former therapist. Whatever pity that woman had felt for me regarding my divorce had been quickly overridden by my inability to continue paying her. My mother once called her my "most expensive friend."

"I'm calm," my mother shouted at my back. I locked the door behind me.

My childhood bedroom was now partly storage space. Boxes took up one corner. Old mops smelling of fake pine took up another. A Popsicle-stick cabin on the bookshelf propped up a family portrait from junior high. The leg of the frame had broken off. My face was all braces, pimples, and blunt home-cut bangs. My mother was vacuum-packed into her wedding *qipao*, which she'd insisted on wearing because tradition something something. My father wore a benign expression. That was how I mostly remembered him—benign like a small faint mole in the crook of a knee. He'd smiled frequently but rarely widely. He said very little to me outside of daily greetings. "Fighting" between him and my mother consisted of my mother yelling and him nodding with his eyes playing over something in the distance as though he were contemplating a different matter entirely. My first year of dental school, he announced over the phone that he was moving back to Taiwan because the climate there suited him more. My mother said nothing (if she did, I didn't hear her). Neither answered any of my questions. They never even got divorced. These days I heard from him by phone a few times a year. Every year for my birthday, he sent a package of Taiwanese confections with a note that read WISHING YOU GOOD HEALTH. For a while I was convinced that he was gay, that he had moved back to Taiwan to pursue a love from his youth. Then I realized that even that scenario was too poetic, too colorful. My parents had simply fallen out of love with each other, or perhaps more accurately they had never been in love in the first place, their relationship having been initiated by their respective families because of his solitary nature, her advancing age and financial needs, and their parents' desire for grandchildren. I could count on one hand the number of times I'd seen them kiss.

I lay down on the pilling comforter, scanning the bookshelf. Tomes sheltered under dust like a child under the covers with a flashlight after bedtime: girl meets handsome stranger, girl discovers she has a special destiny, girl becomes someone better than she thought she ever could be. I'd moved down to Los Angeles after leaving school to make it, *it* being some combination of commercial and critical fame that would afford me the Italian marble fireplace on which I could display my awards. Then I'd met Allen, who was handsome in his own hawkish way and an up-and-comer in his firm, though I told myself I would have felt the same way even if that second part hadn't been true. He was very direct, some might say gauche, so whenever he praised me for my appearance and talent, which he did a lot in the early days, I couldn't help but believe. Soon the Cinderella fantasy was underway (the thing about Cinderella is that, unlike many of her counterparts, she didn't start out a princess—her happy ending was not a birthright but a reward). All that was left was waiting for my fairy godmother to send me a role that would wing me skyward.

A book from middle school, *Stories of Adventure from Around the World*, caught my attention. The plastic hardcover, made to look like leather, was limned with barely legible curlicue script and smelled of cheap floor mats left in the sun.

When I came back out, she was sitting in front of the television, watching a Chinese period drama that she'd watched before—she had a tendency to repeat her dramas to the point of being able to repeat lines, partly because she couldn't afford the premium channels from East Asia and partly, I suspected, because she had grown wary of surprises. I even recognized the scene that was on. The main female character had just had her pinky finger cut off as punishment for supposed infidelity (the accusation turned out to be false, of course, because audience members sympathize only with female characters who are blameless). Covering the stump was a thin cone made of gold foil. It looked like the curled, pointed slipper of a sprite who had sprung from a flower.

"What about the one with the white snake?" I said, shaking the book at her.

"That's not a fairy tale."

"Why not? It's got a romance, a happy ending."

"What?"

"Ugh, just listen." I opened the book.

LEGEND OF THE WHITE SNAKE

Once upon a time, there was a scholar named Xu. One rainy day, while crossing the bridge into town, he met a beautiful woman named Bai. She had flowing, lustrous hair, hands that were as if carved from white jade, and delicate red lips like a drop of blood in a porcelain bowl. He had found her standing in the rain and lent her an umbrella because he couldn't bear to see such a beautiful woman suffer. They fell in love and married. Unbeknownst to him, Bai was actually an ancient snake spirit who had meditated for many centuries to develop the ability to take on human form. Though her love for him was real, she hid her identity from him out of fear that he would leave her if he learned the truth.

One day, a powerful Buddhist monk passed by their home. Sensing that Bai was actually a spirit, he swore to free the young scholar from her grasp. First, he approached Xu in his monk's robe and said, "Though she appears a lady fair, of her lies you must beware." But Xu dismissed his words and banished him from his home. Then, he approached Xu dressed as a fellow scholar and said, "Clear the mind of your lady fair, from your true path you must not err." But Xu dismissed his words and banished him from his home. Finally, he approached Xu dressed as a peddler and convinced Xu to serve Bai a poisoned wine. He said, "To honor well your lady fair, let her take of this wine so rare." Bai drank the wine and was transformed back into a snake. Seeing his wife's true form, Xu passed out from shock. The monk seized the opportunity, capturing Bai and imprisoning her in a temple.

When Xu awoke, he realized that he still loved Bai despite the secret she had kept from him, so he enlisted the help of Bai's lady-in-waiting, who had revealed herself to be a fellow snake spirit when Bai was taken. They defeated the monk, freed Bai from her prison, and Xu and Bai lived happily ever after. Love conquers all. The end.

"Who got you this book?" my mother said after I had finished. "That's not how the story goes at all. That's how an American would tell the story."

"You got me this book. For Christmas."

"No I didn't."

"I wanted a Tamagotchi. This book was in the clearance bin. I remember this very well."

She rolled her eyes. "You're misremembering. It's not even supposed to be a love story. It's a fable about staying on the right path, about obeying the order of the universe. First, the white snake defies nature by becoming human—she's a snake and should accept that she's a snake. Second, the scholar runs from his own responsibilities by giving into worldly temptations. And then the two of them think they can be together? Ridiculous." She crossed her arms and smirked, daring me to contradict her.

"So how does the story end?" I asked.

"The monk defeats the white snake, and the scholar goes back to studying."

"That's the dumbest ending I've ever heard."

"The ending is not the important part," she said. "The important part is everything else."

On the television screen, the woman was wailing into the sleeve of her robe, staining the dark-pink fabric red. Her husband, or some other man in the household, had deliberately kicked over the pail of water with which she'd been washing the floor.

"She married him to pay off her family's debt," my mother explained, even though I hadn't asked. "She's actually in love with a young man from her village. But they couldn't be together because he was too poor."

I said nothing. Before my parents met, my mother had seriously dated someone else, if the gossip of my extended family in Taiwan was to be believed. The whole thing had ended abruptly; she never told anyone what happened.

"This show reminds me of another Chinese legend," she said. "The one about the butterfly lovers. Do you know that one?"

I shook my head.

She stood and began rummaging through the drawers in the house. I asked her what she was looking for, assuming the answer would be a book, but she mentioned something about a folding fan. I asked her if she was feeling hot, which earned me a scoff. Looking a little dejected, she returned a few minutes later empty-handed. "I guess I don't need it," she said, "but it would have been nice for effect." And then she just stared at the ceiling for a while, muttering to herself.

"What are you doing?" I asked suspiciously.

"I'm telling a story," she said. "Did you think I was going to just read it? The way something is told matters. I took oral storytelling classes when I was in college and spent time at traditional storytelling salons with friends. A good storyteller interacts with the audience, makes the story come alive with commentary and examples. So much is lost when you rely on text."

I left her to mutter. On the screen, the main character had just run into her true love in the marketplace. He was going away to war. Inconsolable, she tore a piece of material from the inside of her sleeve and pressed it into his hand. She made him promise to carry it for luck.

My mother loudly tapped her hand on the coffee table once.

LEGEND OF THE BUTTERFLY LOVERS

Wet with tears, in unfinished dream
In deepest night before the voices of the palace sing
Her red cheeks still youthful, her first love severed
She reclines in incense smoke until dawn

In year 300 of the Eastern Jin dynasty, in the wealthy family Zhu, there was a young woman whose heart was full of the love of learning. But as a woman, she was forbidden from attending school, so she decided to enroll as a man. She wound her long straight hair into a single bun atop her head and put on a loose gray robe that hid her slim figure. At school, she met the young scholar Liang, whose pale skin and fine-boned hands indicated one who had spent his life around scrolls. He had the air of a kind, thoughtful man, always gazing at the birds in the trees.

Now everybody from my generation knows—young folks these days don't quite seem to grasp this—that love is a seed that must be nurtured, not a peony blossom that falls from the stem in full bloom. My childhood friend Min waited eight whole years before even planting a kiss on her husband-to-be! Anyway, the two scholars grew close over the years, and one day Zhu realized that she had fallen for Liang. But the inexperienced Liang misunderstood all of her attempts at disclosing her secret to him. Finally, she told him that she planned to set him up with her sister. I hope he will not be troubled by my deception, she thought.

When Zhu, posing as her own sister, revealed her true identity, Liang was overjoyed. The two lovers swore their loyalty to each other. But the revelation came too late. Zhu's parents had already promised her hand to a man from a wealthy family. Heartbroken, Liang fell ill and died a few months later.

On the day of the wedding, Zhu went to Liang's grave to pay her respects. She prayed to join him. Suddenly, his grave opened up, and she threw herself into it. The spirits of the two lovers emerged as butterflies and flew away together. Human will is powerless in the face of fate. The foolish fight fate; the wise accept.

She said the last part quickly and softly, signaling the end of her performance. I was taken aback and trying to hide it: she'd gestured, stood up at dramatic points, and contorted her features into a dozen expressions I'd never seen on her before. She'd even spoken Zhu's thoughts in a different voice. An American child who did such things might have been told that she should become an actress when she grew up. "So it's okay for a woman to dress up as a man?" I said finally. "She's not 'defying the universe' or whatever?"

"It's okay if she's doing it to study. Zhu is a sensible girl. She wants to apply herself. She doesn't confess her secret until she has finished school."

I groaned. "Yes, and because of that she gets married off to some guy she doesn't love, and Liang dies. How is that supposed to encourage anyone to follow in her steps?"

"Life's not fair."

I sat down on the far end of the couch, pulling my legs into my chest. Without turning away from her show, she reached out to pat my bare feet before covering them with a pillow. Her hand felt like a piece of tofu, chilled and slightly clammy. The woman on the screen was wailing again, this time over her son, who had died shortly after being born.

"I don't understand how all Chinese girls are not horribly depressed," I said.

"We have happy stories, too, like the one about the cowherd and the weaver girl. They're just not fairy tales." Once more she began staring off into space and muttering. Had she wanted to become a professional storyteller when she was a girl? She hardly ever talked about her past, as if, in leaving Taiwan behind, she'd also left her former self, the self that gushed and pantomimed and stayed out late at storytelling salons with friends. Maybe she didn't want to give me any ideas, or maybe she just didn't want to reopen any wounds.

A messenger from the battlefield had arrived. With him he carried the piece of material, now stained with blood. He delivered the fabric to the main character.

My mother tapped her hand on the table.

LEGEND OF THE COWHERD AND THE WEAVER GIRL

With deftness she weaves faint clouds
Stars in flight shine in grief
Ferried across the distant Milky Way
They meet in secret

("Wait, I think I know this one from somewhere," I interrupted. "Doesn't it go like this?")

A long, long time ago, two stars in the sky fell in love, even though they were forbidden from being together. When the wicked Queen of the Sky discovered their love, she banished one star to earth to be reincarnated as a cowherd. The other star was condemned to weave clouds forever.

("So you've heard this one," my mother said. "Except the Empress of Heaven wasn't wicked. The star Vega was her granddaughter. She simply didn't think the star Altair was good enough. It's like this.")

The star Altair was reborn as a sturdy young cowherd with clear eyes. He was poor, possessing nothing except a small house, a broken cart, and the faded blue tunic and trousers he wore. His only companion was an old ox that had once been the Golden Ox star, whom the Empress had cast down to earth for siding with the cowherd and the weaver girl, but the cowherd did not realize this. One day, the ox spoke. "Go to Bi Lian Lake today. You will find celestial maidens bathing there. If you take a maiden's dress, that maiden will be become your wife."

As fate would have it, the weaver girl was visiting the lake with the other celestial maidens that day. She had received a vacation from her duties from the Empress of Heaven. Who can say how the old ox knew this! When I was a little girl, there was a dog in my village who only barked when someone was about to die. Maybe animals sniff out secrets we humans can't! The cowherd did as his faithful companion suggested, stealing a red dress from a rock. Please let my faithful ox be right, he thought, for I wish to have a wife. At this point, any good listener would be able to guess to whom the dress belonged.

("I'd forgotten this part," I said. "The cowherd just seems like a creep now.")

What are you talking about? When the weaver girl saw him, she was so happy because she was finally being reunited with her love."

"He was looking to coerce her. Actually, he didn't even set out to coerce *her*. He was just looking to get some celestial-maiden tail. Any one of them would have been fine by him. It's so typical."

"It's just a story."

"No, you called it a *happy* story."

"Fine. You tell it."

"Fine.")

Tricked by the cowherd—don't roll your eyes, I'm just stating the obvious—the weaver girl married him and had two children. But soon enough the Empress of Heaven learned what had happened and ordered her guards to abduct the girl from her home. This poor girl just couldn't catch a break between her husband and her grandmother. It's like when you threatened to not attend the wedding because it didn't include any traditional Chinese elements, and instead of compromising, Allen just dug his heels in deeper because he didn't want to open the door to your demands. Anyway, wearing the magical hide of his old ox, the cowherd chased the guards into the sky. But when he had almost caught up, the Empress of Heaven waved her wand in a wide arc and created the Milky Way, permanently separating the cowherd from the weaver girl.

(My mother sighed loudly. "It was a hairpin. Chinese people don't use wands. Let me finish it.")

The lovers gazed at each other across the Milky Way and cried and cried. Witnessing this, the Empress, who is not wicked but simply burdened with having to keep order, softened her heart. She transformed the family into stars and decreed that, once a year, the cowherd and the weaver girl would be allowed to reunite by crossing a bridge of magpies. The pair lived happily ever after because one night of transcendent love a year is better than the slow decay that happens to even the most passionate relationships here on earth. This world does not permit things like unending love.

On the screen, the woman threw herself off a bridge. The end. I rubbed my feet, which had fallen asleep under the pillow while we were talking.

Dams burst in the veins and capillaries.

"Maybe it's culture, maybe it's just that she's younger," my mother said. "I don't really know. All I know is that when you called me crying at three in the morning that day, before you even told me anything, I already had a feeling. And I worried about what was going to happen to you. The house was in his name. You had no stable career. This is why I'd pressured you to go to dental school. Why I'd begged you to just settle down with someone stable."

Rage overtook me so quickly that I felt almost violated by it. "And how did that work out for you? Finding someone stable? Dad wasn't some hotshot lawyer like Allen. He just sold mattresses at the mattress store every day until he decided he couldn't fucking look at another mattress ever again and moved back to Taiwan. You stood behind a counter bagging doughnuts until pain from varicose veins forced you to quit. Why is it so crazy that I might have wanted to take a chance on some things?"

"Because you didn't have the good fortune to be able to take a chance! Your dad and I tried our best to give you the fortune to go out and chase your dreams, but sorry, we couldn't. You insisted on doing it anyway, probably because of all those stupid movies with the princes and castles. You were so busy daydreaming about your fairy tale that you forgot about the oldest story in the world."

She had fished a corner of the couch coverlet from the seams and was dabbing at her eyes with it. Suddenly she seemed broken, helpless. I hadn't been there when my father broke the news to her. Perhaps she had worn the same expression in that moment, or perhaps she'd simply nodded and gritted her teeth as though preparing to heft an immense weight, because she'd never really expected a happy ending. The ending was not the important part. The important part was getting through each day, putting dinner on the table, saving money for my college education, and sleeping in a divided bed with someone who never quite stopped being a stranger. The important part was accepting fate because if one wasn't a sick, starving child in a telethon, then one had no right to want anything else.

I felt terrible, but I didn't want to tell her that, not that she would have accepted my pity anyway. I offered her the pillow she'd placed on my feet. She took it and hugged it, resting her chin on it in a way that made her look almost childlike. I didn't say anything to comfort her out of fear that I would injure her further. I might have wrecked my life by taking chances, but in never taking chances, she had resigned herself to a life of unmet expectations. Confined herself to the tower, bolted the door, boarded the shutters.

No one can save you if you never stick your head out the tower window, but then, you never really think you're going to fall.

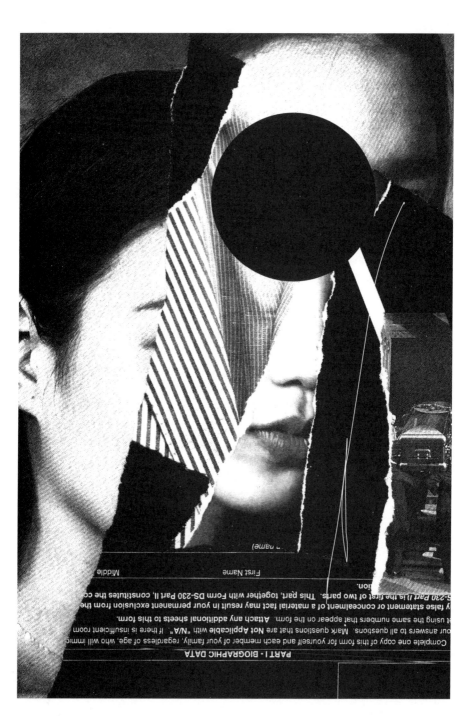

BRANDON

NOEL ALUMIT

B RANDON SILVERIO HEARD THE phone ringing. It was the special phone, located in the hallway, meant only for communication to and from the Philippines. He knew it was his mother. Who else would be calling him at three in the morning? He had moved to Los Angeles in 1962, twelve years ago, and since then he'd had to put up with occasional early morning calls from his mom. They were usually calls ordering Brandon to mail some product that wasn't available in the Philippines. ("Send some of that Jean Naté?" his mother said. "I think Revlon makes it. An American woman said it was big in the States. Send me some of that!") That was the price for being the only one in his family to move to America—he would have to buy things for them and send it home, he knew.

As the phone rang, Brandon thought of ignoring it. His son, Eric, could sleep through anything. His wife, Jane, could not. Jane stirred but he patted her shoulder letting her know that he would get it.

Brandon stumbled out of bed and made his way through the dark hallway.

"*Ano nang yari?*" Brandon said into the receiver.

"Why don't you properly greet a caller? Instead of saying, 'What happened?'"

"Sorry, Mom. Hello. Now, what happened?"

There was a pause, then his mother said, "I have to tell you some bad news."

Brandon leaned against the wall, the phone cradled in his shoulder.

"What's the matter, Mom?"

Brandon heard his mother sobbing, "It's Dad. Heart attack. He died this morning."

He dropped the phone, then reached down to get it. He stayed on the ground, sitting cross legged.

"Come home," she said. "You have to come home."

Home. Brandon looked at the pictures on the wall. There were photos of his new American life with his new American family. Brandon and Jane and Eric. His father would have been proud of the kind of husband and father he was making.

"Let me see what kind of time I can take off work," Brandon said. "I'll find the next flight back."

Brandon went to his bed, thinking about his father.

"Everything alright, sugar?" Jane said.

"No, my father died. I'm going to have to go home, back to Dagupan."

"Oh, baby, I'm sorry. I know how much you loved him."

Brandon kept photos of family members in their living room. It was fair to say photos of his father were the most prominent.

"Anything I can do?" Jane said.

"No. I'll be alright," he said. He wanted to cry, but didn't. He fingered the seams of his pajama pants, clothes he had made himself. He knew his father would be proud of the craftsmanship. He sat in bed, wondering how he'd make the trip back home work. He looked at Jane, who had resumed her sleep.

Brandon had met Jane at a concert in MacArthur Park in 1968. Meeting Jane was the best part of that year, one that saw the death of Martin Luther King, Jr. and Robert Kennedy.

Brandon had been with Jane for six years now, took an active part in raising Jane's son, Eric. He almost didn't want to date a woman with a kid, but Jane wore flowers in her hair, the way hippies did back then, and he couldn't resist how a daisy petal had fallen onto her face, appearing like a tear under her right eye.

Jane was also Filipino, born and raised in San Francisco. They didn't make Filipino girls like her in the Philippines. Jane said that she was proudly atheist and hadn't bothered marrying Eric's father, a white man from Sausalito. Jane was a carefree, open-minded woman. That meant a lot to Brandon.

Within twenty-four hours Brandon had made arrangements to return to the Philippines. Other Filipino men talked with Brandon, offering memories of the passing of their own fathers.

"You'll be one of the pallbearers, then?" one man asked.

"Yeah, sure," Brandon quickly replied.

Jane had packed his suitcase for his trip home. One suitcase belonged to him. Another suitcase was packed with gifts for his family. Brand-new Levi jeans that his brothers would love. American gossip magazines for their wives. Stuffed animals and candy for his nephews and nieces. Bath products for his mother. Not even a funeral diminished his role as gift-giver from the States.

"All set?" Jane asked.

"Yup," he replied. "Where's Eric?"

"In his room."

Brandon called out to him. "Eric, say good-bye to me."

"Bye," Eric hollered from down the hall.

"Eric," Brandon called, with a bit of grit in his voice.

A door opened and slammed. Eric showed up with his arms crossed. Brandon looked at the boy who was slowly becoming a man. Eric was ten and looked like his mother, a wide face with a small mouth. Brandon was grateful. He didn't know if he could look into the face of the boy if he resembled his father, an irresponsible lout hitchhiking through Canada.

"Take care of your mom," Brandon said. "You're the man of the house now."

"I'm always the man of the house."

"Eric, please," Jane said.

Brandon looked at Eric and squinted. With that squint, Brandon took away the new skateboard he had promised Eric for his birthday, the new camera he wanted for Christmas, and the extra cash he slipped him in addition to the allowance.

"Sorry," Eric said, slumping against the wall, his arms falling to his side.

Brandon detected genuine remorse from the boy. He tousled the youth's hair, letting him know that he was forgiven. He straightened the shirt Eric was wearing, adjusting it so it hung properly.

Brandon landed in Manila at two in the morning. He had chosen to land late so his relatives wouldn't greet him en masse. On other visits, he'd landed during the day and a busload of relatives greeted him at the gate. It was overwhelming. This time it was just his brother Edwin. Brandon knew that Edwin would love the chance to leave Dagupan and spend a few days in Manila.

Edwin was only a few years older than Brandon. Next to his father, Edwin was the second most loved man in Brandon's life. As children, they walked to school together, played together, even slept in the same bed until it became clear one mattress could not sustain two growing bodies.

At school, when Brandon got teased for playing sports better than most, Edwin came along to set the other kids straight. Unfortunately, one of those kids was Bing, a distant cousin on their mother's side. Brandon still got chills just thinking of his cousin Bing, a skinny, trouble-making boy who enjoyed sniffing glue.

Brandon had always tried to distance himself from Bing. Even as a child, he wanted to know why they let an idiot like Bing come around. Mr. Silverio explained that Bing's family often bought clothes from the shop. During the holidays, Bing's family bought enough dresses and trousers to keep them busy for weeks. For this reason, Bing, despite his ways, would always be treated well around the family.

Brandon smiled when he exited the plane, seeing Edwin standing there. He gave his brother a huge hug. He barely winced when Edwin called him the name that he was born with.

"Brenda," Edwin said, "you're looking well."

"Brandon," he corrected.

"Ay, sorry. It's hard to change."

"Tell me about it."

They went to a bar near Manila Bay. Brandon raised a San Miguel beer to his lips, then asked, "How's Mama?"

"The same. Dramatic. Ordering everyone here and there."

"Sounds like the woman hasn't changed."

"No, but you have. Your hair, clothes… Mom is not going to be too happy."

"Don't worry. I'm prepared."

"Are you sure, Brenda? Sorry, Brandon."

"That's okay. Call me Brenda. I might as well get used to it."

In the morning, Brandon woke up at his hotel, ready to take the five-hour trip to his hometown. That was another reason he had wanted to arrive in Manila late at night: so he'd have time to adjust to his new surroundings before taking that long bus ride home.

Brandon got up from his bed and pulled out the luggage. It was filled with his old clothes: blouses, some pants, a few skirts, and pumps. They were the same clothes he brought back to the Philippines every time he visited. He sighed at the sight of them. Maybe the garments were a little outdated, but they would do. After twelve years, he could still fit into them. He supposed he should be proud of that, but he wasn't.

Once Edwin exited the bathroom, Brandon entered and dressed. He was thankful that he had small breasts, but they were breasts nonetheless. In America, he did everything he could to hide them: bind them, slouch, and wear those billowy barongs. He didn't put the pomade in his hair. He let it fall across his face. Before leaving he had taken some of Jane's cosmetics. He applied a little bit of lipstick, a little bit of mascara. His hand shook as he brushed his lashes, but he knew that his mother would lay into him if he didn't apply at least an ounce of makeup.

With the exception of Edwin, no one in his family knew about the life he led in America. Brandon squirted a bit of lotion into his hand. It was cocoa butter. To Brandon it was the most feminine of scents. He looked into the mirror and put some earrings on. He smiled and saw a tinge of sadness in his face.

Brenda Silverio was the last of six children, born in a small town outside of Dagupan City, Pangisinaan Province, in the Philippines. She was the only girl and the biggest hope for her mother, Miss Pangisinaan, 1939. As soon as she was able to walk Brenda was adorned with a paper crown and sash. Brenda held the crown long enough for a photo to be taken, then immediately ripped off her sash and crumpled her crown. She was two years old.

Mrs. Silverio laughed, thinking the child precocious. No one knew that would be the beginning of the girl's rejection of anything overtly feminine or garishly frilly.

It took, under the direction of Mrs. Silverio, the strength of three maids to prevent young Brenda from running out with her brothers to play ball. By the time she was ten, no army could hold Brenda down. She burst from her home with a fury to race her brothers to school, staying late into the afternoon under the burning sun to run, swim, jump, tumble.

When she arrived home, her mother screamed at her for returning darkened and sweaty.

"Brenda, you will never be Miss Philippines if you keep acting like that," she said.

Matters became worse when cousin Bing had no problem telling Mrs. Silverio how Brenda often behaved at school.

"She fights the boys, Auntie," Bing said. "She picks fights with them for no reason."

"They pick on me," Brenda cried, swinging a fist at Bing.

Mrs. Silverio slapped her daughter for being so violent, then pulled Bing close to her.

"Oh, Auntie," Bing said, "what perfume are you wearing? You smell like flowers."

"Oh, just something I used to wear during my pageant days."

"You are still the most beautiful woman in the province."

Brenda wanted to vomit at the sight of her mother hugging this wretched boy.

To her father, Ernesto Silverio, Brenda could do no wrong. When she was small, he recognized the girl as a headstrong creature with a spirit for adventure. She'd throw on his old suits and stumble around in his loafers, acting like a big shot. The sight of this little girl wearing his clothes made Mr. Silverio bend over with laughter, then pick her up and swing her in the air.

Brenda preferred hanging out with her father in the tailoring shop to cooking at home. She loved seeing the men come into the store, try on various coats and hats. Her father would measure, mark, and pin clothes on some of the most distinguished men in town.

There wasn't a wedding, a graduation, a funeral that his father didn't know about. He dressed men the way he wanted to be dressed: with complete dignity, style, and practicality. Mr. Silverio showed up for work in a suit that he had made himself, knowing that he was his own best advertisement. He wore suits of emerald green or sea blue or cloud white, mostly in linens appropriate for the tropical weather.

Brenda's favorite suit was the one Mr. Silverio wore when someone truly important came into the shop, like the governor. It was a gray sharkskin that Brenda thought her father looked best in. The fabric had been delivered from Hong Kong and it was easily the most expensive suit Mr. Silverio had ever made for himself.

Allowing her to work in her father's shop was the only concession her mother made. Brenda learned how to operate a sewing machine, which fit into Mrs. Silverio's idea of femininity. Her brothers knew how to operate a sewing machine also, but Brenda really took to it. By the time she was thirteen, she was the one sewing the best suits for the finest men.

By the time she was sixteen, Brenda was sure that her life would not be in that town. She preferred pants to dresses and tried to wear them as much as she could. Mrs. Silverio wouldn't have it. When Mrs. Silverio made Brenda wear a hideous white dress and veil to a mass, Brenda couldn't stomach it anymore.

Somehow her father knew this. Mr. Silverio had encouraged his sons to stay, help with the family business, but he encouraged Brenda to leave.

"Go," he said, "go to Manila. You might be happy there."

Brenda almost cried. She took it as permission to truly be himself.

One year she returned home and sat with her father. Brenda's long hair had been shortened to her shoulders. "I'm going to move to the States," she said. She remembered her father's long pause.

"What will you find in America?"

"I don't know," she said. "But I won't find anything here."

Again, he said, "Go." He extended his hand, his knuckles facing her, a major sign of his blessing. Brenda got down on her knees and lowered her forehead to meet his hand. She filed paperwork to go to America the next day.

The bus ride back to her town was long. Her brother Edwin sat by her side. The bus pulled into the main square of town. She exited the bus and the smell of her former life came rushing back to her. The food from local vendors made her smile. She saw the big church where all the passages of life happened, from christenings to funerals. She held her bag close to her when a thin, jittery man approached and gave her a hug.

"Brenda, welcome back," the man said.

Brenda pulled away. It was Bing. He took her bag and led them to a car.

"I'll drive. I like to drive," Bing said.

Brenda sat in the back watching Bing's head bounce to music on the radio. The road they drove on was a dusty and lonely one. A few times they swerved. Brenda knew that he was intoxicated.

"In America they're starting to take driving drunk seriously. You can go to jail," Brenda said.

"Thank goodness we're in the Philippines," Bing said with a snort.

Asshole, Brenda thought.

The Silverio home was part of a compound: several houses clustered together to let others know that this was not just a family, but a series of families who looked out for each other. They had all been tied together by marriages or births. Ask anyone living there and they could count back at least four generations how each family member was related.

The compound occupied six acres of land, half a mile from the beach. It was a green, lush area with colorful flowers dotting the grounds. All of the homes had furniture made locally. Indeed, Dagupan City was known for its woodwork.

Mrs. Silverio stood at the opening of the compound, her arms outstretched. Brenda embraced the old woman and gave her a kiss on the cheek.

"America has been good to you," Mrs. Silverio said. "You don't seem to be starving. You've gotten fat."

Brenda sighed. "Actually, mom, I weigh the same as when I left."

"Oh, Auntie," Bing said. "Even under difficult circumstances, you still manage to remain beautiful."

"Thank you, Bing," Mrs. Silverio said. "You always know what to say."

Brenda rolled her eyes.

"Let's see your father," Mrs. Silverio said, walking her through the crowded house. A wave of relatives hugged and kissed her. Brenda returned their affections. She was truly grateful to see them. She was led to the middle of the room, where her father rested in a mahogany casket.

It took less than a second for Brenda to fall to her knees sobbing. No one saw the slight smile on Mrs. Silverio's face, who approved of her daughter's fine display of grief.

Away from the main house, where Mrs. Silverio wanted to stay with the guests, Edwin brought Brenda to his house, where she unloaded her American gifts on her family. Her brothers (in addition to Edwin, there were Marco, Ryan, Joel, and Cesar) graciously accepted the new jeans. Their wives (Grace, Erlinda, Nina, Marites, and Joanne) planted kisses on Brenda's face upon receiving the lotions and perfumes.

They ate rich meats topped with garlic rice and desserts of sweet beans and fruits. They caught up on neighborhood gossip and sang songs they used to hear on the radio. San Miguel was brought out and the memories of their father followed.

"I messed up on a suit," said Joel. "One pant leg was longer than the other. Dad cut it up and fixed it like that. The customer even gave a generous tip."

Cesar chimed in, "At school, people gave me respect because they knew dad was a good man."

"He was the first one to welcome me to the family," said Grace. "I felt like I was his daughter immediately!"

"Me, too," said Joanne. "Your father was always so kind. Your mother, on the other hand…"

They all burst into knowing laughter.

"I felt like he just wanted us to be happy," Edwin said. "Isn't that right, Brenda?"

"Yes, that's true," Brenda agreed.

There was a very long pause, so long Brenda knew that it was meant for her.

"He wanted you to be happy, too," said Marco.

"I know," Brenda said.

"Is there anyone in the States you're seeing?" asked Marites.

Brenda remained silent. She looked to the ground and nodded slightly. Marites continued, "Do you want to tell us?"

Brenda looked up and saw the faces of her family. Her father raised good fine sons; in turn they chose fine wives. She wiped the lipstick from her face and said, "I met this girl in 1968…"

Brenda walked about the house. Her shoulders slumped over. Her head bowed. Her father was gone. The concept was settling in her bones and, with that understanding, the weight of who she was disappeared. Empty. Cold. Lifeless. She looked into the mirror and saw the fabric of her pajamas on her body. Who is that? she wondered. All she saw was a scarecrow: clothes on some propped-up creature, void of feeling and purpose.

She heard her mother talking, a faint determined voice at the kitchen table. Brenda walked toward the sound and found her mother with a notepad in front of her.

"Make sure there's enough food," Mrs. Silverio said. She was talking to the maids, preparing for the funeral gathering. "I don't want to hear about how people left hungry. Is that clear?"

"Mom, what can I do to help?"

"Brenda, I need for you to tell people about dad's passing. Make sure everyone knows."

"Of course."

"We need to gather and let people know their duties. All of your five brothers will be needed. They'll carry the casket. We need one more pallbearer."

Brenda looked down at the floor, then said, "I'll do it."

"What? No. The casket will be heavy. We need a man to do it."

"Mom, if my five other brothers will be there, I can hold up my end."

"Brenda, only men are pallbearers."

"Mom, this is the 1970s. It's a different world. I want to help carry Dad's body."

"Nonsense."

"I want to do it."

"Your cousin Bing will do it."

"Bing? He's not good enough to wash Dad's shoes, let alone lift his body."

"Why are you always so hard on him?"

"Mom, there are a million men who should be a pallbearer over Bing.

We can find somebody else."

Her mother didn't respond.

"Why Bing?"

"Funerals are expensive..."

Brenda clenched her fists. Bing's parents were helping pay for the funeral, she surmised. Brenda wished she had the money to chip in. She thought of the music lessons, the baseball uniforms, the Christmas gifts she gave to her son in the states. She didn't regret it for a minute, but it meant she didn't have money for unplanned expenses, like a funeral. She left the house to think.

She knocked on the door and heard scuffling. A prostitute opened the door. There was one whorehouse in town and Brenda knew she'd find Bing there. The prostitute was young, maybe fourteen.

"Yes?" said the girl.

"I know Bing's here. Where is he?"

"Let her in," a voice said.

Brenda entered and saw her half-naked cousin on the bed. He was skinny, really skinny. He didn't seem to have an ounce of muscle on him.

"Get out of here," Bing said to the whore. The girl obliged.

"I want to talk to you," said Brenda, taking a seat on a wooden chair by the wall.

"I figured that. If you come into this place, you must want to talk to me pretty bad."

"It's about my father. I want to carry him into the ground."

"That is reserved for the men of the family."

Exactly, Brenda thought, and you don't even come close. She said, "Bing, it would mean a lot to me if I could help carry the casket."

"It would mean a lot to me to carry the casket, too. Your father was always good to me. Unlike you."

"We may not have gotten along in the past, but now is not the time to go into that. I'm asking if I could take your place as one of my father's pallbearers."

"I might consider it… if you beg."

"What?"

"You always thought you were better than me. You love your father? Beg me to take my place. If you get on your knees and beg, I'd be more than willing to give up my spot."

"If I beg, you'd let me be a pallbearer for my father?" Brenda sat there for a long while. "My father didn't raise me to beg for anything." She got up, picked up the wooden chair she was sitting on and threw it at Bing, then sauntered out the door. She heard cursing as she walked out.

"Brenda," Edwin said, "I know you feel obligated to do this, but I'm not going to give this up."

She decided to approach her brothers to see if one would be willing to give up his spot beside the casket. Predictably, each one sympathized but ultimately said no. She was dejected.

"We're packing up some of Dad's clothes," Edwin said, "See if there is something of his that you might want to keep."

Brenda went through the box of clothing. She went through the garments carefully, smelling the musk of her father and the mildew of time. She saw his old T-shirts and slacks, thin dress socks, and leather belts. The denim jeans and short-sleeved oxfords. Brenda sat there and remembered sitting on her father's lap and pulling at the collars of some of these shirts when she was a child.

She found another box, carefully packed. She examined it and smiled. This was filled with his old suits, thin-lapel coats and narrow-legged pants. Linen garments with a bit of wrinkle. Khakis that still maintained a crease on the leg. Brenda lowered her head, bringing the clothes to her face, inhaling them deeply. She reached the bottom of the box and her eyes widened. It was the gray sharkskin suit—her father's favorite. She put on the coat and yes, it was too big. She didn't bother trying on the trousers. She could tell that they were too large for her size.

She folded the clothes, as if handling a small child. She cradled them in her arms and left the room.

Brandon opened the door of the church. His hair was slicked back and his face free of makeup. He walked down the aisle of the church, preparing to sit by his family. His father's casket in the center of it all. He wore an altered suit, the gray sharkskin that had belonged to his dad. He had been up all night refitting the garments to match his body. He heard whispers as he walked through the crowd.

It wasn't until he joined his family in the front pew that someone said in a very loud whisper, "Is that Brenda?"

Brandon felt the stares of his siblings and the intense fury of his mother, but being in front of God, wearing threads that his father had once worn, Brandon felt the handsomest he'd ever felt. His shoulders were back, his hands folded in front of him. He followed the rituals of the mass, waiting for the moment the casket would be led down the aisle, out the doors of the church, and through the hundred yards to the cemetery.

"Would anyone like to come up and say something about our departed Ernesto Silverio?" the priest offered.

There was a brief moment of silence, then one by one members of the audience got up to share a fond memory or two of Mr. Silverio. Each one of Brandon's brothers shared memories of his boyhood with their father. Mrs. Silverio dabbed tears from her eyes. Brandon could feel his mother's fury abate with each person who spoke sweet words of Ernesto Silverio.

Brandon looked around and saw that cousin Bing was at the far end of the pew, dozing off. From his moments of nervous twitters, Brandon knew the asshole was loaded.

The bastard's high at my father's funeral, Brandon thought.

"Is there anyone else who'd like to speak?" asked the priest.

Brandon got up and approached the podium. "I'd... I'd like to say that I was raised by the best man in the world. If... if I could be half the man he was, I'd be satisfied."

After the final prayer, the priest asked the pallbearers to arrange themselves around the casket. The men lifted the coffin and proceeded down the aisle. They all had calm expressions, except for Bing who was sweating, wiping his forehead with his coat sleeve. Bing tripped and the coffin heaved forward with an audible gasp heard from the mourners.

Brandon walked behind the pallbearers, his mother a few feet away, silently weeping. She seemed to forget that her daughter was now a son. Despite what differences they may have had, they both loved the same man. When she appeared too grief-stricken to walk, Brandon scurried beside her and touched her elbow, letting her know he was there for her.

The church doors opened and the six men walked down the several steps of the church. Bing lost his balance and fell, and his end of the casket sank, causing the other five men to stop briefly and collect themselves. Bing began to chuckle and it became clear to everyone that he was drunk.

Bing tried to stand, but Brandon stepped forward. He firmly put his hand on Bing's shoulder, guiding him away and depositing him into the crowd. Brandon took hold of the casket. It was heavy, but he knew he could carry his end.

WHEN GOD WAS A TREE WITH A GLASS EYE IN THE MIDDLE

by MGBECHI UGONNA ERONDU

M Y GRANDMOTHER WAS BORN of a cassava in the days when god was a tree with a glass eye in the middle. I am told also that during this time animals spoke and walked upright like you do now. She had ten children, my grandmother. And each of those children had ten children in turn and so on.

Back then children were both grown and eaten. A man would urinate on thick soil and pack it into the underside of a woman. She would sit knees bent while other men would add their own handful of soil until her legs were buried. To protect a germinating woman from rain and sun we learned to build houses—first dry palm fronds on stilts and then real corrugated-iron roofing on clay. Our mothers knew it was time to give birth when their bellies hardened into stone and the overlying skin became thickened and itchy. Worms and centipedes slithered down their inner thighs and the midwives needed to be careful when swatting them away to avoid getting stung. With heads full of leaves or grass, we exited the womb buzzing like bees and whirring like cicadas, sometimes accompanied by a bird or two that would have to be chased away.

The juiciest of us were kept in a barn for nine months under the watchful eye of our fathers until we grew legs and were strong enough to fend off hungry family members. Then we were kept in the sun until our skin darkened into colors that ranged from dark television wood to sand. Some of our mothers wanted their children to have red skin and so rubbed us with ochre. Some of our mothers wanted their children to have dark skin like oil and so rubbed us with charcoal and ash until we glistened like gold. When we were of age, the tree of knowledge with its glass eye decided who would become male and who would become female. Often we disagreed with our assignment but said nothing because those who questioned the television tree—humans and animals alike—were turned into leather shoes.

Like everyone else, I was born with white skin and red eyes but I was kept too long in the barn—a full five years—and my skin never turned and I remained the color of young coconut flesh, of cassava soaked in water. When most fathers did not care into which woman they had packed the most soil, my own father insisted that I was his child and killed many a hungry passerby to prove it. This is how Umuororie were given the reputation of both cannibals and decapitators. In truth, my father had dug up an entire mountain and buried my mother with it so that no other man could add a speck. I am told it required the entire community to extract her. I am told that she was the first woman to experience love.

Because of my delicate skin my mother thought it prudent to protect me, to bathe me in milk and feed me precious things like eggs and cocoa beans. In those days, the days after my grandmother packaged up the tortoise, human beings were also discovering that they could eat animals as well as vegetables. This is why animals ceased to speak to humans.

When my own time came, the television tree called me ugly and decided I was neither man nor woman. Still, I was considered the most beautiful and most desired of all beings in the land. In those days, an unlucky woman could be infested by termites while germinating so that her belly would grow and grow until she was consumed by it. I refused all suitors and, by fiddling with atoms and such, I discovered that woman did not require man for reproduction. I taught each woman that she could grow butterflies and komodo dragons and sequoia trees from her womb. That we could, each of us, be gods.

Perhaps I will tell you tomorrow how I chopped down the television tree and smashed it until its glass eye became the very river that divided your people into nde ororie and nde ohuhu.

ONCE A CELLIST

by WILLIAM PEI SHIH

I T WAS MY DAD who first taught me how to play the cello. My lessons began at five years old. My dad had a vision for me, and I was there to fulfill it. That was that.

We lived in Dongbei, the northeastern part of China. I was born there. The winters were difficult. We ate spicy soups and kebabs. One day, my parents separated. I was only seven. My mother was an opera singer and could not abandon her own ambitions. Before I got my hands on my first full-sized cello, she had already gone on to tour the western provinces. Years later, the tour turned out to be a lukewarm endeavor. She soon married an admirer; he was much older, a wealthy businessman from Sichuan. This hurt my father. After that, I rarely heard from my mother other than a letter here and there, reminding me to be a good girl. Perhaps if I'd been born a boy, or perhaps if my parents had been allowed to have another child, it would have been different. I remember crying. I remember days when I felt alone. To my dad's delight, I turned to my cello. I developed calluses on my fingers. In between practice sessions, my dad was sure to tell me that I should be proud of myself. He would say, "We Zhengs are descendants from Manchurian nobility." Later on he claimed that we were distantly related to a Qing princess. But that was a different time for China—before the war, the Communist Revolution, and the Great Leap Forward. Our little tale meant nothing under a China after Mao Zedong.

That was why my father had to start from scratch. He was a music teacher. He had made a reputation for himself as a cellist. In private, he would often remark on how difficult it had been to play Johann Sebastian Bach in a country that had no tradition or minimal appreciation for Bach or Mozart or Beethoven or Brahms. To give an example of what the musical climate was like, a colleague of my father's was thrown in jail for playing Prokofiev during the Cultural Revolution. He was never heard from again. But my dad had managed to charm his audiences with his sound, his stunning technique that was all at once effortless and beguiling. He would play in the park. In the distance, a group of elders might be practicing tai chi. There was something amazing about the way my father's thick fingers would travel up and down the body of the instrument with such blind confidence, such brilliance and light speed. I used to wonder how any woman could leave a man like that.

"You will, too, Xiao," my father said to me one morning over breakfast: rice porridge and steamed buns, bought from a stand down the street. We ate over the foldout table. It was the middle of a brutal winter. We were in our cold apartment. There was no heat—my father did not like to waste electricity. Laundry was strung along the walls. There was a faded calendar taped up as well. Then my father went on, "I mean that you will accomplish such feats on the cello, you'll see."

Even back then, how could I not believe him?

* * *

Years later, I was our one-way ticket to New York City. We rented a one-bedroom in a walk-up apartment building in Flushing, Queens. It was grimy. We barely had any furniture: a tattered sofa, another foldout table, metal chairs and stools. Several rusty music stands that creaked each time they were adjusted. Our view was a brick wall across an alleyway. For the first few weeks, all I wanted to do was to take the 7 train into Manhattan and visit the Empire State Building and the Statue of Liberty. I also wanted to walk the trails of Central Park and fly a kite. But according to my dad, there was no time to waste playing tourist. My audition for the Juilliard Pre-College Division was only a month away, and I had to impress the admissions board. Though I had been practicing nearly every day of my life, there was still more practicing to be done—according to my father, that is. There was still much to fine-tune, down to each and every note of a minor scale. Now was not the time to get carried away. I was to play the cello from dawn to dusk. That was that.

My dad had decided on what I should play for my audition to Juilliard: the Cello Suite in C Major by Bach to show off the clarity of my phrasing. Beethoven's Sonata no. 3, op. 69, to exhibit the maturity of my musicality. To top it off, I was to play a piece after my father's own heart—the Concerto in D Major by Franz Joseph Haydn. It was a calculated move (the piece was of greater difficulty than the more popular C Major Concerto). It was also meant to separate me from the rest of the pack.

Last but not least, my father had personally composed the cadenza himself—that final moment when the composer's music comes to a halt and the musician's improvised solo takes over.

"This is where you shine big, Xiao," my father told me.

I looked at the score, at my father's convoluted scribblings in dark ink that only I seemed to comprehend. There were split-second changes in position, chords that broke like the parting of clouds, a final cadence holy enough to end a church service at St. Patrick's Cathedral (another landmark I had not been allowed to see yet). My dad referred to the passage as a final moment of transcendence, an instant before one descended back into the known world.

"In short, cathartic," my father said.

I was embarrassed for him. I thought he was overestimating his contribution to the canon of cadenzas. After all, wasn't he only prolonging Franz Joseph Haydn's original work?

"Yes, Xiao, but a cadenza is how a musician extends the life of a concerto," he explained. "Is it not the final blaze of a movement? Is it not like holding on for dear life?"

"Well when you put it that way…"

My father instructed me to commit each note to memory. "Leave no stone unturned." "A syncopation is nothing without its pulse." I told him that I already knew the music by heart—I needed only to hear it once. I showed him. He was pleased. He was so pleased, in fact, that he said I was to pass off the cadenza as my very own work. Now I could see the extent of his grand scheme. He wanted to give me more than a good head start. He wanted me to…

"You're asking me to lie?" I said.

"Did not Leopold Mozart do the same for his dear little Wolfgang?"

"No, he didn't."

"One can't be quite so sure." He paced back and forth in our kitchen; I could hear the excited shuffling of his slippers. He muttered something about the early symphonies of Mozart. He couldn't believe that a four-year-old could be responsible for something like a symphony. At least not without help.

"Baba, this is wrong," I interjected. "This is dishonest."

He looked at me, incredulous. "Xiao, my little one. This is love. Remember that."

*   *   *

I was accepted into the Juilliard Pre-College Division. The admissions board marveled at my abilities. They marveled at my age (I was twelve). They marveled at my perfect pitch, at my meticulous comprehension of music theory and counterpoint, at my ability to play even the most difficult passages on sight (I was playing Kodály and Paganini transcriptions as if I had been toying with them for years). Foremost, the admissions board was floored by the cadenza. "How splendid." "How charming." And, because they had thought it came from me—a petite girl with a long ponytail and wide eyes and fair skin—it was only all the more astonishing. "You are extremely gifted," they told me, and I smiled as broadly as I could.

A week later, on my first try, I made the unprecedented move to the most senior of orchestras in the Pre-College Division. Not only was I first chair, but I was also the first stand. My father was ecstatic. "Perhaps you'll win the concerto competition this year, imagine that," he said. "On your first try?"

Many of my music teachers were beyond impressed, the conductor of the orchestra as well. Then there were others who didn't take kindly to my arrival. My stand partner was five years older than me. She had been at Juilliard for nearly a decade (her entire childhood). Her name was Frieda. She had red hair. She had sad and faded green eyes. In orchestra, we barely talked. She would give me a dirty look with those same green eyes each time she had to turn the page—even though her demoted position now required it. At times, during concerts, she'd purposely miss a page turn or two. She didn't seem to have any qualms about undermining a century's worth of orchestral etiquette. But it didn't matter. By then, I could have played anything from beginning to end with my eyes closed.

"You play so fast," my private teacher, Dr. Garrett, said to me. We were in the middle of a lesson. I had played a piece by Boccherini at twice the speed.

"Tell me something I don't already know," I replied. I almost blew on my fingernails, but somehow knew that would be a bit much. Besides, I was still holding my bow, and I didn't have time to put it down, in case Dr. Garrett had planned to ask me to play it at three times the speed.

Then he clarified, "It's *too* fast."

Dr. Garrett had salt-and-pepper hair. He had long expressive fingers. Sometimes his fingernails were dirty, and I'd wonder if he picked his nose in private like I would at home. Like me, he was rarely impressed. He interpreted this as a kind of refinement, evidence of taste and intelligent insight. In actuality, it was all affectation because he did not have the vision to take his playing to the next level (Dr. Garrett only performed once a year at the faculty concert, which I would, more often than not, sleep through). And yet, Dr. Garrett still somehow made me aware of that infinitude I had yet to absorb. He made me take another agonizing look at my fingering and my bowing. He made me rethink my articulation and depth of sound.

"I've seen many youngsters like you come and go throughout the years," he said. It was during a later lesson. It was now January. Outside, snow was falling lightly. The sky was a gray overcast. "But alas, child prodigies are like shooting stars."

"What does that mean?"

He leaned in. His hair was a little longer now. He could do with a shave as well. His murky blue eyes took on a deeper hue. "They never last."

"Oh, I see."

He had me look again at the Bach that I had auditioned with.

"You can't rely on your lush vibrato in lieu of gradation, you know."

"But my father taught me to do that."

Dr. Garrett chose not to comment. I contemplated what his silence meant. I looked at the walls of photographs in his office: all the cellists he had taught throughout the years, the best of whom were now playing the solos of concertos all over the world. "Okay," I said. "I think I see what you mean."

*   *   *

Dr. Garrett taught me other things as well—like posture, voicing, articulation. There was so much that my father hadn't been exposed to in China. But was it my father's fault? I realized that it didn't matter when few people ever forgave him for it. Not the critics. Nor other musicians, other connoisseurs of music—people who didn't even play the cello themselves, but had strong opinions on what they thought a suite or sonata should sound like. But my father *did* manage to collect a handful of students in Flushing. They would come to the apartment for lessons. When they did, I'd hide in my room and cover my ears. I was afraid that their tone-deaf playing would only seep into my consciousness. They were mostly beginners, children who were easily distracted and had to be showered with compliments in order to make any strides during a lesson. God forbid they'd practice seriously throughout the week. More often than not, their parents would cancel lessons until inevitably giving up on their children altogether.

Some of my father's other students were middle-aged men who had once played the cello and were now returning to music as a pastime. But still, my father complained that he was never given the attention and respect and credit he was due: those of a true musician.

"No one has the presence of mind to give me the benefit of the doubt," my dad would say at his lowest, which came more and more frequently now. "If only they knew what I have been through."

"Baba!"

"I do my best. I play German music better than most Germans. And don't let me get started on the Italians. You know that. And yet, they say that I don't play with feeling, that I only play with technique. I'd like to see some of them try their hand at Chinese music for once. Then we'll see who's most musical."

"With that attitude, you don't make it any easier on yourself. Or me."

To this, my father raised his head in that all-knowing manner that I had come to resent (Dr. Garrett had taught me to beware of fake musicians). But my father said, "Xiao, it is a miracle that you are even here at all. And that's thanks to me."

The following year, as my father predicted, I won the concerto competition at Juilliard. I played the Concerto in D by Franz Joseph Haydn. I played my father's cadenza as well. He could not have been more thrilled by my achievement. There were actually tears in his eyes when he said, "To think that our very own cadenza will be performed at Lincoln Center, for all to listen to."

"You mean *my* cadenza," I reminded him.

"Of course, yes. You know what I mean." He waved me away, too excited to really argue.

But my father saw my debut at Lincoln Center as if it were my debut to the rest of the world. From here, he imagined that my ascent would only be exponential, limitless. He saw me playing at Carnegie Hall and Royal Albert Hall and at the Konzerthaus Berlin and even the White House and the Palace of Versailles.

"They're not going to close down the Palace of Versailles just for me to play," I told my father.

"Why not?" he said. "They did it for Yo-Yo Ma. I've always wanted to see the Hall of Mirrors, and now I will."

"But Baba, I'm not Yo-Yo Ma."

"No, you're not," he admitted. And then he added, "Not yet."

Almost more important than the performance, for the prize, I was awarded a loan of the Lord Weston cello. It was given to me by an anonymous donor in Idaho. The instrument was a semi-mythical piece. It dated from 1707, Venice. It had a deep and sweet and velvety sound. It had a strong reddish varnish, a sheen that only deepened under the spotlight of a stage.

It was as if each part of the instrument responded to even the slightest of my touches. I felt suddenly capable of a universe of nuances—sensitivities that were now available to me, and furthermore, the amplification of such things. My dad was left staggering in amazement at the cello. He said that he had never been this close to anything so precious in his life. He carefully plucked a string, and the room resonated and filled with such intense sound that the few pots and dishes and glassware in our old and crumbling kitchen seemed to sing in harmony with the note.

"Don't you forget this generosity, Xiao. Be humble. Be thankful, always."

"Okay, alright, I know."

But he didn't believe me, and the weeks that led up to the concert were an intense endeavor. My dad and I argued over every single detail of my playing. We argued over the dynamics, the proper tempo. We even argued over the dress I would wear in order to hide my heavy sweat stains. I just wanted him to stop criticizing each gesture and move. But I could see that he was nervous for me, and that he would cope by going on and on about my bowing, my vibrato, my intonation, my fingering, until one day I couldn't take it anymore.

"It's pronounced *three*," I said to him as he counted off the beats in the tenth measure of the second movement. "Not *swee,* you idiot."

I said this in a voice that I could barely recognize. But by then, I knew how to make my dad feel stupid. He gaped at me.

"If you have something to say, then say it," my father pushed back.

I told him the truth: I couldn't bear to listen to him play anymore. I told him that he overindulged when he played Beethoven. I told him that he was gratuitous with Saint-Saëns's *Swan* ("It's not a holy missive"). He countered by telling me that these pieces were already a part of his repertoire—music that had survived the test of time, music that was gold, forever. I told him that he could call it what he wanted, but he was actually stuck in his old ways. This meant a slow and gradual descent that he was stupidly blind to.

"And please don't touch my cello," I concluded. "I don't want your oily fingerprints all over my instrument. It was given to me, after all, not you."

I could see that this stung. Up until then, my father had been using the Lord Weston for run-throughs of his own pieces in between my practices. We ate meals at different times. We practiced at different hours. But my dad quickly retaliated.

"Child, you always butcher Brahms, and if the composer were to hear how you treat his music today, the man would roll over in his grave and die, again."

"I'd sooner butcher you than Brahms, old man. So what do you have to say about that?"

"I've spoiled you," my father shouted as I slammed the door to the bathroom. I turned on both the faucet and the shower. Full blast. I knew how much it would pain my father to know that I was wasting water, not to mention the precious moments of my practice time.

Outside he continued to bang on the door. "At this rate, you will never be ready!"

On the day of the concert, I stepped onto the stage at Lincoln Center to a booming round of applause. There was the orchestra behind me, all dressed in black and white. I wore a sleeveless red satin dress. The conductor, who was also dressed in black and white, held his baton in the air. He was ready to give the downbeat for the first note, an F-sharp. I took a moment to savor the hushed atmosphere. An audience member coughed. I nodded my head, giving the conductor permission to begin. In the midst of the first movement, I couldn't help myself. I snuck a glance at the audience. In that sea of alert and expectant faces, I saw my dad. He was sitting in the front row and on the edge of his seat. Why was I not surprised? How could he resist? Throughout the rest of the concert, I could see him sway his right arm continuously this way and that, as he emulated each and every stroke of my bow.

Afterward, I found myself in a throng of excitement. I received an offer to play at Carnegie Hall. I was asked to give a recital at the 92nd Street Y, to make an appearance on WQXR. Several benefactors invited me to give concerts in their homes on the Upper East Side or in the Hamptons. Somehow I knew to keep my father away from this lot. I had asked him to wait for me outside.

He met me later with a paper bag of takeout dinner and a smile. "Ready to go home, maestro?"

"Oh, yes."

And then it was Monday. I was back in high school. My dad had enrolled me in the school across the street from Juilliard. It was convenient. I would be able to make my afternoon music lessons. When I didn't have lessons, I could spend the afternoon in a practice room. What my father didn't know was that it was difficult for me to make many friends at school. I wasn't exactly popular. I'd once caught my reflection in the pane of a display case for trophies. Did I really care that I had not developed into the beautiful woman my mother had been? The other girls in my class teased me. They pointed out my "mannish face" and "thick nose" and "heavy glasses" that somehow "matched" my nose. In essence, I could not escape resembling my dad. But they were wrong. I had gorgeous hair. It was long, thick, and black. I wore it loose. It reminded me of the photographs of my mother because she would wear her hair the very same way. Besides, I couldn't understand the stratosphere of the school. These same girls were fixated on superficialities: the clothes that they wore, whom they associated with, and what parties they were invited to on the weekends. I felt excluded. I felt left behind, and that it was already too late for me to catch up. A part of me somehow held out hope that my talent would make up for my heavy accent, for being an anomaly.

It didn't.

Each day, I was put in my place. I was a nobody from Dongbei. None of my classmates even knew where Dongbei was. I saw that no one wanted to be friends with someone who lugged around a case as hard and life-consuming as a tumor. I missed China. I felt silly for missing China because so many of my relatives and friends there wanted to be where I already was. But how could I explain? They always insisted that *I* was the lucky one. Sometimes I wondered if I had the heart to ruin their idea of the life they thought I was living—a life that they could pick and choose what to imagine and vicariously live through. I thought of the roadkill I'd see on the highway during drives to Dr. Garrett's Long Island home (which was where he would conduct lessons in the summer). The squashed and bloody bodies of dogs and cats and raccoons and opossums. Sometimes, the bodies were so mangled that I couldn't even tell what animal they had been. I remember wondering why these poor creatures wanted so badly to cross such a dangerous highway. What did they imagine was on the other side? Something better? It was only the same, more or less.

One day, I left my cello in the locker room after gym class. It was Mr. Swarovski, my gym teacher, who called my home. I watched as my dad slammed down the receiver and glared at me. He had been ready to call the police.

He pointed to my cello (Mr. Swarovski had been kind enough to drive it to our apartment). My dad was all but shouting at the top of his voice, "Don't you understand? That is a Lord Heston, Goddamn it."

"A Lord *Weston*, Baba. You're confusing it with Charlton Heston. Say it right." I was starting to sound like some of the girls in my class, and I liked it.

"You got it on loan," my dad said.

"Yes, and so what?"

He raised a hand. I couldn't help but wince. But that was enough for my dad; he would always be a man who would come up short. "Don't you ever be so foolish again," he said.

Then I met Dominic. He came backstage to introduce himself after my recital at the 92nd Street Y. I was impressed; he was not the least bit intimidated by the company that surrounded me. A rich benefactor. The director of the program. The renowned violinist Gil Shaham. The host of WQXR. Dominic said that he had an appreciation for the cello. Great, I replied. He said that there was something special about the way that I played. I nodded in what was by then habitual agreement.

Later that week, we were at a café when Dominic informed me that he played the cello a little himself, in fact.

"That's wonderful," I said, stirring my glass of iced tea.

His red pimpled face looked hopeful, perhaps a touch too eager. "I like to quote the first few measures of the great concertos. Elgar, Dvořák, Schumann, you name it."

I soon learned that this was typical of Dominic. He echoed the initial lines from books he didn't finish reading. He had dropped out of high school after his freshman year. He now ran a startup computer-licensing company that, according to him, made a ton of money. He ran it out of his parents' home in Whitestone. In his spare time, he hacked into other people's email accounts. "You wouldn't believe how many nude pictures I find these days." One time, he'd discovered child pornography on a neighbor's computer, and tipped off the police.

Dominic was shorter than me, and I was already not especially tall. He also tended to slouch, and maintained a perpetual frown which he believed denoted sincerity, though to me it looked more like an odd scowl. He was not very handsome either. My dad held that against the boy.

"His face is plagued with acne," my dad said. "It's like he's diseased."

"So what? I like him."

"His breath always smells like Caesar salad."

"Okay, well, what do you want me to do about it?"

"End this nonsense."

But Dominic persisted. He had audacity. He was convincing. He was the kind of person who got his way because he wasn't afraid of pushing his luck to the limit. It was a kind of privilege that he seemed oblivious to. If I were to send a plate back at a restaurant or agonize about how I wanted my coffee prepared at the counter of a Starbucks, I'd be filled with inelegance and guilt. I would not be able to live it down. I'd feel cheap. It'd be like playing the theme of the Lalo concerto the same way each time without even a hint of variation. It'd be like only playing the opening of the Lalo and never nearing the rest of the piece.

And yet, I was flattered by Dominic's attention. We went on several more dates. Soon, I had a boyfriend. I was actually delighted. I could see that my dad would never know how to be like Dominic, someone who was not afraid to promote himself, who was unafraid of a gratuitous amount of self-indulgence. In public, my father was always deferring to his own humble mannerisms. And I thought that this was likely what contributed to how he was a failure now in music. For in the real world, no one wanted to listen to failures. No one gave failures a second chance.

One day, my dad put his foot down. He told me that I wasn't allowed to have a boyfriend. He reminded me that my work and my career were of the utmost importance. My cello. That was that, or didn't I remember?

Then he said, "Don't you see? Once a cellist, *only* a cellist."

"Bullshit, Baba."

"With that attitude, you will never be the best."

We were in the practice room at Juilliard. I could hear someone at the piano in an adjacent room. The music was melancholy, a Chopin etude. Whoever was playing was also off the beat. I told my father a kind of half-truth. "What if I was thinking of giving up the cello? What if I wanted to do something else for a change? Concentrate my energies elsewhere?"

"Then you wouldn't be you," my dad replied. "You wouldn't be my Xiao."

"Why can't I be something different?"

"Like what?"

The music outside had reached a turning point; the piece was supposed to shift from somber to a kind of acceptance of finality and beauty in sadness. But the pianist was playing too slowly, which only belabored the sentiment. "I don't know. Play soccer? Go to the YMCA? Swim in the pool?" Then, "Summer is just around the corner."

"Summer is when you can go to music camp."

"That's not what I mean."

Then my dad told me to stop acting like a child. I told him to stop sounding like a desperate old man. His face became ever graver. Suddenly it was too quiet. I noticed that the music had stopped. Perhaps the pianist had finally given up.

My dad said, "Please don't say such garbage."

"Actually, I'm saying what I want to say for once." In the silence, I sounded louder than I'd intended.

"You can't mean that."

"Oh, but I do."

He shook his head. "Then get out of my sight."

I left home. I left the Lord Weston cello behind. This I did on purpose. I knew how much it would hurt my father to see the instrument sitting there in the living room each day, unplayed. But I didn't care anymore. I thought that maybe then my father would get the idea: he might learn what it felt like to have one's fate already predetermined. It was like having your hands tied behind your back, and trying to navigate through life while crossing the narrowest of beams. I thought of my mother. I wondered if she would have ever led me down such a tortuous and endless path. I've often imagined not.

I stayed with Dominic and his parents. His mother, Lana, was a tall woman. She was slender. She had frizzy auburn hair. She was a former dancer of contemporary expression. She now ran a gourmet chocolate shop down the block. Each evening, she would bring back different chocolates for Dominic and me to try. Milk chocolate, Mayan cacao from Mexico. Bittersweet chocolate. Dominic's father also worked in computers, though Dominic insisted that there was no correlation between his father's and his own aspirations.

"I'm completely self-taught," he told me. "Unlike you."

We'd have dinners together in an actual dining room and at the same time (6:30) every evening. We'd watch TV in the living room. They enjoyed shows like *Law & Order* and *Law & Order: Criminal Intent*. It was great. One evening, Lana showed me baby pictures of Dominic. They were of the embarrassing variety. We were sitting side by side on the couch. There was an infant Dominic taking a bath. A five-year-old Dominic at the front row of his kindergarten class. There was a Dominic dressed as a fireman for Halloween.

"When Dominic was four, he wanted to be the biggest, strongest fireman," Lana said. "Don't you remember, my little Domino?"

"Domino?" I said.

Dominic couldn't help but blush. He tried to change the subject, but I wouldn't let him.

"That's what my parents used to call me." Then he said, "Did you always know that you wanted to be a cellist?"

"For as long as I could remember," I replied. I could hear my father's voice echoing through me when I said, "Once a cellist—well, you get the idea..."

Dominic shook his head. "Actually, I don't. Why *don't* you play anymore?"

I didn't know what to say. My dad always believed that he had given me the greatest gift that a father could ever give a child—talent, but even more than that, the insight to cultivate such a phenomenon. "As miraculous as Beethoven," he'd say. "As incredible as Mozart." Now it only made me cringe to reiterate these phrases. But Dominic seemed to lap them up. Then I said, "I hate the cello."

"I don't believe you."

I kissed him on the nose. He playfully bit mine back. I gave him a look. "Then don't."

September came around, and then it was my birthday. I was born in the year of the dog. It meant that I had a good nature. It meant that I was loyal. It meant that I was trustworthy, and apparently removed from the ugliness and evil in the world. Lana wanted to throw me a birthday celebration. They would take me out to their favorite sushi restaurant in Little Neck. It was my senior year of high school. I was about to turn eighteen. As I buttoned up the new purple top that Lana had bought for me at a boutique in Manhattan, I heard the doorbell ring. Lana called me to come downstairs.

"It's for you," she said.

"Oh?"

I went downstairs. There, on the doorstep, was my cello. Its black case was freshly polished and reflected the light of the afternoon sun.

"Well this is a birthday surprise, isn't it?" Lana said.

"Not really," I replied. And then, "My dad's never been the subtle type."

Still, I opened the case. I felt the cool and humming wood of the instrument. It was as if every part of the cello were trying to communicate with me.

"You should call your father. Don't you miss him?"

I grasped the neck of the cello with a strength that paralleled my determination. "No," I replied.

I expected the Lord Weston and me to pick up where we'd left off. But that was not so. For the first time in my life, I felt stiffness in my fingers. I heard the dullness that had somehow infiltrated my once deep and exquisite sound. It hit me instantly. My father was right: we were continuously remade and unmade. I could see that each day I didn't play the instrument was like walking backwards through a jungle that I'd have to find my way out of again, blindfolded. Once again, I had to regain ground. I had to rediscover what I had mistakenly thought would always be there, what I had thought I would always know like the back of my hand. My dad used to say, "If you're not practicing now, remember that someone else is."

A statement like that could make my stomach hurt, badly.

I called my dad. At first, our formality felt like that of two long-lost acquaintances trying to get to know each other again. But soon enough, we were back to discussing the wretched cello. My father told me that he was taking on fewer and fewer students.

"I want to perform more—stretch out these old muscles."

I humored him. It was the least I could do. I told him that it seemed like a good idea. But in the back of my mind I also wondered who would want to see him, let alone hear him play.

"You just have to use your coconut," he said. I could picture him pointing to his wide forehead when he said this, his hair as thin as his career.

The next time we talked, my dad told me that he had started playing on the subway platform at Grand Central Station. "I'm playing for the rest of the world now. You wouldn't believe how many people pass through during rush hour."

"Are you serious?" I felt my face redden. "That's embarrassing. I'm embarrassed for you."

"The money's good. And I could always use help with the rent."

"Oh Baba, no, Baba."

What more could I say? From then on, each time I rode the subway, I'd be afraid of running into my father. Whenever I'd hear the soaring notes of a stringed instrument echoing throughout the tunnels with the sudden rushing and warm underground wind, I'd turn the other way.

Sex with Dominic was something I had to get accustomed to at first. It wasn't what I'd expected. Dominic did it ravenously, as if he were worried that I might suddenly change my mind each time. His sweat, after a while, didn't smell so unpleasant. His labored breathing wasn't so disturbing. Sometimes, he would even allow his gerbil, Wellington, to watch us.

One day, Dominic proposed. He was proud of the ring that he'd picked for me, a half-carat diamond over a rose-gold band. He had asked his mother for input. She did good.

"You have no idea how pricey this was," he told me.

"I can't imagine," was all I could reply.

He'd already posted pictures of the ring on Facebook; that was why it hadn't been a surprise. I told him that I needed more time to think about it.

But this caught him unawares. He said that he had expected me to say yes.

"I didn't say no."

"I think you'll change your mind. Give it a week or two."

The weeks led to months. Suddenly it was nearing the end of the winter. Snow that once covered the yard gave way to the streets and grass outside. One afternoon, I was at the computer when I discovered Dominic's profile on a dating website that was in the search history of his browser. A picture of his gloating face (minus the pimples and blackheads and greasy skin). The picture had clearly been Photoshopped. I clicked through his page. There was a selfie of him with the Lord Weston, along with the hashtag #MusicianLife. I realized that he must have taken it one morning when I was still asleep.

I confronted him. He didn't exactly apologize.

"Xiao, you have to understand. I'm looking for someone who's going to take me more seriously, someone more decisive. I'm not sure if you realize, but you don't know how to connect with anything besides the cello."

I was taken aback. When I didn't respond, he mentioned that my auditions for conservatories were coming up. I was going to graduate high school that very year.

"I don't appreciate these digs," I finally said.

"They weren't meant to be digs." Then he said, "Perhaps we should take a break."

I moved back in with my dad. He agreed to let me purchase a secondhand computer. I wish that I could say that things were better. We continued to butt heads. We continued to argue. An interpretation of Grieg, a passage in a Mendelssohn sonata. I couldn't help but feel claustrophobic in our tiny apartment, and was annoyed that I had to practice pieces with my father's hypervigilant ears always listening in while chopping vegetables from the kitchen or while he watched Chinese historical films on mute in the living room. Of course, he would practice his cello as well. But by then, it was clear that we had become drastically different players. It was as if we spoke two entirely different languages altogether, barely able to communicate.

I had never felt more the urgency to get away for good.

I got into Juilliard. I got into the Curtis Institute of Music. I got into the Manhattan School of Music. I got into Le Conservatoire de Paris.

I got into the Berklee College of music. I got into Mannes. I got into
the New England Conservatory. I got into the Cleveland Institute of
Music. I got into the Boston Conservatory. I got into the San Francisco
Conservatory of Music. I got into Peabody. I got into Eastman. I got
into Oberlin. I got into the Jacobs School of Music. I got into the Royal
Academy of Music. I got into the Los Angeles College of Music. I got into
the Moscow Conservatory. I got into the Sibelius Academy in Helsinki.
I got into the Vienna Conservatory. I got into the University of North
Texas College of Music. I got into the Madrid Royal Conservatory. I got
into the Colburn Conservatory. I got into the Berlin Academy of Music.
Full scholarships to all.

I got into USC also. Again, full scholarship. But by April, I was still
undecided on what to do next. My dad didn't understand my hesitation—
Juilliard, the College Division, of course. "Only the best," he said. He
made the word *Juilliard* sound as if it were the highest rung on the ladder
of goals, entirely oblivious to other heights.

"Who the hell ever heard of USC for music?" he asked. He was pacing
back and forth; the sound of his slippers now carried a desperate drag. I
had to admit that a part of me felt that watching him was as enjoyable as
the slow movement of a Mahler symphony. Then he said, "I don't understand it, what's keeping you from making the right decision? Why move
all the way across the country to California?"

"Because why not?"

He kept pacing, shuffling his slippers. He started muttering to himself.
Moments later, he turned around to me and said, "We're Chinese. It means
that no one cares about us. It means that we have to stick together, you
and I. It means that we have to work twice as hard for half the reward,
and then know how to swallow the bitterness of that contentment. Why
make it more difficult than it already is?"

When I didn't answer, he then added, "You're a young woman, and it's already hard enough for a woman to make it in a man's world—let alone a cellist. Don't you feel it your responsibility to undo an injustice like that? Don't you want to be a role model?"

Still, I refused to reply. My father continued, "Think of your mother, think of all her years of hard work, only to be accepted by a small degree." And then, "God gave you a talent to use to its full capacity. It's your moral obligation to nurture this gift in the appropriate place and setting." Then, "No one will ever listen to what you have to say, you only have the cello to speak for you. Why banish yourself to the middle of nowhere?"

I kept my gaze on his hands. They were more callused than ever, riddled with brown spots and thinning skin. The nails were yellowed and bitten to the quick. He threw them up into the air. Finally he said, "Stay: Dominic is in New York."

I couldn't take it anymore. "There's a teacher I'd like to study with at USC."

"But who better for you to study with than your own father?"

"You know that's not true. At least not anymore."

He slammed both hands onto the linoleum countertop. This rattled the plate of half-cut vegetables he'd been preparing for dinner. "Your teachers have turned you against me. They've turned you against yourself. Your teachers are racists. I've seen the way Dr. Garrett looks at me."

"Stop it."

I watched as my dad pressed the top of his nose with two fingers. It left a bright red mark. "Xiao, I know that I've never been very good at expressing how much I've always wanted the best for you, but I have, always, 100 percent. Even more, if that's possible. But if you're hesitating now only because it hasn't been easy for me to say the right things at the right times, then please, I beg of you—don't do this. It's not worth it."

I could tell that it was difficult for my father to make this admission.

But what else could I respond with besides "I guess"?

"So will you go to Juilliard?"

"How should I know?"

He stepped into the next room. Then he fell into his practice chair and twisted away. I saw his broad back; it was turned toward me like a wall. I watched him slouch forward in what had become his usual pose—defeat, humiliation, not humility. I saw him sigh. I realized that he had run out of arguments. There was only one more thing for my father to do. He picked up his cello. He began to play. Instantly, I recognized the music. Franz Joseph Haydn. The cadenza. I heard the glissandi, the lyrical solo voice, double-stops. After all this time, he, like me, could still remember every note by heart. Well, almost every note.

Still, I suppose that it was a sort of apology from my father. As the notes continued to soar, one after the next, I gazed upon the small area we used as our living room. There was still the gray tattered couch, the secondhand coffee table. There was the worn-out desk with the missing leg that my dad had rescued from a street corner because he thought it was a crime to throw away anything that could still be of use. In my absence, he had become a bit of a hoarder.

When my father broke his last chord, he was elated. There were actually tears in his eyes.

"What do you think?" he said. "Not bad for your old Baba, right?"

He held his bow in midair. The dust of the rosin floated like mist in the light. What else did he expect? But still, I turned and said what I thought my father needed to finally hear: "You were flat the entire time."

USC turned out to be a mistake. The teacher whom I had wanted to study with was on sabbatical that year. Southern California wasn't exactly the music capital of the world. There was too much sun. There was too much beach, too many days of blue skies that gave off the essence of paradise. I found that my pale skin was easily sunburned. Everyone wanted to be outside or go to the mall. Drives along the coast that never seemed to end up anywhere. More roadkill. There was no place like Carnegie Hall. No Lincoln Center. I felt like a big fish in a feeble bucket—and the water was lukewarm. What I mean is that I didn't need to practice much to stay ahead. I sought other distractions. I had a fling with a pianist who only practiced finger exercises from Hanon and Czerny. I dated a trombonist who could scarcely play in tune. I went out with a violinist who played as if his fingers were drenched in grease.

Then one day, I decided—no more musicians.

I met Rufus through an oboist in the orchestra. He had hazel eyes and dirty blond hair. The loose jeans he wore only emphasized his gauntness. According to Chinese superstition, he would have been considered unlucky. But it was a plus that he was studying to be a vet. In the beginning, we would meet for ham sandwiches at a nearby delicatessen and talk about our childhoods. I told him that I'd always longed to have a pet—a cat—but there never seemed to be any time. Practicing and performing always got in the way. He'd grown up with four older brothers and a plethora of pets. Fish, birds, reptiles. He said it was never too late to adopt. A few weeks later, he brought me a shoebox. Inside, a sleepy orange and white kitten. I named her Fifi.

Rufus didn't really know much about music. When he attended my concerts, he'd fall asleep. He slept through Franz Joseph Haydn's Concerto in D—all three movements. *Allegro moderato. Adagio. Rondo.* He slept through the cadenza as well.

Afterwards, he admitted to staying up late studying for exams. Organic chemistry was getting the best of him.

"It was a pretty long solo," I told him. "It's kind of gotten me some attention through the years."

He gave me a small smile, shrugged in the way that would always leave me weak in the knees. "Sorry," he said. "This world is pretty alien to me. I like *you* very much, though."

I couldn't help but be moved. He was honest. He was without airs.

I didn't mind that Rufus eventually stopped attending my concerts altogether. He had another string of exams to study for; his science classes and volunteer schedules were rigorous. I told him that I understood.

"I just want someone who will take me out to a nice meal from time to time," I said.

His uneven smile gradually became more endearing. He had crooked teeth. "Alright," he said. "I can do that."

Rufus got into vet school. At the same time, I graduated from my program. I accepted positions playing for several orchestras based in Los Angeles. I played on the scores for various films about comic-book superheroes and aliens. I also performed backup for a Celtic band that would appear on nightly talk shows and clubs in West Hollywood. I was giving lessons to intermediate cellists in the area. Inspired by Rufus, I even volunteered at a high-school music program. Life was good.

A year later, my dad visited. I took him on a tour of the house Rufus and I rented. It was only a half hour's drive from campus. I introduced my dad to Fifi and another recent addition, Sha Sha, a shy black-and-gray tabby. I showed him my garden in the backyard, where I'd planted marigolds. I had long since decided to take some pride in this. They were coming up quite nicely.

My dad tasted my cooking for the very first time. I made us veggie omelets and potatoes. I had to use Rufus' coconut cooking oil. We didn't use much seasoning either. The food wasn't very good, but we ate it anyway. I explained to my dad that brunch was a meal between breakfast and lunch, and that it was my favorite meal of the day now. Afterwards, he watched me load the dishes into the Maytag dishwasher.

"You know how to work that thing?" he asked. I took off my apron. It was pink with roses. It had been a birthday present from Rufus's mother.

"Yes, of course."

"That's good."

We talked of the weather in California. How nice the people were. There were strangers who said hello to you in the streets and meant it. My father's voice was weary and strained. He told me that playing in Grand Central Station wasn't as profitable as it used to be—so he was thinking about relocating to Times Square. Soon we ran out of things to say, and for a moment we just stared in each other's direction, but not quite at each other. We listened to the squishy hum of the dishwasher. My dad looked as if he were suffering from a kind of nausea.

"Are you okay?" I said. "Was it the spinach? It might have gone bad."

"No." He seemed to flinch.

"I can whip up some ginger tea if you'd like." I started searching my cupboards, which had been recently refurbished with cream-colored frames and glass panels. I pushed aside Rufus's collection of mugs from local races and triathlons. I pulled out a tin canister and shook out a tea bag. I could feel my dad watching me.

"What is it?" I almost burst.

"Nothing." Then he said, "You know, you could have really been something."

"Okay, I know."

Ten years later, I was in Prague. I had decided to stay a couple of days longer after my concert at Smetana Hall. I postponed my flight. I thought of how it would feel good to be in another country and to actually see it for a change.

I tried goulash at a museum cafeteria. I crossed the Charles Bridge several times. I rubbed the statue of St. John Nepomuk for good luck. I watched

Don Giovanni at the Estates Theatre. An usher told me that it was where Mozart had premiered the opera himself. He had conducted it as well, over two hundred years earlier. Did I know I was in the presence of greatness?

I visited the Lobkowicz Palace. There were some of Beethoven's original scores. I saw the *Eroica Symphony*. The stack of pages, all in the maestro's own fierce hand. I thought of how my dad would have liked to see this. I took a picture with my phone. I thought that maybe I might send it to him in the future. We had gone months without speaking, until one day we no longer spoke to each other at all. Neither of us felt the need to interrupt the rest. At least not yet.

"I miss you," Rufus texted. He sent me a picture of a wise- and aged-looking Fifi (Sha Sha had succumbed to feline leukemia a year ago). Then Rufus texted, "How was the performance?"

I was already back at the hotel. It was located along Panská, on the border of the New and Old Towns. It was after dinner. I didn't answer. I was in the middle of packing. There was the Lord Weston beside the bed. It looked like a dead body. I imagined leaving the cello where it lay—a little out of the way, undisturbed. What was that saying about letting sleeping dogs lie? I entertained another delicious thought that I always somehow returned to: by this time tomorrow, maybe I wouldn't be a cellist anymore. Maybe I would imagine having my mother at my side instead. The endless and aching possibilities.

I thought of my flight. I thought of how I'd already reserved two seats. One was for myself, and one was for Lord Weston. As always, the cello would sit next to me, positioned upside down. I'd hoist the instrument on the seat and then buckle it in as if it were some enormous child. People always stopped to ask me, "Is that a bass you're carrying?" Or "How long have you been playing?" Once in a while, someone might say, "Is it tough to lug that thing around everywhere you go?" I'd smile and say no, but think yes. Oh, yes.

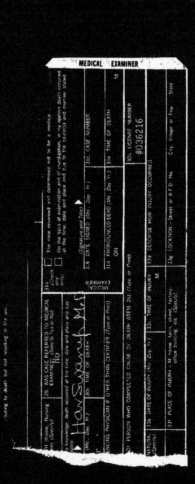

MEDICAL EXAMINER

...bting to death but not resulting in the un...

H (Home, Nursing
...e) (Specify)

29 WAS CASE REFERRED TO MEDICAL
EXAMINER? (Specify Yes or No)
NO

31a (Check
one
only.)

☐ The case reviewed and determined not to be a medical.

☐ On the basis of examination and of investigation, in my opinion death occurred
at the time, date and place and due to the cause(s) and manner stated

(Signature and Title)

MEDICAL
EXAMINER

Han Seward M.D.

31b DATE SIGNED (Mo. Day. Yr.)

31c CASE NUMBER

...knowledge, death occured at the time, date and place and due

31d PRONOUNCED DEAD (Mo. Day Yr.)
ON

31e TIME OF DEATH
M

(Mo. Yr.)

30c TIME OF DEATH

RNING PHYSICIAN IF OTHER THAN CERTIFIER (Type or Print)

32 LICENSE NUMBER
#036216

2? PERSON WHO COMPLETED CAUSE OF DEATH (ITEM 26) (Type or Print)

NATURAL
(Specify)

33b DATE OF INJURY (Mo. Day Yr.)

33c TIME OF INJURY
M

33f DESCRIBE HOW INJURY OCCURRED

33d PLACE OF INJURY – At home, farm, street, factory,
office building, etc. (Specify)

33g LOCATION – Street or R.F.D. No   City, Village or Twp.   State

MANY SCATTERED A BENCH ALONG THE BANKS OF CORALVILLE LAKE

by NOVUYO ROSA TSHUMA

H E APPEARED TO ME yesterday afternoon, my father, a day after my biweekly session with M at the Eastwind Healing Center, opposite the Iowa City Public Library, where she suggested that I have, for the past fifteen years since he died, been searching for him, and that I ought to work through my memories of him if I don't want to end up in the psych ward at Mercy Hospital again. He materialized in my kitchen on the chair across from me, his large hands palm-down on the table I found on the sidewalk last week and which Shào Mingli helped me drag all the way from Summit Street, near his place, to my apartment at the corner of Bloomington and Dubuque. The sunlight poured through the window behind my father and splashed against his back, flaming his tanned leather jacket, the one I last saw him in the year before he died, when I visited him in Rome for two weeks, and which I always imagined he was wearing on the day of his death. The sun washed over his hair, lightening the dark-brown kink, but failed to burrow into the depression on the right side of his head where I imagined he had slammed into the windscreen in the car accident that caused his death. The whole of the right side of his face was smashed in, pushing his eye deeper into his skull and pulling his upper lip away from his mouth. I began to cry softly, trying to sniffle into my shoulder so that Mingli, whose laughter rumbled from the bedroom, probably talking on the phone, wouldn't hear me. I wanted to stand up, to lean over and wrap my arms around my father's broad shoulders. To bury my face in the lapel of his jacket and feel the grizzled warmth of his good cheek pressed against mine. I half got up out of my chair, my hand sliding toward his, which was dark brown against the ash wood of the table. But he began to fade, and I was afraid he would disappear. I snatched my hand away and tucked it beneath the table.

"Say something."

But he said nothing.

"Won't you say something? Please?"

I was afraid to move. We sat there for a good fifteen minutes, in what was at first an anxious silence on my part but which, gradually, took on a texture of serenity, disrupted only by my sniffling, the whirring of the aircon in my bedroom, and the rhythmic padding which I assumed was Mingli tap-dancing to the music of his conversation.

"Did you say something?" Mingli called out. "J?"

He began to dissipate, my father.

"J?"

The next moment, the chair before me was empty.

I turned to Mingli. He was standing by the bedroom door, in a rill of sunlight, his gray towel wrapped around his slim waist, his hairless chest glistening with water, his hands rubbing my pink towel across his damp hair.

"Did you say something?" he asked again, and then noticing my tears, "J? What's wrong?"

I tried to glare at him.

"J? What's happened?"

"You'd better make sure you put my towel in the laundry," I said, getting up.

I brushed past him, moved into the bedroom, and disappeared into the adjoining bathroom, slamming the door.

I left early this morning and went for a walk. I left Mingli still slumped beneath the duvet, snoring softly, his back to me, darkly pale in the withering darkness. He had his arms wrapped lightly around his slim torso, which means I must have slapped him away at night when he tried to touch me, something he says I do in my sleep whenever I am angry with him or we've had a fight, but which I never remember doing.

He died on this day exactly fifteen years ago, my father, August 15, 1999. It was a gloss-tinged summer day. I was eleven years old. I was playing Stuck in the Mud with my neighbors Zinzile and Stha when two men rumbled into our yard just as the light was paling, flickering between the garnet-colored leaves of our msasa tree. At first, I paid them no mind, sloshing in our self-made muddy patch beneath our tree, water trickling from the hose pipe we'd secretly fastened to the garden tap. Our eyes fluttering about for Mum, our lips sly with smiles.

The men rumbled into our yard in a Mazda 323 and whispered something to Mum that made her face undo itself and redo itself and fall apart all over again. She was standing by the car, one hand gripping the front passenger door, the other folded on her waist, making her tie-dye dress ride up the small of her back. She blink-blinked, shook her head, blink-blinked, shook her head.

"Mummy?" I called out.

"Go into the house," she ordered.

"Mummy? What's wrong?"

"I said go into the house. You too, Zinzi and Stha. Go and watch TV. Ask Sisi to give you ice cream."

I remember, with a little guilt, how we sucked greedily on those lollies, how they filled our mouths with giggles and icy sweetness, painting our tongues orange and green and red, dribbling down our chins like things already lost.

It was Khulu, my mother's father, who came to pick me up the following day and took me with him to his house in Queenspark East, where I usually spent the weekends, sitting beneath the lemon tree at the back of the garden beside him, my khulu, my math and English books spread across my lap. And though my eyes flitted about for my father as we alighted from the *khombi* in Queenspark East, I didn't ask after him. I'd been asking after him the evening before and, failing to get an answer, had resigned myself to awaiting his call, trying to sniffle back my tears, my lips pursed in mock petulance.

The jacarandas seemed unusually purple that day, their leaves curled into fists, the petals bruising under my feet. I was chattering faster than a chatterbox, like the puppets in *Barney & Friends*. I didn't know what I was going on about, I was just going on and on and on, because that's what I do when I'm nervous, and the worry lines on Khulu's forehead, the set line of his lips, made me nervous. My breath reached my ears in sharp rasps.

"What's that?" I asked, pointing to the piece of black cloth pinned to his scotch jacket, one of his numerous District Administrator of Education jackets.

After a while he said, "It's a sign."

"A sign? A sign of what?"

"A sign we wear when somebody close to us dies."

"Who died, Khulu?"

He didn't reply.

"Khulu, who died?"

When he didn't answer, I shrugged. He squeezed my hand. I tried to squeeze his big hand back, stumbling to keep in step with his rapid strides.

I remember that house in Queenspark East with such fondness now, sitting well back from the gate, my gogo's garden of gloriosas flanking the gravel driveway, the patch of grass to our left a shaggily decent height, the same color as the spring-green walls of the house, its viridian asbestos roof glistening with a fresh coat of paint. "Colonial style" was what my teacher called the houses of Queenspark East, with their generous rooms and equally generous gardens. It was eerily quiet that day, Khulu's house, and I remember this only now, or perhaps this is how I like to remember it, so befitting in retrospect, the usual laughing and shouting, thudding and dithering failing to reach my ears. He had twelve children all in all, my khulu, some, like Mum, grown; others, like my aunt Sihle, the last born, only three years older than I, and a handful of grandchildren and grandnieces and grandnephews, so there was never a dull moment in that house.

But I don't remember bumping into a soul as we went in through the back, past Gogo's kitchen with the ancient blue fridge that belched and farted incessantly, although meat was boiling on the stove, a beef-smelling steam rising from the huge black pot, a squad of flies hovering nearby.

He took me straight to his room, Khulu, where he made me remove my Bata sandals and sat me on the edge of his bed, my feet pressing against the cool, shimmering maroon floor. He dragged a chair from his desk, where his District Administrator things sat, arranged neatly in sheaves of papers and piles of books, his reading glasses resting on their leather case, a tin of Vicks Vapor Rub next to it, its minty scent filling the room. There he sat, opposite me, my Khulu, his eyes angled not at me but at the polished floor—where if you looked hard enough you could see your reflection—suddenly a crumpled old man.

"*UsekaJ kasekho. Kube le accident...*"

It was as though he were not speaking to me even though he was speaking to me. He said I should not cry, that it was not good to cry and cry and cry, that if I cried like that, endlessly, I would end up crying myself sick.

I dragged myself out of his room, to the bedroom next door where we girls slept. It was midmorning, and yet I remember this moment as dusk. I went to sleep even though I wasn't sleepy. I simply lay my cheek against a pillow. It was soft, the pillow, my cheek—my cheek sunk into the pillow, the pillow sunk against my cheek.

My daddy. Is dead.

So that means. I shall never see him again.

But I spoke to him. Yesterday. Did I not speak to him?

The words stumbled across the pages of my mind, clear scribbling, no mistakes. Yet, in my eleven-year-old mind, they were just another tale in a storybook, a horrid tale in a horrid storybook I had to tear and throw into the dustbin.

My father was the world. He could not die. The world could not die. But?

But nothing.

I recall hearing stories about my father, about his birth, his boyhood. My gogo must have told me. Now these stories have become memories, mine, as though from my own subconscious, saturating my heart with the warmth and recognition of personal experience, as though I were there with him, my father, watching him grow up, and myself through him, in Empandeni Village in Plumtree, in the Bulilimamangwe District of

Matabeleland South Province in Zimbabwe, the fourth of nine children, sprouting under my gogo's unyielding grip dunking him and scrubbing him and baptizing him in rivers of water. They were Catholics of the staunchest kind, never missing mass or baptism or confession or the last rites, but never deigning also to slaughter a cow for the ancestors whenever necessary. In my memories, I see her polishing him, my gogo, lathering him in the sacred oils of Vaseline Petroleum Jelly until his gangly limbs glisten like a pecan in the sun. Always, he tries to scamper off, this svelte young Horus, he's seventeen and the hairs have bunched up on his chin and his heart beats wild in his chest. She grips him, my gogo, grabs his arm even though he's a head taller than she and even as he tries to wrench himself free. She tugs him toward her and holds him close, and if he continues snarling and gnarling like a crazy thing without a mother's guiding hand to instill some *ubuntu*, some love, she's not above unthreading him with a slap that I can hear ringing, even now, *pa!* in that tranquil afternoon of my father's youth, double-ringing *pa pa!* in my ears in my father's ears, stopping me stopping him dead in our tracks, me trembling from the shock of the vividness of it, he no longer trying to run, although his gaze upon my gogo is fierce even as he never dares do to her whatever impiety the passions of youth are imploring him to do. He begins to cry. I begin to cry. I sniffling abashedly, he bawling ashamedly, hiding my tears in the collar of my blouse, burying his eyes in the pockets of his fists, shaking whether from the shock of her slap or the force of his passions or the glow of my memories. Those deep-throated, heart-slitting wails of a man-child make my gogo laugh even as she holds him close and even as he tries to turn his streaked face away from her, yielding eventually to her embrace. He lurches suddenly, ducks and manages to slide out of gogo's grip, laughing-crying as she yells for him to stop, hey *wena*, stop, *mani*, come back here, if I catch you, I'll... It fades, gogo's voice, a whisper, as he scampers off. He's laughing now, and it swells my heart, walking in downtown Iowa

City, the humidity hanging thick and oppressive, although the August sun is still just at the threshold, the morning relatively pleasant, to hear my father's adolescent laughter as though he were walking right here next to me, or I scampering back then next to him, privy to this unruly croak of a boy teetering into manhood, boisterous and yet unsure. He slinks off to the river Shashi, all gangling pecan limbs, ashy cedar at the elbows, darker at the knees, those knobby knees bunched up like fists, ready to punch the ground where he crouches by the riverbank, squinting at the verdant bushes teetering on the banks opposite, threatening to dump their wine-dark berries into the water, their roots all tripped up by the sedges that sprout indiscriminately from underground rhizome colonies and cling to whatever offshoot they happen to curl around. There he raises his long face to the sun, which shines flame-hot and eggshell-colored, and I imagine he imagines we imagine I can taste he can taste we can taste those plump berries bursting warm and wet in my his our mouths. Spit roils about on my tongue.

Walking down Dubuque, past Church Street and Brown, toward Park Road, I see, past the fraternity and sorority houses, to my left, the gray skin of the Coralville Lake, skimmed by the morning light like cream over a steaming cup of rooibos. It's my second year here, at the University of Iowa, where I'm beginning to wonder why it is exactly that I'm studying toward an MA in Italian, the language that my father spoke so fluently but which isn't, for all intents and purposes, a "practical degree." M suggested, during one of our sessions, that my never having mastered the language makes me feel locked out of an important part of my father, unable to access him fully or meaningfully, the way one can perceive the mind of a writer through the sensibility of her language.

I take a left onto Park Road, across the bridge and down the Iowa River Trail. The benches scattered along the banks of Coralville Lake are empty. There's hardly ever anyone here at this time of the morning, save for the occasional sprightly jogger or the power walker puffing up the trail, past the university construction site to my right. I settle on one of the benches and watch the sun, lusty with the heat of summer, as it rises above the sorority houses sloping up Dubuque on the other side of the lake. The gray, messy construction on the university site that stretches behind me as I sit facing the water, with its suspended cranes and cement slabs, detracts from the moment's tranquility. It reminds me of the alien invasion in the movie *Edge of Tomorrow*. I imagine my father dying over and over again, caught in an eternally recurring time loop, like Tom Cruise. The memory of his death is raw, as though it just occurred yesterday, as though it shall keep recurring in all the yesterdays I shall live.

According to his death certificate, my father died on the 94 km peg along the Bulawayo-Gweru road. It says, under *cause of death*, that he died of *head injuries*. That is what it says, but the truth of the matter—whether I overheard this from Mum or some other person or whether someone actually told me, I can no longer recall—is that his car was forced off the road by a truck. I imagine it was one of those Optimus Prime Peterbilt-379 models with the big heads that haul behind them one and sometimes even two partitions, like the carriages of a train. The driver was trying to overtake my father's car—probably something unflamboyant like a Mazda 323—when he swerved back onto the left lane too soon, so that one of the carriages of his truck rammed into the smaller vehicle, elbowing my father off the road. The truck driver did not stop. He was never apprehended.

I imagine that the truck driver glimpsed my father's car careening off the road through his rearview mirror. I see him, every time I close my eyes, his eyes enlarging as he realizes what he has just done. His grip on the steering wheel tightens. His body goes stiff. He jabs at the brakes with his right foot, the tires of his truck mewl, the protest of rubber against tarmac stinking up the air. Then, realizing that they are alone, he and my father, on that dry stretch of tarmac, with only refractions of light playing mirage with the heat in the distance, with nobody, nothing, only the savannah grass shimmering in that stupor, brown and crisp along the sides of the road, he releases the brakes, rights his truck, and speeds off.

I hope, at least, that he called an ambulance.

I hope my father died a quick death.

I visited the 94 km peg where he died, along the Bulawayo-Gweru road, once several years ago, when I was eighteen, and I will never go back there again. I can still see it now, the emptiness of that road, its unremarkableness, how there was nobody standing on that uncultivated stretch of land on either side of the road to witness my father's death. I have been trying to ponder the significance of this number, ninety-four. It has been guiding me, like the lead chromate-coated road markings that illume under car headlamps at night.

How, exactly, does a person die? I have spent inordinate amounts of time hunched over the computers at the Iowa City Public Library, away from my MacBook and Mingli's censorious gaze, googling death. Up to seven minutes for the brain to shut down. Those valiant cells of the body acting as soldiers, fighting for the nation that is the brain, tumbling one by one under the rifle of that notorious assassin, death. Or perhaps the cells, shorn of the fictions of the superheroic, are closer to the civilian, the pedestrian, the human, like those villagers in Matabeleland in 1984—men, women, children, and the elderly—splattered by the bullets of Mugabe's notorious Fifth Brigade Army. They rupture, the civilian cells, to form a messy terrain of remembrance, a bloody torrent of memories that flood the prefrontal cortex.

Did he think of me as he died, my father?

Delirium. Disorientation. Liquid flooding the lungs. How is it, when a man dies? Does the fading light lap like a postcard sunset at the fading consciousness? Trapped in hypnopompia—the state leading from sleep to wakefulness—does the dying victim, *death's* victim, fight the current, dragging himself toward that beach of wakefulness, wrestling against death's tide, trying to cling to the solidness of the world he has always known? I hope my father did not have to experience death this way. I hope his experience was closer to hypnagogia—the slipping from wakefulness into sleep—inspiring little resistance. What could be more beloved than sleep? To be dazzled by random speckles and geometrical shapes, all in mosaic, shifting colors. These would offer something pleasurable as he went under.

I picture him dying, and the very last image he glimpses, as he dies, is my face. Or sometimes, I imagine him, after having driven for almost four and a half hours, something he is not used to, finding himself dominated by this activity he has just been performing, afflicted by the Tetris effect, mercifully prevented from realizing what is happening by the illusory feel of the upholstery of the Mazda 323 warm against his bum. The smell of a lemon-scented car freshener, this, surely, would be preferable to the rusty smell of blood. I picture him taken over by hypnagogic hallucinations, hearing, once again, our very last conversation, which we had a few hours before, just after his flight landed in Harare. His features spread and tighten. Affected by synesthesia, the last thing he sees before he dies is the proverbial streak of blinding, angelic light.

And somewhere in all of this, maybe, my face.

What I remember most vividly about my father's funeral is Mr. C. He was towering, he was alpine, he was lofty, he was colossal. He was big— hefty—and big—weighty, the way fathers are. His face was wide and solemn and pimpled—and taupe-colored, like my father's. He filled the charcoal suits he wore, filled them and filled the world and filled my world and on that day when we first met at my father's funeral he looked down and enveloped my little hand in his big hand and bent over until his wide face was close to mine, filling the whole of my world, and he said, "I'm sorry, really, really sorry…" And he kept saying this, that he was sorry, and when he straightened up and turned to Mum to tell her this, that he was really sorry, I looked up at him and was met by his broad nose, so large, that nose, but handsome, trembling with grief and nose hair, each breath and sigh trembling, trembling through every fiber of that man. He had this habit of tapping his gold-rimmed oval spectacles as he spoke, and sometimes in my teens whenever I lost myself in quixotic reveries of my father doing the everyday things that fathers do, those humdrum things that in teenhood are likely to elicit some dramatic eye-rolling and lip-pouting but in my daydreams took on the stuff of bliss, that terribly quotidian stuff like sitting slouched on a couch reading a newspaper, legs crossed at the ankles, face creased from a long day's work, he would come to me, my father, dressed in charcoal suits and wearing gold-rimmed oval-spectacles which he'd tap incessantly on his broad nose with its trembling nose hairs. He'd bellow my name—"J!"—slouching on his couch, perusing the *Sunday News*. He'd ask for a glass of water, and I'd rush to the kitchen and pour him water in his favorite glass and walk steadily back to the sitting room, making sure not to spill, and as I handed it to him I would curtsy and watch as he raised it to his lips and tilted his head back, his Adam's apple going *guru guru,* some of the water dribbling down the sides of his mouth and sliding down his chin, his hand moist from holding the glass as he tapped me on the shoulder and asked for a napkin.

He took up *space*, Mr. C.

That day at my father's funeral I saw the grief almost topple him. He was helping the coffin-bearers carry my daddy's coffin from the Doves Funeral hearse to the grave, that ivory box whose embroidered edges caught the glint of the steel-blue clouds, clouds so resolutely steely that when you stared at them your eyes hurt, almost as if you were looking into the sun. He was helping the coffin-bearers and taking the weight of my father in one hand, the other stretched out for balance, when he peered into the grave, and what he must have seen there, that oblong hole in the ground in which my father was going to be entombed, overwhelmed him (it must have been a terrifying vertigo, the kind that has assaulted me time and time again over the years) and his Kenneth Cole shoes lost their grip on the soil. There was a moment when he seemed to be slipping into that frightful hole. Then, thankfully, he teetered. In all of this, he did not let go of the coffin. He held on to it. His grip was determined. A look of dread came over his face, a dread of the kind which evades language, which, like all highs and lows of human emotion in their purest forms, is so genuine as to be terrifying, and endurance of which, were such endurance possible—like the proverbial looking into the face of God—would be of an intensity that could only lead to death. It was very brief, that peculiar dread on Mr. C's face, but in that brief moment—probably less than a second—I recognized in it something close to what I felt and had been feeling ever since that day sitting on Khulu's bed in his house at Queenspark East but did not have, in the way of children, the vocabulary to articulate, only a numb, overwhelming dumbness. Then he regained his balance and the moment had passed, and some of the Ladies of Roma, who were dressed in the chocolate skirts and tortilla blouses of their Sunday uniforms with their matching Catholic berets angled carefully on their heads, smiled relieved smiles. Their voices tintinnabulated in that death-still afternoon, seeking those soprano peaks and contralto watersheds and tenor valleys, relentless, relentless. They dragged out sorrow as though it were death or its occasion that had given them the wisdom to mine our deepest pits of woe and reflect them back to us in songfuls of unbearable feeling, imploring us nevertheless to bear it. And it was beautiful to hear, and awful, too, so very awful.

My gogo was there, inconsolable, lying on a *cansi*, for she could not stand, my poor gogo, beckoning me every so often and pressing me to her bosom. Mum was there, too, as were both my khulus, and so many faces most of which I cannot remember now. But it's Mr. C who comes to me now, Mr. C bending over and confiding, "I don't know what to say. I don't know what to do... It was only yesterday that Frank and I were at law school together. And now. I just can't—"

Mr. C weeping into his charcoal jacket, wiping his snot-bubbling nose on his arm.

He placed his big, warm hand on my little shoulder. I just stood there, looking up at him.

"I'm sorry."

He spoke with a whiff of an accent, something cultured, like our version of the British intonations, with that familiar, clipped stoicism which the British like to exude in the face of feeling, recognizable in the men of his age, men like my father who, in their youth, were experiments in and rebellious products against a Macaulayist type of education.

"I'm very sorry..." Trying to put himself back together now, sniffling, half-turning away from me, dabbing his eyes with a handkerchief. "It's just...I'm sorry."

I did not know what to do with this, what it was expected I should do with sorry.

He was there after the funeral at my babomdala's house in Lobengula West when I finally cried as they shaved my head; it had to be done because my father had died. I felt my face tighten when they told me this, becoming pinched the way one's face does when one bites into a lemon, and before I could stop them they were chopping off my hair with a razor blade and the tears were gushing. They cooed to me and gently urged me not to cry. I think they thought once I started I wouldn't be able to stop, though I did, I did manage to stop, after a while.

He was there again, Mr. C, when we drove down to Empandeni for the traditional rites, to my gogo and khulu's homestead, across those dusty plains of Bulilimamangwe where my daddy had grown up, cow-herding and rabbit-hunting and river-bathing, before he turned thirteen and was sent off to boarding school at Empandeni Mission, coming home only during the holidays. Mr. C was right there, squatting beside me with his large hands balanced on his knees as the local *nyanga* performed the rites, leaping from side to side, the bells fastened to the *amaShoba* on his arms and legs tinkling, his white-painted face glistening as he swished up and down before me, eyes opened wide, so frightfully wide, leaping away, then back again, then away, chanting the ancestral liturgies. He carried on this way for a long time, until my legs began to burn from crouching, and when he spun for the last time, he was carrying a smoldering bucket with his bare hands, which he thrust toward me and huffed into, sending ashy clouds of smoke into my face, and though I tried hard not to, I broke into a fit of coughing, I couldn't help it, and Mr. C rubbed my back.

Mr. C carried his grief with him everywhere. Seated with Mum and my gogo and my babomdala in the boardroom of his law offices on Selous Avenue in Harare three months later, in that air-conditioned air that swirled cool and hazy in the torrid November afternoon, I felt the weight of his grief, in the grave glint behind his spectacles, in each carefully clipped word as he spoke, saying how he lacked the words to express how much of a great loss Frank's passing was to him. And not just a loss to *him*, but a loss to Africa as a whole, a loss to the academic community, to all those who had known him and loved him. Frank had loved people. His love for learning and commitment to knowledge had been infectious. He had been kind—an inspiration to all who had known him. A truly brilliant and exceptional human being. His old university, where he had done his LLM, in London, was naming an award after him. It would be awarded each year to the most outstanding LLM student in the Emerging

Markets Law course. A book of essays on law was being compiled, too, in his memory. This was the kind of impact Frank had had. It was not to be taken lightly. Frank had been truly outstanding. He had had an incredible inner strength. You did not meet someone like him every day.

He spoke to us in this way, as though schooling us in a matter whose magnitude and significance we were not able to fathom and whose significance we were at risk of not being able to grasp. He, Mr. C, would make sure Frank's wishes were fulfilled. He had left a will, though it was unsigned, written just before the accident, as though he had seen death coming. He had meant to sign it on his trip home. He had meant to appoint Mr. C as the executor of his estate. He, Mr. C, would make sure that we did what Frank had wanted. We had to honor Frank. We would keep his memory and his legacy alive. This was what Frank would have wanted; what Frank *would want*.

Mr. C began to cry. His eyes rapidly became wet behind his glasses. He blink-blinked, blink-blinked, as though dazed, finally excusing himself and rushing out of the room.

And when I think of this now, it seems incredible that things soured between us, that they even *could* sour, bound as we were by the superglue that was my father. And yet, that first afternoon in Mr. C's office was the beginning of my lesson in the oppressive weight of my father's achievements—this supposedly meta-human excellence that was rubbed, as death does to memory, smooth of any ruts, scars, or weaknesses, those marks through which we bear our humanness—and of whose brilliance I was the unbefitting genetic inheritor, as I was to later learn through Mr. C's malice and also that of his friend who claimed to have known my father, that cruel, terrible woman, Mrs. G. And though it was Mum's fallout with Mr. C when she got married three years later that led to Mr. C's attempts to shut us out of my father's estate, it was, ultimately, the sense of disdain with which he began to treat me, as though there weren't any difference between Mother and me—causing me, for a time, to despise Mother and seek to distance myself from her in a bid to regain Mr. C's affection—which caused me to shrink from my father whenever he appeared to me, in my teens, while eating or sleeping or just walking down the street, his smashed-in face appearing with its raised upper lip and rolling eye on the right side of his head—where I imagined he had slammed into the windscreen in the car accident that caused the injuries I so wished I could clean and bandage yesterday afternoon when he appeared in my kitchen, if only he would've let me.

The sun becomes blinding as it rises over the sorority houses that slope up the incline of Dubuque Street, on the other side of Coralville Lake, turning the lawns, which are shamrock green in the shade, into a sharp emerald, and polishing the copper letters of the Greek alphabet adorning the grass into a shiny brass. Its rays become sharper, rippling across the lake, stretching ghostlike, as though dazzled, like Narcissus, by its own golden-yellow reflection.

CONTRIBUTORS

AYA OSUGA A. was born in Japan and raised in Los Angeles. She received a BS in computer science from Yale University, where she also had the privilege of studying under some of the most influential writers of our time, including the late Amanda Davis, who was a great friend to *McSweeney's*. Aya left a career in banking to refocus on writing and currently resides in the countryside of Panama, on a beach called Playa Venao, with her husband, her children, and lots of monkeys. This is her first publication.

NOEL ALUMIT wrote the novels *Letters to Montgomery Clift* and *Talking to the Moon*. He's currently in Buddhist divinity school trying to get enlightened—and failing miserably.

ZEEVA BUKAI was born in Israel and raised in Brooklyn. Her stories have appeared in *december, Flash Fiction Magazine, WomenArts Quarterly Journal, Lilith, Calyx*, and the *Jewish Quarterly*. She was a fellow at the Center for Fiction in New York City, and holds an MFA in fiction from Brooklyn College. Her work has recently been nominated for a Pushcart Prize. She teaches writing and is at work on a novel.

MARCUS BURKE is a graduate of the Iowa Writers' Workshop. He is the author of *Team Seven*. He is currently at work on his second novel.

RITA CHANG-EPPIG is a writer and psychologist in the Bay Area. Barring any trickster-god antics or global catastrophes, she will soon be receiving an MFA from NYU. Her stories have appeared in *Calyx* and the *Kenyon Review*.

MGBECHI UGONNA ERONDU is a physician and writer of fiction. She holds a BA from Princeton University and an MFA from the Iowa Writers' Workshop. Currently she is an anesthesiology resident at the Baylor College of Medicine.

MERON HADERO was born in Ethiopia and, via Germany, came to the United States as a refugee when she was a child. Her writing appears in *Best American Short Stories, Selected Shorts* on NPR/PRI, the *Missouri Review, Boulevard*, and the *New York Times Book Review*, among other publications. She has been a fellow at the MacDowell Colony, Yaddo, and Ragdale, and has an MFA in creative writing from the University of Michigan, a JD from Yale Law School, and an AB from Princeton in history with a certificate in American Studies.

ESKOR DAVID JOHNSON is a writer from Trinidad and Tobago.

CASALLINA KISAKYE is a Ugandan-American writer living in Los Angeles and working in television.

MARIA KUZNETSOVA was born in Kiev, Ukraine and moved to the United States as a child. "I Pledge Allegiance to the Butterfly" is the first chapter of her novel, *OKSANA, BEHAVE!*, which will be published by Spiegel & Grau/Random House in 2019. Other chapters from the novel appear in the *Southern Review* and *Kenyon Review* online and her other work appears or is forthcoming in the *Threepenny Review, Indiana Review*, and the *Iowa Review*.

SANAM MAHLOUDJI's fiction appears or is forthcoming in *Passages North* and *Crab Creek Review*. She was recently nominated for a PEN/ Robert J. Dau Short Story Prize for Emerging Writers. She lives in London.

ILAN MOCHARI's Pushcart-nominated debut novel, *Zinsky the Obscure* (Fomite Press, 2013), earned flattering reviews from *Publishers Weekly*, *Kirkus*, and *Booklist*. His poems have appeared or are forthcoming in *Hobart*, the anthology *Spectral Lines* from Alternating Current Press, *Specter*, and *The Release*. His short stories have appeared in *Keyhole*, *Midway Journal*, *Stymie*, and elsewhere.

JOSÉ ANTONIO RODRIGUEZ, born in Mexico and raised in south Texas, is the author of the poetry collections *The Shallow End of Sleep* and *Backlit Hour*, and the memoir *House Built on Ashes*. He teaches writing at the University of Texas Rio Grande Valley. Learn more at www.jarodriguez.org.

MINA SEÇKIN is a writer and editor based in New York. She is pursuing her MFA in fiction at Columbia University School of the Arts, where she received the Felipe P. De Alba merit fellowship. She is the web editor of *Apogee Journal*.

WILLIAM PEI SHIH is from New York City. His stories have been recognized by the Flannery O'Connor Award for Short Fiction, the John Steinbeck Fiction Award, the Raymond Carver Short Story Contest, the Alice Munro Festival of the Short Story, the Masters Review Short Story Award for New Writers, the London Magazine Short Story Competition, the Bridport Prize, the AAWW North America Asian American Short Story

Contest, *Narrative*, *Glimmer Train*, and others. A graduate of the Iowa Writers' Workshop, he has been awarded fellowships to the Sun Valley Writer's Conference and Kundiman, and a Carol Houck Smith Scholarship in fiction to the Bread Loaf Writers' Conference.

EDVIN SUBAŠIĆ was born and raised in Bosnia-Herzegovina and now lives with his wife and daughter in Boise, Idaho. His work has appeared in *Out of Stock* and The Cabin's Idaho's *Writers in the Attic*, and more is forthcoming in *B O D Y Literature*. He was also shortlisted for the 2017 Disquiet Literature Prize for Fiction and earned an honorable mention in *Glimmer Train*.

NYUOL LUETH TONG is co-founder and editor-in-chief of the *Bare Life Review*, as well as editor of *There Is a Country* (McSweeney's, 2013). Tong studied philosophy and comparative literature at Duke University, where he was a Reginaldo Howard Memorial Scholar. He received his MFA from the Iowa Writers' Workshop, where he was a Truman Capote Fellow and a Teaching-Writing Fellow. Tong's writing has appeared in *McSweeney's*, the *Baffler*, *Transect Magazine*, NPR, *New Sudan*, and *Gurtong*, among other publications.

NOVUYO ROSA TSHUMA is the author of the novel *House of Stone* (Atlantic Books, UK June 2018; W. W. Norton, USA January 2019). She is a graduate of the Iowa Writers' Workshop, and has received fellowships from the Kimmel Harding Nelson Center for the Arts and Imprint, as well as a prestigious Bellagio Literary Arts Residency Award from the Rockefeller Foundation. She serves on the editorial advisory board of the *Bare Life Review*.

McSWEENEY'S WOULD LIKE TO THANK THE FOLLOWING DONORS FOR THEIR BOUNDLESS GENEROSITY. YOU MAKE OUR WORK POSSIBLE.

Aaron Sedivy · Adriana DiFranco · Adrienne Esztergar · Aiden Enns · Aimee Kalnoskas · Alan Rintoul · Alexia Schou · Allan Fix · Amy Foster · Andrea Lunsford · Andrea Winnette · Andrew Benner · Andrew Crooks · Andrew Hirshman · Andrew Kaufteil · Andrew Martin · Anita Hatter · Anita Wylie · Ann Haman · Ann McKenzie · Anne Germanacos · Annie Ganem · Anonymous Donor · Atsuro Riley · B Basheer · Barbara Cauble · Barbara Murray · Benjamin Russell · Betsy Pattullo · Betty Joyce Nash · Bill Spitzig · Bradley Harkrader · Bradley Rickman · Brandon Chalk · Brendan Hare · Brian Dice · Brian Downing · Brian Geraghty · Brian Grygiel · Brian Pfeffer · Brian Thurston · Brooke Prince · Carl Voss · Carol Davis · Carole Fuller · Caterina Fake · Catharine Bell · Cathryn Lyman · Celeste Roberts-Lewis · Charles Irby · Charles Spaht, Jr · Charlotte Locke · Chelsea Voake · Cheryl Petersen · Chris Roe · Christian Rudder · Christine Brown · Christine Kobayashi · Christine Rener · Christopher Fauske · Christopher Maynard · Christopher W Ulbrich · Cindy Lamar · Clark Newby · Claudia Mueller · Cleri Coula · Cloe Shasha · Cody Dublanica · Cynthia McDonagh · Dana Gioia · Dana Skelly · Daniel Golding · Daniel Grossman · Daniel Kamins · David Nahass · David Tulis · David Zarzycki · Deborah Goldsmith · Deborah Goodman · Deborah Jackson Weiss · Debra Bok · Derek Stoeckenius · Devin Greene · Devon Voake · Diane Fitzsimmon · Dianne Wood · Dom Baker · Don Walters · Donald Woutat · Donna Green · Dorothy Malloy · Douglas Kearney · Duane Murray · Earline Ahonima · Edward Carle · Edward Crabbe · Elizabeth Davies · Elizabeth Keim · Elizabeth McQuire · Ellyn Farrelly · Elske Krikhaar · Emil Volcheck · Emily Ostendorf · Emily Schleiger · Eric Brink · Eric Heiman · Eric Kuczynski · Eric Ries · Erica Portnoy · Erica Seiler · Ethel Watson · EVA Rimbau Gilabert · Faisel Siddiqui · Femme Fan1946 · Fiona Hamersley · Greg Prince · Greg Vines · Greg Weber · Haiy Le · Hans Zippert · Hans-Juergen Balmes · Heather Myers · Heidi Oates · Heidi Raatz · Hilary Sasso-Schleh · Ian Glazer · Ian Shadwell · Irma Noel · Isaac Lauritsen · Isabel Pinner · J.P. Townsend · James Brandes · James Klein · James Moore · James Pabarue · James Tibbitt · James Whitehead

· Jason Seifert · Jay Traeger · Jean Decker · Jeff Campoli · Jeffrey Johnston · Jeffrey Podis · Jenni Baker · Jennifer Dait · Jennifer Ta · Jennifer Morris · Jeremy Ellsworth · Jeremy Radcliffe · Jeremy Rishel · Jerzy Jung · Joan Thompson · Joe Sou-Baba · John Ebey · John P Monks · John Pancini · John Repko · Jonathan Patton · Josue Nieves · JP Coghlan · Julia Slavin · Julie Nudd · Kate Berry · Kate Bush · Kate Schreiber · Katherine Sherron · Kathleen Einspanier · Kathleen Hennessy · Kathryn Farris · Kathy Phillips · Kelly Browne · Kelly Bryan · Kelly Heckman · Kermit Eck · Kimberly Harrington · Kingslea Bueltel · Kristi VandenBosch · Kristina Tacou · Kuang-Yi Liu · Kyle Jacob Bruck · Landy Manderson · Laura Tiffany · Lauren Colchamiro · Laurence Saviers · Lawrence Bridges · Lee Harrison · Lee Smith · Leslie Maslow · Leslie Power · Libby Carlson · Lila Fontes · Lila LaHood · Lindsay McConnon · Lisa Parsons · Lois Lowenthal · Louis Loewenstein · Lucinda Sabino · Lydia Ship · Lynn Farmer · Mackenzie Clark · Margaret Park · Mari Belfort · Mariana Almeida · Marielle Smith · Mark Aronoff · Mark Beringer · Mark McEwen · Marshall Hayes · Martin Cielens · Mary Durbin · Mary Gioia · Mary Mann · Matthew Mullenweg · Maureen Stinger · Maxim Michor · Megan, L Hoover · Michael Gavino · Michael Gilchrist · Michael Gioia · Michael Greene · Michael Gwynn · Michael Jones · Michael Kuniavsky · Michael Mikula · Michael Muratore · Michael O'Connell · Michelle Curtis · Micquelle Corry · Mitch Major · Mr Pancks · Nadine Schwartz · Nance Maiorino · Nancy Folsom · Nate Arnold · Nathaniel Missildine · Neva Purnell · Nicholas Bergin · Nicholas Calabrese · Nicholson Baker · Nicole Ryan · Nigel Dookhoo · Nion McEvoy · Nion McEvoy · Nizam Maneck · Oliver Kroll · Patricia Gainer · Paul Bielec · Paul Fanning · Paul Ghysbrecht · Paul Nixon · Penny Dedel · Peter Baggenstos · Peter DiChellis · Philip Kors · Philip Scranton · Pia Widlund · Polly McKinney · Rajeev Basu · Randy Woodhead · Rebecca Cox · Rebecca Gillespie · Rebecca Schneider · Rebecca Wilson · Rhian Miller · Rivkah K Sass · Rob Knight · Robert Conrad · Robert Nelsen · Robert Washburn · Ross Solomon · Ruth Madievsky · Sairus Patel · Sairus Patel · Sarah Bownds · Sarah Brewer · Sarah E Klein · Sarah Fishtein · Scott Stelter · Sean Beatty Oaktown SS · Sharon Bronson · Sir Carlisle · Sonia J Cabrera Ullon · Stephanie Anderson · Stephen Berger · Stephen Cole · Steven Blunk · Steven Powell · Steven Schreibman · Stuart O'Connor · Susan Nathan · Susheila Khera · Swati Puri · Tammy Ghattas · Tanya Ruckstuhl-Valenti · Theodore Gioia · Thomas Green · Tim Hedeen · Tim Perell · Tom McDaniel · Tony Solomun · Tony Sweeney · Tracy Cambron · Tracy Thomas · Uttam Kumbhat Jain · Virginia Atkins · W Floyd Olive Jr · Wendy Goodwin · Wendy Salome · Wes Wes · Wesley J Ginther · William Mascioli

THE BEST OF

M^cSWEENEY'S

INTERNET TENDENCY

INCLUDING:

IT'S DECORATIVE GOURD SEASON,
MOTHERFUCKERS.

ON THE IMPLAUSIBILITY OF THE DEATH
STAR'S TRASH COMPACTOR.

I REGRET TO INFORM YOU THAT
MY WEDDING TO CAPTAIN VON TRAPP
HAS BEEN CANCELED.

HAMLET (FACEBOOK NEWSFEED EDITION).

I'M COMIC SANS, ASSHOLE.

IN WHICH I FIX MY GIRLFRIEND'S
GRANDPARENTS' WI-FI AND AM HAILED
AS A CONQUERING HERO.

AND MORE OF THE BEST OF FIFTEEN YEARS
OF THE WEBSITE.

Edited by CHRIS MONKS *and* JOHN WARNER

THE BEST OF McSWEENEY'S
INTERNET TENDENCY
edited by Chris Monks and John Warner

"{The Best of McSweeney's Internet Tendency} *is just like
those chocolates that hotels put on pillows, if the chocolate were
laced with acid.*" —Michael Agger, the *New Yorker*

THE BEST OF McSWEENEY'S
edited by Dave Eggers and Jordan Bass

"The first bona fide literary movement in decades." —*Slate*

"An inimitable retrospective on modern storytelling."
—*Publishers Weekly*

FLOWERS OF ANTI-MARTYRDOM
by Dorian Geisler

"Flowers of Anti-Martyrdom... *is exactly the book you need
to read right now... a mix of cautionary wit, a dash of profound
sadness, and a heavy dose of quiet empathy.*" —Dorothea Lasky

SEARCH SWEET COUNTRY
by Kojo Laing

*"Exuberantly reels with language and imagery
reminiscent of the early Joyce."*
—Library Journal

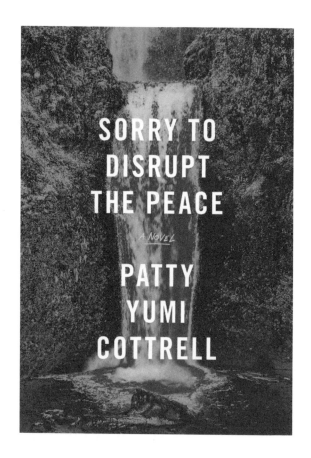

SORRY TO DISRUPT THE PEACE

by Patty Yumi Cottrell

*"Her voice is unflinching, unforgettable, and animated
with a restless sense of humor."* —Catherine Lacey

ALSO AVAILABLE FROM McSWEENEY'S

store.mcsweeneys.net

FICTION

HUMOR

The Secret Language of Sleep .... Amelia Bauer, Evany Thomas
Baby Do My Banking .... Lisa Brown
Baby Fix My Car .... Lisa Brown
Baby Get Me Some Lovin' .... Lisa Brown
Baby Make Me Breakfast .... Lisa Brown
Baby Plan My Wedding .... Lisa Brown
Comedy by the Numbers .... Eric Hoffman, Gary Rudoren
The Emily Dickinson Reader .... Paul Legault
All Known Metal Bands .... Dan Nelson
How to Dress for Every Occasion .... The Pope
The Latke Who Couldn't Stop Screaming .... Lemony Snicket, Lisa Brown
The Future Dictionary of America .... Various
The Best of McSweeney's Internet Tendency .... Various; Ed. Chris Monks, John Warner
I Found This Funny .... Various; Eds. Judd Apatow
I Live Real Close to Where You Used to Live .... Various; Ed. Lauren Hall
Thanks and Have Fun Running the Country .... Various; Ed. Jory John

POETRY

In The Shape Of A Human Body I Am Visiting The Earth .... Various; Eds. Ilya Kaminsky, Dominic Luxford, Jesse Nathan
City of Rivers .... Zubair Ahmed
Remains .... Jesús Castillo
x .... Dan Chelotti
The Boss .... Victoria Chang
Tombo .... W. S. Di Piero
Flowers of Anti-Martyrdom .... Dorian Geisler
Of Lamb .... Matthea Harvey; Ill. Amy Jean Porter
The Abridged History of Rainfall .... Jay Hopler
Love, an Index .... Rebecca Lindenberg
Fragile Acts .... Allan Peterson
The McSweeney's Book of Poets Picking Poets .... Various; Ed. Dominic Luxford

COLLINS LIBRARY

Curious Men .... Frank Buckland
Lunatic at Large .... J. Storer Clouston
The Rector and the Rogue .... W.A. Swanberg

ALL THIS AND MORE AT

store.mcsweeneys.net

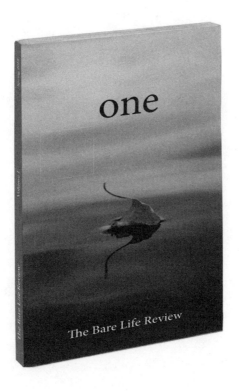

"Uprootedness has been a determining fact in my life, and that clearly informs *In the Distance*. But my personal experiences are just one material among others—and I tried hard not to fetishize any of my materials, from language itself (because the novel takes place in the nineteenth century, I didn't want to abuse words with an historical aura) to contextual facts (I avoided direct contact with the territories where the book takes place)."

—excerpt from *The Vanishing Point: A Conversation with Hernán Díaz* (*The Bare Life Review*, May 2018)

www.barelifereview.org

Founded in 1998, McSweeney's is an independent publisher based in San Francisco. McSweeney's exists to champion ambitious and inspired new writing, and to challenge conventional expectations about where it's found, how it looks, and who participates. We're here to discover things we love, help them find their most resplendent form, and place them into the hands of empathic, engaged readers.

THERE ARE SEVERAL WAYS TO SUPPORT MCSWEENEY'S:

Support Us on Patreon
visit *www.patreon.com/
mcsweeneysinternettendency*

Volunteering & Internships
email *interns-sf@mcsweeneys.net*

Subscriptions & Store Site
visit *store.mcsweeneys.net*

Books &
Quarterly Sponsorship
email *kristina@mcsweeneys.net*

To learn more, please visit *www.mcsweeneys.net/donate* or contact Director Kristina Kearns at kristina@mcsweeneys.net or 415.642.5609.

All donations are tax-deductible through our fiscal sponsorship with SOMArts, a nonprofit organization that collaborates with diverse artists and organizations to engage the power of the arts to provoke just and fair inclusion, cultural respect, and civic participation.